"**What are you talking about?**" he demanded, unable to comprehend her swift change in mood. "What's galled you now?"

She jutted her chin angrily in the direction of the whaler, and his eyes followed her gaze. "Aye. 'Tis a ship at anchor. And?" he prompted.

"And in less than two months that ship will be the *China Maid*. And here I'll stand while Zacch and Papa and thee go aboard and sail out of sight. And here I'll be, alone, for how many years, Jake?" She turned to descend the slope, her wrath renewed at the injustice of her fate.

Before she'd taken a step, Jake's hand closed over her arm in an iron grip and yanked her around to face him. His grin had faded; his blue eyes were serious. "Don't be daft, China," he said quietly. "Don't spoil the present with thoughts of the future. We've not gone yet. *I've* not gone yet. I'm still here. If you don't enjoy today while it's here, you'll have nothing but empty memories of missed chances. Don't waste today, China; don't let today go for naught."

"An exciting, pulsating reading pleasure . . . unforgettable."
—*Brooklyn Record*

"Laura Simon writes from, and for, the heart."
—*The Inquirer and Mirror*, Nantucket, MA

UNTIL I RETURN

Laura Simon

W🌐RLDWIDE

TORONTO • NEW YORK • LONDON • PARIS
AMSTERDAM • STOCKHOLM • HAMBURG
ATHENS • MILAN • TOKYO • SYDNEY

UNTIL I RETURN

Worldwide Library Trade Paperback October 1986

Worldwide Library Mass-Market Edition July 1987

ISBN 0-373-97051-X

For Jonathan

1

NANTUCKET
May 1839

"IF THEE DOESN'T BELAY that scrubbing, thee'll wear a hole in my best porridge pot. And thy eyes will chafe two holes in the window, staring through it as thee is," Aunt Judith said tartly. When her words brought a flush to China's cheek and her grandniece's attention back to the present, the lanky Quaker spinster added in a more kindly tone, "When thee's finished thy chores, thee may scud out upon the heath. 'Tis a waste of time to try and keep thee indoors on a fine morning like this."

"Aye, 'tis," China agreed, grinning. She shook her glossy black bangs out of her eyes, sloshed the scouring sand out of the breakfast kettle and admitted, "In truth, I was just wondering how to pass the day. The water is too cold, still, to be wading about after quahogs, and the eels have all left the mud in the Creeks. Perhaps I'll see if I can hook a mess of pickerel out at Long Pond." Her large gray eyes grew dreamy and distant again.

Aunt Judith nodded briskly, busying herself with preparations for breadmaking. She knew China's mind was focused not on the fish, but on the thought of stretching her long legs along hidden paths through the moors and on releasing her vibrant delight in life beneath mile-high blue skies.

7

"'Tis about time for the fiddleheads to be unfurling," she suggested. "A touch of something green and fresh would be welcome after this winter's fare of potatoes and dried apples. To be sure, it would mean a long hike out to Squam Swamp, or thereabouts, but I doubt that prospect will faze thee. A good airing might make thee bend thy back to the spring cleaning with more cheerfulness."

She paused a moment to peer meaningfully across the kitchen at China before continuing, "Of course, thee might have some nearer spot for picking fiddleheads. 'Tis a proper shooler thee has become, sailing out upon the commons and along the shore, finding fresh provisions. I'm convinced thee knows every rock, rip and rose bush about this island.

"'Twas astonishing to hear thee telling Jedediah Baxter after Meeting last First Day where the best hole is for flounder fishing. And he has lived here for all his sixty-three years, and thee came here at the age of nine, scarcely eight years ago."

As Aunt Judith vigorously scooped flour onto the big, wooden breadboard, her benevolent mood turned more severe. "'Tis not only impertinent for thee to correct thy elders, and frivolous for thee to discuss such worldly topics on First Day, 'tis also becoming unseemly for thee to tack back and forth across the island. Thee is no longer a coltish child."

She looked up before kneading the spongy yeast mass into the mound of flour, assessing her grandniece and ignoring the scowl that was pulling at China's striking features with this impending lecture. She nodded knowingly at the curves in China's tall, slim body, only half hidden by the gray muslin gown and the snowy white kerchief knotted carelessly over her breasts.

"Aye, thee is no longer a child," she repeated, turning back to pound the dough. Her voice assumed the slappity slap rhythm of the bread on the board as she went on, "'Tis time for thee to start acting as a young woman and not as a foolish girl. Time for thee to learn patience and tolerance. Time for thee to stop fretting over thy stitching. Time for thee to prepare for marriage and thy own household. Time for thee—"

"I've no wish for marriage and a house to manage," China interrupted this familiar litany. "I've no wish to be anchored ashore, endlessly mending and scrubbing and attending my husband's whims."

Aunt Judith never lost a stroke. She had heard this argument many times before. "Thee must come out of the clouds, China. Use thy common sense. What other course can a young maid chart? What would thee do instead?"

China didn't know how to respond. Even without turning around, she could see Aunt Judith, stern and unbent, despite her seventy-two years. She could see her square, sober face, which lines were only beginning to erode, and her blunt brown eyes, somewhat obscured behind steel-rimmed spectacles. How could she explain to this plain-speaking, practical woman what she hardly knew herself? The dreams of adventure and independence that stirred through her head while she was striding through the heather would sound foolish to Aunt Judith. They scarcely made sense to her.

She was spared any further thought by the shout of a small boy racing up the lonely lane toward their house. He vaulted the neat white fence to their yard before shouting his news again, "Thy ship is at the Bar! The *China Maid* is at the Bar! She's set her anchors not one hour gone. There's no mistake. The lighters are on their way to her now!"

All thoughts of fiddleheads, fish and Aunt Judith's arguments instantly vanished from China's mind. For a moment she seemed frozen in disbelief, and then her heart began beating frantically as excitement sent her into motion. Her hands splashed through the rinse water, flew across the flour sacking towel and plucked her bonnet off the peg by the back door. In an instant, she, too, was racing, pausing only long enough to open the gate and go through it, rather than over it.

She left Aunt Judith to dole out the traditional silver dollar reward to the breathless bearer of this good news, and to shout in vain, "China, come back here! Thee must return at once! The wharves are no place for thee. Decent women wait at home for their menfolk. China, does thee hear me?"

Tearing out of their lane and onto the newly cobbled Main Street, China vaguely heard Aunt Judith's admonition, but she ignored it. Sheer happiness propelled her toward the waterfront, lending speed to her long legs. Their ship was at the Bar! The *China Maid*, her namesake and her home for five blissful childhood years, was anchored just beyond the sandbar at the mouth of the harbor. And on board the beamy, old whaler were her father, Captain Zaccheus Joy, and her brother, her beloved twin, Zacch.

Usually alert to every detail of her surroundings, China hardly noticed today the huge houses she was passing. The clapboard, brick or shingled mansions, built with wealth wrenched from whales in every remote, watery corner of the world, whisked by without any of her normal speculation as to what grand goings-on were taking place in their parlors. A dray, laden with newly coopered barrels, lumbered along, eliciting no questions from China as to their far-flung destinations. Old Asa Harkens, stumping by on his wooden leg with his basket of codfish for sale, received only a hurried wave rather than an audience for his ritual recitation of tides, temperatures and fishing conditions.

The crisp May breeze stirred China's straight black bangs and chin-length hair as her bonnet swung from her hand instead of covering her head. Her creamy, clear skin, not yet browned by the summer sun, was rosy from the fresh air and inner elation. And her unusual gray eyes, beautifully outlined in charcoal and set off by thick, dark lashes, were alight with the anticipation of seeing her family again.

It was nearly three years since she had seen them; three long, lonely years since she had shared secrets with Zacch. They were so close always, almost able to sense the other's feelings. Twice in their lifetime he had sailed away with their father, twice leaving China stricken by their separation. But now he was returning to complete the natural extension of her that seemed somehow empty without him. It was as if her feet couldn't go fast enough. After three weary years of waiting, they would be each other's shadow again.

ZACCH WAS BORN just minutes before her in a small stone cottage near Le Havre, seventeen years ago. Their fragile French mother named him for their American father, then thousands of miles away in pursuit of whales. When China followed Zacch into the world, she was named for the Nantucket ship carrying her father to fortune and home to her. For the next nine years, the twins were never far apart in either thoughts or action.

From the time they were old enough to toddle, they had helped Josephine, their mother. Together they had fed the skinny, brindle cow, plucked persistent weeds out of their rocky garden and toted endless buckets of water for the wash Josephine took in to support them. The money her husband had left, before the twins were born, had long since disappeared, most of it flowing down the throat of her father in the form of hard cider. He drank to forget the poverty in which he lived, the pain in his war-injured legs and the memory of his three strong sons, all dead for God, country and Napoleon. M. Briaud drank a little too much one bitter February night, fell into a ditch as he staggered back to his tiny stone cottage and died of exposure before dawn.

Through all adversity, the petite Josephine had persevered. She was sure that Zaccheus would return one day, and she was just as sure that she would never allow them to be separated again. She had met him one sparkling June day when she was stealing a few free minutes from her chores and he was stretching his long legs on the pebbly beach below the bluff. They had fallen very much in love.

All of this mattered very little to China and Zacch, who had never met their papa, had never spoken English and had never seen Nantucket. That changed shortly before their fourth birthday when Zaccheus finally returned, and Josephine, with a determination unexpected in one so seemingly delicate, convinced her adoring husband to take his family on board. Where once their clog-shod feet had clambered in unison after butterflies or buttercups, the twins' bare toes had then trod oak decks and had stubbed against huge coils of rope.

They had spoken not only French and, now, English, but also pidgin Portuguese, and a few phrases of a Polynesian dialect. They had climbed the rigging, rowed boats, studied the stars and sailed through the world's southern seas searching for whales and for idyllic happiness.

They had been successful on both counts until, sixty days out of Nantucket, with a hold full of oil, Josephine had taken ill during a wicked storm and had succumbed to pneumonia, Zaccheus's name on her dying lips. The twins had been stunned, but Zaccheus had been devastated by grief and guilt. When next he had sailed, a grim and somber man, Zacch had gone along as cabin boy, but China had been left ashore.

To no avail, China had argued that she, as well as Zacch, had inherited their father's long-legged build, his hardy Nantucket health and his love of the sea. Zaccheus hadn't listened. He had seen only her mother's silky black hair, her porcelain complexion and her gray eyes with their seductive charcoal accents. She was a rare beauty to be protected. For her own safety, he had left China in Nantucket, in the care of his elderly Aunt Judith.

Aunt Judith had been aghast by her first encounter with her grandniece, eight years ago. Her plain, pious soul had been truly offended by the sight of China dressed in duck trousers, a sailor's jersey, a bright red neckerchief and a string of shells and shark's teeth. The girl's Dutch Boy cut hair had set her teeth on edge, her colorful combination of languages had made her flinch, but the gleam of unabashed independence in China's unusual eyes had set Aunt Judith's jaw in determination to turn her young kin into a proper Quaker girl.

She had confiscated China's masculine wardrobe, replacing it with flannel petticoats, high-buttoned boots, drab gray dresses and coal-scuttle bonnets that somewhat hid the girl's sinfully seductive eyes. It was to take Aunt Judith many years to view China's beauty as natural and unalterable, not a vain affectation that could be stowed in a locker like a bejeweled bonnet or a red satin gown.

China had been dragged to every First Day Meeting. In the winter, she had frozen her toes and had felt like shouting into the frosty silence, and in the summer she had itched under her layers of petticoats and tight-sleeved dresses and had ached to be outside in the whirring sounds of sunshine. She had been berated, belayed and corrected until she straightened her speech and substituted thee and thy for you and your, though her tongue still tripped and she always had the feeling she was tiptoeing rather than talking. She had been sentenced to long days on hard benches at the Cent School where learning had soon lost the magic it had had in the captain's day room on board the *Maid*, and where she no longer copied her lessons from old issues of newspapers from New Zealand and the Sandwich Islands, but struggled instead with the dreary morality of *The American Speller*.

China had been miserable. The constricting clothes had made her feel as if she were choking, the long-brimmed bonnet had made her feel like a blindered dray horse, and the lessons, in and out of school, had made her feel dense, for they hardly penetrated. But more important, she had been almost totally friendless. Other children her own age had regarded her with suspicion. The whispered stories of her French birth, her exotic looks and her enviable experience at sea had conspired against her. The boys, whom she had been able to outrow and outrun, had rejected her because she was a girl, while the girls, with the exception of Harriet Swain, had excluded her because she looked and acted like a boy.

Only gradually had she come to accept her situation. And as she had acquiesced, to her surprise, Aunt Judith had also relented. It had been give and take. China had ceased complaining about the dreary color and the confining fit of her clothes, and Aunt Judith had withheld her comments on her niece's chin-length hair, first cut for convenience somewhere off the coast of Africa. China had submitted to stitching samplers and hemming handkerchiefs, and Aunt Judith had stopped throwing out the shells, arrowheads and odd beach jetsam that the girl collected. China had dutifully read the Bible, and Aunt Judith had let pass the pages of French poetry China had hidden between the chapters.

She now lived in a state of unspoken compromise with Aunt Judith. When she was home, or on an errand for her aunt, China behaved as a circumspect young Quaker lady. In return, Aunt Judith would frequently release her on fine days, allowing her to disappear into the moors or over the dunes, to kick off her shoes and to toss away her bonnet, to spend her day as she pleased. If a mess of clams or a bucket of berries resulted, so much the better. Aunt Judith learned to accept this part of her grandniece's personality with the tolerance that made Nantucket as famous for its eccentricity as for its piety.

CHINA WASN'T THINKING, NOW, of solitary expeditions in search of fish and a few hours freedom. Nor was she concerned with the turned heads and disapproving stares as she left the residential end of Main Street behind and plunged into the crowd of shoppers, vendors and off-duty sailors in the commercial square. Only one thought occupied her mind as she dashed past Samuel Cary's furniture shop and Valentine Hussey's emporium and nearly crashed into a portly Quaker man in a beaver hat just coming out of the Manufacturers and Mechanics Bank. Only one thought pounded in her heart as, now short of breath, she sped past William Rotch's warehouse and Mr. Tuck's chandlery and Gideon Hussey's huge sail loft looming along the crushed shell street and wooden walks of Straight Wharf. Only one thought filled her as she pushed through the throng of astounded men rapidly gathering at the end of the dock, as she threaded between the outgoing casks of salt beef and the incoming casks of oil, and as she caught her breath in gulps of air redolent of tar and salt and sweat.

"Zacch!" she cried, and ran right into her brother's arms as he stepped off the lighter.

15

Her tall, strong twin showed as little care for constraint as she as he delightedly hugged her tightly, then lifted her in an exuberant swing that sent her petticoats whirling and the onlookers hooting their glee. "Good God, China, you've grown into a proper young lady," Zacch exclaimed as he finally held her off for examination. "Just look at you. Next you'll be telling me you're married and have a babe. Have I really been gone that long?"

"Aye, thee has," China replied, returning his scrutiny. He had grown, too. His long, lean frame was filling out and the boyish softness was receding from his face to reveal fine, straight features. Like China, he had thick, black hair and wide eyes the color of a Normandy fog, though his were without her intriguing charcoal outlines. "Thee wasn't shaving when last I saw thee," she said, rubbing her fingers along his firm jaw. "Besides," she added, as he laughed, "I'm not quite the proper young lady that thee thinks. Aunt Judith says that all decent women wait at home for their menfolk."

"And right she is, too," her father said severely. China whirled to face Zaccheus, her dismay at his tone evaporating when she saw the smile tugging at his lips. Although his wavy chestnut hair was now liberally salted with gray, and his face showed signs of weather and life's vicissitudes, he was still a hardy, handsome man. His rigid grief had mellowed somewhat over the years, and his pride in China's spirit overcame his chagrin at her lack of decorum.

"Zacch has read the chart quite correctly. You've become a beautiful young woman, China," he said admiringly. "However, I fear that you are making life hard for Aunt Judith with your harum-scarum ways."

China blushed for the second time that morning and said softly, "Welcome home, Papa." She held her hands un-

16

certainly at her sides, and Zacch reassuringly gripped one. Where once she had been sure of her father's love and warmth, ever since her mother died, Zaccheus had been remote and unreadable.

"Thank you, China," he said seriously. "We'll say our hellos at home, as is fitting. In the meantime, scud along and take your brother with you. I imagine he won't be good for anything, anyway, until he has had a good gam with you. I've business to discuss with the owners." He started off into the crowd, and then looked back. "Tell Aunt Judith I'll be home for supper," he added, as casually as if he had just been to 'Sconset for the scenery, instead of halfway around the world hunting whales.

"Aye, Papa," she called to his disappearing back. Then she gave an amused shrug and turned toward home, tugging her twin with her. "Now I've two people to reef my sails," she said ruefully to Zacch.

"And I'll wager neither of them can make you turn into the current," said a deep voice at her side. Astonished, China turned to stare into a pair of eyes as startlingly blue as Nantucket Harbor on a clear day in March. Like those bright waters, they were alive with surprises and strong undercurrents. China felt a warm flush rise to her cheeks, and a shiver run down her back, riveting her to the dock.

The owner of those eyes stood as tall as Zacch, an inch over six feet, but his shoulders were broader, while his hips stayed slim. His skin after years of exposure to the tropical sun was almost the color of mahogany and his hair, curling down the back of his neck and over the tops of his ears in an unruly fashion, was thick and dark. His nose was straight, his chin was strong, and in his right ear was a little gold hoop.

He carried himself with ease, almost with insouciance. At first glance he might have seemed just another unkempt sailor, albeit a very able-bodied and handsome one, but closer scrutiny showed keen intelligence in his arresting blue eyes and loosely checked passion just under his carefree exterior.

As if aware of the unnerving effect he was having on her, the stranger grinned sassily and added, "Though to my eye 'twas a fine set of petticoat sails you just unfurled and in no need of shortening at all."

Before China could sound her indignation at such audacity, Zacch laughed and said, "China, meet Jacob Swan. Jake, I guess you know that this is China."

China swung around to stare, now, at Zacch, incredulous that he was actually introducing her to this rake, instead of taking exception with his familiar speech. A warm, work-hardened hand seized hers, and she swung back to face Jake Swan. With her heart suddenly, and inexplicably, hammering, she sought to extract her hand, but he would neither relinquish it nor cease his bold grinning. "How does thee do?" she finally stammered.

"I do well enough, thank you," he answered. Then he laughed and said, "I'm afraid I've got the advantage of you. I feel I've known you for years, while you've never set eyes on me before."

"Jake skipped with us in Valparaiso," Zacch explained, as China tried to pull around to face him. Jake would not release her hand. "He was on the beach after his own whaler, a barkentine out of New Bedford, was condemned. And we were an officer short since Mr. Gardner slipped on the cutting stage attaching the hook to a blanket piece of blubber. He was quite lucky. He only broke his leg. But we put him down to mend in Valparaiso and took up Jake in his stead."

"Poor Mr. Gardner," China said, finally yanking her fingers free.

"Nay," Zacch said, shaking his head, oblivious to China's struggles and to Jake's devilish grin. "I think we got the best of the bargain. Mr. Gardner was too fond of his rum and too quick with a sharp word. No one liked him. Not even Papa. But everyone likes Jake." China could tell by the warmth of Zacch's tone that he was not the least of Jake's champions. Somehow the thought was disquieting.

A deep laugh from Jake brought China's gaze back to him. "We're not on board ship, now, Zacch," he said. "I'm no longer your officer, so you needn't speak softly around me and about me. You're finally free to say exactly what you think."

"'Tis true," Zacch protested. "All the hands forward think you're as fair a mate as ever they've sailed under. They all say the same: that you'll not ask any man to do what you can't do yourself. Though you can do a deal more than most ordinary men!" His admiration was evident. China's discomfort increased.

"And you're the first person Papa has talked to so much in years," he continued. "Why I've seen you two gamming for hours. He enjoys being able to discuss politics and business, not to mention the matter of whaling, with someone who has as much knowledge as you. He hasn't been so easy since Maman died."

The discomfort became a sharp pang of jealousy. Who was this man? How dare he captivate her brother and beguile her father, while she knew nothing of his existence.

Jake seemed unaware of her resentment as he replied, seriously and sincerely, "It goes two ways, Zacch. I've learned a lot from your father. And I've come to understand a great many things I never had the patience to sort out before. He's a wise man is Zaccheus. He's weathered many a gale in life." Then his grin came back and he added in a bantering tone, "To say nothing of all I've learned from you, Zacch. Most of it about China."

China looked sharply from one to the other. "How's that?" she demanded.

"Your doting twin is forever talking about you, writing you letters or doing you a bit of scrimshaw." Jake ignored the color rising in China's face as he continued, "I've heard all about your years on board the *Maid*. I know about the time you fell overboard in Honolulu Harbor, trying to catch the phosphorescences in the water, and about the time you nearly burned down the galley baking a coconut cake. I know that your favorite color is the pink inside a conch shell from Christmas Island; that your favorite spot on the ship is hanging off the bowsprit; and that your favorite island in the Pacific is in the Galapagos, because you like to ride the giant tortoises."

He paused a minute, squinted appraisingly at her, then said, "The only thing Zacch didn't tell me is how beautiful you are. He had me believing you were a rag-tag tomboy; a shorter, skinnier, beskirted version of himself."

His teasing tone masked the actual intensity of his surprise. When he first saw her, with her arms wrapped tightly around Zacch's neck, a shiny tear of happiness in her sensuous eyes, and her dress swirling around her slim, but definite, curves, he felt an instant rush of desire that he tried, not quite successfully, to squelch. Such lust was fine for tavern girls or South Seas wahines, but not for Zacch's twin sister.

In fact, before meeting her, Jake had almost come to think of China as his sister, too. He had grown extremely close to both Zacch and Zaccheus in his three years on board the *Maid*. Despite an initial reluctance to accept any emotional encumbrances, he suddenly had found himself part of their family. Eight years older than Zacch, he had become the boy's elder brother, showing him the fine points on a variety of subjects from celestial navigation and Shakespeare's sonnets to shore leave in Samoa. Simultaneously, he had become Zaccheus's older son, a companion and confidant, a capable shoulder to lean on, an understanding ear to fill.

Once his early hesitancy was overcome, Jake had found himself hungrily welcoming this new sensation. The scars created by his own cold upbringing were forgotten as he had thrown himself heart and soul into the Joy family. He had almost felt himself mourning Josephine, missing Aunt Judith's oyster stew and chuckling indulgently at thoughts of China's escapades. His feeling of brotherly benevolence ended abruptly at the sight of her, however, and he attempted to cover his ensuing confusion with a careless air.

China's feelings at this moment were more easily defined. She was angry. Angry at Jake's insinuation into her father's and brother's confidences, angry at his impudent stares and arrogant words, angry at Zacch's conspiratorial chortle, and most of all, angry at herself for blushing like the sky at dawn and for feeling thrilled that Jake thought she was beautiful.

In her coolest, most correct manner, she replied, ''Perhaps I will have the same opportunity to become acquainted with thee and to learn thy favorite color. Although I'm sure thee is anxious to regain thy home in New Bedford and will not anchor here long.''

''On the contrary,'' Jake answered, his eyes crinkling in amusement as he picked up the challenge, ''I'm not bound for New Bedford, at all. I'm from New York, but I've no reason to rush back there.'' There was determination in his voice, even though he spoke lightly. ''I'll be cruising Nantucket shores until the *Maid* sails again. Your father has promised me a berth.''

"Oh," China said, disappointment apparent in her tone.

"Aye," Zacch chimed in enthusiastically, "you'll have plenty of time to become friends. Jake's to stay with us. He'll be sharing my room."

"Oh," China said again, in alarm this time. The thought of Jake sleeping only a closet width away from her, made her heart leap to her throat.

"Aye," Jake repeated, goadingly, "we'll have plenty of time to become friends. But in the meantime, I'd best see to the cargo and to a shipkeeper's crew. Someone has to mind the *Maid* while we all come ashore. Don't wait for me, I'll come home with Zaccheus." He turned to saunter off down the dock, his path made clear by men automatically stepping aside in respect of his height and of the undefinable air of authority that seemed to envelop him.

China watched his hip-rolling gait, the sea chest riding easily on his shoulder, and the sun glinting off the gold hoop in his ear. As if he knew she was staring, he turned from ten yards away to grin and to call, "By the way, China, my favorite color is fast become gray. With a touch of charcoal."

Once more color flooded China's face and once more her anger flared at his insolence. With a swish of her skirt, she whipped around and headed for home, hardly waiting for Zacch to shoulder his own sea chest and stride along beside her. He seemed unconscious of the tension between his twin and his friend. He hadn't caught the baiting in their speech.

"Heave to, China," he said genially. "Give me a chance to accustom my legs to the land again. 'Twas eighty-four days ago that I last stood on firm ground, and that was a miserable cove in South America where we took on fresh water."

"I'm sorry, Zacch, I forgot," China apologized. She slowed her pace, feeling contrite. She hadn't meant to lose patience with Zacch. Without Jake's piercing blue eyes to unsettle her, her happiness at her brother's homecoming started to return. "After so long asea, 'tis easier to roam the deck during a howling gale than to take a few calm steps on land," she said. "The ground simply won't stay in place. 'Tis a bit like being an infant again, just learning to walk."

"You're right about that," Zacch replied, starting to get the rhythm of his feet, as they put Straight Wharf behind them. "And we've roamed many a stormy deck this voyage, too." He shifted his chest more comfortably and continued. "Did you get the letter I wrote about the typhoon we weathered on Japan? Probably not," he answered himself. "I left it in the letter box on St. James not even a year ago. But that was a storm for the records.

"When we were down in the trough of a swell, the crest was higher than the mizzen crosstrees. We were cruising in the company of the *Alice Brattle*, out of New London, and we'd lose complete sight of her. Then up we'd go on the crest and we'd sight her so far down she looked like one of those miniature ships that are stuck in bottles. We came out with only a ripped jib, but the *Brattle* lost two boats overboard when they yawed. Broke off their waist davits, as well. The way her helm was handled, she was lucky to be afloat with all hands alive by the end of the storm." Here he paused for a breath and a disgusted shake of his head. "There must have been a greenie at the helm. 'Twas sheer carelessness. Papa let naught but himself and Jake handle the wheel throughout the whole three days."

China caught her breath at the mention of Jake's name and was again tense with hostility. The news that Jake's seamanship was so eminently respected only added to her resentment. Fortunately, Zacch was too excited to notice his sister's face go grim. While she clutched frantically at her fading gladness, Zacch rambled on about his adven-

23

tures at sea, but the damage was done. Jake had ruined her mood.

Despite a glorious afternoon sprawled in the warm sand atop a dune at Dionis, exchanging stories of the past three years, China was still feeling irritated by supper time. Her edgy feelings increased as Jake easily wrung smiles and second helpings from Aunt Judith with appreciative comments about her quahog chowder and humble apologies for his intrusion.

China had just cleared the plates from the table and was soaping them in the sink, when Zaccheus announced, with typical Nantucket understatement, "I've talked to Daniel Ray today and have proposed to buy the *China Maid* from him. He agreed."

The tureen nearly slipped through China's fingers as she started in astonishment and pleasure. Before she could voice her delight, Aunt Judith sniffed and said, "'Tis a fine thing to own a ship if thee has the money, but the *Maid* is an old one and might not warrant the investment. I know thee has sentimental attachments to her, Zaccheus, but thee must be practical, too. If it is a ship of thine own thee yearns for, have one built anew."

Zaccheus shook his head. "The old *Maid* is a good ship," he insisted. "Both Jake and I have been through her with a fine-tooth comb. Aye, she needs a bit of work to put her absolutely to rights, but she has a lot of life in her yet. Wouldn't you agree, Jake?"

"She's a fine ship," Jake said earnestly, resting his arms on the oak-planked table and leaning forward. He directed his conversation toward Aunt Judith, but his eyes were on China who was standing stiffly by the sink. "She was overbuilt to begin with. Her first owners designed her to fish the Bering Sea where she'd constantly be battling ice floes. There's very little rot in her and only one cracked rib. The telling inspection will come when she's hauled on the ways and we go over her bottom. But from the looks of her on the inside and from the way she handles, I'm guessing we won't find much damage from the worms. You'll not find a more sea kindly vessel, that's for sure. And the price is very fair.''

China could not bring herself to turn and face the table. She was seething. She could understand how her brother, being younger and less experienced, might be blinded by Jake's seeming superiority and self-assurance, but how could her father be?

Behind her, Zaccheus nodded. ''Indeed the price is fair, though it'll cost something to refit her properly. She'll use up all my savings, Aunt Judith. There might be a few lean years for you and China before we come in with our first cash cargo. I'll take her out for only three years, and I'll surely save aside some money for your expenses, but you'll have to be prudent and sail close to the wind.''

''I know all about lean years,'' Aunt Judith snorted. ''I've been through more lean years in my life than not. For most of my girlhood, we were at war with England, with no ships of any size or purpose going in or out of this harbor because of the British blockade. And was it not lean years after the second war with England that sent thee to France? Does thee remember the soup kitchen on Gardner Street that kept Nantucketers fed during those lean years? Thee swore thee'd never ask for charity and so off thee went to Le Havre to find a berth and meet thy wife.

'''Tis not the lean years that bother me, Zaccheus. 'Tis the thought of thee spending all thy money and thy time on a ship that may be worth neither. If she is such a fine vessel, why is Daniel Ray so quick to part with her? He hasn't the name for being a fool.''

"Nay, he's no fool, and neither are you, Aunt Judith," Zaccheus said, with a gentle chuckle. "But he's using the same reckoning that you are. He sees that she's old and needs some attention, and so he's glad to be rid of her rather than risk any investment in her. She's paid for herself many times over. For him this will just be a bonus."

"He hasn't sailed her, either," Jake said. "He's looking only at the ledger, not at the ship. To be fair, he's probably making a wise business move. But so is Zaccheus."

Aunt Judith gave a shrug of submission. Zacch gave a whoop of glee, and Zaccheus settled back with a sigh of satisfaction. Jake's feeling of pleasure was mitigated by the sight of China's still-turned back. He felt almost annoyed with her. Why was she being so contrary? She should be over here, congratulating her father, rejoicing with her twin, not stuck in the corner ignoring them. Surely the dirty dishes weren't that fascinating.

China was hardly aware of the dishes as her hands mechanically ran the rag around and around. Her rigid anger was being replaced by a sensation of utter loneliness. The happiness she should have felt by having her namesake finally in the family was diluted by the obvious addition of Jake, as well. She felt unneeded. It was Jake's opinion that was important, Jake's presence that gave pleasure, and Jake's knowledge that was necessary. Jake and Zacch and Zaccheus were a trio; they formed a circle she could not enter. The abandonment that had begun eight years before when Zacch sailed away to sea was now complete. Jake was stealing her father, her twin and even her memories of the *China Maid*.

2

NANTUCKET
June 20, 1839

CHINA WAS THE FIRST ONE UP this morning, her bare feet hitting the pine plank floor even before the sun burst over the horizon. Today was Shearing Day; anticipation of the festivities to come urged her out of bed early. She dressed quickly and tiptoed down the narrow staircase, careful not to wake Zacch. Part of her lightheartedness was a result of Jake's absence. He had received an official-looking letter from New York ten days ago and had left on the packet that afternoon. She could look forward to a whole, happy day in Zacch's company, just like it used to be.

Ever since her father had signed the papers for the *China Maid*, China had seen precious little of her twin, with or without the omnipresent Jake. The three men spent almost every waking hour at the Marine Railroad on Brant Point, overseeing each inch of the ship's refitting. On his own, Zacch might not have been so vigilant, but Jake had admonished, "You can never learn too much about shipbuilding—not if you mean to spend your life at sea. What if you are wrecked on some uninhabited island in the South Seas? Why, you could grow old and perish there, completely alone, for want of knowing how to caulk a seam."

After that, Zacch was just as diligent about observing every timber, trunnel, mortice and tenon as Jake. Together they watched, and helped, as the keel was refastened, the planks replaced, the old oakum reefed out and the new ironed in, the hull copper sheathed, the bulwarks rebuilt, the topsides redecked, the masts restepped and the hold scarved with stanchions not yet scalloped by chafing casks. Except for breakfast and supper, China never saw either one. And even at those times, their conversations revolved around the *Maid*.

Today, however, would be different, China thought triumphantly, as she splashed water on her face at the kitchen sink. Today would be a day devoted to feasting and to fun. The whole island would gather in the meadow by Miacomet Pond, arriving by foot and by calash and by the curious two-wheeled Quaker cart. For the past three days, shepherds on horseback, aided by long leather whips, had rounded up the sheep that roamed freely about the island and had driven them into the mile-long pens by the pond. Yesterday, they had been thoroughly dunked and scrubbed. Today, while all of Nantucket celebrated this annual event with a jubilance not often seen among the serious-minded Friends, the sheep would be shorn. Humming happily, China dried her face on the soft sacking towel and waited for her family to rise.

"You're up and about at an early hour," came Jake's voice from the back door. Arms akimbo, he leaned casually against the frame.

China looked up, startled. Then her heart sank. "What is thee doing here?" she wailed. "I thought thee was in New York."

Jake laughed at her obvious dismay, white teeth gleaming in his tanned face. "You needn't sound so glad to see me," he said sardonically. "I *was* in New York, but now I'm here. I wouldn't want to miss Shearing Day, would I? After all that you've said about the good things to eat and the two-headed calves on view? How often do I have a chance to see one of those?''

"Ho, Jake," Zacch said delightedly, as he entered the kitchen. "When did you get back? And what don't you have a chance to see?''

"The packet came in late last night, but I didn't want to wake you, so I slept on board and came around just now. China and I were discussing some of the marvels we'll see today at the Shearing."

"Aye," Zacch said. "It should be a jolly day. I've never been to one before, though I came close in thirty-five. We made port just two days late. We'd best not be late today, though. I promised Franklin Folger I'd help some with the sheep. You can lend a hand, too. Papa and Aunt Judith will come along later."

Jake laughed again and came fully into the kitchen. "I'll do what I can, but I scarcely know one end of a sheep from the other. Perhaps I'd do better to help China fix our breakfast so we can be off."

"'Tis an unnecessary offer," China said loftily. "We'll eat breakfast there." Some of her enthusiasm returned as she continued, "There's always fresh broiled salmon and whole roast pigs, as well as veal and mutton and beefsteaks swimming in butter. And donuts. And blackberry pie. Thee won't lack for something to eat."

"Stow that talk," Jake groaned, in mock desperation. "You're making me weak just thinking of it. Let's set sail for this squantum."

As Jake and Zacch set the pace, chatting amiably about the progress on the *Maid*, China loped along, a half step behind. Her annoyance grew as she hurried to keep up. Whenever Jake appeared on the horizon, she seemed to disappear from view.

Although her twin might have been less than alert to China's presence, Jake was in no way unaware of her. He kept up his curious questions about work in the boatyard, but his sharp blue eyes were constantly swinging in her direction, absorbing every detail about her. He saw the anger clouding her clear brow and turning down the corners of her full lips. He saw her softly curved breasts heave as she caught her breath at the quick gait. He enjoyed watching her. Despite his relentless teasing, he realized how much he was attracted to her. He had missed her while he was away.

They could hear and smell the festival long before they were upon it. The sound of eight thousand bleating sheep and the aroma of roasting meats hovered over the whole meadow. China's irritation dissolved as she allowed the excitement to envelop her. They wound their way through the fast-swelling throng in search of Franklin Folger's pens. When China once threatened to be cut off by the crowd, Jake reached back and yanked on her. A thrill ran through her at his touch, and she looked at him in surprise and wonder, but he seemed to pay her no more mind than he would a lagging child. China felt an inexplicable stab of disappointment.

They found the pens at the same moment that Harriet Swain found them. "Ho, China," she called. "I've been looking for you all morning. Mother and I just returned from visiting Aunt Phoebe in Philadelphia, not three days ago, and I haven't had a chance to come and call. Father told us that the *China Maid* came in. I was so happy for you. Is that really Zacch with you?"

"'Tis indeed Zacch," China answered. "I didn't think thee would miss Shearing Day, even for all the merry times in Philadelphia. Welcome home." She leaned across to kiss her friend's cheek.

"What do you mean, am I really Zacch?" her brother demanded jovially. "Who else would I be? Hello, Harriet. I wondered why you weren't waiting for me at the wharf with China." He too planted a kiss on her cheek, sending a blush of color across the pale skin.

Harriet was the daughter of Benjamin Swain, a wealthy shipowner and merchant, a man of blunt looks and a compassionate nature. Harriet had inherited both qualities from her father, although the plainness of her features was softened by the natural sympathy in her brown eyes. She was the kind of person who set food out for stray cats, splinted the broken wings of sparrows and freed butterflies from the nets of naughty boys. It was this instinct that had made her take China's hand, as China had stood all alone and miserable, on her first day of school, eight years before. They had been friends ever since, bound by mutual admiration. Harriet was in awe of China's adventurousness and independence; China was impressed by Harriet's tolerance and patience.

"You know that even if I had been here, I'd never have had the courage to greet you on the wharf the way China does," Harriet said, shaking her head in wonder at China's nerve. "I shall be put to the test, though, when my own brother returns from England, shan't I, Zenas?" she asked a slender young man at her side.

"What's this?" China asked. "Is thee going to England? I hadn't heard."

"I am," Zenas replied with a touch of excitement and pride in his mild voice. Though actually two years older than the twins, Zenas looked several years younger than the sea-strengthened Zacch. Blond hair fell softly across his pale forehead. "I'll be gone six years, some spent in the university, and some employed by a British shipping firm. They act as our agents in England and in Europe. Father

31

thinks it would be wise for me to learn the business from the other side of the Atlantic, too.''

A half-disguised snort of disgust brought China's gaze around to Jake. A look of disdain filled his rugged face. China's eyes narrowed in irritation. Although she had never much noticed Zenas, other than his being Harriet's brother, she knew he was a kind person and undeserving of Jake's contempt.

"I don't think thee has met Jacob Swan," she said in a cool tone. "Jake was second mate on the *China Maid* this last trip. Perhaps some day, if he proves himself, thee can find him a berth on one of thy ships."

Zenas failed to notice either the ice in China's voice or the sardonic amusement in Zacch's eyes as he replied seriously, "Of course. We're always looking for good men."

Any further comment on the issue was cut off by the arrival of a small group of young people. By virtue of their stature in the community, to say nothing of their agreeable natures, the Swains attracted a crowd. Today, though, as always in recent months, Obed Hussey's attention was centered squarely on China. The solid, stolid son of a sailmaker gazed with inarticulate longing on her lovely face, oblivious to the adoration in Harriet's gentle eyes.

Jake's attempts to monitor this new threat were interrupted by the artless giggles of the Coffin sisters, Liddy and Sarah. The two girls were opposites in every way. Liddy, the older, was dark haired and vivacious, while Sarah was a porcelain doll, blond with wide, innocent blue eyes that instantly ensnared Zacch. He was so bowled over by Sarah's delicate features and guileless grace, he hardly saw Barzillai Cartwright, a ruddy-cheeked seaman of his own age and build, hovering solicitously by her side.

China, already uncomfortable under the silent stare of Obed, and oddly irked by Liddy's flirtatious overtures toward Jake, felt her heart sink at the enthralled look on her brother's face. Here was another claim on his attention. It was with great relief, therefore, that she heard Franklin Folger call from the midst of his pen, "Zacch, where has thee been? We've nearly all finished, but some extra hands would still be welcome."

Reluctantly, Zacch tore himself away from the sweet Sarah, first extracting a promise that she would wait for him to finish his duties. With much more willingness, Jake unwrapped himself from Liddy and entered the melee of bawling sheep, swirling dust and flying fleece. As they were completely unskilled in shearing, Zacch and Jake were assigned the task of capturing each sheep and holding it still while the shearer whisked off its wool.

The sheep, accustomed to browsing alone and unmolested on the commons most of the year, were little better than wild. It had been a terrifying few days for them, and none of the brutes was in an obliging mood. While the others looked on with increasing hilarity, Jake and Zacch wrestled with the shaggy beasts, often ending up with no more than a handful of fluff and a mouthful of dust. Forgetting her anger and apprehension, China laughed until tears rolled down her face and she clutched her side.

When the last sheep stood naked and protesting, Jake slapped the dirt off his clothes and demanded of China, "What do you find so funny? Haven't you ever seen a man work before?"

She laughed again and shook her head, her cheeks rosy with mirth. "If thee chases whales with the same deftness that thee chases sheep, the spermaceti need have no worry. They are safe from thee."

A grin split his face despite the growl he tried to put in his voice. "There's a good reason I'm a whaler and not a farmer," he said. "There's not many a whale I've set my sight on still swimming in the sea. And now, how about some of that breakfast you've promised."

"Haven't you eaten yet?" Liddy asked, her voice full of sympathy. She slid her arm through his and started toward the tents in the field. "'Tis a shame for a man like you to go unfed. Come. There's any number of booths where we can get a bite to eat."

"Aye," Harriet agreed, hastily swinging in behind them. In her own quiet way, she had sized up the situation and had decided that Jake was a strong enough man to handle China, and humorous enough to make her happy. She wasn't about to let Liddy get away with him. "We could all do with some refreshment. Laughing is hard work, too. Jacob Jones, the whitewasher, has his booth again. I'll wager he has some quahogs baking and some butter melting, ready to douse them in. Maybe some oysters and pickled onions, too."

"I saw a booth with the best-looking shearing buns," Sarah said, accepting Zacch's proffered arm with a sweet smile. "They had a sugar glaze and currants in each of the three corners."

"I saw it, too," Obed said suddenly, then said no more as he tagged along beside China.

It was nearly noon when the little group had wandered from booth to booth and all had had their fill of roasted ham and huckleberry pie, fried chicken and cranberry tarts, broiled salmon and poached bass, coffee, tea and lemonade.

"'Tis time for the Big Tent," Liddy announced, decisively. She looked up at Jake and asked, "Do you know about the Big Tent?"

He winked at China and answered, "Is that where they keep the two-headed calves? I've heard a good deal about them."

"There's a striped pig and dancing dogs, as well," Zenas said.

Liddy waved away these spectacles with a sweep of her hand. "'Tis where there are gypsies who tell your fortune and Blind Frank, the fiddler, all come over from the continent. They've laid a wood floor down and there's dancing. Although," she added, a pout playing on her face, "Blind Frank only knows two tunes. 'Tu you can't and tu you can, all the way down to the shearing pen.' 'Tis monotonous after a while." Nevertheless, she took Jake's arm again and led the way to the Big Tent sitting in the center of the field.

The others followed without hesitation. Only China stopped short of the entrance. The Big Tent, with its frivolous attractions, was forbidden territory for Friends. While Aunt Judith might forgive her impetuous dash to the docks to greet Zacch after a three-year absence, she would be deeply insulted if China indulged in music and dancing simply for the sake of an afternoon's pleasure. Contentment draining out of her, she watched the group disappear into the tent without a backward glance. Only Harriet lingered, torn between her loyalty to China and her desire to trail Obed. Sensing her infatuation, China shooed her along.

Feeling very bereft, China wandered away from the gaiety. She made her way down the length of the sheep pens toward the beach beyond. Her dejected walk was momentarily interrupted by a call from one of the pens.

"Ho, Chi-China. Where are you going today?" The booming voice belonged to John James Henry Wannaleana, a giant of a man from the Society Islands. When the twins were only five, the *China Maid* had rescued him in his storm-damaged pirogue, a thousand miles from home. In eternal gratitude, John James Henry had pledged himself to Zaccheus, becoming the captain's self-appointed protector and harpooner. He had adopted the Christian names out of respect for his new life, though his spiritual beliefs remained unchanged.

He had taken a special interest in China, fascinated by watching this white girl child grow up. As if she hadn't been spoiled enough by the rest of the crew, John James Henry had showered her with trinkets and toys, and, as his peculiar command of English increased, he had regaled her with tales from his native island, as well.

China's spirits lifted at the sight of her huge friend. "Ho, John James Henry," she answered. "I'm going down to watch the sea."

"Chi-China, you going alone? Where your rascal twin Zacch?"

"He's gone dancing with a pretty girl," China replied, trying hard to keep the resentment out of her voice.

John James Henry eyed her shrewdly. "I go to watch the sea, too. Might be bad spirits. Might be sharks to take you away."

She laughed at the thought of bad spirits on Nantucket. "Nay, I doubt that very much. The town fathers would never let them land. Thee needn't fret. I'll be perfectly safe. Anyway, thy strength is needed here to help with the sheep." So saying, she waved and continued on her way.

Despite China's reassurances, John James Henry was unconvinced. Nothing must happen to his charge. He was about to leave the sheep to their own devices, when he saw Jake, a quilt thrown over his shoulder and a sack in his hand, following the path that China had taken. A big smile relieved the worry on his face and he muttered to himself, "Ho Ja-Jake. Good. Good. Good."

As Jake had entered the Big Tent, the tenacious Liddy on his arm, he had glanced over his shoulder to make certain China was not far off. He had felt a little too old for this sophomoric group, but he had tolerated it for the sake of seeing China. He had meant to unlatch himself from Liddy as soon as Blind Frank struck up one of his two tunes, and to whirl China away in a dance. He had looked forward to the chance of clasping one hand around her slim waist and the other over her soft fingers. But she had gone.

Seeing the puzzled look on his face, Harriet had quietly explained, "The Quakers don't approve of music and dance. I doubt that China minds a good tune, but her aunt would surely object. 'Tis not worth it to rile her over an afternoon's merry-making."

Jake had looked at Harriet with new respect. He hadn't suspected this ordinary-appearing girl of such perception. "You're a good shipmate, Miss Harriet Swain," he had said.

With the scantiest of excuses, he had removed Liddy's arm and had left her fuming. He had gotten out of the tent just in time to catch a glimpse of China's back, disappearing down the path toward the sea. Knowing that there was only one place she could be headed, he had taken the time to grab a quilt from Zaccheus's high-wheeled cart and to fill an old flour sack with fried donuts and a few earthenware bottles of spruce beer.

Immersed in her loneliness and taunted by the distant sounds of revelry, China followed Miacomet Pond as it flowed toward the ocean. She felt betwixt and between, not quite a Nantucketer, but not really a coof, as the off-islanders were called. She was no longer a seafarer, but still not a landlubber; she mouthed the Quaker beliefs, but didn't feel them in her heart. It seemed indisputable that her girlhood was gone, the careless days when her life was inseparable from Zacch's, but she wasn't sure what had come in its place. She felt adrift.

A pathetic baaing broke her gloomy introspection, and China turned to see a small lamb, up to its neck in water, snagged in the reeds along the pond's edge, pinned in place by a jumble of branches and brambles. "Ahh, thee poor creature," China said softly. "*Pauvre petit*. Thee has lost thy way, just like in the Bible."

The lamb blinked at China and bleated again. China left the path and came over to the edge of the pond, studying the situation with her hands on her hips. "Don't distract me while I am trying to think. I must free thee of the briars and pull thee ashore, but how shall I do that without getting wet?"

Again the lamb bleated, more hoarsely this time. "I know, I know," she soothed. "Thee is feeling abandoned and helpless. I feel that way myself. Would that my troubles were as simple as thine. If all I had to do was haul myself out of a pond, I'd do so in jig time, shake myself off and go along. But 'tis not so easy for me. I'm caught in a pond that has no water; one I can't swim in. But there, I'll pull thee out and hope that I'll be pulled out of mine, in turn."

Squatting on her heels at the very edge of the water, China alternately pushed at the brambles with a stick and pulled at the lamb. The little beast made no headway, but succeeded in splashing the sleeves of her dress. Exasperated, China leaned farther forward and gave another yank on the soggy fleece. With a wobbly leap, the lamb burst free, sending China face first into the still icy waters of the pond.

The frigid water took her breath away. Instinctive fear made her fight for the surface, her panic easing only when she righted herself, coughing and sputtering for air. At that point the pond was no more than waist deep, but the banks were sheer and slippery, and the brambles that had snared the lamb now secured China. Reeds snarled her petticoats, mud sucked at her shoes. As the initial shock of the plunge wore off, the coldness of the water penetrated to her bones. The more she struggled to pull free, the more tangled she became. *"Pauvre petite,"* came a mocking voice above her. "You've lost your way, haven't you?"

China stopped her futile flailing and looked up to see Jake balancing on his heels a safe distance away. His insolent grin was more than she could bear. All the lonely disappointment of the morning, all the frustration and discomfort of her current fix, found focus in rage. "How dare thee?" she hissed. "Thee was eavesdropping. 'Tis a sly, cowardly trick."

"How can you say such a thing?" Jake protested in pretend horror. "On my oath, I never heard a word that the lamb said."

"Thy conceit is odious!" China shouted, splashing about once more. She longed to be able to turn her back on his arrogant expression and to stomp away, but she was stuck in place.

"If I were you, China, I wouldn't be frolicking in the water and thinking of unkind things to say to me. I'd be hauling myself out of the pond in jig time. At least before that snapping turtle that's headed your way gets a bite of your beautiful flesh."

With a gasp, China turned to see a turtle swimming leisurely toward her. She turned back to Jake and demanded, "Help me out of here. If thee had even the barest acquaintance with common courtesy, thee would have offered assistance long ago."

"Ahhh," said Jake, as if in sudden enlightenment, "you need a hand, do you? You should have sung out straightaway, instead of being so shy." He inched toward the edge and mused, "Now how can I pull you out without getting wet? Don't distract me while I think."

China cast a frantic glance over her shoulder at the approaching turtle and said furiously, "Thee has made thy point. Now just extend thy arm that I may get a firm leverage against the muddy bank."

Ignoring her instructions, Jake leaned forward and slipped his hands underneath her arms. In one easy motion he stood up and swung her free to solid ground, leaving the turtle to chomp at the empty air in her wake.

China's eyes widened at the suddenness of her release. "Oh," she said, then gritted her teeth and added, "thank thee."

"Such sweet words are ample reward," Jake said, with a low bow. His bantering stopped when he saw her shivering from the effects of the icy water and the deceptively fresh June breeze blowing on her wet skin. Her usually lush pink lips were nearly blue.

"Bejesus, that water must have been colder than I thought. You should have said so, China. Come on." He caught up the quilt and the sack and took her by the hand.

"Where is thee taking me? Let go. I've no further need of thy help." The cold shaking through her had dulled her anger and her attempts to pull her hand from his warm grip were weak.

"Don't struggle," Jake commanded. "I'm steering for the lee of that dune. You can sit in the sun 'til you dry."

They rounded the hill and found a slash of hot sand, protected from the breeze and facing the sea. China sank unceremoniously to the ground, her teeth still chattering and her fingers numb. His bright blue eyes were serious as Jake knelt before her and took both her hands in his, chafing them vigorously. When shivers continued to ripple through her, he said, "You'll have to take your clothes off and wrap yourself in the quilt while they dry. You'll never get warm this way."

"Ha!" China retorted, between clacking teeth. "Does thee take me for a simpleton? Even silly schoolgirls know better than to take their clothes off in front of a sailor. My clothes will stay in place, thank thee. I'll be warm shortly."

"Silly schoolgirls know better than to fall into ponds, too," Jake said, with an impatient shake of his head. "And silly schoolgirls know better than to wander off by themselves. They also know that they'll never get warm while they are head to toe in wet clothes. Now do you take them off or do I take them off for you?" He yanked one shoe free from her foot and reached for the other before she could react.

"Fiend!" she cried. "Where does thee get the nerve to toss me about as if I were a child?" One arm shot out to push him away, but he caught it easily and held it between his hands.

"When you act like a child, so shall you be treated. If you don't get warm soon, you'll get sick. You're absurd if you think I will attack you, tempting as you might be. Here, you have my word that I won't take advantage of you without your clothes on. That's a fair bargain, isn't it? Now what's it to be?" He waited a moment, still holding her hand, watching her seductive eyes turn stormy, and thinking that he would be hard pressed to keep his promise. Even in her miserable state, her exotic beauty aroused him.

"Come, come," he coaxed. "I'll give you my coat, too. My coat and my word. What better protection could you want? I'd offer you my shirt, as well, but you might try to take advantage of me with no clothes on." He pulled off the other shoe.

China jerked away, snapping, "Thee is despicable. Thee judges all the world by thy lowly standards." Part of her outrage was caused by her own uncertainty. The feeling of his hand, firmly gripping hers, the thought of having nothing between them but a quilt, somehow unsettled her. Despite her earnest desire to detest him for his intrusion into her family, she found herself intrigued by him. Even while she longed to slap the mocking grin off his face, her hand wanted to linger on his bronzed skin.

Again a shiver ran through her, only partly due to chill. Jake made another move forward, and she made another move back. "Very well," she said, abruptly. "Give me thy coat and take a walk down the beach."

Jake looked genuinely relieved. "Here is my coat," he said, stripping his arms out of it at once, "but I'll just turn my back." He arched his eyebrows suggestively. "You might need some help."

With a provoked sigh, China snatched the proffered coat and retreated as far as possible down the dune. In truth, she could have used some help because her fingers were numb and her arms were shaking and there were eighteen buttons down the back of her dress. She would have shredded the fabric, though, before she asked Jake to come to her aid. Eventually she overcame the buttons and the soaking laces of her petticoats and let them all drop to her feet. She slipped on Jake's coat, wrapped the quilt around her body, dug her toes into the hot sand and sat down with a thud. She felt warmer, already.

"Done?" Jake asked, turning around. He gathered up the sodden heap of clothes and spread them over bayberry bushes to dry in the sun and the breeze, then came back to sprawl next to her in the sand. "And now for a bit of refreshment," he said, pulling the donuts and spruce beer out of the sack.

China eyed the bottles of beer suspiciously. "Does thee now mean to ply me with strong spirits?" she asked, with a sudden return of her sense of humor. With the cessation of her shivering came a restoration of her enthusiasm. For the first time, she felt equal for Jake's teasing.

"Actually, I mean to ply you with donuts until you beg for mercy," he responded. "The beer is for me, to restore my strength after a vigorous afternoon rescuing a maiden in distress. But you may have one if you like."

"Hmph," China said, reaching her hand through the folds of her bulky bunting to snag a sugary donut. "I'll not dispute the rescue, but most of my distress was caused by thy wretched behavior. 'Tis ill-mannered, in the first place, to listen in on the conversations of others. And secondly, 'tis most unkind of thee to throw my words back at me."

Jake laughed and raised his arms in a gesture of surrender. "I didn't think you had such private thoughts to share with a lamb," he admitted. "You're right. I apologize. It wasn't nice of me to rag you so." He took a swig of beer, then added, as a wicked gleam lit his eyes, "But it *was* fun. You were such a perfect target. It isn't often I can pin you in place. Here." He extended another donut to ward off the temper sparking in her great, gray eyes. "A peace offering. You can wash it down with some of this beer."

Still dubious of his sincerity, but desirous of the treat, China accepted both donut and beer. She neither acknowledged his apology, however, nor scolded him further. She wanted to forget the whole discussion.

Jake seemed content to let the subject drop, and for a while they munched donuts and drank beer in an easy silence. Lulled by the sun and the mild brew, China leaned back against the eroded face of the dune and studied the sea. Waves rolled endlessly in to shore, slapped against the sand and scudded away, to be carried by deep currents beyond sight, to the Azores and Africa. Propped on one elbow, Jake sifted sand through his fingers and studied her.

"If I am not mistaken," he said finally, "your thoughts are a long way away. What do you see out there, China? Do you see France? The little cottage where you were born? Would you rather be sitting on a beach on that side of the ocean?"

A slight flush colored her creamy cheeks at being caught daydreaming, but her mellow mood remained. There had been none of his usual sarcasm in Jake's questions, and she answered him honestly. "Aye, I was across the Atlantic, but not in France today. I barely remember living there, though it seems to me that the beach was not so fine and soft as this one, but covered in small smooth pebbles."

She paused to swirl sand in her hand before leaning back again and continuing, "Maman once told me that she used to sneak away to the beach whenever she had a free moment. She would stand at the edge of the water and skip flat stones across the surface, wishing more than anything she could see what was on the other side of the horizon. And then one day Papa came down the beach and took her across many oceans and beyond many horizons. She said that it was as if the sea had heard her prayers and had sent Papa to answer them. She felt blessed."

China stopped, rolling her head to look at Jake. His face was serious now, intent on hers. "And is that what you see when you stare at the sea, China?" he asked. "Are you praying that the sea will send you a sailor to take you off beyond the horizon in his whaling ship? To pull you out of your waterless pond?"

With a soft laugh and a shake of her head, China answered, "Nay, I've no wish for a whaling man in my life. 'Tis a bloody, brutal business and I'm heartily sick of it. The men go off to sea for years at a time to hunt and kill giant beasts, who bear no malice toward anyone, while the women wait on shore with their fatherless children and their lonely thoughts and worries."

Catching sight of Jake's eyebrows raised in astonishment, China laughed again. "Do I shock thee?" she asked in a slightly teasing tone. "Does thee think it is a sacrilege for a Nantucket woman, daughter and sister of whaling men, to speak so bluntly?"

"Perhaps not a sacrilege," Jake answered slowly, "but a damned foolish attitude for someone who seems to love the life of the sea as you do. What of all the years you spent on board a whaler? How else do you propose to see the other side of the ocean and other ports?" He raised himself higher to better watch her face as she responded.

"I'll not deny that the years I spent on the *China Maid* were very fine." That distant look clouded her eyes again as she retreated into her memories. A sea gull circled overhead and the breeze ruffled the bright fuchsia flowers of the wild rose, sending a sweet scent through the salty air. With a toss of her silky hair, China brought her attention back to the present. "'Tis not my wish for a whaling man to come down the beach, though. If I could wish for the very best thing—and I may as well wish for the most as for the least— I would wish for a ship of my own."

Excitement made her sit up straighter. She had never told anyone about this pipe dream before. Not Zacch, who loved the life he led; not Harriet, who was content to stay on shore. Somehow it seemed natural to be telling Jake, however. "It would be a merchant ship," she said. "And I'd not stay home while it sailed. I'd go along to London and Le Havre and buy beautiful silks and precious porcelains, then sail back to Boston and Philadelphia to sell them. Perhaps I'd carry sugar and spices from the Indies, or cotton from Egypt, or tea from the Orient.

"'Tis canny of Zenas Swain to spend some years in England. He'll learn about more than oil. He'll be able to deal successfully on many counts."

The doubt that had been darkening Jake's eyes as she spoke now led him to laugh scornfully. "Aye," he snorted. "Hidden safely behind ledgers and ink pots, he'll watch the world go past.

"He'll never know what a barrel of oil means, save in dollars or pounds. He'll not know the challenge of the sea or the excitement of the chase. He'll never sit in a tossing whaleboat, not a quarter as big as the beast he's stalking, nor stand dripping with sweat and soot as he tries out the blubber. The life of a merchant is for the weak spirited." He jabbed his finger into the sand for emphasis.

Insulted by his bitter response to her cherished secret, China squirmed around to face him and to ask in a scathing voice, "And where did thee, a beached sailor, the second mate on a whaling ship, gain such vast experience? I think thee speaks through thy hat. Or—" she paused a moment to consider, then finished bitingly "—perhaps thee is envious of those who can make their way with their brains rather than with their backs."

To her surprise, Jake neither flared back in anger, nor more probably, goaded her with a sarcastic remark. Rather, he sat very still, scrutinizing a scallop shell that lay shattered in the sand. It seldom mattered to him what others thought of his opinions or his actions. And there were very few people who knew more about him than what they could perceive at the instant. But it suddenly seemed important to him that China understand. "I'm not envious and I'm not talking through my hat," he said quietly, turning his gaze to rest squarely on hers. Below wind-tousled bangs, her eyes lost their look of fierce displeasure and became puzzled.

"I come from New York," Jake started calmly, almost as if he were reciting. "My father was a very shrewd businessman who lived for his work. He owned any number of ventures, from Hudson River trading packets to wool mills in Rhode Island. He was considered a great success. He made a lot of money. And he died at the age of fifty-three, in his office, clutching a ledger and clawing at the pains ripping through his heart."

"Oh," China murmured, much subdued. She hunched forward in her quilted cocoon, now full of sympathy. "Is that what called thee to New York? Is it grief for thy father that makes thee so bitter?"

A smile crinkled the corners of Jake's eyes as he reached across to tenderly brush a strand of hair from her sunpinked cheek. He was touched by her concern. "Nay, China. Randolph Swan died five years ago and it was not grief I felt even then. It was guilt." As her brow furrowed again in bafflement, he explained. "At the moment of his heart attack, we were having a tremendous argument. Although I've since realized that it was merely the last strand in an already frayed halyard, at the time I was convinced that my temper had brought on his death. As penance I took over his business.

"I shackled myself to a desk. I spent ten, twelve, fourteen hours a day with papers and meetings and account books. Seven days a week I was surrounded by clerks and scribes and bankers and lawyers. And I was a success, too." He stopped, then added, "I felt as though I couldn't draw a breath. It was as though I were drowning."

He fell back on the sand, covering his eyes with his forearm, as if reviewing that time. After a while he started speaking again. "I stayed with it almost two years, until finally I realized that no one really cared. The bankers didn't care. I was just another source of money for them to juggle. The clerks didn't care, because one employer was pretty much the same as the next.''

His voice got softer and harsher. ''My mother never cared. She was only interested in her charity balls and her afternoon teas. After she remarried and moved to Baltimore, I realized the only person truly affected was me.'' He removed his arm from his face and shrugged. ''I packed it all in and went back to sea.''

''Back to sea?'' China probed. ''Does that mean, then, that thee had already spent some time at sea? Is that what thee was arguing with thy father about?''

Jake gave a surprised chuckle and turned his head toward her. ''Aye, China, it was. 'Tis very clever of you to guess that. I ran off to sea when I was fourteen—old enough and tall enough to secure a reasonable berth on board a whaler. I made two voyages to the Pacific, the first in the fo'c'sle, the second as fourth mate. I might have gone back again, but the ship was sold to London and I didn't like the thought of working as a British seaman. Instead, I went back to New York and tried my hand at my father's business. I'd been there eight months and was ready to quit when we had the fight.'' He rolled back on his stomach and rested his chin on his crossed hands.

China regarded his long form intently. The breeze plucked at the broadcloth shirt stretched across his sinewy shoulders and played with his dark, unruly curls. The afternoon sun twinkled on the little gold hoop in his ear. She felt an unexpected urge to lose her fingers in his hair and to slide her hand along his back. Instead, she tucked her hands more firmly into the quilt and asked, ''Why did thee choose the sea? Was thee also curious about what lay beyond the horizon?''

He nodded and raised up on his elbows. ''My grandfather lived with us until I was eight. He was a rare one. He founded the family fortune as a privateer during the Revolution—some said pirate. 'Twas but a hair's breadth of difference, in any event," he said with a grin. "He filled me with stories of his seafaring days, even as he filled himself with rum. I knew it was just a matter of growing big enough before I'd be up the rigging, too. And so it was."

A silence fell between them again. It was almost as if a spell had been cast, woven with the intimacy of their shared secrets and the salty, sweet scent in the air. Abruptly, China rose and went to gather her clothes, now dry but badly wrinkled. She felt flustered by her tremendous attraction to Jake, confused by the sudden turn in their relationship. She wasn't sure how to sort out the conflicting emotions that were tumbling around within her, but she could no longer sit still.

She took her clothes behind the dune and quickly stepped into them. As she was fumbling with the eighteen buttons at her back, she heard Jake approach from behind, swishing aside the long beach grass and thistles. His strong hands closed over hers, and lightly pulled them to her side. Her heart seemed to stop, then began beating like the wings of a trapped wren. As his fingers slowly slipped each button through its hole, grazing her skin through the thin cotton of her camisole, she stood stock-still, paralyzed by his touch.

She was scarcely breathing when he reached the last button and kept creeping up. Strand by shiny strand, he moved her hair to one side, exposing the graceful curve of her neck. She could feel his face lowering, feel his dark curls brush her head, feel his warm breath on her smooth skin. Then his lips touched her and electrified her body. She was suddenly filled with a glorious ache, a flush of heat.

In the same instant, she drew a sharp breath, hunched her shoulders and whirled away, frightened by the powerful throbbing his caress caused.

"Don't!" she gasped. "Thee promised."

Frustration collided with desire, still darkening Jake's eyes. "What did I promise?" he asked in a hoarse voice.

"Thee promised not to take advantage of me. Thee gave thy word."

As Jake regained control of himself, he resumed his insouciant stance. "Ah no, *ma pauvre petite*," he said, mockingly. "I only promised not to take advantage of you with your clothes off. I made damn sure every button was in place before I kissed you."

The taunting in his tone doused whatever remained of the delicious sensation his lips created. It was almost a relief and a refuge to return to their familiar pattern of bickering and baiting. "Thee is a scoundrel, Jacob Swan," China said, hotly. "'Tis a twist of words worthy of the New York lawyers thee holds in such contempt." So saying, she smartly knotted her neckerchief and marched off toward the meadow, her chin high, her great gray eyes gleaming.

Despite the smug grin on his face, Jake was fuming. Already irritable with repressed desire, China's allusion to the past he had unfolded for her further aggravated him. By the time they reached the field and its diminishing activities, he was in a thunderous frame of mind. Without a word, he left China by her father's cart and went off to drown his anger at a tavern.

Determined not to be affected by Jake, China wandered among the thinning crowd looking for Zacch or Harriet or even Aunt Judith, someone, anyone, with whom she could pretend she was having a merry time. She spied John James Henry, but he was busy drinking spiced rum with his friends at the completion of their labors, so she only waved from a distance. The more she roamed, the more melancholy she felt. When she finally found her father, engaged in a gam with another captain, she waited quietly a few feet away until he finished exchanging tales.

As they rode home, Zaccheus casually remarked, "You seem unusually demure this evening, China. Are you ill?"

China looked up quickly from the folded hands she was studying in her lap, but his face was unaccusing. She looked down again and answered, "'Twas a long day is all."

"Your dress looks a bit weather-beaten. Were you trampled by some sheep?"

Her eyes fixed on her hands, China shook her head. "Nay, I fell into the pond rescuing a little lamb," she said truthfully. "Then I sat in the sun at the beach to dry."

Zaccheus sensed that something was deeply troubling her, but, unaccustomed to the ways of young women, he didn't know how to approach her. Anew, he mourned Josephine who would have set their daughter to rights. She would have solved China's problems and then soothed away his own worries. By the time they reached home, far from drawing China out from her gloomy thoughts, he had retreated into his own.

Late that evening, as China lay sleeplessly in bed, eyes tracing the shadows the moon made in the eaves, she heard Zacch come home. His feet stepped quietly up the narrow stairs, then paused at the top. "China?" he whispered, tapping lightly at her door. "Are you awake?"

China hesitated, then muttered, "Aye, I am."

Zacch pushed open the door to her room and came over, setting his candle on the plain pine bureau by her bed. He pulled over a chair, straddled it backward and told her confidentially, "I've just come back from Sarah Coffin's house, China. I brought her home from the Shearing and she invited me to stay for supper. 'Twas a wonderful evening. She is so pretty, don't you think?''

Without waiting for her to reply, Zacch continued, "'Tis like watching a flower in a gentle breeze to watch her move. And she is so sweet. She believes the best of everyone. When Liddy would have criticized an acquaintance, Sarah admonished her ever so gently. She cannot bear to hear unkind words said. She is like an angel.'' He paused. "China?''

"Aye.''

"Don't you think she is wonderful?''

Tears were aching at the back of China's throat, but she forced herself to make a level reply. She could not disappoint her twin. "I know her only in passing, Zacch. But if thee thinks she is wonderful, I'm sure she is.''

After Zacch had gone blissfully to bed, China let the tears pour down her face. She felt doubly devastated. First Jake had captured her beloved brother's affection, and now this delicate girl, who moved like flowers in a breeze, was stealing his attention. She was all alone.

3

NANTUCKET
July 1839

As THE SUMMER SET IN, China became reconciled, at least on the surface, to the new routine. The three men left for the shipyard after breakfast and seldom returned before supper. Most evenings, while Zacch went off to be with his sweet Sarah, Jake played chess with Zaccheus or wound wool for Aunt Judith, and China sat quietly in the corner. Sometimes Jake, seeming tense, would disappear, too, leaving the Joy parlor in silence.

China spent more and more time on her solitary excursions around the island, and Aunt Judith, sensing a deep disturbance in her grandniece, let her go. Only on her own, examining the flotsam on some deserted beach or following a deer track over the moors, could China find any peace. Even Harriet, her usually loyal and sympathetic friend, let her down.

"He seems to be a very admirable man," Harriet had said, speaking of Jake. "Father says his nautical abilities are much praised. I found him to be quite humorous and discerning. And, while of course it is a bit impetuous of me to make judgments on such short acquaintance, I do not think I am mistaken in perceiving a very kind heart behind that saucy grin. He seems to have his eye on you, China."

When China hadn't answered, Harriet added slyly, "Certainly Liddy Coffin was much taken with him."

"She's welcome to him," China had retorted darkly. "He's a rogue and a bully, with too great an opinion of his own worth."

"That may be," Harriet had said, placidly, suddenly intent on the lace she was tatting. "But he didn't appear so to me."

The more others praised Jake, the more China resented him. She chose to ignore that afternoon on the beach when it had seemed so natural to share her secrets with him and to listen to his, when his fingers stroking her hair and his warm lips against her skin had taken her breath away. Instead, she focused on his insidious hold on her family. He became an obvious target for all her frustrations.

Every evening she watched Zacch bolt down his supper and scud out the door, with just a friendly farewell. Unable to vent her pique against the object of his attention, Sarah, whom she seldom saw unless by accident while on an errand in town, China blamed Jake. Daily, she heard accounts of the *China Maid*'s progress, the memory-laden whale ship that finally belonged to her father. Knowing that Zaccheus was more removed than ever from letting her come live on board, China held Jake responsible. Very often she fled from the house, anxious for diversion, staying away longer and later. When her absence caused no comment, evoked no regret, she accused Jake for Aunt Judith's lack of concern.

Although China was convinced that Jake derived some devilish enjoyment from engineering her exclusion, that was not quite the case. He was constantly thinking of her, wanting her. In vain, he tried to forget the memory of her satiny skin beneath his lips, the clean smell of her shiny black hair, the sympathy in her alluring gray eyes. Her very presence in the parlor of an evening caused him to lose more chess games to distraction than to Zaccheus's skill. Often the sight of her would drive him from the house in search of sublimation. He tried to tell himself that she was too young and innocent, too much a member of his self-adopted family.

When he was honest with himself, though, he knew her age should not be measured by her short accumulation of years, but by how she had filled them and what she had seen. He knew that her innocence was just a thin screen, behind which simmered strong emotions, eager to be expressed. He knew that she could never be simply his sister, a dispassionate companion, an innocuous sibling.

He woke early one morning, his dreams as disturbed by images of China as his waking moments were. While he examined the ceiling and listened to Zacch's peaceful breathing, he heard the door to China's room creak open and then her soft footsteps on the stairs. He rose instantly and pulled on his clothes, intent on taking this rare opportunity to have a few minutes alone with her.

His bare feet made no noise on the worn oak treads or across the thick rag rugs of the parlor. When he reached the door to the kitchen, he paused a minute, studying her graceful form with deep pleasure. She was leaning with her shoulder against the cupboard, her hip carelessly cocked, gazing out the back window and gulping down a breakfast of leftover biscuits and cold milk. Although somewhat reluctant to interrupt this engaging pose, Jake stepped into the kitchen and closed the door behind him.

The click of the latch made China start and spin around. At the sight of Jake standing there, hair tousled, clad in just a shirt and trousers, color flooded her cheeks. His presence cut short not only her breakfast, but also her thoughts, which had centered totally on him. In the tranquil gray dawn, in the muffled peace that enveloped a slumbering house, her vigilance had slipped and her attraction to him had surfaced. Thinking him safely asleep, she had allowed herself to feel his strength again as he had pulled her effortlessly from the icy water, and to sense his vulnerability again as he had recounted his past.

Far from following through with her cordial thoughts, however, she let her startled embarrassment turn to irritation. "Thee is forever sneaking up on me," she snapped. "I must grow eyes in the back of my head to guard against thy stealthy appearances. Has thee no sense of decency? Thee should be abed at this hour, not lurking about the house like a rat in the cheese bin."

"If you grew another pair of eyes as smoky as the first, the Lisbon bell would be forever ringing the fire alarm, and you'd be half drowned in buckets of water." Jake wasn't sure exactly what he had intended to do in his moments alone with China, but any soft impulses were quickly extinguished, and his usual mocking manner took over.

"As far as decency and bed are concerned," he continued, "I might remind you that *you* were up first, creeping down the stairs and secretly stealing breakfast. If anyone should be abed, 'tis you. In fact, I'll be glad to help you return, if you like." A goading grin broke over his face, and he stepped toward her extending a hand.

China edged off, her cheeks now rosy with rage. "Keep away from me!" she commanded. "'Tis like thee to make such lewd offers. 'Tis also like thee to accuse me of stealing the very biscuits I baked last evening. Thee has such a lowborn mind, thee can only think in terms of thievery and lust."

"How you sidestep the issue, China," Jake jeered. Crossing his arms on his chest, he strode forward, propelling her nervously backward until she collided with the rear door. "And how quick you are to give my innocent words such villainous meanings. 'Methinks the lady doth protest too much.' Could it be your own guilt that makes you speak so loudly against me? Although you didn't hesitate to accuse me of indecency for rising so early, I've yet to hear what drew you from your cozy bed. Is it a clandestine meeting with some tongue-tied boy, perhaps? A clumsy embrace behind the barn?"

"Beast!" China hissed. "'Tis blueberries, not boys, that I am going to meet. I'm sure it is a difficult thought for thee to grasp, but I mean to spend the morning picking blueberries. The best bushes are by the head of Hummock Pond and I want to arrive before the heat of the day has settled into the thickets. So you see," she finished, with a triumphant flourish, "my motives are completely moral."

"Moral, perhaps," Jake said, glancing out the window at the heavy gray sky, "but sensible, nay. Surely an old salt like you can tell that there's weather making. 'Tis not the day to be larking about the island. Spitting fire as you are, you'll no doubt attract lightning, from pure affinity."

As if to prove that he was wrong about her temper, China bit back her hot retort. She drew herself up and inched her hand behind her back until it rested on the door latch. In her coldest, most correct Quaker tone, she said, "'Tis not amusement I seek, but food that can be put by for the long winter. 'Tis barren here by November. Often in January the harbor ices over, and there are no boats for weeks. If we are not provident now, we will pay for our sloth later on. A summer shower is poor excuse for indolence." With that, China flung open the door, swept up the waiting pails and sped out.

Jake rushed to the open door with his right arm raised and his finger pointed, but any reply he might have shouted at her back was cut off by the emergence of Zaccheus from his room next to the kitchen. Curious, he joined Jake at the open door, then frowned as he recognized his daughter's long legs carrying her rapidly out of sight.

"Is that China?" he asked. "I thought I heard you talking to someone out here. Where's she off to at this hour?"

"Blueberrying," Jake answered, shortly, struggling to get his anger under control. It was one thing to taunt China until her eyes were as dark and stormy as the sky. He was only amused by the names she called him in return. But this facade of piety infuriated him.

Beside him, Zaccheus shook his head grimly. "She's sailing single-handed too much," he said. "And always into a head wind." Shaking his head again, he turned away from the door and moved to the stove, where he began to shift out the ashes of last night's fire and to set the kindling for today's.

"There was a time when she'd run to me with every little problem she had and we would talk it away together. Now she's grown away from me. I don't know how or what to say to her."

He stopped again, but Jake still made no comment. Zaccheus lit the kindling, closed the stove door and brushed the ashes off his hands. "She's not unlike her mother was at that age." He looked over at Jake, but his eyes were seeing into the past. "Josephine was just China's age when I met her. And just as stubborn. Of course, it took me a while to realize that, since I didn't speak French, but I learned soon enough. When she set her helm, there was no changing her course. But Josephine knew not to head into rough seas with all her sails up. I'm not sure that China does." He walked slowly back to his room. Behind him, Jake set a pot of shaving water on the stove, a bleak look on his face.

Breakfast was a comparatively quiet meal that morning. Only Zacch remarked on China's absence, and he seemed satisfied with Jake's terse explanation. Sensing the tension around his father and his friend, he ate his way through a stack of corncakes in puzzled silence. He was just as content to fill his mind with thoughts of Sarah, anyhow.

As he worked that morning at the shipyard, Jake's anger increased. With each stroke of the boat slick against the mighty spruce log that would be the foremast, he muttered another curse at China, involved in an inward argument. His hands gripped the huge chisel harder as he longed to grip her and shake the smugness off her beautiful face. His mood grew darker with the rolling clouds, which reinforced his conviction that a storm was on its way. When, at midmorning, he badly burred the slick by jabbing it against a knot, he realized his fury was interrupting his concentration and impeding his work. He put his tools down and took off in search of China.

He checked first at home, but Aunt Judith, ceasing her sweeping and shaking her head, said China hadn't yet returned. "She's out on the commons, making her peace with life," the Quaker spinster said. "She'll come home when her heart is calm." Despite the confidence with which Aunt Judith spoke, she cast a dubious eye at the threatening sky.

"Aye," Jake grunted. "I think I'll just fetch her home early."

Following Aunt Judith's careful directions, Jake stomped his way through the fields, across the hills and along the trails toward the blueberry thickets. The overgrown sheep traces and often prickly underbrush did nothing for his dark humor. He finally found her, fast asleep against a sun-bleached log. Her sleeves were rolled up, her neckerchief unknotted and her long legs bare. To one side of her sat her boots and two pails brimming with blueberries. Around her mouth was a smudge of purple.

The sight of her sprawled in such heedless indulgence made Jake's temper explode. Roughly seizing her bare foot, he shouted, "'Tis not the time for sleeping, now. If it's rest you need, stay abed later in the morning. Wake up, wake up!" China's eyes flew open wide and she gasped, even as she was pulled away from the log, her shoulders bumping the ground, her toes trapped by Jake's hand.

"What sermons have you now, little hypocrite?" Jake asked harshly. "What self-righteous hymns are you going to sing? I'm sure you have a good excuse for lying spraddled in the berry patch like a fat seal in the sun. What's the sanctimonious reason, Miss China? Are you storing up fresh air for the barren winter?"

From her position on the ground, China just stared at him, her eyes full of bewilderment, her mouth a perfect, purple O. Her silence only incensed Jake further. Shaking the foot he still held, he said, "You're doubly dishonest, China Joy. First because you are pretending to be a proper Quaker, and second, because you are pretending *not* to be yourself. You're high spirited and hot blooded, you're stubborn, sassy and smart. You grew up half wild on a whaling ship, in every ocean of the world, and now you act as if those years had never happened."

Some of the steam escaped from Jake, and his tone became less hard. Still he gave her foot another small shake and continued, "You're denying yourself, China. And your behavior is an insult both to real Friends and to you. There's no Inner Light in you, no calm heart and tranquil nature. There's just the same overwhelming will to live as in your twin. You were rightly named Joy, and it's as much a sin and a fraud to hide that joy behind your theeing and thying as it is to shroud your beauty in these wretched gray frocks."

Jake stopped, waiting for her boiling wrath to bubble over at him. To his immense astonishment, China simply stared, then gave a heart-wrenching shudder and burst into tears. Roused so abruptly from sleep, she did not have the time to assemble her defenses against Jake's verbal bombardment. Her confusion and frustration of the past few months lay right on the surface, vulnerable to attack. The vehemence of his accusations and the roughness of his touch were the final, unfair straws.

Whatever remained of Jake's ire instantly evaporated. He dropped her foot and sank down beside her, pulling her weeping body close to his as he leaned back against the log. Her efforts to free herself were weakened by the force of her tears.

"Good God, China," he muttered, guiltily, "I didn't mean to make you cry so. I was angry and I have a terrible temper, I know. Don't squirm away; just let me hold you. I won't hurt you anymore."

China's struggling ceased, and for a few minutes she lay in the strong circle of his arms, her sobs soaking his shirt. When her racked breath began to draw more evenly, he softly stroked her shiny hair and said again, "I didn't mean to make you cry. I only wanted you to see what you were doing to yourself."

"Doesn't thee think I knew?" she gasped, suddenly pulling herself away from his chest. His hand cupped the back of her neck and his intense blue eyes regarded her seriously as she spoke.

"Does thee think it is by my choice that I live here as I do? Does thee think I like these wretched gray frocks, as thee calls them? Does thee think I enjoy going to Meeting and speaking plainly and avoiding music and dance? What else can I do?"

She snuffled and wiped at her wet cheeks with the back of her hand. Jake reached into his pocket and found a rumpled handkerchief with which he blotted at her tears. China took it from him and blew her nose vigorously.

"What else can I do?" she asked again, and paused. "Jake," she blurted out suddenly, "they left me here. They sailed away and left me here!" Tears started again as she confessed out loud, for the first time, to that dreadful sense of abandonment eight years earlier. "I wanted to go, too," she said between sobs. "I pleaded with Papa to take me. I wanted life to be just as it always had been. I didn't want to stay on a strange island with an aunt I hardly knew. And when Papa wouldn't let me go with them, I begged Zacch to stay with me, at least. But he left, too."

Her beautiful gray eyes were blurry and the dark lashes around them were wet as she looked at him hard, as if willing him to understand. "Doesn't thee..." she began, then shook her head firmly and corrected, "Don't *you* see, Jake? It was hard enough just to be here. After a while I had to stop bucking the head wind and come about. I *had* to make it easier for myself. I *had* to accept the situation I was in. If it meant wearing a few dreary dresses and saying a few Biblical words, then I had to do it."

Jake reached out and pulled her close to him again, tenderly kissing the top of her head. "*Pauvre petite*," he murmured. "I didn't think it out properly, did I? I just lost my temper and lashed out at you." He gently brushed a damp strand of hair from her cheek. "You're a shipwrecked sailor marooned on a distant island, and I came along and criticized you for managing to survive. I'm sorry, China." He rested his chin lightly on her head and hugged her tightly. He was suffused with a strange, sweet desire to hold her forever, protecting her from the injustices of life.

Mollified by his apology and beguiled by the warmth and shelter of his embrace, China lay quietly in his arms, her cheek pressed against the hard muscle of his chest, listening to the steady beating of his heart. Wrung out by her emotional release, she allowed herself to be soothed, mesmerized by the soft, even stroking of his fingers in her hair. She soaked up the strength he imparted with his hugs, absorbed the sympathy in his light kisses. When at length she gave a deep, shaky sigh, he sensed that she was ready, again, to talk.

"Is it so very bad here, China?" he asked. "Do you have no happy moments? I must say that before I roused you so abruptly just now, you were the very picture of bucolic contentment." He chuckled softly and traced the purple circle around her full lips. "Surely there is some pleasure in picking blueberries. Aunt Judith says you are out here on the commons often, 'making thy peace with life.' Is that so? Do you find satisfaction out here?"

"Aye, I do," China replied, after a moment's thought. She raised her head to look at him. "Sometimes it reminds me of the sea. Sometimes when I sit high on a hummock, when the wind is rippling the broom and the heather and the bayberry brush, I look across the moors to where the horizon meets the sky. 'Tis like the roll of the ocean, only I know it is not really moving as the ocean moves. But nay—" she let her head fall back against the comfort of his chest "—'tis not so very bad. Not now. Not all of the time." Her fingers crept up and played with a button on his shirt.

"If I went back to sea, I would miss Aunt Judith, despite all our battles. And Harriet."

"And picking blueberries."

"And picking blueberries. And eating them," she chuckled, too. "In truth, I'd miss more food than blueberries. Though 'twas a delight to provision in the South

Seas and get fresh mangos and coconuts and bananas, I made more meals than I care to remember of lobscouse and salt horse.''

"Boiled hardtack, pork fat and molasses," Jake said with a groan. "If we could only change the daily fare from lobscouse, there would be little to complain about."

"Nay," said China, looking up again and grinning. "There would still be meal and molasses and potato scouse and dandyfunk, that poor excuse for a Sunday pudding."

Jake grinned back, running his thumb over China's chin. "We'll stow a few barrels of Aunt Judith's quahog chowder on board," he said. "And a bushel of those roast eels she made last night. What else could anyone want?"

The smile faded from China's face as she pondered the question. Letting her head sink to his chest again, she answered, in a murmur, "To carry cargo instead of hunting whales."

"I don't understand that, China," Jake said, in mild exasperation. He slid his palm under her chin and lifted her face up toward his own. "Aye, we kill whales, but 'tis not as though we do it for the sheer pleasure of killing. The oil is needed to light the cities of the world. 'Tis like killing a sheep for the mutton. I don't hear you objecting to that."

"I don't deny the oil is needed," China said. She regarded him steadily for a moment and then looked down, her dark lashes making a fringe against her lightly tanned cheeks. "But I don't want any part of it."

He let go of her chin, and her head slipped back to its resting place. With arms tightening around her, he half shook, half hugged her. "But why? Why? I can't fathom your reasons. If your years on board the *Maid* had been miserable, I could accept your aversion. But you were happy. Why?"

China sighed and toyed with the button of his shirt, again. "'Twas just off the Azores," she finally began. "We had taken on water and food in Fayal and were following the Trades. We were four years old, Zacch and I, and had left France not one month gone. When the cry came from the lookout, 'There she blows!' we ran to the rail, caught up in the excitement. 'Twas a small pod, just three spermaceti." Her voice quavered and she paused. "There was a dam and twin calves."

Jake felt a twinge of apprehension run through him.

"'Tis not usual that a whale has twins," China continued, in a resolute voice, "but 'tis not unheard of, either. Nor is it usual that the hunt should be played out so close to the ship, but this one was. I saw it all."

She pulled free of Jake, suddenly, and sat up, wrapping her arms around her raised knees. She looked off across the moors, seeing that day thirteen years before. "As whalers often do, they harpooned one of the calves first, to keep the mother close at hand. Oh, she was gallied. She swam to and fro, backing and filling, not knowing what to do. They got a harpoon into her, too, but she didn't even take them on a sleigh ride. She just stayed right there by her calf until she turned fin up. The sea was red with blood."

China buried her face in the crook of her arm. In a voice muffled by the fabric of her dress, she intoned, "The other twin escaped."

For a long moment, Jake regarded her hunched form in silence. He rubbed one hand across his forehead, distressed, then he reached for her again. When she was nestled against his body, once more drawing comfort from his strength, he said gently, "They were whales, China. They weren't people."

"I know," she whispered. That fact didn't change her mind.

He sighed and said no more. It was enough just to hold her, to keep her safe in his arms. He bent his face over her head, savoring her clean scent, brushing his lips across her silky hair. He could have stayed that way for hours, but their embrace was interrupted by a resonant clap of thunder and a ragged bolt of lightning.

They scrambled to their feet and grabbed the pails of blueberries, suddenly realizing how dark the sky had grown. Before they could cover even a quarter of the distance toward home, the rain came. It spilled out of the sky in blinding sheets, instantly soaking them to the skin.

Spying a scraggly scrub oak, Jake guided China under the dubious protection of its boughs, increasingly aware of the way her wet dress was sculpted to her body. The gray muslin fabric clung to her curves, sensuously outlining her long, slim thighs, the flat slant of her stomach, the firm swell of her breasts, nipples erect in the beating rain. Again desire rose in him, but not the benevolent feelings of before. Again he pulled her to him, but this time it wasn't to soothe her. He held her body tightly to his, tangled his fingers in her streaming hair and kissed her.

With the rain battering her face, and with her soul swept clean and clear by her recent tears, China responded. She felt the heat and the hardness of his body under the clothes plastered to him; she felt the urgency of his fingers as they pressed against her back and wound around the thick strands of her hair. When his mouth met hers, an unknown throbbing spread through her, a delicious ache. Her hands gripped his powerful shoulders and neck, holding him closer, while her lips returned his fierce kiss. Then his tongue touched hers, hot in the cold, driving rain, and wonderful new sensations burst within her.

"Ho, Chi-China!" came a voice bellowing through the din of the storm. So consumed was she by the desire pulsing in her, the words barely penetrated. Then with a gasp, she pulled free of Jake's bewitching embrace and whirled to see John James Henry bearing down on them through the brush. "Chi-China, where you be?" he scolded anxiously. "'Tis rain, rain, rain. 'Tis day to batten down the hatches and stay snug in port."

He looked at Jake sternly, then his eyes narrowed in speculation as he saw the unspent passion in Jake's face and heard his short, fast breathing. "Ho, Ja-Jake," he said, more gently, thrusting his chin in Jake's direction. "You lost your reckoning? 'Tis no day to keep Chi-China in the rain. Keep her safe. Come home."

"Aye," Jake growled, snatching up the buckets of blueberries. "Let's go home."

Any ardorous feelings that might have remained in China died a while later as she stood dripping in the kitchen, before the eyes of her assembled family. Only Zacch looked amused, grinning widely at her drenched state. Both Aunt Judith and Zaccheus looked distressed.

Thinking for the thousandth time about the storm that took Josephine from him, Zaccheus said reproachfully, "I thought you had more sense, China, than to set sail in a gale. You should have known not to risk it. The berries would still be there tomorrow."

"'Tis only rain," China protested. "And in the midst of summer."

"Aye, 'tis summer, but you're soaked and shivering and you've caused two good men to leave their dry berths to go searching for you. If you don't want to think of your own safety, you might think of others'."

While China's mouth fell open in astonishment, Zaccheus turned to Jake and said, "You have my thanks, Jake. 'Tis good of you to worry about my improvident daughter. I'm sorry you had to go out and rescue her in such weather."

Jake's surprised reply was cut off by China. "The two good men needn't have stirred from their dry berths," she snapped, as all her frustrations returned in force. "I had no need of rescuing; I was perfectly safe. I'm quite capable of tending my own traps, as I do for all the long years that thee is away at sea. If they chose to come search for me, 'tis not my look after." With that furious remark, China turned abruptly and stomped off to her room, leaving behind a grim-faced group and a trail of water.

4

NANTUCKET
August 1839

CHINA ALLOWED HER FURY to carry her along for more than a week. Ruthlessly pushing aside the memory of Jake's body crushed against hers, of his lips, warm and vital in the cold, beating rain; callously disregarding the sense of safety and comfort she had felt as he had wrapped her in his arms and had tenderly wiped her tearstained cheeks, she focused, once more, on his unwitting role in her family's preoccupation. With renewed resentment, she recounted the injustices in her life, and with pique almost verging on self-pity, she held Jake at least partially responsible for her latest feeling of abandonment.

The more China fumed, the more disgusted she became with herself for having allowed him to catch her in such a vulnerable state by the blueberry thicket. To make up for her moment of weakness, she now deliberately, and haughtily, avoided all contact with him. She did not come down to breakfast in the morning until she was sure that the whole family was assembled, and she went up to bed at night when the chess game was several moves from finished. She even ignored Jake's increasingly exasperated attempts to capture her eye.

If, in carrying out her boycott of Jake, China also managed to further remove herself from her puzzled father and her oblivious brother, she didn't mind. She felt a perverse sort of triumph at having, for once, initiated the separation. Aunt Judith often said that temper made a poor substitute for tolerance, but, for now, China was savagely savoring her isolation.

By the end of the week, though, her mood began to shift. She maintained her pose of indifference, but she no longer took any pleasure from it. The spell of temper, which had originally galvanized her, was fading for lack of reaction from her family, and, in its absence, China was once again feeling lonely and left out. She longed for Zacch to clasp her around the shoulders conspiratorially, and to propose an adventure as he used to, or for her father to sit gravely by her side, testing her skill at tying knots, or even for Aunt Judith to admonish her for her lack of humility. She longed for some sign, *any* sign, that they cared about her, but they seemed as indifferent to her as she was pretending to be toward them.

The only person, in fact, who was quite willing to approach China was Jake, but she continued to avoid him. Although she felt her face turn fiery under the unwavering gaze of his arresting blue eyes, she acted as if he weren't there. When he tried to corner her, after dinner or before leaving for the boatyard, she always managed to find urgent business in some other room. The more China mired herself in her exile, the more frustrated Jake became. He thought they had gone beyond that stage.

EXCEPT FOR THAT ONE DOWNPOUR in late July, the weather remained hot and dry, deepening China's depression. She felt as if her myriad layers of modest clothing were glued to her, pressing her into the ground, restricting free breath. Her movements became more mechanical.

One morning in town she was so immersed in her private thoughts, so weighted down by the heat and by the heavy market basket over her arm, that she hardly heard Harriet calling her name. It wasn't until her friend ran after her and seized her by the hand in front of the Pacific Bank, that China turned in surprise, the glaze receding from her great, gray eyes.

"You've your head in the clouds today, China," Harriet teased. "You were not three feet beyond me when I came out of Gardner and Hallet's Dry Goods, but you might as well have been in Madagascar for all you heard me calling. I've been chasing you up the block."

China glanced guiltily down the broad Main Street, her eyes coming to rest on the plain clapboard front of Gardner and Hallet's, halfway down. "I promise thee, I never heard a word," she said, looking back toward Harriet. "'Tis the heat I think. I've been distracted all week." She failed to add that there were other reasons for her distraction, but Harriet almost guessed as much. She knew it took more than the weather to quell China's spirit.

"You should see the new summer hats Mr. Wolth has in then," she said, taking China at her word. "They came in with the schooner *Ariel*, I believe he said. There's a very pretty palm leaf with a pink ribbon, and one a bit plainer in willow. They'd be much cooler than that dusty old bombazine, I'd wager." Harriet nodded briefly, in reference, at the faded gray bonnet jammed on China's head. Although Harriet was resigned to the fact that no amount of silk and lace would ever make her beautiful, she, nonetheless, liked to present a neat appearance. In fact, today she looked fresh, despite the heat, in a sprigged muslin gown with a ruche around the collar and pearl buttons down the bodice.

"Aye," China answered, pushing off the scoop-brimmed bonnet so it bobbed down her back, anchored to her throat by its tattered ribbon. "And 'tis cooler still to do without, letting the head catch a stray breath of breeze, instead of luffing in the doldrums. I tell thee, 'twas either a madman or a fiend who invented this wretched headgear. It was surely no one who ever had to wear it in either the heat or in a hurry, for it shuts out both air and sight. 'Tis no wonder females tend to swoon."

Harriet laughed, too familiar with China's views to be shocked. "I can see those newly arrived goods leave you unimpressed. Perhaps this will please you more," she said, rooting around in her basket until she found what she was looking for. "See? 'Tis Underwood's Raspberry Syrup. And I've a bottle of Lemon, too. Papa promised to shave a block of ice for us to pour the syrup on, after supper. 'Tis so cool and sweet. You must come sit with me in the garden and have a cup."

"Perhaps I shall," China said with decision. The combination of raspberry ice and Harriet's own special sympathy suddenly sounded very appealing. "I shouldn't mind at all a change of scenery, and it has been a tidy amount of time since I've had a good gam with thee. It would please my ear to hear about something other than whale ships and whale men."

Harriet laughed again, a congenial sound that made her plain face merry. "You'll have to go farther than Gardner Street for that," she said. "'Twas bad enough when Papa and Zenas went on for hours about this ship and that ship, but now that Zenas has gone to England poor Papa doesn't know who to talk to. Mama won't listen, or if she does, her answers are all a muddle, so *I* must hear all about the sailings and arrivals and the doings in between. Nay, if it is different conversation that you want, you'll be better off in Madagascar after all. I may even come with you."

Before China could answer, a deep voice above them asked, "Who is cruising on Madagascar?" They turned in unison to see Jake on the broad, tiered stairs of the stately brick Pacific Bank. The seven stone steps faced down the street, providing both overview and delineator for the commercial part of town.

Above the bank, Main Street swerved and narrowed, becoming residential, but below the bank was the heart of Nantucket. Either side of the street was lined with two-story clapboard and shingle buildings, their lower floors shaded by awnings, their unadorned signs and straightforward window displays hinting at the hoards of merchandise for sale within. Almost everything arrived from "away," by packet or schooner or oceangoing clipper.

If the Pacific Bank was the head of Main Street, William Rotch's big, brick warehouse, two blocks down, was its foot. It capped off the square on the lower end of the street and acted as a gateway to the wharves, with all their hustle and confusion, with their cooperages, sail lofts, ropewalks, and grog shops, with their forest of masts and their jungle of rigging. Sweaty dock laborers, industrious artisans, somber, beaver-hatted Quaker shipowners, and sailors from the Azores and Brazil, the South Seas and Malaysia, from China, Japan, Ecuador and the Sandwich Islands all spilled off the wharves, into the square, and along the wooden walks of Main Street. They mingled with matrons doing their morning errands, many drably dressed in their plain grays and browns, others more appealing in swishing Swiss muslins or French mousselines; they passed by serious-faced businessmen hurrying to important meetings, and scampering boys stealing freedom from lessons and chores, lured from birth toward the excitement of the sea.

The wide, cobbled street was athrong with barrel-laden drays freighting whale oil to candle factories or refineries, buckboards piled high with sacks of Ohio flour and Havana sugar; with farm wagons bringing in fresh produce from Polpis and Cisco, out of town; with two-wheeled carts loaded with cod caught in dories off 'Sconset, seven miles over the island; with carriages carrying ladies and gentlemen, and with horses, mules and barking dogs. Despite its inbred modesty, Nantucket was plainly the world's wealthiest and busiest whaling port, and on that hot August morning, in his commanding position on the bank steps, Jake seemed a vital and natural part of the famous port.

If nothing else, his clothes marked him as a whaling man. Though his coat was cut from fine blue kerseymere, its long lines tailored perfectly to his tall, strong frame, it was of a style more suited to the practical life at sea rather than to any pursuits on land. The well-laundered white of his linen shirt, loosely wound with a simple necktie, set off his weather-tanned face and made his blue eyes appear more stunning. The gold hoop in his ear seemed to emphasize his disdain for the dictates of fashion. Despite herself, China felt a thrill.

A grin crept across Jake's ruggedly handsome features as he descended the bank steps, repeating his question. "Who is cruising to Madagascar?" he asked. "Are you planning a voyage?" He came straight to China's side and pulled the heavy market basket from her arm before she could answer or protest. "Do you need a ship's master? I know of an able fellow who'd be happy to oblige."

As China's face suffused in anger at his intrusion, his grin grew wider and he said, "Nay, eh? A mate then perhaps?" Gray eyes snapping dangerously, China reached for her basket, wishing to be rid of him, but Jake sidestepped, saying, with the tone of a huckster making his final offer, "A porter. A porter it is. I'll sign articles as your porter for your trip to Madagascar."

"Nay, Jake, we're not bound for the Indian Ocean," Harriet said hastily, stemming a sharp remark from her friend. "I was just teasing China because her attention seemed thousands of miles away."

"Aye, she does seem a bit adrift these days," Jake agreed, stepping farther out of China's reach and surveying her critically. "Do you think she needs a dose of Dr. Rolfe's Aromatic Pills?" he asked Harriet with mock seriousness.

Harriet shook her head, a smile on her face despite China's fierce look. She liked Jake and she wished China would, too. "Just a few kind words, I think," she said. She knew that China yearned for someone with whom she could share certain attitudes and ideas that went beyond everyday Nantucket. Harriet could sympathize, but she couldn't completely understand those desires. Yet she felt, somehow, that Jake could. And would, and should.

"I must scud," she said. "I promised Mama I would drive with her to Madaket to visit Cousin Miriam Chase. 'Tis her ninety-second birthday today. Imagine, she was married with four children when we were still a colony of England. And she's just as sturdy as ever. She still chops her own kindling and hoes her own garden. I wonder if I shall be able to say the same in another... goodness! In another seventy-five years."

"Thee shall be tatting lace collars for all thy great-grandchildren and fixing treats for half the dogs and cats in Nantucket, just as thee does now," China said, a bit tartly. She guessed at Harriet's intentions and was annoyed that her friend would so deviously desert her. Harriet just laughed, acknowledging Jake's farewell bow with a wave of her hand as she started up Liberty Street toward home.

"I must be off as well," China said uneasily, reaching once more for her basket. She had a difficult time sustaining her anger, and restraining her memories of that afternoon in the rain, when she was alone with Jake.

He shifted the basket to his other arm, out of her reach. "I'll fetch it home for you," he said.

"I can manage it alone," China said, a trace of her irritation returning.

"I'm sure you can," Jake responded equably, starting up Main Street. "But I haven't spent the past three mornings stalking about town in hopes of sighting you just to talk about Harriet's cousin Marion."

"Miriam," China corrected automatically, falling reluctantly in beside him.

"Eh?"

"Miriam. Harriet's cousin Miriam."

"Aye, just as I was saying. I think we have more to discuss than Harriet's cousin *Miriam* or the sweetness of Aunt Judith's corn chowder, which was the extent of our conversation yesterday. This morning, at breakfast, we managed a few words about the lightness of her buttermilk muffins. Come, China, why have you been avoiding me? I thought we had that all sorted out."

"I haven't been avoiding thee," China mumbled, her eyes intent on the smooth cobble beneath her feet, nervously ignoring Jake's gaze. She was suddenly aware that it was quite convenient to be upset with him. It kept her from examining any other feelings she had. But now was not the time to try and make sense of the delicate chills of pleasure that ran through her every time he touched her, or of the feeling of intimacy and understanding whenever she confided in him. She had to think this revelation through on her own, without the distraction of his presence.

Jake suppressed a flicker of frustration and tried again. "Perhaps not, but you've made damn sure there have been at least two other people in the room with me before you've entered it. We haven't exchanged a word in private since the day I pulled you out of the blueberry patch. Why, China? It seemed to me we were sailing smoothly, then suddenly things went aground. Did I say something that offended you?"

"Nay." China wished he would stop probing and leave her to try and decipher the situation by herself. Confusion kept her eyes on the ground.

Jake took a deep breath to steady his temper, studying her down-turned profile at the same time. Thick strands of glossy hair fell softly against her cheeks and brow, now lightly tanned from the summer sun. All that could be seen of her wonderful gray eyes was the dark fringe of her lashes as she continued to examine the toes of her brown leather boots emerging from the folds of her brown muslin dress.

Having gotten her alone, he wasn't exactly sure what he wanted to say to China. Alone, except for an occasional carriage clacking over the cobbles or the servant girl sweeping the steps of the newly built brick Starbuck mansion. He only knew that she was constantly on his mind, that he had felt completely absorbed and enthralled by her, both the day on the beach and the afternoon on the commons, and that he had to keep exploring these feelings.

What's more, he was sure that she shared his attraction. He had felt the ardor in her response when he had kissed her. He had heard the eagerness in her voice when she had confided in him. He had even sensed their matching spirit when they were bickering. What he couldn't understand was this uncharacteristic listlessness. A thought struck him.

"Perhaps I shouldn't have joked about the Aromatic pills. Perhaps you are truly feeling poorly. Are you ill?"

"Nay, I'm quite sound."

"Are you in need of Harriet's prescription, then? A few kind words? Have I been thoughtless in providing them?"

China just shook her head.

"By God, China, I've seen a seasick greenhorn display more spirit than you! I'm getting tired of this one-sided conversation. If you don't want to talk, perhaps you'd enjoy a good kiss on the lips."

China's head finally shot up, her emotions able to focus once more in anger. "Thee wouldn't dare," she hissed. "'Twould create a scandal. If thee doesn't care for my company, thee has no need to stay. I'd be much happier alone. 'Twas thy own idea to follow me home. Here, give me back my basket before the gossips start chattering."

"Ahh, much better," Jake said, ignoring her outstretched hand. "For a moment I thought I was speaking to the wrong person, but then I saw how truly concerned you are with convention," he said wryly, patting the bombazine bonnet hanging languidly down her back, "and I knew I wasn't mistaken."

China flushed, half in annoyance, half in embarrassment. She looked away again. "'Tis too hot to wear it," she muttered.

Jake laughed. "Aye, 'tis truly hot. Which puts me in mind of some addled adventure Sarah and Liddy Coffin, and your brother Zacch, have cooked up. They want us to row out to Coatue on Saturday for a picnic. For some reason they have decided that that empty stretch of sand and sea gulls across the harbor will be cooler. I tried to tell them that there's no patch of shade bigger than a blade of beach grass, but they think it will be a grand lark. *Now* what?"

78

China had stopped in the middle of the street, her eyes wide and hurt. As Jake casually related the details of the intended outing, she felt genuine pain searing through her. She felt betrayed. She and Zacch used to borrow Amaziah Folger's old catboat and sail up and down the harbor on hot summer afternoons. Often they packed a picnic lunch and ate it on Coatue. Now Zacch was taking Sarah, and, worse yet, Liddy, in her place. And he wasn't even telling her. She had to hear it from Jake. She was filled with misery, with long-buried feelings of abandonment.

"China, talk to me. What is the matter? You look as if you mean to swoon." Jake grabbed her limply hanging hand and was shocked to feel it icy cold. He set down the market basket and turned to face her. With one warm hand he held her cold one, with the other he tilted up her chin and studied her face with worried eyes. "What happened, China? Is it the heat?"

Warmth flooded back through China's veins as she turned her injury into protective anger. Cheeks that were pasty only a moment before were suddenly flaming. She snatched her hand out of Jake's grip and brushed his fingers from her face.

"Nay, 'tis not the heat," she snapped. "'Tis listening to thy foolish gabble that gives me such a headache. I can't imagine why thee thinks I should want to hear about thy silly excursions. First thee forces thy company on me, then thee fills my ears with nonsense. 'Tis no wonder I feel faint. If thee wishes to do me a good turn, kindly steer clear of me in the future."

While Jake stood speechless in amazement, she grabbed up her basket and broke into a run for home, unmindful of the nutmegs that bounced out onto the cobblestones. She was half a block away before Jake collected himself in rage.

"Damn you, China!" he shouted at her back. Then he waved a hand in disgust and furiously promised himself that he would do just as she asked. He was done with her unfathomable moods. He would have nothing more to do with her. Yet even as he stalked back to the shipyard, boiling with wrath and with the August sun, he knew it was a promise he would not keep.

CHINA NEVER MADE IT to Harriet's house that evening, to be soothed by raspberry ice and a relaxing chat. Zacch intercepted her as she stood morosely by the sink, after supper, washing up the dishes. "You've looked as gloomy as a day in November all through supper, China," he said, seizing the dish towel and vigorously wiping dry the plates. His fine, clear brow wrinkled in puzzlement as his sister simply shrugged, her eyes not meeting his.

"I've an idea that ought to perk you up," he continued hopefully. "How does a Saturday picnic on Coatue sound to you?" When China only shrugged again, he elaborated enthusiastically. "Think how pleasant and cool it will be to get away from town. Remember how we used to spend hours in that leaky old catboat, then run ashore at Second Bend for lunch? Aunt Judith would pack cold ham and soda crackers and we'd spend our pocket money buying oranges. Do you remember?"

China felt her misery miraculously lifting when she realized Zacch hadn't entirely forgotten the fine times they'd shared. "Aye, I remember," she said happily. "Sometimes we even bought lumps of rock candy and pretended it was sugar cane."

Zacch laughed. "That was when we were supposed to be marooned on a desert island, wasn't it? And the crackers were breadfruit and the ham was wild boar meat.

"And, ho, do you remember how we used to pretend that there were savage cannibals on the island so we had to sneak around in the grass? And one day we slithered over a dune on our stomachs and there were two half-naked Indians butchering a deer that had broken its leg and drowned. They were splattered with blood and looking very fierce. Oh my, didn't we scud for that boat in jig time."

The tension completely left China as she joined Zacch's laughter. She warmly recalled how, much chastened, they had stuck close to home for a few days, but, inevitably, they were off again. For the next half hour, they stood in the kitchen recounting old adventures and reaffirming their old relationship. China hadn't felt so close to Zacch since the day he'd returned, and Zacch suddenly realized how little time he'd spent with China this summer and how much he missed her. For a while their thoughts ran together, almost inseparable, as they had all their younger years.

The sound of their laughter and reminiscing drifted back through the door to the parlor. In her straight-backed chair by the unlit hearth, Aunt Judith mended a stocking and nodded her approval. She was glad to hear the happiness returned to her grandniece's voice, though she hoped China was paying attention to her chores, too. In his oak rocker by the window, Zaccheus put aside the account book he was studying and leaned back, his eyes staring through the small panes but hardly seeing the sun dropping down behind the green and gold commons. He was content. Sprawled on the horsehair sofa in the middle of the small, spare room, Jake was hidden behind yesterday's *Inquirer*, but not really reading about the arrival at the Bar of the ship *Bunker*. Despite himself, he felt his anger lessening and his great affection for both twins returning. When China sounded so alive, she was irresistible.

The grandfather clock that stood by the front hall chimed half past seven and Zacch jumped to attention. "Uh oh," he said, regretfully. "I've promised Sarah I would come by this evening to make final plans for Saturday. You'll come with us, China, won't you?"

At the mention of Sarah, China felt her happiness deflate. She shook her head uncertainly. "Nay, Zacch, I don't think so. I'd only be an extra hand."

"Don't speak nonsense. It wouldn't seem right without you. Besides, Jake told me this morning that he wouldn't consider setting sail without you in the crew." As China's eyes widened in surprise, he added loyally, "And neither would I. If you don't come, it's all off." Zacch crossed his arms as a sign of finality.

"'Tis a fine bit of guilt to foist on me," she said with a little laugh. "Very well," she relented, "I'll come on thy outing, but I'll not buy the oranges."

Zacch uncrossed his arms and wrapped them around her slim waist in a hug. Her own arms clasped his neck. For a few moments they held on to each other, as if to hold on to the warm, close years of the past. Then Zacch placed a kiss on each of China's cheeks and said, a shade huskily, "I'll take care of the oranges. And the rock candy." With another kiss on her shiny bangs, he broke away and went out the kitchen door, leaving China feeling unaccountably melancholy.

BY SATURDAY, China was regretting her acquiescence. Zacch had had no more time for cozy gams and Jake had resumed his mocking grins. She was again feeling unneeded and unnecessary. She half hoped for foul weather so the whole excursion could be canceled, but the day dawned clear and hot.

As she sat waiting, a few hours later, in the parlor of the huge Coffin home on India Street, her regret and insecurity deepened. She felt uncomfortable among the formal silk and mahogany furniture, slightly stifled by the thick Chinese rugs. When a serving girl carried in an elegant willow hamper full of food, China felt completely out of place. She and Zacch had always stuffed their lunch in a flour sack.

Then Liddy swept in, her dark beauty wonderfully highlighted by a full-skirted gown of yellow and white handkerchief linen. An instant later, as if staged, Sarah daintily followed, looking as pretty and fresh as a violet by a stream, in a lavender dimity dress trimmed with Robinette lace. China felt her cheeks burn in great embarrassment. Not only was her own dress a very ordinary quality of cotton, colored a very dreary Quaker gray, it wasn't even one of her good ones. It was an old shabby gown she only wore when she expected to get it dirty or torn. No one seemed to notice her, though.

After a brief, but friendly, greeting for China, Sarah's big blue eyes eagerly followed every move Zacch made. Liddy seemed too busy to acknowledge China at all. She sailed between Zacch and Jake and the lunch hamper, gaily organizing the day's events. When Mrs. Coffin, a tall, aristocratic woman with becomingly dignified streaks of gray in her perfectly coiffed dark hair, came in to wish them an enjoyable day, she cast no more than a cursory glance of dismissal at China in her much-mended frock.

China was used to feeling lonely or unusual, but she wasn't accustomed to the overwhelming sense of humiliation she felt now. She was just about to mumble her excuse and to run for home, when the little party got ready to go. As expected, Sarah clung gracefully to Zacch's arm, and Liddy wrapped her hand around Jake's. The unexpected spasm of jealousy China felt stab through her might have gotten lost if Liddy hadn't turned at that moment and said, with a malicious light in her eyes and a condescending note in her voice, "Coming, China?"

The humiliation vanished instantly. China silently berated herself for allowing these girls to get the better of her. "Most certainly!" she snapped. Then she drew herself up regally and stepped in front of Liddy and through the door Jake held open for her, her cheeks coloring slightly and her eyelashes dipping fractionally in response to his wink.

Her smoldering hauteur took a downturn a few minutes later when they settled aboard the borrowed whaleboat. Anxious to demonstrate her superiority and nautical expertise, China offered to take an oar. When Sarah and Liddy artfully arranged themselves under parasols in the bow, she immediately realized her mistake, but by then it was too late.

Oblivious to the undercurrents of emotion, and accustomed to rowing in unison with his twin, Zacch accepted China's offer. From his seat, steering in the stern, Jake saw the whole situation and grinned in appreciation. With perspiration pasting her bangs to her forehead, with her bonnet, as usual, halfway down her back, and with the rhythmic exertion bringing bright color to her face and an enticing heave to her breasts, China was a rare, strong beauty.

Unaware of her effect on Jake, China's spirits dropped even lower when they made landfall. While Sarah and Liddy waited demurely under their parasols in the boat, Jake and Zacch erected a two-sided tent on the beach that created a cool square of shade. Under the awning they set cushions and a low table, laid with a damask cloth. When all was ready, the Coffin sisters came ashore, chivalrously carried over the line of damp sand and wave foam by Jake and Zacch. Looking cool and lovely, they spread themselves out on the cushions and began setting the cold chicken and pâté on the table.

China stood by the edge of the tent feeling the first signals of sunburn on her cheeks, on her nose and on her forearms, where she had rolled the suffocating sleeves of her dress out of the way. The hem of her dress was dragged down with saltwater and sand, its bodice stuck to her with sweaty glue. She felt too tall and too awkward, too frumpy and too hot. She wished she were anywhere else.

"For heaven's sake, China, you'll get sunstroke standing out there. That's what this foolish tent is for," Jake said, coming up beside her. As soon as they had left the dock, he had stripped off his coat, unsnapped his collar, unwound his cravat and rolled up his sleeves. His chest and arms were hard and tanned in contrast to the snowy, soft linen of his shirt. He gave a little push to propel China into the shade and she clumsily stumbled forward, collapsing on the corner of a cushion, her flush of embarrassment blending with her sunburn.

"You look so hot, China," Liddy said pointedly. "Perhaps a glass of lemonade would cool you down after all that rowing. My, my, I'm sure I would have fainted if I'd had to do it." She handed China a crystal glassful of lemonade, letting go an instant before China's fingers grasped the goblet. It spilled in her lap.

"Oh no," Liddy cried, "how inattentive of me. Oh dear, please forgive me. Here, let me mop it up." She reached an embroidered lace napkin across Jake's chest and dabbed at the puddle in China's lap. "Do say you'll forgive me," she said sweetly, perhaps mindful of the dark look Jake was giving her.

"'Tis nothing," China muttered, staring helplessly at the mess.

"Go sluice it off in the sea," Jake ordered, pushing Liddy's arm and ineffectual napkin away. "You'll attract ants otherwise."

While Liddy and Sarah giggled softly at the thought, China obediently trudged to the water's edge feeling as odd and graceless as a land tortoise. She cursed herself for coming along. Better to have borne the guilt for a canceled trip than to suffer this mortification. At that, she doubted if Zacch's threat would have come to anything. He probably made it in a moment of pity. Right now, he didn't seem to care about anyone but Sarah, looking, if anything, exasperated when the lemonade fell in her lap. Jake, too, was treating her like an overgrown child. She couldn't imagine why he had wanted her along, unless to save himself some rowing.

The rest of lunch was little better, except now Liddy and Sarah completely ignored her. She mechanically ate whatever Jake put on her plate, otherwise she sat in silence. After what seemed like unending hours, the last lady finger was finished and the table was moved to one side. Sarah, made drowsy by the heat and by the food, and lulled by the tempered surge of sea upon sand, snuggled against Zacch and fell into angelic slumber. He gazed at her in unabashed adoration, tenderly brushing a golden strand of hair from her pink and white cheek. China could take no more.

"I'm going for a walk," she announced, rising abruptly and setting out before her comment could be acknowledged, if anyone were so inclined.

Certainly Sarah didn't hear her, and Zacch was only aware of the precious bundle in his arms. Jake glanced quickly China's way, but Liddy pulled his attention back toward her with a delicate yawn and a graceful stretch of her arms that managed to brush along his thigh.

"How sleepy this salt air makes me feel," Liddy said, suggestively.

"Aye," Jake responded dryly, "'tis vastly different from the air on India Street, all of a quarter mile inland."

Liddy had the grace to blush, but recovered quickly. "'Tis easy for you to tease, accustomed as you are to sailing all the seas of the world. You are so strong you scarcely notice ferocious storms and scorching sun. I can't imagine how you endure it. I would . . ."

"I know," Jake interrupted. "You would faint if you had to do it. Well, don't faint," he said, rising. "We don't need to haul a limp body back to town. I won't keep you from your nap any longer." He followed China's tracks down the beach and over the dune, leaving Liddy with her mouth, rather unattractively, open.

Jake caught up with China half a mile away, on the side of Coatue facing the Sound. The waves were somewhat more authoritative here, slapping along the sand, shoving small stones and scallop shells up and down. She was so absorbed in her misery, she didn't even hear him approach. She looked up startled when he was suddenly by her side.

The teasing remark Jake had intended to make never left his lips when he saw the genuinely woebegone expression on China's sun-flushed face. He felt the same sense of protective desire that he had felt that day by the blueberries.

"If you could see your face in a glass, right now, your heart would break," he said, sliding an arm around her shoulders. He held her tight when she tried to move away. "Or maybe it already is broken, and that's why you are in the doldrums. What's amiss?"

"'Tis none of thy lookout," China said gruffly, twisting away from his grip. The nearness of him set her heart soaring, but she had only to imagine Liddy draped gracefully

87

by his elbow to restore her grimness of spirit. It was impossible to think straight in his presence. "I just want to be alone."

"I grant you this squantum is not as gay as it might be, but that's no reason to be so discouraged," Jake said, ignoring her last remark and closing the gap between them again. "Why so glum?" He took hold of her hand and refused to let go.

China dared not look at him. "I told thee," she said to the sand, "'tis nothing to trouble thyself about."

"But I *am* troubled, China. It hurts me to see you looking so unhappy. What is it? Was it something you ate? Was the chicken too greasy? The mutton pie too rich?"

China just shook her head.

"The fish cakes, then. It must have been the fish cakes. Were they too old?"

"Aye, that was it," China lied, in an effort to quell his prodding. She still stared at the sand. "They must have been a bit rancid."

Jake stopped abruptly, bringing China up short. As she looked around in surprise, he seized her by the shoulders and said, gently, "There were no fish cakes, China. And there was nothing wrong with the food. In truth, 'tis the one agreeable thing that has happened today. You've been miserable since we left home this morning. Why can't you tell me why you are so downcast?"

China looked up at his face, amazed by the warmth in his sea-blue eyes and by the concern on his rugged face. Flustered, she looked down again. When she didn't answer him, he gave her shoulders a little shake, until finally she muttered, "I'm not downcast. I simply shouldn't have come."

"Aye," Jake said, grinning, "nor should I have. I told you from the start I thought it was an idea with very little sense to it.'' He tenderly pressed the back of his hand to her sunburnt cheek.

Now that she had started to explain, she felt the need to clarify. ''I only mean that I am an extra sail on this ship,'' she said, staring furiously at her feet again and struggling to keep her thoughts away from the fingers that were now swirling her hair behind her ear. ''Thee didn't need me here to spoil the congeniality of the party.''

The fingers stopped their soft stroking. Jake's voice was full of surprise as he asked, ''Now why do you think that *you* are the extra sail? And why do you think that this ridiculous junket would have been congenial without you?'' His fingers tucked under her chin and lifted it up. A tear clung to her long lashes, threatening to spill down her face.

She suddenly spun away from him. ''Thee needn't pretend, Jake,'' she said in a choking voice. ''I have eyes. I can see the set of the sails. Thee doesn't need me here when thee has Liddy and Sarah. They are so pretty and delicate, and they've beautiful dresses and fancy hampers full of food.

''I'm like an old *corbeau*—the crow that used to eat Maman's garden in Normandy. It was big and dreary and awkward.'' She grabbed a fistful of the gray cotton cloth of her skirt and shook it fiercely. ''Thee doesn't need a crow when there are dainty canaries.'' She sank down on the spot, crossed her arms over her knees and stared forlornly out to sea.

Jake was astonished. It was plain enough that China and Liddy weren't the best of friends, but it hadn't occurred to him that China could think herself inferior in any respect. He sat down next to her. ''I've never been particularly partial to canaries,'' he said, conversationally. ''They're shrill and silly and not an especially pleasing color.''

China glanced sideways at him but didn't say anything.

"Aye, China," he went on, more forcefully, "you do have eyes. And they are about the most beautiful eyes I have ever seen. They are full of life and intelligence and they are set in a lovely face, which rests on a graceful and long-sparred body."

He gave a smile as he fingered a fold of her dress. "I'll have to agree with you about the frock, but we have been through this discussion before. However, I've never been one to judge a parcel by its wrapper. Not that a wrapper can hide your charm. You're a special one, China Joy, and I'd much rather spend my time with you than with those noodle-headed Coffin girls."

China stared hard at her knees while her heart swelled in happiness at Jake's words. The lonely ache that had enveloped her disappeared. Her emotions tumbled over themselves in a rush to be expressed. As a result, she sat tongue-tied and motionless. Jake's hand brushed against her cheek, pushing back her hair and sending thrills through her body.

"What are you thinking now, *petit corbeau*?" he asked, trying to peer into her down-turned face.

China swallowed and fumbled for something to say. "'Tis very hot," she finally managed to blurt out. Action following impulse, she hastily kicked off her boots, peeled away her stockings and rose, heading for the water. Hitching up her skirt, she cooled her overheated toes and ankles at the edge of the sea.

Still seated, Jake grinned and shook his head. He was getting used to her quicksilver moods, to her unfathomable changes of humor. She was like a firefly, all aglow one moment, and gone the next. As he appreciatively eyed her slim legs and shapely ankles, splashing comfortably in the water, his feeling of protectiveness turned to playfulness.

He pulled off his own boots and socks, tossing them in a heap, next to China's.

"Aye, 'tis fearful hot," he agreed, rising. "And any South Seas sailor worth his salt wouldn't be standing around in the sun on shore leave, he'd be cooling himself off with a swim." So saying, he stripped off his shirt and his trousers and dived cleanly into the clear sea, clad only in his cotton underdrawers.

China watched him surface fifteen feet in front of her, the sun sparkling on his wet skin and off the gold hoop in his ear. "Come on, *corbeau*," he called. His teeth looked very white as a smile split his face. "''Tis time to change into a *canard*. Or perhaps I shouldn't say a duck, but a swan. Come *mon cygne*." He splashed in the water invitingly.

Standing only ankle-deep, China was transfixed with shock at his scandalous daring, and with desire at the sight of the sea caressing his bare, bronzed skin, and with envy at the thought of the cool ocean dispelling the heat of the sun. "Come on, China," Jake called again, treading water out of reach. "The sun must be boiling your brain."

It must be at that, she thought, as she almost involuntarily unbuttoned her dress. I must be suffering sunstroke, she thought, as she pulled it over her head and tossed it to shore. 'Tis folly, she thought, as her petticoat joined the pile. I am mad, she thought, as she waded up to her knees, wearing only her pantaloons and chemise. "Come on, China," Jake said. His voice was husky and mesmerizing. Then she slid into a wave and didn't think again; she felt.

She felt the water close over her, washing away the sweat, absorbing the heat and cleansing her spirit. She felt all her chockablock emotions floating away, felt the loneliness and the misery disappear, felt the uncertainty, the shyness, the clumsiness, the self-consciousness sink to the sandy bottom of the Sound. As she swam with long, sure strokes toward Jake, she felt an exultation she had never known, a jubilation, a freedom.

Then Jake's arms circled her waist underwater, his legs rubbed against hers. She felt cold shivers and hot shocks, felt the soothing slosh of the sea, the scorching broil of the sun, felt Jake's face pressing near hers, his lips covering hers with salty kisses. Her hands slipped up the hard muscle of his arms, over his broad shoulders, around his neck. Her fingers tugged at his dripping curls, traced his eyebrows, trailed down his wet cheek. Her mouth clung closer to his, demanding and receiving, longer, more intense kisses. Her body, naked but for worn cotton underclothes, strained against his, urgent and vital. She did not feel shame or doubt, did not feel any Quaker doom. She felt sure and strong and alive.

An aberrant wave washed over them, suddenly filling their searching mouths with sea, sending them under. They let go their embrace and drifted apart, as each instinctively fought for air. They surfaced, coughing and spluttering, the spell not broken, but put in perspective.

"He's telling us something, is old Neptune," China said, with a laugh.

"Aye," Jake agreed, with mock sourness. "He's giving us a reprimand and no mistake. Anyone would think he's taken up religion."

For nearly half an hour they played in the water like two young seals. They swam and dived and shot to the surface. They clasped together in an embrace, tasted the salt and the desire on each other's lips and allowed themselves to be pushed apart by the rhythm of the ocean swells. The sun beat down, the water refreshed. It beaded on their eyelashes, ran down their faces, molded their scant garments and their dark hair to their skin.

For half an hour there was only the sun and the sea and the scraggly spit of sand and coarse grass behind them. There was only the mile-high blue sky and a gull wheeling across it. Then from the beach came a shout. "Ho there! Why didn't you tell me this was where you were sneaking off to?" They turned to see Zacch standing on one foot, tugging his boot off the other, a huge, delighted grin on his face. In a minute, his clothes lay next to Jake's and he was erupting from the water beside them.

"Ahh," he sighed, ecstatically. "This is more like it. I thought I was going to expire. Trust you two to have the right idea."

Surprisingly, China felt not pleasure at her twin's presence, but mild annoyance at his intrusion. Although all summer she had been longing for just such a lark with Zacch, she had, in half an hour's time, surpassed it. Suddenly she felt older, more mature, and in that moment she let her childhood go, to bob and drift, like a shell in the sea, and to sink beyond reach. It added to the clean, elated feeling that buoyed her up as much as the waves.

"I'm surprised thee didn't think of it thyself," China answered. "'Tis not like thee to behave so decorously. I should have thought thee'd be over the side before this."

"I didn't want to leave Sarah and Liddy," Zacch explained, rolling happily on his back and allowing a swell to lift him.

"And where are the fair Misses Coffin, now?" Jake asked. "Have they rowed back to town without us?" He scooped a handful of water across Zacch's blissful face.

Zacch righted himself and swam out of Jake's reach, laughing. "Nay, they haven't marooned us. They're both napping. I nearly fell asleep myself in this heat, but this is much more refreshing. Won't they be jealous when they wake up and find out what a good time they've missed?"

Jake snorted his disbelief and dived down to grab Zacch's legs from below. While the two friends wrestled noisily, China giggled and treaded water. Zacch's artless comment reinforced her feeling of greater wisdom and emphasized her awareness of Zacch's relative innocence. She had little time to contemplate it, though, for suddenly two hands seized her paddling feet and she was forced under. She pulled free of Jake's and Zacch's grip and broke through the surface, gasping and laughing.

The three of them played in the water another ten minutes, then came ashore to collapse on the hot sand. They chatted and joked, amiably and aimlessly, while they waited for their undergarments to dry enough to dress. China's sense of uninhibited exhilaration seemed inextinguishable.

Even the Coffin sisters' reaction failed to faze her when they returned a short while later, still damp and bedraggled. Sarah's big blue eyes were wide with horror, but Liddy's looks were positively murderous. China added a most uncharitable sense of triumph to her high spirits, observing with some satisfaction the girls' wrinkled linen gowns and their wilted coiffures.

HER FEELING OF EUPHORIA had not abated two days later. China stood in the yard hanging basketfuls of laundry on the line. It was not that she had really stopped to understand all the thoughts and feelings hammering at her head and at her heart, but now she was no longer oppressed by them. She felt on the verge of something grand and wonderful. She had been like a sounding whale, diving deep into the quiet, dark bowels of the infinite ocean; now she was breaching, shooting for the surface, ready to spout rainbow geysers against the wide, blue sky.

As she shook the wrung-out garments and draped them over the line, she half hummed, half sang some songs in French she remembered from her mother. A team of horses clopping down the lane interrupted her tunes and she threaded through the flapping clothes and around the corner of the house to see who it was.

"Ho, Chi-China," boomed John James Henry, as she appeared on the front path. He was seated on a buckboard piled high with coils of old, heavy rope. The huge, collarless shirt he wore was untucked over his duck pants, and his feet were bare. A happy smile was spread across his broad, brown face. Sitting next to him, holding the reins, and looking only slightly more civilized, was Jake.

"Ho, John James Henry," she responded warmly, leaning her elbows on the gate and peering into the buckboard. "Thee has enough rope there to rig a fleet. Does thee mean to start thy own navy?"

John James Henry chuckled, a low, rumbling noise that sounded something like a long dormant volcano arousing from slumber. "Nay, Chi-China. 'Tis not for me. 'Tis for Adam Ray, out to Polpis. He swop with the Captain. You want to come along?"

"Is thee delivering it? Is thee driving out to Polpis?" China was a bit puzzled by John James Henry's explanation and invitation.

"Aye, China," Jake spoke up. "Your father is trading the *Maid*'s old rigging for salt pork and dried apples. It really only needed John James Henry to haul it out to Adam's farm, but I'm feeling lazy today and would rather sit behind a team of horses than raise a sweat at the boatyard. What do you say? Can we convince you to come for a drive in the country?"

"Oh, indeed thee can," China answered, happily. The idea of another excursion with Jake blended perfectly with her present mood. As she turned hurriedly away from the gate, she called over her shoulder, "I'll just be an instant. Thee can turn the team around while thee's waiting."

She ran back to the clothes basket, tossed the remaining clean wash haphazardly over the line and flew into the kitchen. Grabbing an empty flour sack from the stack in the cupboard, she shouted toward the parlor where Aunt Judith was cleaning the soot from the lamp chimneys, "I'm going with Jake and John James Henry for a drive to Polpis." She flung a fresh loaf of bread and a large wedge of cheese into the sack. "'Tis an errand for Papa," she added, as if to give justification for enjoying herself.

"Thee needn't sing out like a sailor in the crosstrees," Aunt Judith admonished, coming into the kitchen. "And don't forget thy bonnet!" Her own voice rose in volume at the sight of her grandniece disappearing out the door, black bangs bare to the breeze. China darted back inside the kitchen, pulled the old bombazine bonnet from its peg and was off again.

It was a delightful drive. Once they'd got past the curious glances and the crowded streets of town, China took the reins while Jake and John James Henry sprawled on top of the coiled line. They sang songs and swapped stories of France and the Society Islands and New York. They rolled up their sleeves and threw back their heads and laughed. They shared the bread and cheese, Jake feeding it in bits to China, whose hands were busy driving.

At Adam Ray's farm, it was mostly John James Henry who unloaded the heavy coils while Jake grunted sympathetically, offering encouragement and advice, and China sat in the shade, grinning. They refreshed themselves with clear, cold water from the well, first drinking it, then dunking in it, then pouring it over each other. While they waited to dry, they raided Adam Ray's blackberry bushes, threw the bread crumbs to the geese and took turns at his horseshoe pitch.

By the time they arrived back in town, all three jostling together on the buckboard seat, their moods were more mellow. China felt the buzzing tiredness that comes in the wake of long, hard laughter. It had been a perfect day. When John James Henry grabbed Jake and her into a crushing tricorner hug as they stopped by his boarding house, China savored the moment, fixing it in her memory forever. She planted a kiss on John James Henry's cheek; Jake slapped his shoulder.

After they left John James Henry, they picked their way through the narrow lanes in easy silence. The methodic clopping of the horses' hooves lulled China even more. It was only when they'd wound through town and were heading over the commons on the other side that China roused from her happy reverie. "Jake, has thee fallen asleep at the helm?" she asked. "Thee missed the turn for home a quarter mile back."

A slow smile filled Jake's face. He had no intention of relinquishing China until he absolutely had to. He couldn't get enough of her. The intensity of her emotions excited him, the quickness of her mind stirred him, and the uniqueness of her beauty, of the sensual charcoal outlines around her wonderful gray eyes, made him ache with desire.

"Nay, *chérie*, I've yet to snooze during my trick at the wheel," he answered. "I want to show you a pretty spot I've found with a beautiful view of the sunset."

"But 'tis hours yet 'til sunset."

"We can wait."

Jake followed a trail curving around Capaum Pond and leading up to a bluff beyond. In a small meadow, he stopped the wagon and tethered the horses, then reached up for

China. As his hands circled her waist, she slid her arms over his shoulders and let herself be lifted, almost floated, down. He set her feet on the ground, but kept her close, brushing his lips along the top of her head, over her flushed cheeks, across her full lips.

The passion that had become lazy and lulled in the late afternoon sunshine came awake again inside China. A luscious warmth swept up her legs and through her belly. She leaned toward Jake eagerly, willingly, wanting to respond to the touch of his lips, but he was in no hurry. "Come," he whispered, removing both her arms from his neck and taking hold of one hand. "'Tis hours yet 'til sunset."

He led the way to the top of the bluff where a small grove of pine trees overlooked a slash of white beach below and the deep-blue Sound beyond. A salty breeze off the sea wafted through the clean smell of pine. It was cool and private.

In almost a trance, China held on to Jake's hand, leaned against his arm and took deep breaths of intoxicating air. She looked off to the west and could see the low profile of Tuckernuck, a loaf-shaped island at the end of Nantucket, where the sun disappeared every evening. She looked off to the east and could see the mouth of the harbor and the break in the smooth roll of the tide where the blockading sand bar lay. As if to confirm this fact, a gunnel-deep whaling ship sat peacefully at anchor just beyond the Bar, waiting for lighters either to unload its greasy cargo after years at sea or to fetch out its crew for the start of another endless voyage.

Staring at it, China suddenly felt herself go cold and blank. The exultation that had sustained her since her swim on Saturday was gone. The flush of desire she felt at Jake's touch evaporated. She quickly pulled her hand free of his and moved a step away. "Is that what thee brought me here to see?'' she asked bitterly, as he faced her in astonishment. "Did thee think I needed to be reminded?''

"What are you talking about?'' he demanded, unable to comprehend her swift change of mood. "What's gallied you now?''

She jutted her chin angrily in the direction of the whaler, and his eyes followed her gaze. "Aye. 'Tis a ship at anchor. And?'' he prompted.

"And in less than two months that ship will be the *China Maid*. And here I'll stand while Zacch and Papa and thee goes aboard and sail out of sight. And here I'll be, alone, for how many years, Jake?'' She turned to descend the slope, her wrath renewed at the injustice of her fate.

Before she'd taken a step, Jake's hand closed over her arm in an iron grip and yanked her around to face him. His grin had faded; his blue eyes were serious. "Don't be daft, China,'' he said quietly. "Don't spoil the present with thoughts of the future. We've not gone yet. *I've* not gone yet. I'm still here. If you don't enjoy today while it's here, you'll have nothing but empty memories of missed chances. Don't waste today, China; don't let today go for naught.''

The angry reply she was about to make was smothered when he brought his mouth down on hers. It wasn't the teasing, gentle caress of before, but an urgent, demanding kiss. His arms were hard as he gathered her to him, pressing her protesting body closer to his. With large, strong hands he held her; with hungry lips he silenced her.

At first China struggled to free herself, but her body betrayed her. As in the past, the feel of Jake's face next to hers, the scent of the sea on his skin, the commanding circle of his arms, drove all other thoughts from her mind. She felt hot, yet she shivered when his fingers trailed up the curve of her waist and around the rise of her breasts. She succumbed to desire.

She returned his kisses, feeling delirious shocks when her tongue touched his. Her fingers kneaded the muscles of his shoulders, traced the length of his neck and entwined in his dark hair. She sank with him to the soft, fragrant bed of pine needles, kneeling in embrace.

"Come, *mon petit corbeau*," he whispered, hoarsely. "Let me see you without your gloomy feathers."

He was suddenly unhurried again as he reached behind her to undo her eighteen buttons, placing delicate kisses on her chin and down the sweep of her throat. And she was suddenly shy as he pulled her gray gown over her head, pulled off her petticoat and unlaced her chemise. She looked down, her lush eyelashes fringed against her heated cheeks, her hands clasped in her lap, as he eased the chemise away from her shoulders, exposing the porcelain white skin of her breasts. Very gently he touched two fingers to her cheek, then bent his head to lay the breath of a kiss on her nipple.

China gasped and arched involuntarily at the brush of his lips, the throbbing of her nerves overcoming her momentary modesty. Her eyes lifted to his, unashamed, bold with desire. His teeth showed white as a smile crossed his face. "'Tis as I thought," he murmured, appreciatively. "There's a beautiful swan hidden underneath the crow."

"Aye," China responded, as her fingers worked the buttons of his shirt. "And what is thee hiding?"

With leisurely hands, they undressed each other, reveling in the feel of unclothed skin. With greedy lips they tasted, with sensitive fingers they felt. When it seemed they would burst with building passion, when they could resist the suggestive teasing no more, they lay on their bed of pine needles, and with just the silky August air for covers, they made love.

A long while later they lay perfectly still, watching the sunset. The lowering sun turned the sky pink and purple, casting a muted glow across their bare bodies. As Jake's feather-light fingertips began to chase the soft shadow along her thighs, over her belly and around her breasts, China closed her eyes, luxuriating in his whispery touch and listening to his heart beat.

It seemed to her it was beating in time with hers; it seemed to her, suddenly, that their heartbeats were inseparable. She was in love with him. She knew that. When he was with her, she was the person she was born to be. He awakened in her not only this delicious new feeling of sensual desire, but he also aroused her exultation in life. He understood her as she was; accepted, even relished, her spirit without wanting to subdue it. Aye, she was in love with him.

She sighed. "Jake?" she said.

"Mmm," he answered, satiated, deeply content.

"I love thee. Does thee mind?"

"Mind?" Her words pierced through his sleepy satisfaction. "Do you think I would mind?"

She shrugged against his shoulder. "Perhaps thee does not want my love. Perhaps it is a bother. Nonetheless, there it is."

"'Tis no bother, China," he said, wrapping his arms tightly around her and rubbing his cheek against her hair. He felt a sensation of peace flood through him, a sense of completion, as if some part of him that had always been missing was now in place.

"'Tis the most wonderful thing I've ever been told." He lifted her face and kissed it. "I love you," he said.

The utter happiness that made China want to run and dance and roll headfirst down the hill stayed with her as she slipped into her clothes, willingly leaving Jake to do up the buttons, and then to undo them again while he kissed her satin smooth shoulders. It stayed with her as she blissfully bounced by his side on the buckboard back to town and as she held on to his hand on the walk home from the stables. It stayed with her as they paused in the twilight for a last embrace before entering the house, already late for supper. It was only as she stepped through the threshold to the kitchen that China even thought to run her fingers through her hair or to think of an excuse for their tardiness.

"Ho!" Zacch cried, in delight. "There you are at last. Wait 'til you hear the news." He seemed unaware of their crumpled clothes or of their high color. In fact, no one remarked on their appearance. A smile erased the grief on Zaccheus's face, and even Aunt Judith looked pleased.

"What news is this?" Jake asked, glad to divert the attention from their entrance. "From the look on your face, you've been made the master of your own ship, with a pirate treasure thrown in the bargain."

"Nay, 'tis even better than that," Zacch said with a laugh. His happy face was the mirror of China's. "I've been given the greatest treasure there is."

"The crown jewels?" Jake guessed. "Joseph Starbuck's vault?"

"Nay, nay." Zacch laughed again. "'Tis Sarah. She's promised she'll marry me."

"Well, now!" Jake boomed, crossing the room in two strides and grabbing Zacch into a hug. "Congratulations! I'm truly happy for you." He stood back and thumped Zacch's shoulders, remarking, "You're right. She is a precious gem. I'm surprised her father is willing to part with her."

"There was naught else he could do," Zacch boasted, stepping free of his friend's pounding. "He saw how much she loves me." His grin was a bit sheepish as he added, "He did ask that we wait until the end of this voyage, though, which is probably just as well. I'll be going as second mate this trip and will have a good lay. It will give us a better start.''

"Aye," Jake said, wryly. "I think you'll need a good lay, or a pirate's treasure, to keep your wife in silk gowns, Zacch. She's accustomed to luxury."

"She'll be happy as long as she's with me," Zacch answered, stoutly. "But I mean to see she's always kept comfortable. We may live with her parents for a while, 'til we have enough money for a proper house of our own, but it won't take long."

The conversation carried on, but to China it was just unintelligible noise. She felt stunned. The ecstatic flush was drained from her face; her hands were cold. It was as if someone had punched her in the stomach so her breath had come out with a whoosh, releasing the buoyant happiness, the magical love, that had sustained her. It was as if this afternoon had been a dream and now she was awake. Reality returned, and it was all the more harsh for having been, temporarily, so heavenly.

She was being abandoned once more. This time Zacch would be leaving for good. He'd go away for years, roaming the seas in search of whales, and, even when he returned it wouldn't be to her, but to his sweet Sarah. He'd never again sleep a chimney's width away from her, never again lean on his elbows across the breakfast table. He'd live in the big house on India Street that had too many carpets and too much furniture. Her twin would be irrevocably taken away from her.

"China?"

She heard Jake's voice by her side and felt his hand on her elbow. In almost a trance she looked at him, not seeing the foreboding fill his face at the sight of her stricken expression. She realized, now, that Jake would be leaving, too. Their hearts would not beat together, inseparably. He would not be there to arouse her senses and to revel in her spirit. Her love would be a shadow, gone before she hardly knew it. The life within her would be stifled once more.

Somehow she managed to kiss Zacch's cheek and to whisper some weak words in his ear. Somehow she managed to sit down at the supper table and to swallow a few spoonfuls of mutton stew. Somehow she managed to wash the dishes and to say good-night and to stumble, dry-eyed and numb, to the sanctuary of her room.

The days went by, but China barely noticed. She couldn't clear her head, couldn't focus her thoughts. She returned to her old routine of avoiding Jake, subconsciously hoping that the less time she spent with him, the less it would hurt when he left.

Preoccupied with the outfitting of the *China Maid* and with end of the season preserving and with the "informal" engagement party that Mrs. Coffin was giving on Saturday evening, none of her family noticed China's unusual gravity. Jake noticed, though. At first he was puzzled by her somber mood, but as the days went by, he became frustrated. He tried to talk to her in private. He wanted to jostle her out of her depression, to respark the passion and the love that poured out of her that afternoon on the bluff above Capaum Pond. That was the China he wanted, the woman who filled his soul. Every time he thought he had his hands on her, she just faded away.

He was determined to find a moment alone with her on Saturday, to slip her aside during the confusion of the party. It wasn't as easy as he thought, however. No sooner had they entered the Coffins' elegant home, than Benjamin Swain and Gideon Hussey commandeered his attention.

"What do you think of the *Bunker*, Jake?" Benjamin asked, steering him into a corner. He pressed a glass of rum into Jake's hand with a wink. "Try a tot of this. 'Tis Jethro's special stock from the French Indies. 'Twill see you through a party better than that peaked punch.

"Now then," he continued with the original thread of his conversation. "She's been gone three years in the Pacific and she comes home with eleven hundred barrels of oil. 'Tis a poor showing. Do you think it is as they are saying? That the whales have all been hunted?"

Before Jake could frame a reply, Gideon Hussey answered, "'Tis in the cold waters you need to fish." He spoke slowly and pedantically, in the manner of his son Obed. "There's sperm a plenty in the Arctic, yet. To the south, too. In the Antarctic."

"Aye," Benjamin said, thoughtfully. He took a swallow of rum. "I've been thinking of buying a small schooner. There's one I know of at New London. She's built heavy, for breaking ice. It might be worth my while to send her down south for seals. There's a market still for seal skins in England and France. What do you think, Jake?"

While his eyes scanned the room for China, Jake shook his head and smiled. The last rays of sun filtered through the lace on the large windows and caught the gold hoop in his ear. "For myself, there's nothing that could induce me to spend a season in the South," he said. "'Tis a mean enough life hunting whales in warm climes. I've no desire to court frostbite as well.

"I'd thought the fur trade between England and China was pretty well finished, especially now that England is about to go to war with China over opium, but if you are thinking about it, Benjamin, you must have good reason. You're too shrewd to make a wrong move."

Gideon nodded slowly and started talking about the long drought that had been plaguing Nantucket. Under the cover of his droning, Jake continued searching for China. He finally spotted her across the room, but she seemed engrossed in conversation with Harriet. He kept his eyes on her while he made some monotone reply to Gideon.

In fact, China was little more attentive than Jake was, as Harriet commented, first on the weather, then on the concert of sacred music given last week at the Congregational Church and then on the grandeur of the Coffin sisters' gowns. Her mind seemed fixed in a fog and it was only when she became aware of Harriet's pointed silence that she groggily blinked and said, "Eh?"

"Honestly, China," Harriet said, shaking her head. "I've been rambling on for almost half an hour and you haven't said two words. I doubt if you've even heard me."

"Nay, Harriet," China said, struggling to concentrate. "I've heard thee. 'Twas something about green satin. And the church. Was it the South Church or the North Church?"

Harriet chuckled. "The South Church, if that matters. Come, China, you've no interest in churches, or concerts, either. You seem deeply distracted. Is it another trip to Madagascar?"

"Aye, it must be that," China said, accepting the excuse. "Just a bit of daydreaming, I suppose."

"Daydreams are meant to be delightful," Harriet said. "The look on your face is anything but. You're positively tragic. I don't mean to stick my nose where it doesn't belong, but it hurts me to see you so troubled. Are you unhappy about Zacch's engagement? Is that why you look so disconsolate while your twin is absolutely shining?"

Harriet's observation hit uncomfortably close, cracking through China's daze. Before she could think of how to respond, the sober voice of Obed Hussey came to her rescue.

"Ho, China," he said. "I see you are without refreshment. Would you like me to bring you a glass of punch or a plate of food? They've just laid a table with cold meats and breads. They look quite good."

"Thank thee, Obed," she said, grateful more for his interruption than for his offer. She was too confused about her feelings to try and explain them to Harriet. At the moment, all she felt was loss. "Really though, I've no appetite just now." She started to excuse herself, but had wits enough to see the shy blush on Harriet's cheeks. She hurriedly added, "But Harriet's just been saying how tempting all the food looks. Perhaps thee should fill a plate for her." She gave Obed a gentle shove in the direction of the buffet, patted Harriet's hand confidentially and slipped away.

She meant to plant herself in the vicinity of Aunt Judith, safe from prying comments, but as she was crossing the room to where her aunt was sitting in disapproving silence, a hand purposely seized her forearm and steered her toward the door. It was Jake.

"Where is thee taking me?" she demanded, a fresh wave of pain overwhelming the pleasure of his touch.

"Mrs. Coffin was just telling me about her garden," Jake answered, evenly. "She's quite proud of her Chinese maple trees. I think we should go see them, don't you?" He led her rapidly down the hall, through the small parlor and out the rear door, before she could protest.

The garden was lovely and tranquil in the early evening light. Beds of phlox and fragrant lavender bordered the neat green lawn. At one end, a willow wept gracefully. In the middle, a wrought-iron bench was placed beneath the prized pair of Chinese maples. It was to the bench that Jake brought China, firmly shoving her to the seat.

"Now," he said, sitting next to her and folding his arms patiently across his chest. "Tell me why you are so miserable."

China sighed. She didn't look at him as she mumbled, "I'm not miserable. I'm fine."

"Is that why you look as if you've been keelhauled?"

"I'm fine," China insisted, stubbornly. She felt uncomfortable.

Jake uncrossed his arms and twisted on the bench to face her. He took one of her hands in both his own and pressed it gently. "I know you better than that, *corbeau*. You are not fine and I am very worried about you."

"Thee needn't be."

"But I am."

When only silence and a down-turned face answered him, Jake felt his patience slip away. He released her limp hand and recrossed his arms, settling back in the seat. "I can play this game as long as you can, China," he said in a steely voice. "You're acting like a child who won't eat her oatmeal. And we sit here going back and forth while you refuse to swallow a bite.

"I'm surprised at you. I thought I could expect more forthright behavior from you. This silly sulking is more suited to girls like Sarah and Liddy, than to someone as honest as you. 'Tis not a pretty thing to see you pouting over petty injustices."

China's chin raised sharply at that remark and her gray eyes took on an angry gleam. "Thee is always so quick to judge me," she said. "Thee always has a smart conclusion to make, an important opinion to render. It must be most gratifying to thee to have so many answers. I just wish I knew by what divine power thee makes thy decisions. How can thee know what is 'petty' and 'silly'?"

Rather than being irritated by China's outlashing, Jake was relieved to see her spirit returning. "I can only know what you tell me," he replied, with a goading grin. "And right now you are telling me you are fine. It seems strange to me that someone who is fine should skulk around for a week wrapped in a black cloud of doom.

"What is it? What is troubling you? Is it Sarah?" When he heard her sharp intake of air, he relentlessly pursued that point. "It is the apple blossom beauty, then, isn't it? You won't tell me, will you?" When she clamped closed her lips and gave a short shake of her head, he said, "I'll have to guess, then.

"It can't be her frock and her frippery, because we've gone all through that and decided that it didn't matter." He paused a minute to see her reaction. When she stared straight ahead, unwaveringly, he went on. "Do you really disapprove of her so strongly?" A thought struck him. "Or do you just disapprove of her marrying Zacch?"

Her eyes widened, almost imperceptibly, in pain, but no other expression crossed her face. Somewhat more gently Jake said, "Perhaps you just disapprove of Zacch marrying. Perhaps you feel he is abandoning you again."

His words were such an accurate assessment, such an exact description of her feelings, she felt her eyes fill with tears. Her chin trembled slightly, but she clenched her mouth harder and continued to stare at a shingle on the side of the building. She felt as if she were going to explode.

Jake saw the anguish on her face and knew he'd finally found out her problem. He uncrossed his arms again and leaned forward, resting his elbows on his knees. His voice was tender, but exasperated, as he asked, "But why? Why should you feel that he is abandoning you? Doesn't he have the right to marry the person that he loves when you are going to do the same?'' The thought formed simultaneously with the words, but Jake suddenly knew, with conviction, that it was right. She was more important to him than any other human being had ever been.

His pronouncement had quite a different effect on China, however. Her roiling grief and heartache bubbled over in fierce wrath. ''What is thee talking about?'' she demanded, turning to look him squarely in the eye. ''What makes thee think I am marrying?''

Jake recoiled from the intensity of her anger. ''Don't be coy,'' he snapped. ''Are you miffed because I didn't make a pretty proposal? Did you want posies and bonbons and volumes of poetry? I apologize,'' he said, sarcastically. '''Tis not my way, nor yours either. When a man and a woman love each other as we do 'tis natural to assume they'll marry and no amount of mealy-mouthed nonsense can change the course of it.''

China's fury literally propelled her to her feet. She was shaking with rage as she faced him. ''How dare thee assume I'll marry thee,'' she stormed. ''How dare thee assume our courses are so surely charted. Is thee so blind, deaf and selfish that without even asking me, without even remembering what I have said to thee, without believing me, thee can simply assume I will marry thee and watch thee sail away for three years or four or more? I told thee once, I'll never marry a man who goes whaling. Never. And I'll say it again. Never.'' China's hand sliced through the air, illustrating the finality of her decision.

''What kind of love is this that you speak of?'' she asked scornfully. ''A love that lasts for three months every few years? What kind of commitment is thee making? Only to satisfy thy whims as thee pleases, I think. I'll stay a spinster rather than become a bystander in my marriage; 'tis not a wife thee wants, but an object, a crockery jar or a lacquered box, that thee can put on the shelf when thee goes away. Thee can look elsewhere for such a wife and not at me.''

For an instant Jake was speechless, shocked not only by her words, but by the force of her ire. Then his disappointment and puzzlement dissolved in an equal rage. He came swiftly to his feet, towering over her slim straight body. ''There's nothing amiss with my hearing, nor with my memory,'' he thundered. ''I quite distinctly remember you telling me that you love me.''

China gasped and stepped backward. ''''Twas a mistake,'' she hissed. ''That whole afternoon by Capaum Pond was a mistake. 'Tis one I'll not make again.''

''''Twas no mistake,'' he said, coming close to her again and taking hold of her chin. ''You may lie with your words, China, but you can't lie with your body. 'Tis love you felt then and still feel now. We're meant for each other and that's no mistake.''

''I told thee…'' China began, jerking her face free of his grip.

''I know what you told me,'' he interrupted harshly. ''Why don't you remember what I told you? Do you expect me to chain myself to a garden patch? Or even worse, to a desk and to ledgers and to airless offices? Is that what you want?'' he asked menacingly. ''Do you want to see me dead in my prime, clutching a pile of vouchers to my chest? Will that prove that I love you?

''Do you want me to break the promise I made to your father? He is depending on me for this voyage. And so is Zacch. They've been the only real family I have ever had. How can I betray their trust? What of my commitment to them?''

They argued bitterly, each motivated by haunting memories of the past, by fear of loneliness and coldness and smothered lives. They couldn't accept the other's view, despite, and because of, the tremendous love they felt. They were at a seething impasse, glaring through the dim light of evening at each other when Liddy's voice tinkled across the lawn.

"What are you two doing out there?" she called gaily. "The dancing has started and everyone is in such good spirits. You must come in and enjoy it. And Jake," she added, pleading prettily, "you know that you owe me a dance from the Sheep Shearing."

Jake stared another moment at China's unrelenting face, then growled, "Aye, I do."

He stomped across the lawn, hardly pausing as he seized Liddy by the waist and pushed her through the door. The vivacious brunette managed a smug glance over her shoulder at China before disappearing. Sharp pangs of jealousy added themselves, unwanted, to the torturous jumble of emotions churning inside China. It was a long while before she could compose herself enough to return indoors and to stonily watch the dancers.

5

NANTUCKET
October 1839

THE WARM RAYS of Indian summer sunshine barely penetrated the chill numbing China as she sat, hunched up, on the bluff above Capaum Pond. The view before her was little changed from the last time she was here. The tall, coarse grass on the dunes below was slightly more bleached, and bright stalks of goldenrod signaled the tail end of summer, but the sea still stretched imperturbably toward infinity, rippling under a hazy blue sky. Again, bobbing at anchor, just beyond the Bar, lay a fully laden whaler, the sun sparkling off her neatly furled new sails, her tightly caulked bow ready to plough through the waves with the morning tide.

This time, though, it was not some nameless ship, not just a vague reminder of heartbreak yet to come. This time it was the *China Maid* and in less than twelve hours she would be rounding Great Point and be gone. This time Zaccheus and Zacch and Jake would haul themselves over her bulwark and sail off into the vast oceans of the world for three years. Or for eternity. Sometime after supper this evening they would shoulder their sea chests and stride away, their thoughts already fixed on far-flung horizons. And China would remain behind, waiting; whiling away the long winters darning socks and sweeping dead ashes from the hearth to spread on the icy spots in the yard; sliding silently through the summers sharing her secret swims and island explorations with no one. Alone.

A little jab of anger poked at China and she smacked her fist into her palm in an attempt to dispel it. She was angry with herself for being so dependent on those three men for her happiness. Especially Jake. She banged both fists against her upturned knees, stopping only when she sank her face into her balled-up fingers. It was just as well Jake was leaving, she told herself. It was just as well his mocking grin and assessing blue eyes would no longer be on the other side of the table every morning and evening. It would be a relief to have him gone, she insisted to herself. It would be a blessed release from the hard, sharp tension and from the few, brief words that had passed between them since the night of Zacch's engagement party.

As she tried to almost physically grind into herself a sense of gratitude that Jake would soon be gone, she heard the soft sluffing of footsteps in the pine needle path behind her. Without turning, lifting her face only high enough to peer over the edge of her knees, she knew it was Jake. Panic suddenly fluttered in her stomach and her mouth felt dry. She wanted to yell, "I didn't mean it," to plead that she really didn't want him to leave, but the words wouldn't come. Instead, she only stared at the ground just beyond the hem of her dress and listened to her heart pound frantically.

Jake reached the top of the bluff and paused a minute, automatically scanning the Sound before him, then sat down next to China, so close his shoulder brushed hers. For a long time he didn't say anything, only continued to study the rhythmic roll of the sea, today so deceptively benign. He had known instinctively he would find her here, and he had sought her out with a sense of urgency. His furious resolution that fateful night, to forget about China, to find someone easier to satisfy him, had faded more and more as his departure date drew nearer. There *wasn't* anyone else who satisfied him, anyone who reached past the coldness of his childhood and the rootless ramblings of his youth, anyone whose spirit was large enough and whose passion was strong enough.

He sighed. He didn't have to see her face, almost hidden in the folds of her skirt; he could tell by the rigid set of her shoulders that it wore the same tight-lipped expression it had worn for the past month. Irritation with her stubbornness put a brisk bark in his voice as he finally said, "This is foolish, China. 'Tis purely nonsensical."

China made no reply. She couldn't. The words still would not come. She tried to swallow, but her throat was too dry. Her whole body was straining in hope that he would stay, yet ready to recoil in grief if he wouldn't.

"'Tis a waste of precious time," Jake said. "'Tis our last chance for three years to talk to each other, to be with each other, and we're sitting like quahogs in the mud with our shells clamped closed."

China felt her hope dissolve as grief overwhelmed her. She tried again to speak, but again no sound came. She cleared her throat and managed a husky whisper. "Perhaps we've really nothing to talk about. Thee won't tell me what I want to hear. Thee won't say that thee is staying. Any other discussion is useless."

Jake grabbed her chin between his thumb and forefinger and yanked it around to face him. "I *can't* say that I am staying, China," he said, exasperatedly. "I gave my word to your father. I promised him this trip." His voice softened as he added, "For now our courses are charted and we must sail them as best we can. There's time aplenty to argue when I come back. And I *will* come back."

The touch of Jake's fingers on her face, even roughly gripping, was more than China could take. Tears spilled out of her great, gray eyes and slid down her cheeks into his palm.

"Nay, China," Jake said, his irritation melting away. "Nay, don't cry." He released her chin and wiped at her cheeks with the back of his hand. When the tears continued to come, he pulled her into his arms, murmuring tenderly, "Hush, sweet China. Don't cry. I'm here now. Don't think about tomorrow. Right now is all that matters."

He held her more tightly, softly rocking back and forth to soothe her silent sobs. His lips brushed the top of her head, his fingers stroked her silky hair. With fingers now gentle, he raised her face from his chest and laid his cheek next to her wet one. "Hush, dear *corbeau*, hush," he whispered into her ear, then slipped a kiss just below her earlobe.

A shudder shook China as raw, rich emotions swept through her. The feel of Jake's face, warm against her cold, wet skin, the breath of his kiss at the curve of her neck, sent shocks of pure pleasure along her legs and up her belly. She thought briefly that she should push him away, that she should scream at him to stop tormenting her, that she should shut him out of her life before he could cause her any more anguish, but instead she pulled closer to him, turning her head until her mouth met his, reveling in the hungry press of his lips against hers. It was too late to send him away. She loved him desperately, and, as he said, now was all that mattered.

With the soft pine needles as a bed, once more, they made love. It was not the leisurely, sensual seduction of before, when it had seemed all eternity was available for their enjoyment. Now they made love with an urgency and an insatiable desire, with an almost ferocious passion. It was as if they were chased, hurrying to blend their bodies while there was still a trace of summer, while they were still together, before winter came, before they were separated.

"My God, China," Jake whispered, when at last they lay still, their skin hot, their hearts pounding. "How much I love you. How very much I love you."

"Aye, Jake, as I love thee," China answered. She let her dark, thick lashes shut slowly over her eyes and a shiver travel along her spine as the late afternoon breeze and Jake's knowing fingers trailed over her breasts and teased her nipple. She strained even closer to him.

Jake suddenly ceased his lazy tickling and rubbed his strong hand the length of her body, bringing her eyes wide open again. He chuckled, drew her into a hug more enthusiastic than passionate and said, "You look like a statue, stretched out in the burnished light of sunset. A bronze statue that should be in a museum. Probably a museum in Cairo. Aye, that's it. With your black hair the way it is, you look like a statue found in the tomb of some ancient Pharaoh." He leaned over and kissed her lightly on the nose. "I'll wager you were a famous queen who lived in Egypt four thousand years ago. You probably swam in the Nile and sprinkled yourself with gold dust."

China giggled. "If that's so, then thee must have been there, too, to slay all the crocodiles. Thee must have been the king."

Jake's whimsical mood vanished as quickly as it had come. He hugged her again, fiercely, possessively, this time. "Aye, China," he said. "I was the king and you were the queen. We were always meant for each other. Four thousand years couldn't keep us apart. Nor can three. Nothing can keep us apart. In our souls, we are already united." He shook her shoulder imperatively. "You know it is true. Tell me that you know it is true."

China looked into his eyes, as blue as the sea, reflecting, now, not cynicism, not insouciance, but love. She felt his arms tightly around her, felt his body pressed next to her, strong and protective. She didn't think about whales or ships or absences at sea. She simply responded to the fullness in her heart and said, "Aye, Jake, 'tis true."

The sun was half gone behind Tuckernuck when they reluctantly rose and dressed. They lingered over each button, every lace, knowing their time together could now be counted in minutes. Clinging to each other, they descended the bluff and followed the narrow path toward home. In the twilight shadows outside Aunt Judith's house, they came together in an embrace. This was their farewell. Later, in front of the family, it would be impossible to do more than politely peck each other's cheek. It hardly seemed real to China as she kissed Jake and heard him murmur, "Courage, *corbeau*." Nothing seemed real.

SUPPER WAS A VERY SOLEMN AFFAIR. There was so much for everyone to say, so many memories of the past and reminders for the future, yet no one knew where to begin. Silence was predominant. China could scarcely swallow. Still dazed, still unable to accept what was happening, she cleared the plates from the table and piled them in the sink. When she turned back to the table, her family had risen and was filing into the parlor. It was time.

She stood with her back glued to the sink, unable to follow them into the other room. Perhaps if she didn't acknowledge their departure, it wouldn't take place. But through the open door she could hear Aunt Judith's characteristically composed voice as she wished Zacch Godspeed. He was going on ahead so he could stop once more at Sarah's, and wring one more moment with his pink and gold flower.

118

The next moment, her twin came into the kitchen, his sea chest on his shoulder. He set it down a few feet from her and said, gently teasing, "You seem to have an affinity for dirty bowls. I can never get you away from that sink." He held out his arms, and China was instantly unriveted. She flung herself into them.

"We didn't have much chance to gam this time, did we?" Zacch commented with a slight catch in his voice.

China shook her head, her face buried against his chest, her hand circled around his neck. Her throat was too choked to talk.

"Still, we managed a few good times," he mused, stroking his hand comfortingly along her back. "I'll never forget that day at the Sheep Shearing. Nor the afternoon on Coatue." China nodded into the heavy blue wool of his coat.

"Besides," Zacch said, hugging her tightly and pressing his own face against the soft folds of her fichu, "we don't have to say anything to understand each other, do we?"

Slowly China raised her head, her tear-blurred eyes wide with surprise. She stared a moment at her twin, at the firm, fine lines of his tanned face, at the sudden wisdom in his expression, at the trace of a tear in his own great, gray eyes. Relief ran through her. Relief that she hadn't lost him after all. Even as he was embarking on another endless voyage, she felt that he'd finally returned to her.

"Nay, Zacch," she said, softly, "we don't have to say a word."

He gave her a smile, a final hug and a kiss on the cheek, then he broke away and hoisted his chest to his shoulder. He was halfway out the back door when he turned to her again. "Tell you what," he said with a wink, "if you look after Sarah for me, I'll look after Jake for you. Is it a bargain?"

China's jaw dropped with astonishment. For all anyone knew, Jake was just a friend of the family. Only Harriet had ever considered him anything more than her older brother. Again she was filled with gladness, even as she was sad. Zacch knew. Truly, they didn't have to say a word. She nodded. "'Tis a bargain," she said. He grinned and was gone.

The cold air that came in with the open door shocked China back to a realization of the present. Leadenly, she made her way into the parlor. Her father sat stiffly in his rocker by the window, Jake leaned carelessly against the hearth. At the small, pine dropleaf table against the wall, Aunt Judith poured cups of pitch-black tea. The only sound was the snap and the hiss of the fire and the ponderous ticking of the grandfather clock, as they waited for John James Henry to appear.

The steam had scarcely cleared off the cups when he arrived, looking very grand, and very large, in a brand-new set of woolen clothes. The tea was forgotten as Zaccheus immediately rose, prepared to depart. John James Henry was not quite ready, however.

He crossed the room to where China stood, almost in the kitchen, extracting from the pocket of his voluminous new jacket a string of odd shells and ivory disks. "'Tis for you, Chi-China," he said, solemnly, stopping only inches from her. She had to tilt her head back to see his broad brown face as he tied the necklace around her throat. While his huge fingers skillfully fastened the string, he muttered sing-song phrases in his own language.

"'Tis a prayer to the gods to bring you good plenty back from the sea," he explained. Without turning his head so anyone else could see, he simply rolled his eyes in the direction of Jake.

China felt another twinge of astonishment, then a rush of gratitude. She gathered as much of him as she could into a hug and said, "Thank thee, John James Henry. My prayers are with thee, too."

He patted the top of her head and turned away. Before swinging Zaccheus's chest to his shoulder, he made a doubtful bow in Aunt Judith's direction. She replied with a stiff nod. She had always been just a trifle suspicious of him.

Then it was Jake's turn. He righted himself from his slouch against the chimney and strode, grinning, toward Aunt Judith. Before she could ward him off, he'd wrapped his arms around her, given her a huge bear hug and released her again. "We'll set the compass for your oyster stew and be home in jig time," he said. Aunt Judith snorted at such nonsense, straightened out the neck cloth he had displaced in his affectionate clasp and wished him a safe journey. Then, in an unusual show of emotion, she laid her hand briefly against his cheek.

In another two strides, Jake was standing in front of China. Neither of them spoke. They only stared, willing themselves not to grab the other in an embrace. China thought her heart would stop. She felt ice cold. Finally Jake lifted his hand and ran his finger over the necklace hanging around her lovely throat. At the brush of his touch on her neck, her eyes shut, then opened again, imploring. Jake gave a scarcely perceptible shake of his head and slid his finger over her lips. With an unusually grim set to his jaw, he dropped his hand, then wheeled and followed John James Henry out the door.

China could barely see, barely draw breath. She hurt terribly. Her heart ached in her chest. She almost cast away her common sense and her pride; she almost gave in to her urge to race after Jake and to plead with him to stay, but just then her father stepped in front of her. Somewhere in the back of her mind it registered that Zaccheus was holding her frigid hand, that he was reciting halting words of farewell. But she couldn't focus on his face, couldn't hear what he was saying, couldn't respond. She could only stand by the kitchen door.

She wasn't even aware that Zaccheus had left, that the house was quiet again, until Aunt Judith's voice penetrated her trance. "Thee looks a fright," she said. "I'll do the washup this evening and thee can go directly to bed."

Without comment, China crossed the parlor and stumbled up the stairs to her room, listening automatically for sounds of Zacch and Jake in the adjoining chamber. There was only the creak of the stair treads under her feet. She lay down, fully clothed, on her bed and stared into the darkness around her.

Sometime before dawn, unable to sleep, she slipped silently down the steps again and almost ran across the moors to the bluff above Capaum Pond. In vain she squinted through the graying morning, yearning for one last glimpse of the *China Maid*, but the pea soup fog lay thick across the sea. "God damn!" she screamed into the heavy, damp air, cursing the fog that blocked her view and the fate that always left her behind. The shriek seemed to unstop the pain frozen in her and she collapsed on the pine needle carpet, racked and gasping with sobs. By the time she rose and returned home, she was numb.

6

INDIAN OCEAN
November 1841

"BLOOOWS! THERE SHE BLOOOWS!" The cry brought shirtless sailors surging up from the fo'c'sle and out from the shady spots on deck. Shubael Brown, captain of the bark, *Sally Ann*, took the ladderlike steps of the companionway from his cabin in two leaps.

"Where away?" he shouted to the lookout in the crow's nest, an iron barrel hoop fastened to the crosstrees of the mainmast. "Sing out, man!" he demanded, as he struggled into his black broadcloth jacket, shiny from hard wear and limited laundering facilities. His once white shirt already clung damply to his body, testifying to the intensity of the tropical heat, but he'd sooner appear on deck naked than coatless. It was a captain's duty to maintain a respectable image.

"Two points off the starboard bow," came the echoey voice from the top of the mast. Another lookout picked up the cry. "Blooows! And again!"

Shubael raked his glossy, almost black hair from his forehead with long, tanned fingers and squinted across the glittering ocean to catch sight of the spouting whales. In repose, his deep brown eyes seemed distant and still, casting a melancholy light across his lean, angular features. On the very rare occasions when he smiled, his eyes became alive, crinkling in the corners, and his face became hand-some and appealing, an ingenuous dimple in each cheek making him seem young and untroubled. These occasions, however, were so infrequent as to be practically non-existent. For the most part, he wore a stern, inflexible expression that made him appear older than his twenty-seven years.

"Fall off two points to starb'rd, Mr. Barnard!" he shouted to the fourth mate. "Ease the sheets, Mr. Pink-ham!" he ordered the third mate. "Prepare to lower the boats, Mr. Stubbs!" he yelled to the second mate. "Ready to dowse some canvas, Mr. Folger!" he called to the first mate. As the *Sally Ann* slowly responded to the turning of her huge wheel and the slacking of her sails, thirty-three men ran across the deck, obeying commands that were almost unnecessary. This was a well-practiced routine. Lines were loosened from their pins, whaleboats swung out on their davits. Sailors raced up the rigging, ready to furl released sails.

"Up top! I cannot hear thee!" Shubael roared. "Sing out! Let me know what thee sees!"

"Aye, sir!" came the reply from the lookout in the crow's nest. "There's naught just yet. Nay! She blows! And again! Dead ahead! 'Tis sperm! And again! She blooows!"

Shubael strained his eyes into the distance and was suddenly rewarded by the sight of three graceful geysers shooting against the horizon. The mighty expulsions of whale breath and seawater went up in the air, dispersing like a cloud of crystal rainbows in the sun. As always, Shubael felt a jolt inside himself at the unsuspecting beauty of the spouts, and, as always, he harshly suppressed his desire to just lean against the bulwark and lose himself in staring. Instead, he calculated the size of the school, confirming from the conformation of the spout that they were, indeed, spermaceti whales, the richest creatures in the sea.

"Now, Mr. Folger," he directed. "Strike the tops'ls and the jib. We'll go with the main and fores'ls. Mr. Stubbs, we'll lower all boats; it looks like a good-sized school. Come about, Mr. Barnard. If we get too much closer we'll gally them for sure. Prepare to turn the helm over to the ship-keeping crew." The orders came mechanically. After fifteen years at sea, Shubael hardly had to think. He instinctively assessed the wind and the weather and the number of whales, automatically forming a plan for the hunt.

"Mr. Folger, get that canvas furled and get thy men down from the yards. 'Tis time to lower for whales. Go find the cook, Mr. Pinkham. The lobscouse can wait; he's needed at the wheel. Fall off, Mr. Barnard. Let her luff."

The crew moved swiftly and efficiently. In no time at all, the one-hundred-and-five-foot bark lay wallowing in the sea, her few raised sails whacking emptily against the wind. The cook gripped the massive wheel, ready to tack slowly to and fro while the cooper, the cabin boy and the smithy— the shipkeepers—manned the sheets. Tubs of carefully coiled manila line were set in their specific spots in the twenty-five-foot-long whaleboats, each tub attached to the next, and the ultimate end attached to a two-fluked harpoon pointing lethally from the Y-shaped "crotch" in the bow of the boat.

An officer leaped into the stern of each boat and a harpooner into its bow. At the order, "hoist and swing," the boats were brought up off the deck and swung over the bulwark on a boom, then lowered into the water by the two men on board slacking off the falls. As soon as the bottom slapped against the sea, the three other oarsmen in each boat's crew went over the rail and down into the bobbing boat. With practiced ease, a mast was stepped and a sail raised, and, while the officer handled the steering oar, they made for the school of whales.

Shubael sat at the steering oar of the larboard waist boat, a familiar tautness hardening his belly. It was as if, somewhere, his body were protesting, wanting him not to pursue this reckless, soon-to-be brutal journey. As he had done on all other occasions since he had risen from twelve-year-old cabin boy, he fiercely thrust these subconscious qualms from him, not permitting them to intrude on his duty. In this, his first trip as master of a whaler, he knew where his obligations lay: to his owner, to his crew and to his family. There was no space for idle reflection.

The little fleet bore down on the seven mammoth beasts lolling lazily in the sun. At a certain distance, orders were quietly given to lower the sails, to unstep the masts and to take up the oars. They crept up on the creatures, taking advantage of their limited field of vision, two tiny eyes in an enormous head.

The starboard bow boat was the first to make contact. It slipped up behind a barely grown bull, only twice as long as the boat. At a sign from Mr. Pinkham, the oars were silently shipped. The harpooner rose and took up his weapon. Bracing his knee firmly against the "clumsy cleat," he aimed for a likely spot at the shoulder, drew back his arm and let fly the iron. Instantly, he snatched up a second harpoon and it followed the other, plunging deep into the flesh of the whale. "Stern all!" Mr. Pinkham cried, and the oars bit down in the sea, sending the fragile boat shooting backward.

As the pain penetrated the shocked whale, its powerful flukes smacked wildly against the water, whipping up waves and foam, and narrowly missing the fleeing boat. Then it sounded, diving untold fathoms in an effort to escape the wound in its side. Line ran out of the tubs so fast, it smoked against the loggerhead. "Wet line!" Mr. Pinkham called, and buckets of water were sluiced over the sizzling hemp.

The line suddenly went slack as the whale started once more for the surface. Sailors quickly recoiled the rope while Mr. Pinkham anxiously scanned the sea for a sign of their quarry. "There she breaches!" he cried suddenly, as the sea rolled and the whale erupted, already spouting blood, a hundred yards away. The mortally wounded mammal thrashed desperately in the sea, too weak for another deep dive. Line was paid out, and recoiled, as Mr. Pinkham and the harpooner hurried to switch places. When the whale was visibly exhausted, they "went in" on it, rowing so close to its side that the larboard oars scraped against it. Now Mr. Pinkham stood. He took up a razor-sharp lance and thrust it, with power and experience, into the whale, piercing its lung. Once the lance was embedded, he gave it an extra twist, to widen the gash and to hasten the end.

Again they backed off while the dying beast went through its final flurry, emitting wheezes and moans that seemed to come from another world. At last it rolled on its side, turned "fin up" and died. They went in on it once more, this time to "waif" it by thrusting a lance, with the *Sally Ann*'s pennant fluttering from the top, into the mountainous side. In this sea, empty of other whaling ships, such a precaution really wasn't necessary, but Mr. Pinkham knew his captain's strict insistence on following rules. Waif set, they restepped the mast, hoisted the sail and chased the gallied school, hoping for another kill.

The larboard stern boat, under Mr. Barnard's command, also had their share of greasy luck. They fastened on and eventually overcame a full-grown bull, a sixty-barrel whale for sure. Deciding not to continue the hunt, Mr. Barnard cut a hole through the head of their prey, attached a tow line, and they began the slow, hard row back to the bark.

They maneuvered their giant catch to the starboard side of the *Sally Ann*, securing it against the slideboards with a heavy chain passing around the flukes, through a hawse-hole forward, to the special fluke bitts. Relieved of their drogue, they then rowed easily around to the larboard, where the crew scrambled up the sides, and the whaleboat was hoisted handily to its home position.

Just as Mr. Barnard's men were about to go below, to change into their oldest clothes for the long, dirty process of "trying out," the cook's shout pierced the air. "My Gawd!" he cried. "'Tis the captain! He's made fast and he's heading this way." All hands rushed to the starboard rail in time to observe the captain's boat on a "Nantucket sleigh ride," streaking behind an enraged beast, not a quarter mile off, and heading unerringly for the *Sally Ann*.

As the crew stood helplessly watching, the whale suddenly sounded. For eight fearful minutes they stood without saying a word. The silence was broken by the heart-stopping screech of splintering wood as the whale breached directly beneath the dead beast chained to the side. The bark rocked crazily, then righted herself, half her starboard bulwark ripped away, her foredeck stove in and planks pulverized.

The grim set of Shubael's face, and the cold, sure tone of his voice as he issued orders, gave no hint of the turmoil within him. He had been horror-struck when the whale they had harpooned had suddenly changed course and had raced for the bark. In a moment, he had run the gauntlet of torturous emotions from futile anger at the *Sally Ann*'s immobility to tremendous guilt at her imminent destruction. The suddenness of events caught him behind his wrought-iron control and he felt himself fill with abhorrence and loathing for the whaling profession.

It was only a moment, though, and when it passed he resumed his concentration on the leviathan in front of him. He played the dazed whale like an oversized bass, sternly restricting his thoughts from anything but the business at hand. Even when the mighty animal finally weakened, even when Shubael went in on it and ruthlessly drove his lance through its lung, even when it spouted clotted red blood all over the sails, even when it turned fin up and died, he ignored the wave of disgust and misery that swept over him. He refused to recognize his sense of overwhelming weariness, which had nothing to do with stiff muscles and scraped knuckles. He simply, and capably, did his duty.

"Mr. Barnard!" Shubael shouted for the highest-ranking officer presently on board, almost as he swung his long legs over the bulwark.

"Aye, sir!" Nineteen-year-old Caleb Barnard, son and grandson of Nantucket whaling men, came quickly across the deck. His curly blond hair was bleached almost white by the southern sun.

"What are the damages? Has thee inspected below? Are we taking on water?" Even as he spoke, Shubael was hurrying forward, eyes fixed on the mass of jumbled lumber and free-flying line ahead of him.

"There seems to be two planks only sprung below the water line," the fourth mate reported. "I've set the men on the pumps, though 'tis a small amount of water we're making at the moment. The foredeck is pretty well stove in and the running rigging forward is snapped where the rail tore away. Some of the deadeyes are smashed and some are split. We've not yet untangled the sheets." They stopped at a gaping hole in the deck and stared down at the shattered bunks beneath them. "And half the fo'c'sle is destroyed," Mr. Barnard concluded.

Shubael fought off the leaden feeling enveloping him. "'Tis the least of our troubles," he said, dispiritedly. "There'll be scant time for sleeping these coming days." He stood staring down at the hole in the deck, as if willing it to mend itself.

"Sir?" Caleb Barnard's voice was a little uncertain as he awaited further instruction. It intruded on Shubael's fatigue-battered mind. He roused.

"Thee has acted coolly, Mr. Barnard," he complimented sparingly. "If thee can find a free halyard, send aloft a signal calling in Mr. Folger, Mr. Pinkham and Mr. Stubbs. Then continue with thy efforts with the forem'st rigging. The most immediate danger seems to be from loose swinging line." He turned and strode away.

One by one the whaleboats returned, bringing extra hands to sort among the ruins. Gradually the rigging got untangled and tied down, the splintered wood got cleared away, and temporary repairs patched the rail and deck. As Shubael promised, little attention was given to the fo'c'sle, the bunkroom for the sailors; the time for sleeping was still a long way off. Once the *Sally Ann* was put in workable order, the business of whaling began again. They had three whales to try out, to wring of their precious oil.

The wooden cutting stage was lowered over the side, and sailors armed with cutting spades descended to a point just above the whale. They carved a deep hole in the beast's neck, releasing gushers of blood and frenzying the sharks snapping in the sea below. Then Mr. Folger, clad only in old trousers, wool socks and a "monkey rope" passed around his waist for safety, leaped onto the wrinkled back of the whale and inserted a hook, half his size, into the open gash.

The men on the stage wielded their cutting spades with dexterity, slicing a six-foot swath through the hide and the blubber. On deck, sailors struggled against the windlass, chanting as they strained, and slowly the strip of blubber, attached to the huge hook, attached to a mammoth block, attached to the mainmast, unwound from the whale like the skin from an orange. Long sections called "blanket pieces" were periodically cut off and shoved down the blubber hatch to the vast blubber room between decks.

When the carcass was naked, its giant head was cut off and secured alongside. The "case," a cavity in the forehead containing pure spermaceti for the world's finest candles, was bailed. Daniel Godfrey, the cabin boy, was lowered into the case so he could fill bucket after bucket with the already congealing liquid.

The head oil was the first to be tried out in the great copper cauldrons sitting in the brick tryworks on deck. As the oil boiled, Shubael carefully skimmed it. Then it was ladled into rectangular copper cooling kettles. When cool, it was spigoted into a deck pot, from which it was poured into casks, around whose shrinking staves the cooper drove his hoops and upon whose lids he branded the ship's name and the cask's contents. Then the casks were stowed deep in the hold where they would remain until removed, years hence, in Nantucket.

Standing six-hour watches, the sailors continued their tasks. They sliced the blanket pieces into narrow "horse pieces," then passed them up onto the deck where they were minced into "Bible leaves" and tossed into the cauldrons for rendering. When the Bible leaves were crisp and shriveled, they were lifted out with the strainer and fed into the firebox as fuel. To light their work in the blubber room, the men coiled lengths of old rope into holes in the unprocessed blubber and set them aflame. On deck, the crackling, snapping fires of the tryworks lit up the night and glistened on the bodies of sweaty, oily, nearly naked workers.

The whole process was repeated twice more, for each of the other whales. When the last cask went down to the hold, there still remained to scour the greasy deck with alkali and sand, to clean out the copper kettles and cauldrons and pots, and to wipe the soot from the yardarms. While the exhausted sailors finally collapsed, Shubael tiredly summoned his first mate to his cabin.

"We're fortunate to have tranquil seas, Mr. Folger," he said, spreading a chart of the Indian Ocean on the table in front of them. William Folger, a middle-aged man whose balding head was more than balanced by the enormous muttonchop whiskers on his cheeks, only nodded.

"We cannot rely on that luck to hold, though," Shubael continued. "We must find a snug port and make better repairs. As we are now, a fair-sized squall, nay, even an overlarge swell, and the whole starboard quarter could take on water faster than we could pump her out. Even if we hadn't put down our carpenter in Payta with jaundice, 'tis doubtful we would be able to put her to rights at sea. We need more lumber than we have on board. The forem'st has a nasty check that will never last the cruise, just for a start." Again Mr. Folger nodded, his face gray with weariness.

Shubael looked with some disfavor on his first mate's listless countenance. The man was an indifferent officer. On his own, he would never have risen above boatsteerer, but he was a relation of the owner, and Shubael was all too well aware of Benjamin Swain's uncritical generosity. He stifled his annoyance.

"I make this group of islands, the Seychelles, our nearest landfall," he said, jabbing his finger at a few specks on the chart, a thousand miles from any continent and a half an inch below the equator. "I know that they are a colony of the British, deeded over to them by Napoleon, but beyond that I know little. Has thee ever put in there?"

Mr. Folger finally spoke up. "Nay, I've never made port there, but I have a cousin who spent some weeks his last trip out. He was on the *Ainsley Gibbs* out of New Bedford, and they called in at the island of Praslin with smallpox on board. Needless to say, the Seychelloise, as they call themselves, weren't overly welcoming. In the end they were sent to a small island that's a leper colony. Not that whaling men draw much water with them at any time. It seems they've had some bad brawls and plundering, though 'twas mostly English whalers and none of our own."

MR. FOLGER'S WORDS were prophetic, as they found out six days later when they limped past a string of lushly green little islands guarding the entrance to Mahé harbor and dropped anchor with a sigh of relief. Almost at once, a longboat rowed alongside and a customs official, with a boiled-red face, came aboard. His naturally officious disposition was not enhanced by the tropical heat trapped inside his heavy uniform. He listened without sympathy to Shubael's explanation, casting a quick, incurious glance over the crudely patched wreckage, finally giving reluctant consent for him to come ashore in search of aid.

While the colonists Shubael encountered ashore were more comfortably attired, they were hardly more helpful. Unwilling to offer any suggestions that would prolong the *Sally Ann*'s stay in port, they pretended lack of knowledge about local craftsmen, or, if they admitted acquaintance with a carpenter, declared him to be temporarily disabled or otherwise employed. One man was more blunt.

"We do not encourage *pêcheurs de baleine*," he said, in his heavy French accent. "Always they drink too much of our caloo and of our bacca and make *beaucoup* problems. I remember in thirty-four when thirty men from the ships *Zephyr* and *Harpooner* came into M. Savy's home on Ste. Anne. They stole many things and broke many things, and they even beat the servants. *Quelle horreur.*"

Yet in the end, out of kindness, or loquaciousness, or a simple desire to rid Mahé of the Yankee whaler's presence, it was he who gave Shubael some useful information. "Take your ship to La Digue," he said, waving his hand out beyond the deep purple waters of the harbor. "It is a *petite île* about thirty of your miles to the northeast. There is *un homme* there of the name Napoleon Mussard. He is at the place called La Passe. Perhaps he can help you. His reputation for making boats is *très bonne.*"

Shubael thanked him for his advice and returned to the *Sally Ann* to assemble his crew before him. "We set sail for La Digue on the tide," he told his men. "I have made some inquiries about it and have discovered that it is a pleasant place with an abundance of fresh foods. There are also," he added with distaste, "two beverages called caloo and bacca. The first is made from the juice of a coconut flower; the second is made by fermenting sugar cane or pineapple. Both are extremely inebriating."

His crew grinned broadly and shifted from foot to foot in anticipation, but the captain's next words, and the uncompromising look on his lean face, dampened their excitement. "If I find one man amongst thee intoxicated at any time, he will be punished severely. Moreover, the entire crew will henceforth be confined on board. I also expect thee to behave with respect toward the local population. However humble their surroundings, thee must conduct thyselves as thee would in the finest parlors of Nantucket. I will tolerate no rowdiness."

His men took him at his word. There were some in the crew old enough to be his father, but they did not deceive themselves into thinking Captain Brown was a gullible youth. Though he was not an unjust man, he was a hard master with the straightlaced morals and austere sensibilities so common in Quakers. They had no way of knowing that Shubael's plain speech and somber dress were more a result of childhood disciplines than of any inner convictions. How could they know, when even he didn't, that the melancholy in his eyes came from continually fighting feelings he'd been taught were unacceptable?

THOSE SENSITIVE IMPULSES were an inheritance from his father, a handsome, agreeable man with a dreamy soul, not well suited to the hard, fast face of reality. Alfred Brown had had little success at any of his ventures, from merchandising to marriage. Prudence, who had been as lovely as a rosebud at dawn when he first had courted her, had become a bitter, humorless wife who had found refuge in religion from her disappointment in Alfred's economic ineptness.

Goaded by Prudence, Alfred had continued to try his hand at various businesses, borrowing money from Benjamin Swain. One scheme after another had fallen through due to bad luck or poor management, or, perhaps, to a real lack of interest. His career had culminated in 1830 when a coastal schooner he had built and outfitted was wrecked off Wellfleet on her maiden voyage. Twelve men died. Alfred was devastated with guilt, but Prudence had been more concerned with the loss of income and with the, by then, enormous debt to Benjamin Swain.

Alfred Brown's only real success was in siring children—eight of them altogether, all healthy, intelligent and attractive. And all, one by one, commencing with Shubael, the eldest, were taught by Prudence to regard life as a joyless burden and their father as a failure. When Shubael returned from his second whaling voyage, shortly after Alfred's last disaster, he had dutifully turned over his lay, or share of the profits, to his mother. Waving the money at Alfred, Prudence had coldly asked, "Isn't thee ashamed? Thy son is a better breadwinner than thee."

Shubael had been embarrassed, but his father had responded by giving him an appraising look he hadn't quite understood. A week later Alfred disappeared, never to be heard from, or of, again.

At the age of seventeen, Shubael had found himself the head of a household that included five sisters and two brothers, the oldest boy being only ten. In addition, there was his father's debt. Though Benjamin Swain was understanding and didn't press for immediate and full repayment, Prudence was another matter. In Alfred's absence, she transferred all her nagging and fault-finding to her son.

Being tall, strong and very bright, Shubael had advanced rapidly from seaman to mate and now to captain. At the end of each voyage he had paid off a small portion of the debt and had turned the remainder of his lay over to Prudence. As quickly as he could he returned to sea, his mother's criticisms and complaints ringing in his ears.

Although it sometimes seemed that responsibilities were closing in on him from every angle, he silently submitted to them. If he ever felt resentment at the shackling of his youth to such duty, if he ever felt the urge to sling his hammock under a tree and do nothing for several months, he could almost hear Prudence's excoriation, and he would feel genuine fear that his father's bad blood was surfacing, and that he, too, was a failure.

FOR HOURS La Digue moved inexorably closer, its high green mountains butting into an almost cobalt blue sky, its clean white ring of beach holding off an endless ocean. Midmorning, a black cloud emptied a blinding sheet of rain on them, then moved on in minutes, leaving behind a rainbow that arched from the bowsprit to the very center of the island. Shubael watched it all, transfixed.

He was unable to turn away, to find some practical task to occupy his hands and to divert his mind. He had sailed up on dozens and dozens of islands, including his own of Nantucket, but none had ever captivated him as much as La Digue. The closer they came, the more detail he could make out. The indeterminate verdancy of the mountain became trees of tropical hardwood and broad-leaved bushes of bananas. Over the circle of spun-sugar sand hung the swaying fronds of lazily leaning coconut palms. And barricading the entire island was a reef, on one side of which dark, deep water beat itself into frothy waves, on the other side of which the calm, shallow sea formed a turquoise lagoon.

They dropped anchor outside the reef, opposite a cluster of wooden huts, half hidden among the palm trees. This was La Passe. An interested crowd gathered on the beach, men standing with arms across their chests and women holding the hands of nearly naked children. None of the spectators made a move to come meet the whalers, however, leaving unlaunched eight or ten long, slender pirogues pulled up on the shore. Instead, Shubael went to meet them feeling inexplicably curious and excited.

He was accompanied by Caleb Barnard, the only man on board the *Sally Ann* with any knowledge of French. *"Bonjour,"* Caleb said, tentatively, eyeing his audience. It silently eyed him back. The solemnly staring faces ranged in complexion from milky white to ebony black and every varying shade in between. These people *were* their history, a mixture of French settlers, African slaves and Chinese merchants dressed in the loose cotton clothing of Indian and Arab traders.

Finally one man responded. *"Bonjour, monsieur,"* he said, without moving, so that Caleb and Shubael had to frantically scan the crowd to locate him. *"Ou besoin queque chose?"* The speaker was an elderly man with mahogany-colored skin and crinkly white hair. His much-laundered knee-length shirt was shabby, but he leaned on an elegant cane of highly polished rosewood, carved in the shape of a sea serpent.

Caleb focused on the man, licked his lips in effort and repeated, *"Bonjour."* He thought another moment and added, *"Comment allez-vous?"*

A smile spread across the old man's face at Caleb's belabored French. *"Ça va bien, merci,"* he responded. *"Mon pas coze français. Mon coze Creole. Ou comprendre?"*

Caleb just stared, stumped. "What's he saying?" Shubael asked in an impatient undertone.

"I'm not sure, sir," Caleb admitted. "It sounds like French, but I don't think it really is. I think he said something about Creole. Perhaps that's it."

"Aye," Shubael said, his memory suddenly jogged. "There was someone in Mahé who made mention of a patois. As I recall he called it Creole."

"'Tis very musical, sir, isn't it?" Caleb commented, not knowing what to say next.

"Thee is not here to analyze linguistics," Shubael retorted sternly, even though he had been thinking the exact same thing. "Thee is here to find directions to Napoleon Mussard's."

"Napoleon Mussard?" the old man asked. He had been following their exchange with alert eyes and had picked out a familiar name. *"Ou pe rode Napoleon Mussard?"*

"Oui," Caleb said, nodding vigorously. "Napoleon Mussard."

"Bien. Mon amene ou cote Napoleon. A cause ou besoin li?" When Caleb responded with a blank look, the old man let out a chortle that revealed one gap in a row of otherwise perfect teeth. He reached his carved cane into the crowd and tapped the shoulder of a young boy, rattling off quick instructions. The boy nodded and approached Shubael and Caleb, making a jerking motion with his head that indicated he wanted them to follow him. They looked uncertainly at the old man, and he nodded, waving his hand in the direction the young boy was taking. *"Aller, aller!"* he said.

"Napoleon Mussard?" Shubael asked, pointing after the boy.

"Oui, oui. Napoleon Mussard. *Aller, aller."*

With an uncharacteristic shrug, Shubael said to his fourth mate, "Let's go." He started off, leaving Caleb to stutter their thanks and to run to catch up.

Their small guide led them up a path through the palm trees to a red dirt road that ran parallel to the beach. Without checking to see that the two men were following, he turned down the road. Arms swinging and bare feet padding, he stepped along, calling to his friends and importantly explaining his mission to questioning onlookers.

They walked past little houses on low stilts made of cedar plank and thatch and scattered indiscriminately along the sides of the road. They walked past a slow-moving ox cart laden with coconuts, past three pigs grunting in a red mud puddle, past a pair of spotted dogs hopefully nosing a pile of fish bones, past chickens scratching among fallen fronds and a rooster crowing on top of a chunk of rose-colored coral, past women in full, loose gowns feeding co-conut husks into cooking fires and stirring spicy-smelling stews, past a young man carrying a string of bright pink fish, past a father peeling stalks of sugar cane with his machete and doling them out to his children, past exotic trees and luxuriant plants and lovely, delicate vines that smelled like vanilla.

They turned in at a cedar-planked house slightly gran-der than most, sitting in a yard full of avocado trees in fruit. Their guide stopped by the stone slab stairs that led up to the open door, and he called out in his singsong Creole. Af-ter a moment a man appeared. He might have been an or-dinary islander of mostly French origin—middle-aged, medium height, unremarkable brown hair—except for the singularly serene expression that enhanced his regular, tanned features and brought warmth and slow humor to his eyes.

At the sight of his two foreign visitors, Napoleon Mus-sard smiled hospitably and came down the six steps. Shu-bael extended his hand, motivated not only by manners but also by an immediate liking for this man. He felt strangely comforted by the contentment apparent in Napoleon's face, almost as if some of Napoleon's tranquillity were trans-ferred to him. He introduced himself, and then waited for Caleb to explain their situation.

In halting, half-broken French, aided by stick drawings in the dirt, Caleb presented their problem. Napoleon lis-tened gravely, occasionally scratching his head in contem-plation or gently questioning the flustered mate. At the end of Caleb's recitation, he walked across the red earth road and threaded through a few palm trees to the beach. While Shubael and Caleb, and their now unshakable guide, trailed after him, Napoleon shaded the sun from his eyes with the flat of his hand and squinted across the sea to the *Sally Ann*, riding easily at anchor.

He shook his head, then nodded, as part of some conversation with himself, then shrugged. Putting the matter to one side for the moment, he turned to Shubael and smiled broadly. *"Après nous alle get sa bateau,"* he said. *"Presente, vine cote moi pou manger."*

Shubael found himself smiling back, almost hypnotized, though he had no idea what Napoleon was saying. He turned to Caleb, who was startled by the benevolent expression on his captain's face. Shubael's smile vanished as he remembered his purpose. "What did he say, Mr. Barnard?" he asked, a touch gruffly.

Caleb sighed. "I'm not sure, sir," he said. "Something about the boat and something about eating."

Shubael frowned and looked back to Napoleon, who was waiting expectantly. With open-mouthed fascination, the small boy looked from one man to the next. *"Venir manger,"* Napoleon finally repeated. *"Manger, manger. Ou comprends. Manger"*. He pointed to his mouth, patted his stomach and waved across the road at his house.

"Oh dear," Caleb said. "I think he's inviting us to eat with him." His tone reflected the provincial horror of many otherwise very adventurous American sailors when confronted with unusual foods.

"Aye, Mr. Barnard, I was able to understand that myself," Shubael said dryly. He gave a short bow to Napoleon and nodded his head. "Tell him we accept, with pleasure."

"Accept, sir?" Caleb almost wailed. "Who knows what manner of swill he may be serving? 'Tis unwise I think. They've very odd tastes, these foreigners."

Shubael fixed a cold eye on Caleb. "In the first place, Mr. Barnard," he said quietly, "we cannot afford to offend him, as we desperately need his services. But in the second place, thee has been eating weevily flour and nearly rancid salt pork for the past year and a half. I don't see how anything that is caught in these waters or grows on these shores could be any odder or more swillish than that. Tell him we accept."

Chastened, though unconvinced, Caleb turned to their host, but Napoleon had already done his own form of interpreting. *"Bon,"* he said, simply, touching Shubael lightly on the shoulder, then leading the way back to his house.

Napoleon Mussard's home was devoid of any architectural details or elaborate decoration either inside or out. Solid cedar planks were laid plainly across the frame; doors and windows were cut in without any fuss, to be closed, when necessary, with unadorned batten shutters. The square structure sat on three-foot stone stilts, to discourage rats, centipedes and the family's two pigs from entering the house at will.

The interior was equally sparse, but also as sensible and as comfortable. A breeze Shubael had barely noticed before drifted between the open windows of the main room. Napoleon motioned them into ladder-backed chairs with rushed seats gathered around a sturdy table of rough cut rosewood. The table was set with bowls fashioned from oversized coconut hulls and with spoons, more like scoopers, made from satiny smooth shells.

Napoleon crossed the room and called out the other door toward the small shack used as a kitchen. A moment later a graceful woman, whose face reflected both black and Chinese blood, entered, bearing several steaming bowls of food. *"Ma femme,"* Napoleon said proudly, as the woman set the bowls on the table and turned to smile at her guests. "Mathilde," he introduced, circling her waist with his arm.

Shubael rose and bowed to Mme Mussard. Beside him Caleb whispered, half in wonderment, half in translation, "'Tis his wife."

"*Ça ma fille, Amedee.*" Napoleon spoke again, gesturing behind Shubael.

"'Tis his daughter," Caleb muttered.

Shubael turned to bow again, but froze in mid-motion, stunned. The girl before him was absolutely beautiful. She couldn't have been more than seventeen, just on the verge of becoming a woman. Her skin was the color of coffee, rich with cream. Thick, black, curly hair escaped in tendrils from her long plait to frame a face that was round but for her delicately pointed chin. Lovely almond-shaped eyes showed her Chinese heritage; her other features were inherited from her French father. Three tiny beauty marks dotted one silky cheek. She was dressed in a white kazak, a simple dress gathered at the yoke and falling unbelted to her bare feet, though hardly hiding the soft curves beneath the thin fabric.

There was about Amedee an air of her father's serenity, but tempered by a hint of youthful mischief. The innocent, open smile of welcome on her face faltered a bit under the intensity of Shubael's stare. Suddenly embarrassed and shy, her round cheeks darkening in a charming flush, she set the platter of fruit she was holding on the table and hurried away. A faint scent of cinnamon remained in her wake.

It was only after Amedee had left the room that Shubael realized how fast his heart was beating and how unbearably hot he had become. Unable to believe that anyone could have such an effect on him, he put his reaction down to the tropical heat hitting on his dark coat and to his usual difficulty in adjusting to dry land. Pushing his damp hair off his forehead, he turned back to his host, composed again.

Despite Caleb's extreme skepticism, the meal was a marvel. There was a curry of octopus so spicy tears ran down Shubael's face, yet the sweet sea flavor and the distinctive texture of the octopus were not disguised. There was a whole fresh fish, steamed in banana leaves and dressed with sliced onions and black pepper, a bowl full of breadfruit chunks fried in coconut oil, a salad of avocado and green mango, sprinkled with salt and squirted with lime, and a selection of bananas and papayas and pineapples and custard apples to wash it all down. The spices brought the inside of Shubael's head to the same boil as the outside, somehow equalizing the heat and making it more comfortable. The flavors blended deliciously on his tongue. He couldn't remember when he had ever enjoyed eating as much.

Napoleon took his time. He rested between courses, savored each spoonful. Shubael was amazed to realize that he didn't mind. Normally he would have chafed at the delay, demanded immediate attention to the problem at hand, but suddenly he felt relaxed, a totally unaccustomed sensation. It seemed that everything about La Digue triggered unusual responses. Ever since he had first sighted it beyond the bowsprit of the *Sally Ann*, he had felt his senses involuntarily awakening.

It was almost with regret that he rose when Napoleon was finally finished. *"Bon,"* Shubael said easily, and to his own surprise. *"Merci, monsieur."* Napoleon beamed and again touched Shubael lightly on the shoulder. Caleb looked astonished.

Napoleon went with them when they rowed back to the bark. In his unhurried way he inspected the damage, pausing occasionally to do some inner calculations or to watch a tern fly gracefully by. Once he pointed to a distant purple swell in the sea and said, *"Tortue."* Shubael followed his pointing finger and saw a hawksbill turtle, at least a yard long, just sinking from view.

It was nearly sunset when Napoleon had seen enough. The sky was turning the color of flames as he bade Shubael, *"Bon soir,"* and slid agilely down to the whaleboat waiting to take him back to shore. Shubael watched from the rail, feeling strangely satisfied, but beside him, Caleb let out a sigh of doubt.

"'Tis a queer form of French they speak," he said, shaking his head. "And a queer way they have of doing business, too. He's still not said whether or not he'll do the work. He didn't even say if he'd be back."

"He'll be back tomorrow, Mr. Barnard," Shubael said, mildly, enjoying the cool breeze that sprang up with the evening sky. "And he'll do the work."

As Shubael predicted, Napoleon returned the next morning, poling alongside the *Sally Ann* in a pirogue. With him was his assistant, Ti-France, a tall, coal-black boy of fifteen, his bare arms gleaming with muscles, his cheerful face fixed in a perpetual grin. Breaking the already elemental Creole into even more basic words, and accompanied by descriptive hand motions, Napoleon explained his plan. Shubael hardly needed his fourth mate's halting translations to understand.

They put all the whaleboats over the side, and all the crew in the boats, then slowly towed the bark through a break in the reef, a channel cut through the coral. About midway to shore, she went fast aground. Napoleon ran the towlines onto the beach, borrowed ten oxen, waited until absolute high tide and tried again. They dragged the bark almost all the way in.

On succeeding days, Napoleon worked with Ti-France up on the mountain, cutting trees and snaking them down to sea level, where he could split them into planks. Feeling a duty to his owner to expedite repairs, Shubael offered the use of his men, but was secretly glad when the Seychellois carpenter turned him down, preferring his own methods and his own pace.

Shubael got in the habit of making a daily visit to Napoleon's house, ostensibly to check on progress, but subconsciously hoping to catch another glimpse of Amedee. He was rewarded twice, and each time his reaction was the same. His heart pounded wildly and his temperature rose. He could no longer blame it on the newness of being on land. He tried to tell himself that he was behaving foolishly, irresponsibly, that Amedee was hardly more than a child. He tried to drive away the images of that sweet face that floated across his dreams, but for once his stern self-discipline failed him.

Shubael arrived one morning to find the yard nearly deserted. Only a pig lay in the dust and some chickens scratched desultorily under the house. From the open windows and doors came the sound of a song. Although Shubael had never heard Amedee's voice, he knew at once that it was hers. It fitted her, slightly husky, very pretty, very warm. He told himself that since Napoleon was nowhere about, he should leave. Nonetheless, he quietly mounted the stone steps and peered inside.

Amedee had her back to him, polishing the floor Seychellois style. Her kazak was knotted up so her slim legs were uncovered below the knee. One bare foot rested on half a coconut husk, split side down; the other foot stepped in time to her song. Her whole body swayed rhythmically as she propelled the husk around the floor, its coarse fibers scrubbing off the dirt, its latent oil sinking into the cedar and making it shine.

As he watched her hips swishing to the songs, her breasts undulating behind the bunched fabric of her kazak, Shubael felt heat spreading up from his groin, felt blood bursting through his veins. She was so beautiful, so perfectly in harmony with this lush, languid, semiprimitive, semicivilized island. She seemed to reflect the passion in the flaming sky at sunset and the peacefulness of the turquoise lagoons. For one instant he longed to slide his hands over her smooth café-au-lait-colored curves, and the next instant he felt deeply ashamed of such a desire. It wasn't dignified, it wasn't respectable; it was more the reaction of a raunchy sailor than of a successful captain. He left quickly, before she caught sight of him.

HE WAS STANDING knee-deep in water, several days later, inspecting the copper sheathing on the hull that the crew was scraping free of barnacles, when Amedee appeared on the beach. She was balancing a giant basketful of avocados on her head, a gift from her father. Although today her kazak came down to her bare ankles, the light breeze from the lagoon pressed the thin cotton to her body. All work ceased as the men turned to gape. Amedee stopped at the water's edge, uncertain and a little scared.

Regretting the fact that he had sent Mr. Barnard ashore to negotiate for fresh provisions, Shubael sloshed forward to meet her, his heart pounding familiarly. *"Bonjour, mademoiselle,"* he said, bowing stiffly and feeling awkward in his soggy pants and sand-filled shoes. He had also just exhausted almost his entire French vocabulary.

His discomfort disappeared, however, when Amedee broke into a smile of relief and recognition. It encompassed her whole face, round cheeks rising and almond-shaped eyes slanting. He was enchanted. *"Bonjour, M. Capitaine,"* she said in her husky voice. *"Mon papa ine evoye sa pour zotte tous."* She swung the basket off her head in an easy motion. When he looked helplessly blank, she held the basket out to him and said, *"Un cadeau. Sorti cotte mon papa."*

He still didn't understand the words, but he guessed that she was giving the fruit to him and he stumbled up to accept it. *"Merci, mademoiselle,"* he mumbled. She smiled again, shrugged shyly, then walked away. He stood, dumbly, holding the basket and watching her disappear down the beach.

"I wouldn't mind ron-day-vooing with her some night," one of the crew commented coarsely behind him. A few snickers of agreement followed the remark.

Shubael felt himself seized by unreasonable anger and he whirled to face the offending sailors. "Stow that talk! Keep thy foul tongues to thyselves," he snapped, thrusting the avocados at the man nearest to him. "I told thee once I'd not tolerate any disrespect toward the locals, and I meant it. That young lady is the daughter of our shipwright, not a tavern wench. 'Tis a week in the brig for the next man who speaks loosely of her."

While the men recoiled from the harshness of his tone, Shubael climbed the ladder to the deck and made his way to his cabin. He slammed the door behind him and ripped off his suffocating coat and his sweat-drenched shirt, then sat in his chair, his head in his hands, tormented. He was no better than those lewd seamen, he castigated himself, allowing lust and animal instincts to overcome his common sense. He swore that he'd put Amedee from his mind, but somehow the memory of her whole face lighting up in a smile at the sight of him, of the delightful scent of cinnamon that filled the air around her, wouldn't go away.

SHUBAEL HAD NOT totally regained control of his iron-bound discipline three days later, when, on his daily visit to Napoleon's, he again found the yard deserted. At the realization, he stopped dead in the path, his heart beginning its frantic pumping. While one hand nervously wiped his forehead, the other instinctively felt in his pocket for the ivory spoon he had carved during a whaleless stretch at sea. He had intended it as a present for his youngest sister, Susannah, but had just this morning slipped it into his coat, telling himself it would be a polite gesture to give it to Mme Mussard.

Shubael had hardly believed himself then, and he was less convinced now as he moved forward with sudden decision, looking for Amedee. He found her behind the house, spreading just-washed laundry over patches of grass to dry. She was struggling with a large sheet, trying to lay the far edge flat, while the ever-present sea breeze kept curling it up, when he came around the corner of the house.

"Thee hasn't spent much time at sea," he said, grabbing the recalcitrant sheet and setting it straight with a snap, "or thee'd know to hang thy sails to the leeward." He looked across the clean square of cloth and smiled, the unexpected dimples in his cheeks chasing away all signs of sternness.

Amedee smiled back, her eyes almost disappearing. *"Mon pas comprende ou,"* she said happily, *"mais mon content écoute ou cozer."*

"I've brought thee a present," Shubael said, coming around to her side of the sheet before his mind could change. He pulled the spoon out of his pocket and held it out to her. The handle was carved in the shape of a palm tree, sanded smooth as silk.

Amedee's eyes opened wide in surprise, her mouth made an O. *"Pour moi?"* she asked, clasping her small hands to her breast, not daring to touch it.

"Aye, 'tis for thee," Shubael said, pushing it closer and nodding.

She slowly stretched out her hand and he laid the spoon in it, his fingertips barely brushing her palm. A shock of pleasure raced through him. "Oooh," she breathed, delightedly. *"Y zolie. Bien zolie."* She looked up from the spoon and said, *"Merci. Merci bien, M. Capitaine."* She rubbed the satiny ivory in admiration, first in her hand and then against her cheek.

"Thee is welcome," Shubael mumbled, overwhelmed by her artless appreciation. He watched her for a moment and then asked, softly, "Amedee?"

"Oui, M. Capitaine." She tore her eyes away from the spoon and looked at him again.

"Will thee call me by my given name? 'Tis Shubael."

She cocked her head quizzically, not comprehending.

"My name is Shubael," he said, trying again. She shrugged apologetically and looked back to the spoon.

"Shubael," he insisted, this time pointing to himself. Inspired by the gesture he added, "Amedee," and pointed to her.

"Ahh," she said, suddenly understanding. Her eyes slanted away in a smile as she repeated, "Shoobell."

The sound of her husky voice singsonging his name sent another wave of heat through his groin. "Aye," he finally choked. "Now thee has it. I mean, *oui.*" Then, not knowing what else to say, he turned abruptly and fled back to the bark.

IF NAPOLEON PROGRESSED at a leisurely pace during the week, stopping frequently to gossip with his friends or to take care of a small job, his work came to a complete halt on Saturday afternoon and wasn't resumed again until sometime on Monday. That Sunday, feeling restless and hot, with no legitimate reason for going around to Napoleon's house, Shubael decided to take a long walk through shady palm groves. He excused the aimlessness of the idea by rationalizing that the exercise and the distraction might clear his mind of Amedee.

Shubael deliberately set out in the direction opposite the Mussard home. For almost half a mile he passed the continuing scatter of cedar and thatch huts, in carelessly kept yards, most of them boasting at least one comfortably inclining palm tree and at least one Seychellois man propped contentedly against it, quaffing caloo. At the sight of Shubael, they all waved cheerily and sang out, *"Bonjour, capitaine."* Shubael nodded in reply and walked on.

When the houses gave out, the dirt road dwindled until it became no more than a trail through a partially tamed palm forest. Jungly underbrush cut off the comparatively cool breeze from the ocean and Shubael was soon streaming. He shed his sweltering coat and slung it over his shoulder, then, still not satisfied, he unbuttoned his shirt and pulled it free from his trousers. He hardly gave a thought to how improper he looked; he was simply responding to the heavy, scented air and the shrieks of alarmed birds, the buzzing of insects in the hot sun and the blessed solitude.

Shubael couldn't remember the last time he had been so utterly alone. Probably not since he'd been a boy. Tensions he wasn't even aware of suddenly eased. Sheltered by seven-foot-high banana bushes and bamboo, by patchouli plants and pineapples, by grasses and flowers and vines, he was momentarily free from the incessant demands people made on him. Despite the press of torpid air, there was not the burden of being responsible for anyone else. There was no mother, no mates, no sailors, no Benjamin Swain. He didn't have to answer questions or set an example or settle disputes or make decisions. He had only to follow the path as far as it would take him.

The end came sooner than he expected, but was by no means disappointing. The thick, green growth simply ceased. Before him was a strip of blinding white beach, broken at frequent intervals by gigantic boulders worn absolutely smooth by tens of thousands of years of chafing sea and wind. The boulder nearest Shubael stood fifteen feet above the beach and had a channel running from its base to a bowl in its top. Shubael tossed his jacket onto the sand and easily climbed up the channel.

The view from the shallow bowl was lovely. To his left the strip of sugar-white beach and prehistoric boulders was undisturbed, except for an occasional palm tree leaning over it, until it turned the corner of the island and disappeared from sight. To his right, the sand showed only his own clumsy footprints and the delicate scratches made by scuttling crabs until it, too, turned a corner of the island and was gone. In front of him, turquoise and lavender, lapped the sea. It grew darker and deeper until it plunged over the edge of the reef in a dramatic display of white foam and purple water. Above him, the sky was cobalt blue and cloudless.

Still alone and relaxed, Shubael sat down at the edge of the bowl and pulled off his boots and his socks and his trousers and his underdrawers and his already open shirt, tossing each item over the side into a pile by his coat. The rock was hot beneath his pale flesh, but he sat a moment, naked and defiant, on the top of his boulder. It felt good. There was a faint breeze on his bare skin, a scorch of sun on his never-before-exposed body. It felt wickedly good.

Savoring every new sensation, Shubael slowly descended and made his way across the hot sand until he reached the water's edge. Prolonging the delicious anticipation of sliding into the refreshing sea, he squatted and examined the cowrie shells and the bright bits of coral glittering just below the surface. He dipped his long fingers in the water, then dribbled it down his burning back. A deep sigh of pleasure escaped him and he let himself pitch forward into the lagoon.

Clear, warm water splashed over him, dousing his broiling body, washing away the sweat and the grime, rinsing off any residual gloom. Facedown in the sea, Shubael grinned. With an easy twist he righted himself, floating only inches off the bottom. He gave another sigh. He was wholly content.

After a happy half hour of swimming and floating in the placid blue pool, Shubael emerged from the water. Dripping wet, he threw himself back against a boulder, reveling in the touch of the hard, hot, totally smooth rock beneath him. He spread his arms and closed his eyes, waiting to dry.

A slight rustle of fallen fronds by the edge of the beach brought one eye lazily open. He lolled his head in the direction of the forest, vaguely curious about which bright bird was making the noise. Fluttering white cloth made him stand bolt upright, shock instantly replacing his luxurious sense of tranquillity. It was Amedee, half hidden among green branches.

For a moment they simply stared at one another, then Shubael, propelled by intense mortification, plunged for his pants. Amedee giggled. Her little laugh cut through Shubael as if it had been a machete. As he frantically hopped on one leg and then the other, pulling up his breeches, her amusement became intolerable. "Heathen!" he shouted, focusing all his embarrassed pride, all his Quaker guilt, all his weeks and years of pent-up emotions on her suddenly still form.

"Thee is a sly little minx," he raged. "Has thee no sense of decency, sneaking up on a man like this? Thee and thy neighbors are little better than pagan; lazy and immoral and godforsaken. All thee would do is gawk at the birds and the flowers and each other all day. Are there no morals here? No discipline? No ambition? 'Tis an island of failures.''

Amedee had no notion of what he was saying, but the anger and the bitterness in his voice were evident. With a frightened gasp, she turned and fled down the path. If Shubael's wrath had been instigated by Amedee's laugh, it was evaporated by the look of terror his outburst caused. Instantly repentant, he raced after her, clad in only half-buttoned trousers.

"Nay, wait, Amedee," he called. "Please wait. Oww! Damn!" A gnarly root, banging against his big toe, made him stagger and lurch, but the pain in his cry made Amedee slow uncertainly. In another stride he was next to her, seizing her shoulder to prevent her from escaping.

He meant to just apologize, to politely beg her pardon, but the words were forgotten when he saw her face. Fear widened her lovely almond eyes and tears trailed down her round cheeks, over the three little dots. "Thee mustn't be afraid of me," he said, humbly. "I mean thee no harm. Truly, Amedee. I love thee."

The words amazed him. His hand slid away from her shoulder, but she didn't move. Slowly, a sense of certainty filled him. "I love thee," he repeated. It was true. She was the essence of these islands, vivid and sultry and smooth, not like the cool, efficient women he knew in New England. Like La Digue itself, she excited him and soothed him, intrigued him, suffused him with a warmth he had never known. "I need thee, Amedee," he said.

Just as Amedee had reacted to the harsh anger in his voice, she now responded to the gentleness. The fear left her face to be replaced by puzzlement. She wrinkled her eyebrows and shook her head to show she didn't understand. *"Qui ou pe dire?"* she asked.

"I love thee," Shubael answered. He touched his fingers to his heart, then to his lips, then laid them lightly on her breast. "I love thee," he said, again.

Suddenly shy, Amedee looked down at his hand. "Oh," she said, softly. At a loss for further words, she feigned attention for his stubbed toe, clicking her tongue sympathetically. She tried to kneel and examine the bruise, but Shubael took her arms and lifted her up.

"Thee gives me joy," he said, as he cradled her face in both his hands. His thumbs slid over her silky brown cheeks, wiping away what was left of her tears. He tilted her face up, leaned slowly forward and kissed her.

His touch was tentative at first, almost chaste, but the feel of her lips beneath his released all his dammed-up desire. His fingers dug deeper into her flesh and twisted among her thick, black curls. His mouth pressed harder, more hungrily, moist. He pulled her to him, his bare chest hot against the cool cotton of her kazak, acutely aware of the soft, round breasts underneath it. An ache, a thrill spread through his groin and settled in his belly as he rubbed his hand down her back and imprisoned her body against his, silently willing her, insisting, that she respond.

With only an instant's hesitation, Amedee returned his embrace, modestly at first, then with a passion matching his own. Her lips parted, welcoming his; her hands wrapped around his neck, then stroked his bare back. She strained closer to him, eagerly yielding to the crushing of his arms.

In a graceful, easy motion, Shubael swung Amedee up and carried her back to the beach, to a spot in the shade of an inclining palm tree. He set her down, slipped off her white shift and buried himself in her light brown, cinnamon-scented flesh. "Shoobell," he heard her croon.

Over the next month, the repairs on the *Sally Ann* progressed at a pace that Shubael found agonizing. Where once his distress would have been caused by the lazy half days Napoleon put in, now it was a result of seeing the work coming to an efficient finish. He could not bear the thought of leaving the Seychelles, of sailing away from the hot, lush islands with their slow, sensuous style of living, away from Amedee.

They met often, on the beach with the boulders, and continued their magical affair. It was like a fantasy for Shubael. When he was with Amedee, he was in another world, where debts and demands and duty didn't exist.

"Thee has changed my life," Shubael said one afternoon after they made love. He lay on his side, lazily fanning a banana leaf over Amedee's naked body, taking immense pleasure, as always, in her beauty. She smiled dreamily and ran her fingers lightly down his chest, no longer pale from lack of sun.

"Nay, 'tis more on course to say thee has given me a second life," Shubael amended. He rolled on his back and fanned himself absently, concentrating on his thought. "When I am with thee, I am a different person. I see more, I hear more. I feel more than I ever knew was possible. 'Tis as though colors become brighter and songs become sweeter, as though I have been stuck in the hold and now have come topside, into the light and the air. I almost have to blink my eyes against the brilliance of this new life."

Amedee tapped him on the ribs. *"En Creole,"* she chided. *"Ou bien capabe doze Creole."*

He turned on his side again and gave her a rapid whoosh with the fan. The banana leaf bent and broke under the pressure and Shubael tossed it away with a grin. "Yes, you're right," he said, in the Seychellois patois. He covered the three tiny beauty dots on her cheek with a kiss. "I can speak Creole. I learned so quickly. I am still surprised at how easily this language comes to me.''

''I'm not surprised,'' Amedee said, trying to capture his dimples with her fingertips. ''I think you were born with Creole on the back of your tongue. It was just waiting for you to come to La Digue so it could be free.''

Shubael laughed and scooped her into his arms, rolling on his back once more. He wrapped his legs around hers, anchoring her on top of him, desire stirring with the weight and the heat of her body. His hands caressed her shoulders and traveled up her neck, to frame her face with his fingers. ''But why do you think it was put there?'' he asked.

Amedee's eyes slanted away, half in a smile, half in seduction. ''So that you could tell me that you love me,'' she answered, turning her face against his hand and trailing her tongue over his salty palm. She turned back. ''And so that you could understand when I say that I love you, Shoobell,'' she added in her husky voice.

Shubael pulled her face down. ''I think that's a very good reason,'' he whispered, as his lips closed over hers. His heart was full.

WHEN SHUBAEL RETURNED to the New England atmosphere of the ship, however, his new second self disappeared like the setting sun into the sea. Surrounded once more by the smell of sweaty men and rancid oil, the cramped space and stark comforts, the greasy stews at suppertime, the need to decide and to discipline, his old self reemerged. He grappled again with his sense of duty, and with the ever present echo of his mother's voice crying, ''Failure!'' Against the gloom of these thoughts was the image of Amedee, her round cheeks engulfing her eyes in an ingenuous smile. He felt torn by guilt.

157

The day came when the repairs on the *Sally Ann* were completed. Her bottom had been scraped and practically polished, her sails mended and remended. The pantry was stocked with every manner of fresh provision, and a dozen live land tortoises were penned on deck for future fare. The masts had been retarred, the rail repainted, the lines respliced, and the bark had been towed back beyond the reef. There was no longer any reason to linger in La Digue.

No reason except Amedee, Shubael thought as he sat leaning against a boulder, his shirt at his feet, waiting for Amedee to meet him for one final time. The next instant she was beside him, sliding down the smooth side of the boulder and curling in the crook of his arm. Her face was woeful and tear-streaked. Shubael held her close and kissed the top of her head.

"I didn't hear you on the path," he said, trying to make ordinary conversation.

"No, I came by way of the beach." Amedee's voice was muffled against his chest. Her breath stirred on his skin. He held her tighter.

"I'll never forget the first time I saw you on the path. You were like a butterfly in the bushes. So very delicate and pretty."

"You were very odd looking, though," Amedee said. She looked up at him, a shadow of her usual playfulness showing in her eyes. "Your hands and face were very brown, but the rest of you was as white as coconut milk." She returned her head to its resting place on his chest and ran her fingers over the hard muscle. "Not now, though," she said. "Now you have been kissed by the sun all over."

"Now I have been kissed all over by Amedee," he said, tenderly, taking her fingers and pressing them to his lips. "Now I have been covered with love. That's much better. It stays forever, while the sun's kisses fade."

A sob shook her at his words and she clutched his neck. "But why must you go, Shoobell?" she asked. "You could stay here with me. You could let M. Barnard be the captain of your ship."

"M. Barnard is only the fourth mate," Shubael corrected automatically. "M. Folger would take command."

"Then you'll stay?" Amedee cried, hopefully, sitting up.

"No." He shook his head sadly.

"But why? Why must you go?" Tears were running down her chin; her voice was almost hoarse with grief.

Shubael gently laid her head against him again. A tear slid down his hot skin and puddled on his lean stomach. He thought about explaining it all to her, of telling her about his father's failure, about the enormous debt he was obliged to accept, about his responsibility to Benjamin Swain and to Prudence and to his sisters still at home. But he didn't. First he didn't tell her because he didn't know how to say words like success and self-discipline in Creole; it was too simple a language, too tied to the fundamentals of living to explain all the conflicting complexities of his life. Then, when he sat with her in his arms, the sea purple and turquoise and infinite in front of him, his excuses seemed foolish, empty. He had only a dull sense of duty to guide him.

"A coze," he finally answered. "Because. I must."

Amedee gulped on her tears. She understood. She lay still awhile, then asked, almost timidly, "Will you come back, Shoobell?"

Shubael almost said no. He almost shook his head, but the idea of never seeing her again, of never smelling the cinnamon of her soft skin or of touching the three luscious dots on her cheek, of never hearing her husky voice musically saying she loved him, made him turn cold in dread. He thought of a life of endlessly hunting whales, sailing and chasing and butchering, of returning to Nantucket to his mother's bitter whining and winter's bleak fog. He leaned his face against her head and said, "Yes."

7

NANTUCKET
November 1842

"UH, UMM, 'TWAS A FEARFUL BLOW we had night before last," Obed Hussey said. He sat stiffly on the horsehair sofa in the parlor, his hands clenched in his lap. "Ammiel Paddock lost half the roof of his barn and William Coleman's side fence was knocked into Silvanus Jenkins's garden."

China stifled a yawn and kept her eyes on the gray stockings she was knitting. This was the third week in a row that Obed had come to call, stuttering and stumbling through hours of clumsy conversation. After all the years of eyeing her from afar, he had finally found the courage to come courting, much to China's dismay. Despite her professed disgust for whaling men, she secretly held Obed's landlocked career at his father's sail loft in some disdain. She couldn't help but compare his square, solid and serious expression with Jake's strong, handsome features and lively blue eyes. He fared badly.

If China hadn't been so aware of how smitten Harriet was with Obed, she would have brusquely cut short the spurts and fits of his stilted conversation on his first visit. For her friend's sake, she tried to tread the line between everyday courtesy and discreet discouragement of his attentions, while attempting to reroute his interest to Harriet.

"Aye, it was a nasty gale," she answered. "Harriet told me that David Chase's dory tore loose from its mooring and was wrecked on the pilings at Commercial Wharf. Perhaps thee knows that Harriet regularly brings toys and biscuits to David and Phoebe's third child, Isaac, who is a bit simple. Harriet is a wonderfully generous and kind person."

This information seemed to sink into Obed without a ripple of response. "Umm, uh," he said, shifting his weight awkwardly on the sofa. "'Twas quite a sight last month when the *Peru* came over the Bar in the Camels. The bells and gunshots and all in celebration."

China ceased her knitting and lifted her head, genuine interest lighting her gray eyes even though they had discussed this grand event on both of Obed's previous visits. "'Tis a clever scheme at that," she admitted, "and I admire Peter Ewer for building the Camels, but they seem too cumbersome a contrivance to be a real boon for the whaling industry."

Obed shrugged his wide shoulders. "Time will tell all there is to know," he said pragmatically. "'Tis very true we need something to get the ships over the Bar when they are fully laden. I've heard more than one owner say in the past year that he's taken his ship to New Bedford or Edgartown for outfitting. 'Tis a nuisance to have to anchor out and have goods freighted backward and forward in lighters."

"That may be so," China replied, vigorously, "but it seems to take almost as much effort with these Camels as with a good fleet of lighters. First they must steam that huge pair of pontoons out to the ship at the Bar. Then they must set them in position around the ship, then let the water run in so they sink, then chain them in place, then pump them out again so the ship rises as the Camels are refloated. And then the whole rig must steam back into the harbor where the pontoons are once again sunk, so that the ship can be released. 'Tis ingenious, but I hardly think 'tis practical.''

Obed shrugged again. "Time will tell," he repeated stoically.

China sighed and dropped her head, resuming her knitting. With a flash of irritation, she wondered what Harriet found so attractive in Obed's stolid, unexcitable nature. She again compared him with Jake, thinking how Jake went eagerly in search of life, while Obed waited patiently for it to come to him.

Across from her Obed again twisted uncomfortably on the sofa, running his finger under the muslin stock wrapped around his neck. Next he tugged at the plain woolen waistcoat buttoned high on his chest, then fidgeted with the buttons of his black broadcloth coat. He cleared his throat. "I've heard it said," he intoned, "that Silas Macy means to sell his house on Trader's Lane. I've been thinking I should buy it."

China's fingers froze in midstitch as panic struck her. Obed had a totally comfortable berth in his parents' big home on Fair Street. There was no reason for him to consider moving out, unless he meant to marry. She nervously sought to ward off any imminent proposals.

"Aye, I know the house," she said, forcing her fingers into motion, again. "It seems quite snug, but I personally don't care for Trader's Lane. Harriet, I know, enjoys being close to town. She's often commented on how quiet and private it is there, while still being only a few minutes to the shops."

While Obed blinked in bewilderment at this answer, Aunt Judith finally spoke up. She had been sitting silently by the window, where the light was strongest for the fine seams she was sewing. She intended to act only as chaperon, to lend the proper air of morality to Obed's visit by her presence, but the edginess in her grandniece's voice prompted her to speak before China could further discourage her suitor.

"Thee has a shrewd head for business, Obed," she said. "A house is always a good investment and a safe harbor in a storm. I've often had cause to clip in on Silas and Abigail, and I know the house to be as tight and tidy as any on Nantucket. Aye, thee could do a lot worse than buy it from them."

She set aside her sewing and stood. "Thee looks in need of refreshment," she said, in a tone that left no room for objection. "I'll go brew some Hyson tea and fetch a plate of cranberry and currant tarts that are in the cupboard. China made them herself and they are a true treat. She's a fine cook."

As Aunt Judith disappeared into the kitchen, China hastened to add, "'Tis a recipe that Harriet gave me. She has such good ideas for foods to cook. Whenever I am not making headway in the kitchen, I go to see Harriet and she sets me on course. I'd have a very dull diet if it weren't for Harriet."

Obed struggled to digest all this information, then said thoughtfully, "I've never liked cranberries."

China sighed again and gave up. For the next few minutes the only sounds in the parlor were the whirr and crackle of the fire and the clicking of China's knitting needles. Obed shifted once more and seemed about to speak, when the southeast wind carried the faint pealing of the Lisbon bell through the closed windows. They both went completely still as they strained to hear the chimes coming from the towers of the South Church on Orange Street.

"'Tis a ship at the Bar!" China exclaimed. She tossed her knitting into a basket at her feet and leaped up, pulse pounding wildly. Color flushed her cheeks and hope lit up her lovely eyes. "Perhaps 'tis the *China Maid*," she said excitedly as she dashed into the kitchen, heading for the back door. She snatched her shawl and bonnet off their pegs, adding, as she bolted through the door, "She's due any time now."

Aunt Judith, whose aging hearing hadn't caught the bell's ringing, looked up from her teapot, surprised, as China sailed past. As the sound came more clearly through the open door, she registered what was happening. She hurried outside and called, "China, come back! Thee knows better than to run to the wharves. Thee is no longer a foolish child, but a full-grown woman of twenty-one years. 'Tis indecent behavior!" Her dismayed words had no effect.

It was obvious that China was no longer a girl, that she had changed since her last mad dash to the dock three and a half years ago. Although she still looked much the same, her glossy black, Dutch Boy bangs and short hair flying free of her bonnet, her porcelain skin glowing with eagerness, her long legs carrying her slim, softly curved body, the thoughts that put the sparkle in her gray eyes were different. It was no longer Zacch whose arms she longed to fly into, but Jake's.

As she tore over the cobbles, images of Jake flooded across her mind. She ached with a desire to see him, to match his half-mocking grin, to breathe in the scent of the sea clinging to his sun-browned skin, to taste his lips, moist and salty, kissing hers, to laugh, to tease, to shout, to love, to come alive in his powerful presence. In this instant of anticipation and hope, she forgave him his desertion of her, she happily withdrew her objections to his career, anything, only let it be he who stepped first off the lighter.

China pounded out of the residential quiet of upper Main Street and into the bustle of the business section. The continued pealing of the Lisbon bell, now only a block away, added to the usual clamor of commerce. China rounded the corner by the Pacific Bank and collided squarely with the well-fed form of Harriet's father, descending the tiered steps.

"Well now, China," Benjamin Swain said, reaching out to steady her after impact. "I'll wager ten cents to a nickel I know where you are headed, but I must tell you, dear girl, that she's not the *China Maid*. 'Tis the ship *Ontario* who's been out only two and a half years."

China felt the excitement drain out of her, leaving only the lonely dullness of disappointment and the suddenly labored breathing from her run. She gulped to contain her panting and to compose her shattered thoughts.

"Don't fret, dear girl," Benjamin said kindly. He patted her arm with his thick fingers. "I know the old *Maid*'s due. Before you know it, she'll be coming around Great Point and your Papa and Zacch will be here demanding a hug and a bowl of quahog chowder."

"Aye," China said, tiredly. "I presume it likely." She didn't want to wait any longer. She didn't want happy reunions around the supper table; she wanted Jake. She wanted him crushed against her in an embrace, not of friendly welcome, but of need and desire. She wanted him, warm, strong and naked, stretched next to her on a pine needle bed. She didn't want him next week or next month or next year. She wanted him now.

Misinterpreting her dejection, Benjamin patted her arm again. "I know what you need," he said. "You need a good gam with Harriet over a pot of hot chocolate. I know she just got a new shipment from Holland, so scud along up to the house."

China nodded and turned in Liberty Street, but bypassed Gardner Street and the Swains' large, comfortable house.

The embers of old anger were starting to rekindle. She could feel the resentment rising, the annoyance and frustration of being left behind. She didn't want to be soothed by Harriet's common sense and cocoa; she wanted to bask in her wrath, to release her roiling emotions in one passion or another.

CHINA'S ANGER WAS STILL STEEPING two days later when the third mate of the ship *Ontario* arrived at their door. They had picked up mail, homebound, in Callao, he explained, and he was delivering it now. China barely glanced at the admiring young man as she grabbed the two letters and the package from him. She brushed off his friendly overtures with the necessary, but brief, expressions of gratitude, then took the stairs to her room two at a time. Sitting on the edge of her bed, she examined both envelopes, then set aside the one addressed in Zacch's familiar scrawl and ripped open the one from Jake.

"It is beastly hot, here," he wrote. "Yesterday I went swimming in the surf, which was quite exciting as well as refreshing. It is a thrill to ride a big wave to shore. You would have enjoyed it, I know. I am sending you a package, my dearest *corbeau*, with some new feathers. I'll imagine how beautiful you look. All my love, Jake."

China stared at the short note in disbelief. She turned the page over and shook the envelope, wondering where the rest of the letter was, where detailed news of the voyage and solemn reassurances that he daily yearned for her were written. It was as if he were sending a quick message from an overnight trip to Falmouth, rather than his sole communication in three long years.

She impatiently threw the letter aside and seized the package. When the oilskin wrapping was unfastened, a magnificent Spanish shawl emerged. The fine, soft wool was a midnight blue with a deep, tasseled fringe around all the edges. Vivid pink roses with rich green foliage radiated from the center. Even after years of being tightly wrapped up, a faint scent of lavender water and luxurious living clung to the cloth.

China's initial delight in the shawl's beauty was almost immediately overwhelmed by the anger that had been slowly growing for two days and was now at a boiling point. She was enraged both by Jake's scanty words and by the brilliantly hued Spanish shawl, which she could never wear. She felt he was once more being selfish and insensitive. He showed neither sympathy for her frustration in being abandoned, nor understanding for the circumstances that curbed her life. It wasn't fair for him to carelessly remind her of what she was missing, to callously disregard the Quaker conventions that confined her. He was taunting her.

In a fury, she stamped on the letter, which had fallen to the floor, and sent it skidding out of sight under her bed. Perversely pleased by its banishment to this dusty dungeon, she flung the beautiful shawl after it. With slightly trembling hands, she opened Zacch's letter, determined to put Jake's out of her mind.

Zacch's lengthy descriptions and friendly tone soothed her somewhat, though she found some of the news quite disturbing. Aunt Judith came heaving up the steep stairs when China was halfway through the letter, so she read parts of it aloud.

"We have been in port for over a week now," he wrote. "We hadn't meant to call in here, but Papa caught a tropical fever in Valparaiso and was quite sick for a time. Jake decided we should make for the nearest doctor and get him some medicine, which is what we did. Papa is now much improved and back in command, and, of course, insists on weighing anchor immediately as we have now been out for seven months and have not a barrel below decks.''

"''Tis foolish to push too hard after a bad fever,'' Aunt Judith chided, as if her worried advice could travel southward eight thousand miles and backward two and a half years. "He must strengthen up or the fever will return.''

China raised her eyes briefly in acknowledgment of her great aunt's concern and continued. ''Jake has managed to delay him a bit, however.'' Aunt Judith briskly nodded her approval. "He has spun some yarn about having to redo some repairs, and Papa is accepting it, whether because he believes Jake or because he is just as pleased to rest, I do not know.

"We had a rough time of it rounding the Horn and had to heave to for three days while a storm blew over. We lost some of the rigging and punched a hole in the deck where a yardarm fell, but no injuries, thank God. We limped up to Valparaiso and got everything mended, but you know how it is in these parts; it is always siesta or fiesta or some other excuse for not doing the work. We were there for over a month to do a week's worth of repairs. None of us minded so much at first because it's always a relief to have some shore leave after a long haul at sea, but after a while we all started to chafe because we came out here to hunt whales, not to drink wine under a tree.''

Aunt Judith clucked ominously and said, her voice heavy with disapproval, "I knew it was a mistake to buy that old ship. 'Tis nothing but bad luck and mishaps. Zaccheus let his sentiment overcome his common sense.''

Aunt Judith's sour words were the final straw for China. First Jake mocked her present life, now Aunt Judith was maligning her past. She couldn't bear to hear harsh words against the comfortable old vessel that had been her happy home for so many years. Nor could she tolerate Aunt Judith's criticism of her father's judgment. She jumped off the bed, her gray eyes smoky with anger.

"Thee has no right to say such things," she stormed, hands on her hips. "I think Papa knows better than thee how to estimate a ship's seaworthiness. He would not risk his life in an unsafe vessel. Even less would he risk Zacch's. The *China Maid* is a good ship, but bad luck can befall even the most cautious person, as well thee knows." She stuffed Zacch's letter in her pocket and clambered down the stairs and out the front door before Aunt Judith could recover from her surprise at China's attack. It had been years since her grandniece had displayed such fury.

Out in the brisk November air, China's wrath cooled. She headed for Sarah Coffin's big house to compare news. In the past three years, mindful of her promise to Zacch, she had made an honest effort at friendship with her future sister-in-law, forcing aside her former distaste for the delicate, blond beauty. She called regularly, if not often, in India Street, sipping tea from Wedgwood cups and listening to Sarah's guileless chatter.

For all her attempts at closeness, however, China could never muster anything more than a casual feeling of amiability. She and Sarah were essentially opposites in everything from coloring and clothes to modes of thinking. And although her dislike of Sarah's sister, Liddy, hadn't abated, Liddy had equally as little use for her and rarely intruded on her perfunctory visits.

Today, though, even Sarah tried China's patience. Of course she received a letter from Zacch on the *Ontario* but she was blushingly secretive about its contents. "Oh my, China," Sarah murmured, her blue eyes cast down in her lap. "He wrote a great many things, but they were intended for me only, I believe."

"For heaven's sake," China snapped, "I don't ask thee to repeat any intimate passages, but surely he gave thee some news of the voyage. Did he mention Papa's illness? Did he tell thee anything he forgot to tell me?"

Sarah still did not look up. She cocked her head to one side and studied the perfect pinkness of her fingernails and the satiny whiteness of her small hands. "He just said your Papa was ill," she said, with a small shrug. She finally lifted her innocent blue eyes and added, "He said there are wild orchids all over Callao and they remind him of me. And that I should carry orchids on our wedding day. Do you think I should?" China gulped down her tea and left without rendering an opinion, more annoyed than ever.

HER MOOD WAS NO MORE SUBDUED at breakfast the next morning, but then, neither was Aunt Judith's. Still smarting from China's abruptness the day before, the grim Quaker spinster confronted her grandniece. "Thy behavior of late has been regretful," she began in a forbidding voice. China dipped her spoon into her cornmeal mush and didn't answer.

"Thee is no longer an impulsive child to be forgiven thy trespasses. Thee must now pay the consequences of thy rash action and defiant attitudes."

"I apologize," China interrupted stiffly. She was not completely sorry for her words the previous day, but she did not want to hear the rest of Aunt Judith's lecture. "'Twas wrong of me to snap at thee, but thy comments about Papa and the *China Maid* provoked me."

Aunt Judith set a steaming bowl of mush at her own place and sat down opposite China. She dolloped a generous lump of butter into her bowl, closed her eyes briefly in silent prayer, then continued, "Anger is always an unworthy emotion and thee should seek to rid thyself of it," she said, vigorously stirring the melted butter into her mush. "But 'tis not thy quick temper I speak of now; I have long since learned to ride out thy squalls. 'Tis thy unwillingness to accept reality that disturbs me. Thy head is in the clouds, in a dream. Thee does not seem to recognize the way of the world.

"Firstly, thee lives on an island whose entire economy derives from whaling, yet thee refuses to embrace whaling. And secondly, thee is of more than marriageable age, yet thee is unaccountably rude to thy only eligible suitor. What does thee want, China? How much longer does thee expect to go shooling across the moors in bare feet and wearing a heathen amulet?"

China's hand flew protectively to the necklace that John James Henry had given her. She didn't know how to answer Aunt Judith's questions so she only insisted, defensively, "I was *not* rude to Obed and he is *not* an eligible suitor."

"Certainly he is," Aunt Judith responded, briskly. She swallowed several spoonfuls of mush. "He is a good man with fine prospects for the future. Gideon Hussey has no other sons, so the sail loft will go to Obed, and he will make it prosper, I'm sure. 'Tis true he is not a Friend, but he is hardworking and steadfast and does not use rum. Since thee must marry, China, thee should be thankful Obed is willing to have thee and not chase him away by jabbering about thy friend Harriet or by bolting out the door while he is calling." She efficiently spooned up the rest of her mush.

China pushed her own bowl away, too upset to eat any more. After her emotional buffeting of the past few days, she was in no mood to explain about Harriet's secret adoration of Obed, or about her own longing to be in Jake's arms. She fought, unsuccessfully, to suppress her irritation as she answered, "I wish thee would cease to badger me. 'Tis my life to decide as I choose. Why does thee continually insist that I *must* marry? Thee never did.''

For an instant Aunt Judith froze. Then she slowly set her spoon in her empty bowl and looked squarely at China. "'Tis not from choice that I did not marry," she said, levelly. "I had but one suitor, Peleg Cary." Her old eyes took on a faraway look behind her steel-rimmed spectacles. "He came from a poor family," she went on, "but he had ambition. He decided to make one voyage to the Pacific before we were wed, to give us a fair stake for the future.

"''Twas near the Marquesas, they told me later, that his boat made fast to a big sperm and was taken out of sight on a sleigh ride. His ship went after them, but though they cruised for nearly a week, not a trace of that whaleboat, or Peleg, was ever found."

She cleared her throat, then quickly stood and turned to the sink. After a moment of fussing with the dirty dishes, she faced China again and continued. "By that time I was twenty-six and well past marriageable age. Besides, my brother's wife, Rachel, thy grandmother, died and left thy infant father in need of care. I made my home here from then on."

Tears came to China's eyes and a chill ran down her spine. She had never known about Aunt Judith's Peleg before. She thought of Jake in that whaleboat, being towed away forever, to capsize and drown, or to be ripped apart by bloodthirsty sharks. "Does thee see what I mean?" she asked, brokenly. "Does thee see my objections to whaling? How many years did thee sit and wait and hope for thy ship to come in, only to have thy life shattered when it finally arrived with an empty berth? How many years of thy youth were wasted in lonely waiting?"

"Oh China," Aunt Judith said, exasperatedly. She sat down opposite her grandniece again. "Why does thee set thy nose to the wind all the time? For a hundred years Nantucket men have hunted whales and Nantucket women have kept the hearths warm while their husbands were away at sea. That is the way of it. Why can thee not reconcile thyself to life as God gave it to us?''

Her great aunt's annoyance first stunned, then stung, China. "Perhaps I do not have thy capacity to overlook death and unhappiness," she retorted.

Aunt Judith sighed. "I do not overlook it, China," she said, softly. "I accept it as part of life. Thee has much to learn." She slapped her hands on the oak table and pushed herself up again.

"In any event," she said, brisk once more, "Obed Hussey is not going to sea, so thy girlish notions have no bearing. I would advise thee to consider carefully. There are not so many courses for thee to chart."

China leaped up, too, enraged. "There is nothing to consider," she said. "I will never, ever marry Obed Hussey. He is stodgy and dull and can't get three words out of his mouth without stumbling over his tongue."

Her face was flushed with anger as she stomped out of the kitchen. She ran up to her room and fished under her bed for the exiled Spanish shawl, wrapped it around herself defiantly and strode out of the house. China wasn't quite sure whom she was spiting, she only knew she was consumed with fury. She was angry with Aunt Judith, with Jake, with Sarah; she was even angry with Harriet for being in love with Obed.

She walked for hours, hardly aware of her surroundings, intent on her inner arguments with first one and then the next. She finally found herself in 'Sconset, the little collection of shanties and fish racks seven miles from town. There was no one about on this cool, cloudy day; the shanties were occupied only when the cod fishermen came from Nantucket to launch their dories in the surf and to dry their catch on the racks.

China finally sank down on the beach, her back against an abandoned dory. The surf was not high here, but it was strong and cold and deep, dark green. As it broke steadily, imperviously, on the clean swept sand, it seemed to squelch the fire raging within her. The rapid, erratic beating of her pulse caught the tempo of the pounding sea; her string-tight nerves loosened. Implacable fog rolled in off the Atlantic, smudging the horizon and blanketing her whirling mind. She let her shoulders sag in surrender, her arguments ended.

Oh Jake, she thought miserably, why isn't thee here now? Why doesn't thee come sailing home on the *China Maid* and take me in thy arms, that I might have life again, too? Why isn't thee here to hush Aunt Judith with thy devilish grin and to discourage Obed Hussey with thy fierce blue eyes? "Please Jake," she cried out loud. "Please come home. I need thee."

Only the strident screech of a sea gull, hidden in the fog, answered her. No familiar figure, tall, strong and tropically tanned, came striding across the unmarred beach. No rich voice coaxed and cajoled and finally taunted her out of her gloomy mood. Jake did not appear, his dark curls tousled by the wind, the gold hoop in his ear rakishly reflecting the light in his eyes. She was alone. Completely and totally alone on a bleak November day.

The raw breezes easily penetrated the pretty Spanish shawl. Shivering, almost numb, she was forced to rise and return toward town. The walk home seemed endless. No longer warmed by her boiling anger, nor propelled by aroused emotions, she moved along leadenly, thoroughly chilled.

By the time China reached the outskirts of town, night was falling, the depressing early darkness of winter. The wind had picked up steadily from the north, whipping the layers of flannel petticoats around her legs, making movement that much more difficult. She cut across Back Street, a rutted little lane, hoping to shave a few steps off her journey. There were only three small houses on the street, all forlorn and decayed looking in the deepening twilight.

From behind a ramshackle outhouse appeared the weaving form of a man, fumbling at the buttons of his pants as he mumbled to himself. China quickened her pace, hoping to pass by him in the shadows before he spotted her, but the muddy ruts and her heavy petticoats twisted her feet and slowed her gait. The man staggered onto the road just as she drew even.

He seemed suddenly, and soddenly, aware of her. "Hey ho," he said. "What's this? A pretty sloop sailing up to me dock?"

As he approached her, China could smell the stench of tobacco, rum and stale sweat clinging to him. She could see the dark stubble on his rough, grimy face, the murky light in his bloodshot eyes. Fear stabbed through her, momentarily paralyzing her legs and making her mouth go dry. Then panic started her blood again, and she picked up her skirts to try to circle around him and run. The road was narrow, though, and he was in the middle of it.

With a swipe of his huge, hairy hand, the drunken man captured China and pulled her close to him. He chuckled gutturally as she fought his grip, but he was stronger than he seemed. "Hey ho," he said. "A regular typhoon, are ye? 'Tis no nevermind, I like 'em with spirit. C'mon now, dolly, gimme a kiss, and I'll getcher warm this chilly night."

He pressed his face next to China's and she twisted her own away in horror and disgust. The rottenness of his breath made her stomach rise to her throat, the evilness of his intentions brought tears of terror to her eyes. As she struggled desperately to free herself, the memory of a waterfront fight she had witnessed years ago in Honolulu flashed through her mind. While the vile-smelling man held her in the crook of his arm and dug his hard fingers into her breasts, she banged her knee into his crotch and simultaneously wrenched out of his clutches.

The violence of her movement and the quickness with which he released her to yowl in pain, and to seize his bruised parts, made China stumble backward and sprawl across the muddy ruts. Before she could rise or scramble away, he lunged for her, raking his dirt-encrusted fingers down her chest, ripping away John James Henry's necklace and tearing both the bright Spanish shawl and her gray dress underneath. The cold November night struck her exposed skin.

"Whorin' bitch!" the man screamed. "'Tis a lesson ye need and I'm the one to teach ye!" He grabbed for her again, but she rolled in the mud and he got only a handful of cloth, further shredding her dress. While he regained his balance after the aborted attack, China found her feet. She'd taken only one step though, when his arm shot out and spun her around.

"Ha! Ye got mud on yer titty!" he shouted triumphantly. "And it'll be much worse afore I've finished with ye, ye poxy whore!"

For the first time since she'd encountered him, a sound escaped from China. It was a low cry, almost a sob, of shame and fear and pain. Then in an instant of pure blind anger she balled up her fist and slammed it into the man's groin. This time the blow was not padded by petticoats or diminished by fear-weakened muscles. This time it landed squarely and with full effect. The man fell to his knees, screaming and retching in agony. China stumbled around him and made for home.

Panting hoarsely, she went in the front door and up the narrow stairs before Aunt Judith could see her battered condition. Finally feeling safe, she collapsed on the rag rug next to her bed, not wanting to soil her quilts with the mud and filth of her meeting on Back Street. She leaned her head against the bed, the coolness of the cotton quilt soothing the burning bruises on her cheek. She felt drained.

It was almost half an hour before China moved, finally forcing her stiff muscles into action. Slowly she stripped off the shreds of her clothes, gasping in grief at the sight of the Spanish shawl, no longer beautiful, but tattered and dirty. She let it drop to the floor with her ruined dress and petticoats and went to her washstand to clean the mud off her body.

She dipped her flannel square in the cold water of her wash bowl, then wiped it, shivering, over her breasts and shoulders. She dipped and wiped, dipped and wiped, until the mechanically moving cloth came to her neck. A burn of pain, when her fingers came to a sensitive spot, suddenly reminded her of that vicious swipe, when her attacker had torn away John James Henry's necklace. "Nay," she cried, piteously. "Nay, nay, nay." Her hands circled her slim neck, now empty of its ivory disks and odd shells.

With a shudder, she dropped the wash rag and found her way to her bed. As she sank into its feathery softness, all her emotions, which had lain still in shock, finally erupted. Great wrenching sobs shook her as she gave way to the horror of what had happened to her, to the fear, to the helplessness, and to the events that led to it in the first place.

When her weeping finally subsided, and her breath came back to her in gulps, she weakly punched her damp pillow and muttered, "'Tis over, Jake Swan. I'll not let thee do this to me anymore." In that vulnerable moment, her body and spirit badly bruised, she said goodbye to Jake. She could no longer endure the waiting, the wild, high hopes, the crushingly deep disappointments.

In her overwrought state, she interpreted the loss of her necklace to mean the loss of her love. There would be not "good plenty" coming back from the sea for her; there would be only what there always was: short weeks of happiness followed by long years of loneliness. Not anymore, she decided. Not anymore. She was a fool to love a man who went whaling, anyway.

8

INDIAN OCEAN
January 1843

"BLOOOWS! THERE SHE BLOOOWS!" At the cry from the crow's nest, Shubael stopped in midsentence. His pen hovered over the ship's log, dropping a blob of ink on the day's entry, while he tried to decide whether to finish his writing or to race immediately on deck and organize another chase.

"Sir! Captain Brown!" Caleb Barnard called, as he pounded on Shubael's door. "She blows, sir. Off the port beam."

Shubael looked regretfully at the blotched page and set down his pen. "Aye, Mr. Barnard," he said, heavily. "I'm coming."

There was very little enthusiasm in his movements as he shrugged into his battered coat and made his way topsides. He could hardly even rally any of his former efficient self-discipline. Ever since leaving La Digue, he had found the business of whaling increasingly distressing. Where once he had been able to harshly block out his sentiments, now they seemed to gnaw on his nerves.

Still, he managed, as always, to assess the situation and to give the right commands. It was a small school they'd come upon, but he ordered all boats lowered, anyway. With any luck, they could fill their hold and turn toward home.

The thought brought small comfort, but at least it was a respite.

Despite Shubael's lack of eagerness, his luck and whaling judgment were still strong, and it was his larboard waist boat that fastened first to an enormous bull sperm. No sooner had the second harpoon left his boatsteerer's hand, than the giant beast took off at full speed for the horizon. Shubael's heart lurched in familiar fear as they were dragged over the vast ocean behind the pain-crazed monster, the planks of their small boat shaking and quivering as it banged against the sea.

Suddenly the whale sounded, diving deeper and deeper, dark silent fathoms. "Wet line!" Shubael shouted, his mouth as dry as the desert, his knuckles clenched white around the steering oar. Buckets of water were bailed over the line, whipping out of its tubs and smoking over the loggerhead. Then the line went slack as the whale started its final ascent, breaching with a snap of its twenty-foot jaw and a flurry of white water.

Despite the roiling sea and the fearful swinging of the whale's flukes, Shubael knew it was weakening. As they closed the distance between the boat and the beast, he changed places with the boatsteerer. When he took up his lance and concentrated on the kill, he felt not fear flood through him, but disgust. He sank the razor-sharp weapon into the whale's hide and gave it a savage twist, not stopping until blood spurted out the wound. "Stern all," he ordered hoarsely, falling onto the seat and wishing that the whale would open its mammoth jaw, just once more, and swallow him whole. It didn't. It turned "fin up," dead.

Two days later they sat down for supper, tired and grimy. It had been a successful hunt. One hundred and four more barrels of oil were tried out and stowed below. Shubael looked around the table while Daniel Godfrey, the cabin boy, set bowls of whale meat stew before them. William Folger was staring dispassionately at his unappetizing portion; Randolph Pinkham was struggling to maintain his usual good-natured mien while fighting off a yawn; Micajah Stubbs was slumped in his seat, his right forearm red and blistered where boiling oil had splashed; Caleb Barnard was absent. As the most junior officer, he always drew deck duty while the others ate.

"Gentlemen," Shubael began, digging his fork resolutely into the bowl before him. "'Tis time to set the helm for home."

Three faces turned toward him, eyes suddenly awake. Even Daniel Godfrey paused on the companionway, unable to resist listening in on this good news.

"We've been out almost three years and have had greasy luck," Shubael continued, after swallowing a mouthful of meat. He grimaced, but gamely speared another chunk. "We've twenty-seven hundred barrels of sperm in the hold. Even those men with a one hundred seventieth lay will make a profit. If we bend on new canvas and have any kind of breeze, we should be home for the Shearing."

"'Tis pressing it a bit," Micajah Stubbs commented. "Oahu is a good seven weeks' sail from where we are. Unless we aren't to reprovision, it'll be five months or more before we round Old Man Shoals and drop anchor at the Bar."

Shubael chewed carefully before answering. He almost took another bite, but stopped, the fork halfway to his mouth, discouraged. The memory of succulent crabs in coconut curry and fresh mango chutney flashed through his mind, and he sighed, shoving the bowl away.

"I've decided to go home around Africa rather than around the Horn," he finally said. "I know we first cruised the Pacific Grounds and meant to return that way as well, but we've been lucky around the Moluccas and off the Maldives. There is no need to recross the Pacific. As thee stated, Mr. Stubbs, it would only add weeks to our voyage. Nay, we'll go around the Cape of Good Hope.''

He paused, contemplating the unsavory stew, then added with sudden decisiveness, ''We'll call in at the Seychelles for fresh supplies. We established good relations our last time in port and we know they can provision us well.'' He looked up briefly, almost defying his officers to comment or criticize, but no one said a word. Though not quite conventional, it seemed a thoroughly logical plan. They accepted it without a trace of suspicion. Shubael suppressed a sigh of relief as he rose and went to his cabin.

SHUBAEL WATCHED the familiar green mountain of La Digue looming larger on the horizon, excitement and apprehension knotting his stomach. His longing to see Amedee was almost a physical ache. It was no coincidence that they had kept to the Indian Ocean this past year, rather than cruising on Japan as he had planned. In the back of his mind he had searched for some excuse to return to the Seychelles; he knew that once he left these waters he would never see Amedee again. And yet, ever since he had finally yielded to his yearnings, he had been plagued by the fear that she would have forgotten him.

Thee is a fool, he told himself, a glorious fool. He assured himself that it was best he came back, for now he would see the situation as it really was. La Digue was a primitive island with half-heathen people. It had been a mistake, before; it had been sunstroke. Amedee would have gotten ugly or fat or she would have married one of her own kind and would laugh at him. Aye, he thought bitterly, it was a good joke at that. Despite the hot, heavy air, his hands were cold and clammy.

It seemed to take an eternity to sail up to the cut in the reef and to drop anchor. Although his face was set in its usual stern, stoic lines, as he had a boat lowered and was rowed ashore, Shubael's heart was pounding furiously. His tense, single-thought trance eased a bit when they reached the beach and the lilting sounds of Creole reached his ears.

It was a much different welcome than the last time the *Sally Ann* arrived. Little children swarmed around the boat shouting greetings, while grinning men grabbed the whaleboat to drag it up on the sand. Women waited under the palm trees, broad smiles on their faces and baskets of fruit balanced on their heads. Raoul Savoyard, the shabby old man with the elegant, sea serpent cane, limped forward to pump Shubael's hand and to say, "*Bienvenue, capitaine.* I knew you would return."

For the first time in months, a smile creased Shubael's face as he replied, "Then you are a better whaler than I, M. Savoyard." The patois came easily to his lips. "I never know where the whales will take me." M. Savoyard chuckled and slapped Shubael's shoulder.

The smile stayed on Shubael's face as he wound his way among the palm trees and onto the red dirt road. As soon as he was out of sight of his crew he shed his coat and rolled up his sleeves. The cedar and thatch houses sitting nearly level on their stilts, the untended animals snuffling and scuffling in the dust, the pineapples and bananas growing casually by the roadside, seemed delightfully familiar. At least this memory hadn't been sunstroke.

When he walked up the path to Napoleon's house, the tension returned. It was impossible that anyone in La Passe did not know of their arrival, but he saw no sign of Amedee. It was an effort for him to breathe normally. As he stood by the stone steps, anxiety lying cold in his guts, Napoleon came to the door. His tranquil face was beaming in welcome.

"Hello, my friend," he said. "Come in. Come in. Mathilde is just bringing coffee. Or perhaps you would prefer bacca? Come in. Don't just stand there." He held out his hand.

Knees moving stiffly, Shubael mounted the steps and grasped the hand in his own. Genuine pleasure filled him at Napoleon's firm, glad grip. "Coffee is fine," he said. "I'm unsteady enough on my legs after so long at sea. If I drank any bacca, I'd have to crawl."

Napoleon laughed and led him into the house just as Mathilde entered from the other door carrying coffee. Shubael automatically returned her cheerful greeting while his eyes scanned the room for Amedee. There was no sign of her. His heart seemed to stop. She was hiding from him. Or his worst fears were right: she was married to someone else. "Eh?" he said, blinking, suddenly aware that Napoleon was asking him something.

The Seychellois carpenter eyed him shrewdly, but simply repeated his innocuous questions. "Was the voyage a success? Did you take many whales?"

"Oh, yes," Shubael answered, sinking into a chair. Pain pressed at him, tore at his heart. Mathilde set a cup of coffee in front of him, smiling. He couldn't smile back. "Yes, it was a successful voyage," he said, dully. "The owner will be well pleased."

"And the bark? She is in good order? Did my work withstand hard use?"

"Yes, Napoleon, your work was excellent. The *Sally Ann* is in fine repair."

"And young M. Barnard? Is he well? Has his appalling French improved?"

"Yes, he is well, but no, his French has not changed a bit."

"Amedee is at Grand' Anse, on the other side of the island. She is visiting her grandmother."

Shubael's head shot up, hope suddenly bursting through his body. "When will she return?" he demanded, before he could think.

Napoleon read the change of emotions on Shubael's face and smiled his approval. "She is not meant to be home for a week," he answered. When dismay filled Shubael's eyes, he added, "I think you had best go to Grand' Anse, right away. She will be upset if she misses even a moment with you. In fact, she will probably scold me for keeping you here long enough to drink a coffee. Go."

Even as Shubael listened to the words, in silent happiness, even as his heart started pounding again with relief and elation, his mouth dropped open in astonishment. "You know," he stated. He had always been ashamed to be having an affair with the daughter of a man he considered his friend. It was dishonorable. He had felt guilty accepting Napoleon's many kindnesses, knowing how poorly he was repaying him. He had dreaded the day Napoleon ever discovered his deceit.

"Of course, I know," Napoleon said, gently. "How could I not know, when I watch my little girl? While you were here, she was floating on the clouds. After you left, her chin was scraping the dust."

"And you don't loathe me?" Shubael asked, incredulously. "You don't wish to kill me?"

This time Napoleon laughed. "And what good would that do?" he said. "If I killed you, first of all, I would lose a friend. And then, Amedee would never speak to me again. So instead of three people being happy, two people would be miserable and one would be dead. It doesn't make sense.'' He shook his head.

"No, Shubael, I don't loathe you for loving Amedee any more than I loathe her for loving you." He paused a minute, then gave a shrug that was typical of the islands, a shrug that accepted the strange ways of fate. "I might wish it weren't so difficult, so impractical, but I can't go inside your hearts and change them. What is, is. Now go."

IT TOOK SHUBAEL almost no time to send a message to his first mate, instructing him to proceed with reprovisioning. He then set out across the island to Grand' Anse. He walked along the overgrown road with a quick, light step, despite the steamy heat, which grew more stifling the farther he went from the sea breezes. He stopped briefly to peel off his shirt and shoes and socks and to bundle them with his coat in a package on his shoulder.

As he penetrated the jungle-lush interior of La Digue, he felt his spirits lifting; it was as if his soul were reemerging after a year's imprisonment. The rich scents of patchouli and vanilla stirred his senses. Scarlet and gold butterflies made his heart leap. All his nerves were alive and alert, ready to receive every sound and impression, appreciating, anticipating.

He felt as if he were a baby bird, building with ever stronger flapping, to his first soaring flight. Step by step along the dusty road, under graceful casuarina trees, past towering rosewoods in festive pink bloom, between half-cultivated patches of coffee beans, along trickling streams red from the rich earth, through the humid shade of the forest, his eagerness mounted, his pace increased.

Then the thick, cloying greenery ended and before him was a cove defined on either side by jetties of haphazardly piled prehistoric boulders. Clean, clear blue waves curled and splashed on the edge of a wide, dazzlingly white beach, utterly empty. Except for Amedee.

She saw him at the same moment that Shubael, eyes blinking against the brightness, saw her. As she ran toward him, his heart swelled until he thought it would burst. He dropped his bundle of Quaker clothes, released, and raced across the beach, arms extended, reaching for her, needing her.

She rushed into his arms, her small feet leaving the sand as she half leaped, was half lifted, crushing into his chest. His nose filled with the cinnamon scent clinging to her black curls, his fingers felt the sensuous curves of her body, naked beneath her kazak, his tongue tasted the sweetness of her mouth. He clutched her to him, embracing her, absorbing her uninhibited passion, hungry for more.

"My Shoobell," she whispered, her face rubbing against his, her fingers swirling the hair at the base of his neck. "You came home to me."

Her husky voice thrilled him, but her words cut through him, bringing reality crashing back. Slowly he set her down, now studying her face and wondering, as always, at her sumptuous beauty. He held her chin in his hands and ran his thumbs across the silky, brown skin of her cheeks, bending briefly to kiss the three tiny dots beneath her eye.

"Sweet Amedee," he said. "I love you more than anything on sea or land. You are the only joy in my life, the only goodness and reason. But I cannot stay. I am only here for a week, and then I must leave."

Tears rose in her almond eyes and spilled down her cheeks, splashing against Shubael's thumbs and burning them with her pain. She gulped and asked in a quavering voice, "Can you stay with me for the week? Or must you return to La Passe? To your ship?"

He kissed her again, tenderly, grazing her mouth and brushing the tears off her cheeks with his lips. "No, my darling, I don't need to return to my ship," he said. "Not now. Not for one week. For those days, I am yours wherever you want me. For this week, my ship doesn't exist. The only thing that matters is you and me."

A tremulous smile slanted at her eyes. She slipped her arms around his neck and gave him a brave hug. *"Bon,"* she said. "For one week you are mine. I shall take you to Anse Banane, where there is no one to disturb us. In La Passe there are too many people. Even here, there are too many eyes. See my grandmother and her servant staring out the window at us?"

Shubael had forgotten all about Amedee's grandmother. When he turned around, he was surprised to see a small house set back from the beach and two curious faces peering past the open shutters. He turned back to Amedee. "Anse Banane sounds very nice," he agreed. "Where is it?" She giggled.

Half an hour later, she led the way. Loaded down with sleeping mats and cook pots, they climbed over the jetty of jumbled rocks and descended into another cove, a miniature version of Grand' Anse, called Petite Anse. They slogged across the sand, pulled themselves to the top of another pile of rocks, then slid down a boulder to the long sweep of beach that was Anse Banane. The surf was gentler here, breaking on the spun-sugar sand and frothing away. A huge field of palm trees sloped down to the beach, and delicate green vines with brilliant fuchsia flowers crawled out of the field and almost to the edge of the warm, blue water.

"This is heaven," Shubael said, in awe.

"No," Amedee corrected, firmly. "It is not heaven. It is home." Less certainly she added, "At least for the next week."

They built a little arbor from fallen fronds and lined the floor with mats. Nearby they set up the kettles and gathered some old coconut husks to fuel the cooking fires. "It's too hot to work like this," Shubael said, lazily. "Let's go for a swim."

He pulled off his pants and turned toward the sea, but when he looked over his shoulder for Amedee, all thoughts of swimming evaporated. She was just lifting her kazak over her head. Sunlight flickered through fluttering palm fronds and spattered across her café-au-lait skin.

Her body arched and curved as her arms stretched up, then twisted to the side, discarding the cotton smock. Seeing Shubael's eyes on her, she smiled slowly and began to unfasten her long, black hair. Freed from its thick plait, it curled down her back and was tossed by the breeze over her satiny shoulders to tease the taut nipples of her breasts. She let her hands ease unhurriedly down her body, smoothing her small waist, slipping over the slight round of her belly, brushing the delicate flesh inside her thighs. Then she lifted her hands and held them out toward Shubael. "Let's not swim just now," she suggested in her husky voice.

"No," he agreed, stepping toward her, "let's not."

It wasn't until a great deal later that they finally slid through the crest of a wave and bobbed in the bathtub-warm water of the cove. Even then, they couldn't stop touching. Wet legs wrapped around each other, bare chests rubbed together, tongues tasted slick, salty skin. They kept a contact, whether it was fingertips hooking as they tumbled ashore with a wave, or limbs totally entwined as they floated over the swells.

They never bothered to dress again, after initially abandoning their clothes. There wasn't any need. Shubael's body, white again after being bound up for a year, turned pink, then red, then a healthy tan. They were like primitive people, or Adam and Eve, completely natural and utterly comfortable.

They made their meals from tender crabs caught on the rocks and from ripe papayas growing in the field. There was a spring with clear, fresh water bubbling through a lush crop of wild cress. They drank the juice of green coconuts and ate the sweet, crunchy meat of sun-cured ones.

During the day, when the sun heated the blue sea to barely refreshing temperatures, they were constantly in and out of the water. At night, when the moonlight and starshine gleamed off eerily blinking phosphorescences just below the surface, they swam cautiously and quietly. Like children, they buried each other in the sand and drew pictures along the broad beach with sticks.

If Shubael had caught glimpses of the person bound inside himself on his last trip to La Digue, he now, finally and fully, set him free. He was like a newly opened spigot, at first dribbling tentatively, then pouring forth without restraint. He laughed until his ribs ached; he sang songs until he was hoarse. He lay for hours watching bees busily sucking nectar or sooty terns wheeling through the air. And he made love to Amedee.

He made love with his body, urgent and hungry, until his skin was glistening with sweat and his breath came in great gulps; or tenderly and slowly while the sea breeze skidded across his skin, tantalizing his tingling senses. And he made love with his heart, cherishing, adoring, giving himself wholly to her. She returned his love equally, deeply.

Just as Shubael was becoming accustomed to his new life, it was time to return to his old one. The reality that he had ignored all week, faithful to his promise to Amedee, intruded on their last night in Anse Banane. An enormous sadness weighed on Shubael, silencing him. He lay next to Amedee, one hand propping himself up, the other hand tracing the outline of her soft body, memorizing it, trying to capture this moment forever, to gain courage for his long, dreary future.

"Perhaps you were right," Amedee said, quietly. "Perhaps this is heaven after all. It is perfect, it needs no improvement. I can't believe that paradise could be any better."

Shubael gave a crooked smile, invisible in the night. "It is better, though," he answered. "It's better because it never ends. In heaven, the mango bush never goes out of season and the monsoons never drive the fish out to sea. In heaven, there is always plenty of everything." He lifted her fingertips to his lips and kissed each one. "Especially plenty of time," he murmured.

Amedee let her fingers fall on his face, finding the spot in the dark where his dimples had so often appeared this week. "Perhaps next time you will stay long," she said hopefully. "Perhaps when you return again we will stay together for a long, long time."

Cold guilt overwhelmed him. He told himself to be honest with her, to tell her now that there would be no next time, that he would not return again. "Amedee," he started, then stopped. Once again, he didn't know how to explain it to her. Where his excuses sounded so crisp and sensible in English, they were only garbled and foolish in Creole. "Perhaps," he finally finished.

Amedee moved closer to him, fitting her body to him. "When will you come next, Shoobell?" she asked, innocently.

192

Shubael lay perfectly still, his hands ceased their soft stroking. He had to tell her the truth, but he couldn't bear to utter the words that cut her off forever. The thought of never seeing her again, of going through decades, perhaps half a century, of life without her was unendurable. For a wild moment he considered taking her with him to Nantucket, but he banished the thought almost immediately. She would wither and die on that North Atlantic island, subject to his mother's scorn and the bitter winter weather. It would be cruel and selfish.

In the end, he answered her with a Digois shrug and a typical Seychellois expression, "Only God knows."

Amedee accepted his answer with the peculiar patience of people in the tropics. She laid her cheek over his heart, lulled by the even beating. "I'll be waiting for you, Shoobell," she whispered. "I'll always be waiting for you. I'll be here when you return, but wherever you are, my love will be with you."

BY THE TIME the *Sally Ann* weighed anchor and started on the long journey home, Amedee's words were more like a curse than a comfort for Shubael. Knowing he couldn't have her, knowing she was gone from his reach, he ferociously wished he had never met her. He dreaded having her love follow him everywhere, tormenting him with glorious visions of a life he could never, and should never live. His harsh sense of discipline returned with a vengeance, sparing no one in the crew, including himself. But he couldn't forget her.

9

PACIFIC OCEAN
March 1843

"BLOOOWS! THERE SHE BLOOOWS!" At the lookout's call, Zaccheus came bounding on deck, Jake, Zacch and Samuel Easton, the third mate, at his heels. Their interrupted meal lay forgotten below. Sailors were clambering out of the fo'c'sle and emerging from shadows on deck. "Blooows!" came the cry. "Dead ahead! And again!"

All eyes swung forward in time to catch three spouts arched against the horizon. "Sperm," Jake pronounced, in satisfaction. Although right whales, humpbacks and bottle noses all yielded oil, only the spermaceti whales had that extra bonus, the "head matter," which turned waxy when exposed to air, and which made the finest candles in the world. Nantucketers rarely hunted anything but spermaceti, leaving the lesser species for Vineyarders and New Bedfordites.

"Fall off, Mr. Worth," Zaccheus yelled to the fourth mate, at the helm. "Fall off or we'll run right up on them and gally them. Mr. Swan," he continued, turning to Jake, "we'll lower all boats. I don't want to lose even one of those whales. We've nothing but bilge water and ballast in the hold now. 'Tis a damned poor showing for three and a half years. Mr. Easton, get ready to strike some canvas." Although Zaccheus always called his young officers by their first names below decks, while topsides, he set an example for the crew.

"Well, Mr. Joy," he said, facing his tall, strong son. "Has it been so long since we've had any luck that you've forgotten the business of whaling? You're standing around as if there's no work to be done."

"'Tis only a small school, Papa," Zacch said, stepping closer to his father and lowering his voice. "'Tis really not necessary that you give chase." Although he didn't say so, they both knew he was referring to the fact that Zaccheus had never properly recovered from the debilitating tropical fever he had contracted in Valparaiso. He looked old and haggard; not even the South Pacific sun could hide the pallor in his skin.

A look of warmth flickered briefly across Zaccheus's lined face, but he quickly set himself aloof. "Must I remind you, Mr. Joy, that I am still the captain?" he asked coldly. "As such, I expect my orders to be obeyed, and right now that order is to lower for whales, not to stand around the deck gamming like a greenhorn." He stared hard at his son until Zacch, tight-lipped, turned away, worry clouding his fine, gray eyes. Zaccheus strode across the deck to his whaleboat where John James Henry was waiting.

FOR A WHILE it seemed to Jake as if the abysmally bad luck that had plagued them ever since they rounded the Horn, was finally broken. His boatsteerer put two irons in a big bull right away, and a surprisingly short time later, Jake was able to thrust his lethal lance deep and true into the whale's lung. By the time he had waifed the mammoth beast and looked around, Zacch's boat was standing off and watching the final flurry of a fat cow. Samuel Easton's boat had also fastened, but he had been forced to cut the line when

195

it bighted as it whirled out of its tub. Jake shrugged. It was a minor mishap. Thomas Worth's boat had missed.

He scanned the ocean again, like a mother hen counting her chicks. For a minute, panic constricted his heart when he saw no sign of Zaccheus's boat, then he relaxed as he caught a glimpse of it almost lost against the sinking sun, being towed over the horizon on a Nantucket sleigh ride. He marked Zaccheus's position in his mind and turned back to the business at hand.

By the time the dead whales were towed back to the *China Maid*, the sun had set with its usual equatorial suddenness, leaving no twilight, only a brilliant display of orange and lavender streaks across the sky. There was still no sign of the larboard waist boat and Zaccheus. As Jake supervised preparations for trying out, he kept squinting into the rapidly diminishing light, hoping Zaccheus would reappear.

"Perhaps we should go in chase, Jake," Zacch said. He too had been anxiously searching the horizon. Unable to contain his feeling of helplessness any longer, he had crossed the deck to speak to Jake. "He's not as strong as he would like to think he is, and a night spent in an open boat can do him no good."

"Aye, Zacch, I know," Jake said. He ran his hand through his dark hair in worry. "But 'tis foolhardy to set out in pursuit at night. We could sail within ten yards of him and never even know we'd passed by. As hard as it seems, 'tis really better to wait till morning."

"He had a lantern on board," Zacch insisted. "Papa's bound to know we're looking for him and keep it lit."

"I doubt that," Jake said, dryly. "He's a stubborn old sea dog and a thrifty Nantucketer, your papa. He's probably sitting there in the dark, with his arms across his chest, not wanting to waste good oil by lighting the lantern. I'll stake my lay that he's reasoning that since 'tis a calm night with only a quarter moon, and since 'tis not terribly unusual for a boat to get caught away from her ship at sunset, we'll do nothing till dawn. He'll have me keelhauled if I go shooling around in the dark looking for him.''

"Aye, you're probably right," Zacch muttered, turning away. Jake watched him go and shook his head sympathetically.

At the first sign of daylight, Jake sent lookouts aloft, then sailed slowly, whales in tow, in the direction Zaccheus had disappeared. The sun was barely showing above the horizon behind them when the larboard waist boat came into view, resolutely guarding the sixty-foot sperm that had cost it a night in the open. Despite his reassuring front to Zacch the evening before, Jake felt relief flood through him at the unexceptional sight. Down the length of the deck, he exchanged a glad grin with Zacch.

When the captain's boat pulled alongside the *Maid* and Zaccheus hauled himself wearily aboard, however, the happy smiles faded. Zaccheus's eyes were glazed with fever; a fine film of perspiration glistened on his forehead although the morning was still fresh; his cheeks seemed sunken and gray. Zacch leaped across to steady his father when Zaccheus stumbled. Jake handed the wheel to a sailor and ran forward. Zaccheus weakly waved them both away.

"'Tis only a bit of stiffness," he said. Even his voice was raspy and faint. "Those whaleboats were not built for a comfortable night's sleep. I'll be fine as soon as I get forty winks." He started, swaying, toward the companionway to his cabin.

"Let me help you, Papa," Zacch said, almost pleading. He slipped his strong, young arm through his father's.

For a moment Zaccheus leaned on him gratefully, then he seemed to gather a bit of strength. He squeezed Zacch's arm briefly, then disengaged it from his. "Nay, Zacch," he said. "Don't fret. And don't waste time coddling me. There's whales to be boiled. Look lively." He moved slowly off, leaving Zacch and Jake to stare after him in dismay.

"Damn whales," John James Henry muttered behind them.

Whether they wanted to or not, they didn't have time to "coddle" Zaccheus with three whales to strip of their blubber and boil into oil. It was nearly midday before Zacch made a free moment to check on his father. He ran quickly down the companionway and pressed his ear against Zaccheus's closed door, knocking softly. No clear reply came, but he could hear mumbled words. When a louder knock brought no different response, Zacch edged open the door and looked in.

Zaccheus lay sprawled on his back across the bunk, still dressed. His face was no longer gray, but blotchy red. His eyes were closed, but his lips were moving. When Zacch came closer, he could hear what his father was saying.

"'Tis a fetching frock, Josephine. You look as lovely as a day in May. When we get to Nantucket, I'm going to buy some ribbons for your hair. Such beautiful black hair..."

Zacch felt his throat tighten in sadness. He gently pulled off his father's clothes and laid him more comfortably on the bed. He was sponging him down with cool water when the door opened and Jake came in. "'Tis bad, Jake," Zacch said, his voice a little rough. "He's talking to Maman."

A deep foreboding filled Jake. His expression grim, he said, "I'll go fetch John James Henry. Perhaps he has another of his magical, island teas to try."

John James Henry's teas had no effect on the fever consuming Zaccheus, nor did the cool compresses that Zacch and Jake applied, in turns, all afternoon and night. Zaccheus's skin continued to burn, his mind continued to travel back in the past, though his voice got weaker and his words less coherent.

The sun was just rising the next morning, lighting the bloody carcass of the last whale still chained to the side and the greasy, nearly nude bodies of sailors tending cauldrons of boiling blubber, when Zaccheus opened his eyes. He looked from Jake, who was standing by his washstand, to John James Henry, whose huge frame was filling up the doorway, to Zacch, who was sitting by his side. A peaceful smile tugged at his mouth as he stretched his hand across the sheet. Zacch grasped it in both of his. "Josephine," Zaccheus said. Then his eyes closed and he died.

For a moment there was complete stillness in the small cabin, then Zacch shook the hand he was holding and cried, "Papa! Papa!"

Jake moved forward and put one hand on Zacch's shoulder; with the other he felt for Zaccheus's pulse. "Nay, Zacch," he said, hoarsely, speaking over the tears in his throat. "He's gone. Your papa is gone."

"He can't be," Zacch insisted, in shock. He shook his father's hand once more, as if he could stir the life back in him. "He's just asleep again."

Gently Jake extracted Zaccheus's hand from Zacch's grip and laid it by his side. "'Tis his final sleep," he said. His chest hurt; it was aching with grief. "He's happier now, I'll wager," he said, as much to console himself as to comfort the young man before him. "He's with Josephine, with your maman. 'Tis what he's wanted since the day she died. He hasn't been happy without her, but now they are together at last. Now he's free to join her."

Zacch barely heard Jake's words. He was doubled over, as if in pain, his arms crossed against his stomach. He couldn't comprehend that his father was dead, his father whom he had seen every day of his life since he was four years old. It wasn't possible he would no longer be there.

Jake laid a hand briefly on Zacch's shoulder, then left him alone. His own sense of loss was enormous. When Randolph Swan died, Jake had felt guilt and regret, but nothing like the grief that was numbing his mind now. Zaccheus had filled a void in his life, one that he had hardly known existed until it was no longer there, replaced by affection, respect and emotional security. Even though Jake had been full grown and long flown from the nest when he had found Zaccheus, he had basked in the warmth of the relationship, allowing himself to lean on Zaccheus more and more, as his captain, as his friend, as his father. And now he was gone.

As Jake closed the door to the cabin behind him, John James Henry stepped forward, his broad face streaming with tears. "Ja-Jake," he said. "I did bad work. Captain Zaccheus saved my life and I do not save his. I am bad. Tell me what to do, Ja-Jake."

"'Tis not your fault, John James Henry," Jake replied. "'Tis no one's fault. 'Twas time and he was ready. Nobody could have saved him. You did good work for many years and I'm sure the captain was grateful. He doesn't blame you, I know."

John James Henry scraped the back of his arm across his wet eyes. "Ja-Jake," he said. "You the Old Man Captain now. You be in command of the *China Maid*. I will work for you like I work for Captain Zaccheus. I have strong arm and true eyes. I will be your harpooner and I will make prayers for you."

Jake was startled, as much by the realization that he was, indeed, the captain, now, as by John James Henry's promise of personal service. He was about to tell the big man it

200

wasn't necessary, but an instinct made him change his mind. "Thank you," he said, instead. "I feel safe now."

When John James Henry nodded his head and gave his version of a salute, Jake knew he had done the right thing. John James Henry had depended on Zaccheus, too. The captain had given his life a purpose, a focus. His declaration to Jake was more than just an offer of labor, or even a pledge of loyalty. It was a transfer of dependence. Jake was extremely touched. He returned the salute, accepting his new responsibility.

THE *CHINA MAID* remained hove to for another day while the crew grimly and mechanically finished the task of trying out the blubber and stowing the oil below. After several hours in the captain's cabin, Zacch had emerged, drawn and silent, to do his part. When at last they finished the grimy work, they scrubbed the decks of grease and soot and sailed out of the bloody water snapping with sharks. When they were once more "cruising the line," ploughing through endless clean ocean along the equator, they buried Zaccheus.

In a somber, but steady, voice, Jake read a passage from the Bible, then said simply, "Dear God, he was a very good man and a damn fine whaler." Zacch and John James Henry tilted the plank, and Zaccheus, sewn into a sail, slid into the sea. The crew quietly dispersed.

Jake joined Zacch in leaning on the rail, staring unseeing at the horizon. After a few minutes he broke the silence by softly saying, "I know 'tis hard to think of business, now, but you must, Zacch. A whaling ship is like its own little country, out in the middle of nowhere, and it can't stop functioning until it makes home port again. And just as a country needs a king or a president, a whaling ship needs a captain and officers."

Zacch slowly turned his gaze away from the sea and settled it, surprised, on Jake. "But *you* are the captain," he said mildly. "And you need only appoint a new fourth mate, for all of us will move up, I imagine."

Jake shifted his weight from one elbow to the other and chose his words carefully. "Don't forget, you are now the owner of the *China Maid*. You've every right to take command yourself, and to appoint your own officers. 'Tis your decision to make."

Zacch's answer was swift and sure. "Nay, Jake. Papa felt you were better able to bring us safely home, gunnel deep with oil, than I. 'Tis why he made you first mate. You're older and smarter. All the men admire and respect you. I'd like you to remain as master." His eyebrows knit together in contemplation and then he added, stoutly, "It wouldn't seem right any other way, Jake."

"And what of China?" Jake asked, with a casualness he didn't feel. His heart beat faster just saying her name. "She is an owner now, too. You must act in her interests as well."

For the first time in two days, a trace of a smile lightened the sorrow on Zacch's face. "I think you are better suited for that task, too," he said. "And I think China made *that* decision a long time ago."

Both men turned back to stare at the sea, each wrapped in his own thoughts, each taking comfort from the other's presence. It was a revelation for Jake. He had gone to sea to escape obligations, to be able to live a careless life, answerable only to himself. And suddenly he was responsible, not only for a four-hundred-ton ship and thirty-three in crew, but for a family, too.

He was responsible for shepherding Zacch the rest of the way to manhood, for providing an anchor while Zacch unfurled his sails and set his course. He was responsible for

Aunt Judith, for making sure the crusty old spinster never went wanting. And he was responsible for China.

His whole body grew taut with longing every time he thought of her. Images of her unusual face and her silky-skinned body filled the hot, airless nights in his cabin. He yearned to hold her and to caress her, to protect her, to give her solace, pleasure and love. As Zacch had inferred, with his twin's intuition, it was a commitment he had made before leaving Nantucket. Now he knew how deeply he meant it.

Oddly, his new responsibilities did not weigh heavily on him. It gave him satisfaction to know he was needed and appreciated. It gave him a sense of belonging, of home, that he had never felt when he took over his own father's functions. Thank you, Zaccheus, he thought. You always were wise. You left your treasures to your family, but you left your family to me. 'Tis all the treasure I want.

10

NANTUCKET
March 1843

THE SMALL GROUP OF FRIENDS silently gathered around the fresh grave disbanded by twos and threes. The raw March wind added impetus to their musings and meditations as they made their unspoken farewells and moved off to warmer places. China felt a hand on her elbow and looked up to see Harriet. Tears of sympathy shone in Harriet's warm brown eyes, despite the biting breeze that turned her lips blue and her plain nose red. "I'll wait for you at home," she whispered. China didn't answer, hardly hearing, wrapped up in her own thoughts. She pulled her brown wool cloak more tightly around herself and returned her gaze to the grave.

China remained, staring at the muddy soil. It still wasn't real to her; it didn't seem possible that Aunt Judith could be dead. At first it had just been a cold, a chill she had caught coming home from Meeting in an unexpected squall. Then it had been a racking cough, then a fever, and now she was laid for all eternity in a markerless grave in a grassy meadow.

In her mind she saw Aunt Judith as she had seen her for the first time, as a raggedy nine-year-old clinging to her father's hand. Aunt Judith's spectacled eyes had raked her in scrutiny, the spinster's stiff spine had registered her rigid disapproval. Defiantly, China had stuck out her chin, returning the assessing stare. Thus had begun their battle of wills, a continuing confrontation that was often no more than a display of obstinacy, but, occasionally, escalated to heated arguments. Compromise or truce was always implemented by either Aunt Judith or her grandniece, but neither one ever surrendered.

Even their last ferocious quarrel, over Obed and China's need to marry, had ended in a draw when China, regretting her tempestuous words and actions, had explained in a steady voice to Aunt Judith that Harriet was secretly in love with Obed and that her kind, patient friend would make him a far better wife than she. And Aunt Judith, sympathizing with China's untamed spirit in her heart, if not in her practical head, had simply said, "Aye, I expect thee is right. Thee would make the poor man miserable."

It was only now with her great aunt gone, and the small house on the edge of town quiet and empty, that China realized how deeply she had relied on Aunt Judith, despite her professed independence. She had leaned on the older woman's strength to bolster her own. She saw now that Aunt Judith's fortitude, her rock-hard faith in life, crustily couched in strict adherence to her religion, had always been more of an inspiration than an obstacle.

Aunt Judith had been the very essence of Nantucket, the bleak and beautiful, severe and serene island that China, ultimately, had come to love. Her stubborn morality could be as harsh as a November nor'easter; her accompanying wisdom had been as tranquilizing as twilight in June. She had shown the shrewdness of the island's Yankee merchants, the backbone of its adventurous seamen, the amazing tolerance of its straightlaced Quakers. Like Nantucket, Aunt Judith had been insular, individual and always enduring.

As China finally turned away from the grave and made her way slowly across the cemetery, it was not prostrating grief she felt, but calmness and resolution. It was almost as if she had absorbed Aunt Judith's spirit, had accepted her legacy, the legacy of Nantucket itself, a sense of continuity, a sense of self-sufficiency, and of strength. With a peacefulness she had seldom felt, China walked down the lane, where she now lived alone, and entered her house.

"China, you look positively frozen. I was just about to come fetch you." Harriet's voice was full of concern as she hovered in the parlor door.

China was startled. She had forgotten that her friend had promised to wait for her at home. "Aye, now that thee mentions it, I do feel chilled," she finally answered, moving toward the fire that Harriet had stoked. She pulled Aunt Judith's ladder-backed chair right up on the brick of the hearth and sat down. "I didn't notice how cold it was, but that damp wind has gone straight into my bones." She extended her numb hands toward the blaze, a slight shiver running down her spine.

Harriet dragged Zaccheus's rocker into position next to China and perched on the edge. She leaned anxiously forward as she spoke. "'Tis always the same with you, China," she said. "You get your head in the clouds and then don't see it when your feet get wet. Why, the fire was cold and the kitchen door was blown ajar when I arrived. I know 'twas because your mind was occupied with other matters." She reached out and gently took one of China's icy hands in hers.

"I don't mean to be unkind or critical, dear friend. I know 'tis a sad time for you." Tears welled up in her eyes again. "I'm simply worried about you, especially now that you are alone." She took a deep breath and then blurted out, "I think you should come live with us."

China turned quickly toward Harriet, surprise widening her gray eyes. "Oh, nay, impossible," she answered, instantly. When she had a moment to reflect on Harriet's suggestion, she hastened to add, "That is to say, I thank thee for thy offer, but I'll manage here very well. 'Tis my home; I can't leave it. Besides, the *China Maid* is due any day and I must be here when Papa and Zacch return." She refused to allow herself to think of Jake, though her friend had no such qualms.

Harriet shook her head doubtfully. "If I felt that were true, if I felt that Zacch or Captain Joy, or especially Jake, were on his way, I might not fret, but I'm not so sure. Oh, China—" Harriet's forehead wrinkled in despair "—'tis wrong to repeat gossip, but they're saying all over town that the *China Maid* is lost. Even Papa looks grim when I question him and sails circles around the point. I know she's only five months overdue, which is not at all odd, but no one has sighted her or heard from her since she left South America nearly three years ago. And that *is* unusual, as well you know."

Amazingly, China was not at all discouraged by Harriet's assessment of the local talk. She was still buoyed up by the calm courage she had found at Aunt Judith's grave. Overlooking Harriet's reference to Jake, she quietly answered, "I've heard the talk, too. I don't know who started it, but everyone seems to believe 'tis true. Even Sarah Coffin has given up. The last time I clipped in for tea, she was surrounded by gentlemen callers and seemed particularly affected by Barzillai Cartwright.

"Does thee remember Barzillai, Harriet?" she continued, attempting to turn the discussion away from herself. "He's that great fellow with the red cheeks and a lopsided smile. He made two trips to the Pacific, but now has had enough of the sea. His father is a ship's chandler and Barzillai has gone to work with him selling deadeyes and blocks and pails of paint.'' Her tone grew more contemptuous as she described Zacch's rival. Though she was secretly pleased that the delicate blond beauty had lost interest in her twin, China was nonetheless indignant about her disloyalty.

It was reassuring to Harriet to hear China sounding like herself, but she was afraid China wasn't being realistic. "'Tis a fine thing to have faith,'' she said, carefully. "But you must try to prepare yourself for all possibilities.''

Now it was China's turn to shake her head and to squeeze the hand still holding hers. "I can hear by thy voice that thee thinks I am avoiding the truth. Perhaps thee even thinks I am like mad Elizabeth Meacham who walks up and down the beach at Dionis, calling for her husband and babies who died twenty years ago.''

While Harriet started to deny this, China continued quite firmly, "I admit 'tis possible that the *China Maid* may have foundered or become disabled, but Harriet, I am *sure* that Zacch is still alive. I would know, I would feel it, if something had happened to him. Thee might think me a witch, but it has always been so.

"Even when we were children, we could tell if the other was hurt or ill. If one had an earache, then the other was bound to get one too. I remember once, when we were six years old, Zacch went racing down the deck, at full speed, and stubbed his toe on the corner of the tryworks. I limped for a week.'' A wistful smile curved at her lips as she remembered less-complicated times. Then she pulled herself back to the present.

"Nay, Harriet,'' she said. "Not even ten thousand miles of ocean can keep me from sensing if Zacch is not well. I know he is all right.'' A little less certainly, she added, "Papa is probably just fine, also.''

"And Jake?" Harriet coaxed.

"Jake, too," China said, grudgingly.

Even though Harriet believed China was right about Zacch, she persisted in trying to persuade her friend to come live on Gardner Street. "'Twould be a simple enough matter to move back here once they've come home," she pointed out. "They would probably even prefer to know you weren't living alone."

"'Tis of little import what they prefer," China replied, tartly, her old anger jumping out before she could stop it. "If they don't wish me to be alone, they shouldn't leave me by myself."

Harriet knew better than to argue. She tried another tack. "But what will you do by yourself all day, China? There will be no one to talk to. How will you fill the hours?"

China gave a little laugh. Her cheeks were rosy from the effects of the hot fire. She looked deceptively carefree. "There's no need to fret on that account," she said. "I'll be employed at a job all day."

"A job?" Harriet was astounded.

"Aye, a job. I may as well tell thee, because thee'll badger me until I admit it. The truth is I've almost no money left."

"Oh, China," Harriet wailed.

"Thee needn't get dramatic, Harriet," China said. She herself was still feeling calm, even proud of her practicality. "Papa used most of his savings to buy and refit the *China Maid*. We knew, Aunt Judith and I, that we had to keep our sails trimmed till he brings home a rich cargo, but we didn't reckon on the roof rotting. We had to have it reshingled last summer and that took a great bite out of the bank balance."

"All the more reason to come live with us," Harriet argued, almost pleading. "'Tis not right for you to have to earn your way. What can you possibly do? What kind of job can you find?"

"I don't know," China admitted, "but something will turn up. The *Inquirer* comes out today. I'll look in it to see if anyone is advertising for help."

"Please, China, please come stay with us. Don't take this on alone." There was genuine anguish in Harriet's voice.

China chose to ignore it. She knew that Harriet only wanted, desperately, to help, that she was motivated by generosity and sympathy. Still, she could not accept. Although the thought of living with Harriet was temptingly comfortable, her pride and independence got in the way. Deliberately misinterpreting Harriet's worry, she said lightly, "Thee needn't fret, dear friend. I promise thee that I'll pull the latch securely, bank the fire before I go out and keep my feet dry. Honestly."

THE FOLLOWING MORNING China had essentially the same conversation with Benjamin Swain when he arrived on her doorstep, as early as decency allowed, to reiterate Harriet's invitation. Although he exhorted and entreated over a cup of tea in the kitchen, China remained adamant. She had no wish to remove to Gardner Street. In a curious way, she was almost enjoying her situation, lonely, precarious and poor though it might be. It was a challenge to her spirit, a test of her autonomy. For the first time, she had control of her future.

Recognizing the impossibility of his task, Benjamin retreated somewhat. "A loan, then," he offered in compromise. "You must accept a loan to tide you over until your ship comes in. 'Tis unthinkable that you should have to seek employment."

"Again, I thank thee, Mr. Swain," China said, politely, but firmly. "But 'twould be most improvident of me to accept a loan with no guaranteed source of repayment. Thee knows the old saying, 'Two lamps burning and no ship at sea.' If indeed Papa's had trouble with the *China Maid*, as the talk around town goes, then the last thing he needs is a pledge against his profits.''

Benjamin pulled at his full chin in frustration. '''Tis interest free, with an open-ended due date,'' he bargained, in a last attempt to convince her. When she started to shake her head again, he exclaimed, ''By gosh, girl, I'm only trying to help you. What will you do otherwise?''

A little twinge of guilt passed through China, along with the vaguely uneasy feeling that she was behaving foolishly. ''I know thee is only trying to help, Mr. Swain, but really I must decline. And I'm no longer a girl, but a full-grown woman who must tend her own traps.

''As for what I shall do, there was an advertisement in yesterday's *Inquirer*,'' she said, reaching for the newspaper to verify her statement. ''See? They are seeking help at the Atlantic Silk Factory on Academy Hill. I intend to go around this morning.''

''The Silk Factory, eh?'' Benjamin said, more thoughtfully. ''I've a few dollars invested there, though I fear 'tis lost money. It seemed quite impressive when Gamaliel Gay showed us the machinery he'd invented for weaving raw silk. It flew along at the rate of an inch and a half a minute, mind you, but I had a queer feeling even then.

''The Lord knows we need to diversify our island businesses a bit with that damn sandbar—oh excuse me, China—with the Bar making it so difficult for decent shipping, but I can't help being suspicious of a manufacturing that depends on growing mulberry bushes and feeding the leaves to the silkworms so they can make cocoons. Mulberry bushes. Sounds like a children's nursery riddle, to me. The botanists say the climate in Nantucket is ideal for mulberries, but I say that if the climate here is so ideal, the good Lord would have planted them long ago."

Caught up in his own analysis of the island's fledgling silk industry, Benjamin continued. "George Easton's got a grove of a thousand mulberry trees in his backyard on North Water Street, and mighty poorly they look, too. Aaron Mitchell planted over four thousand on his property, none of them thriving, in addition to all the money he's put in to get up the company in the first place." He shook his head, despairingly, before he suddenly remembered the object of the conversation.

"Well," he said. "None of that should affect you, for 'tis no money you'll be putting in, but money you'll be taking out."

China nodded, glad that he was finally accepting her point of view.

"Mind you," he added, eyeing her as sternly as his benevolent features would allow, "it will be a miserable job. 'Tis infernally noisy in that big building, what with the steam engine wheezing and huffing and the looms all rattling and clanking. You'll not be happy there."

BENJAMIN SWAIN'S PROPHECY proved completely correct. China had no trouble securing the position, standing behind a twelve-foot spinner that held five hundred bobbins swirling delicate strands of silk, but her promised "apprentice wage" was a pittance, hardly worth the effort. Benjamin hadn't underestimated the cacophony either. China could hardly hear the supervisor as he shouted that she should present herself for work at seven o'clock.

Her enthusiasm dampened, but her determination still intact, China rose the next morning. Almost from the moment she swung her legs over the edge of the bed, the day was a disaster. It started with a small annoyance: while her feet fumbled on the icy floor for her slippers, they got kicked underneath her bed. It escalated from there.

Anxious not to be late, China hurried into her dress, fastening the buttons as she went downstairs. She had gone up and down those steep steps hundreds, even thousands, of times, slowly, quickly, two at a time. Brought up on a whaling ship, agilely climbing the rigging, she had never once missed a step. Until today. As she set her foot on the penultimate tread, simultaneously twisting to reach the last button, her heel slipped off the worn oak edge and she bumped to the bottom, cracking her elbow against the riser as she went.

For a moment she lay in a heap in the hallway, too surprised to move. When her shock receded, she struggled to her feet, suddenly sore all over. Cradling her tingling elbow, she limped into the kitchen.

Perhaps because her arm was still stiff, or perhaps because the day was simply ill-fated, when China opened the door to the cast-iron cookstove, a little later, meaning to add wood to the already roaring kindling, the piping hot door banged into her wrist, not only bruising it, but burning it as well. With a cry she leaped back, colliding with the table and ricocheting off a chair.

"Damn!" China swore, finally sinking into the offending chair and kicking closed the stove door with her foot. When she regarded her wrist, bright red and starting to blister, tears welled up in her eyes and clung to the dark fringe of her lashes. She suddenly missed Aunt Judith very much. Just thinking of the old spinster, though, stiffened China's resolve.

The pain of her burn effectively took away her appetite, but she managed to bathe her wrist in cool water before setting out for work. Not only did she skip eating breakfast, but she also forgot to pack a lunch, and she arrived at the Silk Factory with a throbbing arm, an empty stomach and a decidedly poor start on the day.

It got worse. The noise, the slamming of looms and the jangling of bobbins, which had only seemed deafening the day before, now was nerve-racking. The five hundred slender silk threads in her custody spun by her blinking eyes with a life of their own. Her supervisor's half-heard instructions and explanations confused, rather than clarified, the mysterious process. By the end of the day her head was throbbing as much as her hand; she was weak and dizzy from the pain and hunger.

As she stepped out of the factory into the reverberating silence of the street, the supervisor stopped her. "Miss Joy," he said. His voice was hoarse and loud, accustomed to constantly speaking over the sounds of the machinery. "I think 'twould be best if thee seeks another form of employment. One more suited to thy particular skills." China only nodded, too exhausted and miserable, precisely as Benjamin Swain had predicted, to even ask for her one day's wage.

It was a slow walk home and nearly dark by the time she opened the gate to her yard and trudged around to the back door. When she entered the kitchen and saw Harriet sitting at the table, a hamper heaped with food in front of her, a warm, welcoming smile making her plain face beatific, China's eyes filled with tears once more.

"Oh dear," Harriet said, her smile fading into a look of anxiety. "Was it really that bad?"

"Aye, it was," China answered, her long body slumping into the nearest chair. She was glad that Harriet had come. Almost as much as she needed a nourishing meal and a sound night's sleep, she needed someone sympathetic to tell her troubles to.

"Before you tell me one word of what happened, I think you should eat something," Harriet decided, rising from her seat and unloading the bulging basket. "You look very pale. I'll wager you didn't feed yourself properly today. Here," she said, extracting a blue-striped bowl covered with a tea towel. "Mama made bread pudding this afternoon, with rum and raisins. 'Tis warm still. This should put new life into you. Wait. I'll fetch you a spoon."

While Harriet rummaged in the pine cupboard for a spoon, China lifted the tea towel and eyed the steamy pudding with pleasure. Her stomach rumbled in anticipation; the sweet, cinnamon-y smell wafted up from the bowl and made her mouth water. "Thee is an angel of mercy," she said, reaching eagerly for the spoon Harriet held out.

Her fingers were barely curled around the handle, her gray eyes never leaving the bowl, when a knock sounded at the front door. China looked up, surprised and annoyed. "Who could that be?" she muttered, reluctantly setting down the spoon and getting to her feet.

"You stay here, China, I'll go see," Harriet said, brushing past her friend on her way into the parlor and across the room to the door.

China needed no urging. She sat down again and dipped the spoon into the bowl, bringing a fragrant bite of rum-soaked, raisin-studded pudding close to her nose. She sniffed. "Ambrosial," she murmured to herself then opened her mouth to receive the manna.

"Well, uh, Harriet," came Obed Hussey's hesitant tones. "I didn't expect, uh, that is, I didn't know, uh....I came to ask China, I mean, I came to see her."

"Oh dear," China said to the pudding, putting it down untasted. Obed was the last person she wanted to see.

"China is in the kitchen, Obed," came Harriet's quiet reply. "Why don't you come through?"

China shut her eyes, seeking patience from somewhere within herself. When she opened them again, Obed was standing in front of her, shifting from foot to foot, and Harriet was standing to one side, her face bent, an air of dejection surrounding her. China felt what little patience she had receding. "Hello, Obed," she said warily.

"Hello, China," Obed replied. He chewed on his lower lip.

China waited a moment for further comment and when it wasn't forthcoming, she prodded, "Well?"

"Well, uh..." Obed's eyes darted nervously toward Harriet.

China felt irritation creeping over her common sense, and certainly over her manners. "Did I hear thee say to Harriet that thee came to ask me something?" she demanded.

"Aye, China, I said that," Obed mumbled.

"Perhaps I should go," Harriet said, hurrying toward the table to snatch up her cloak. "'Tis getting quite dark now."

"Nay!" China snapped. Harriet froze in place. "Well, Obed? What did thee mean to ask me?"

"Uh, umm..." Obed's honest face turned bright red. His expression was desperate. "Um, how are you, China?" he finally sputtered.

"How am I?" she repeated, momentarily stunned. Then her temper boiled over, every bump, bruise and burn, every jangle and clang, every disappointing, discouraging and disastrous moment of the day came pouring out. Obed happened to be in the way.

"Does thee mean to tell me thee came all the way here to ask me how I am?" she shouted, pushing herself to her feet. Pressure on her throbbing wrist further incensed her. "Is that all thee wants to know? How am I?"

"Nay, China," Obed said, hastily, retreating before her anger. "I meant to say, I mean, now that your Aunt Judith is gone. That is, uh, now that you are all alone in the world . . ." His voice trailed off, his eyes were almost begging her to understand what he couldn't quite say. He was hoping that she was feeling vulnerable and unprotected and that she would look more favorably upon his suit.

China understood perfectly well what he wanted, but she was in no mood to make it easy for him. "Aye," she stormed, repeating his words, "now that my Aunt Judith is gone and I am all alone in the world, I no longer have the time to untangle thy tongue-tied thoughts! There are more important matters that need my attention. I have not the time nor the inclination to guess what is on thy mind. If thee has come to ask me something, then ask away, so I can make my answer and thee can go home!"

Total silence greeted her outburst. Obed's expression was a mixture of intense mortification and tragic disillusionment. Harriet looked alarmed. China waited, wanting to underscore her eruption with a dramatic finale. In the end, unable to think of a way to make her point any plainer, she turned on her heel and stalked into the parlor, slamming the door behind her as she went.

She strode to the window, arms across her chest, shoulders back, gray eyes looking not seductive but smoldering. She stared out the window a moment, not really seeing anything, then strode to another window. She expected Harriet to come sliding through the parlor door, saying soothing things and settling her wrangled nerves. When the door remained closed, China turned abruptly away from the window and strode to the cold hearth. And then to the pine hutch and then back to the hearth.

As the minutes went by, China's straight shoulders sagged. Through the door she could hear the soft whirring of voices, though she couldn't make out the words. She leaned her head wearily against the mantel. This wasn't right. Harriet should be in here with her, not out in the kitchen giving comfort to Obed. Her stomach growled emptily, and she thought about the bowl of aromatic bread pudding in the other room. A wave of self-pity engulfed her. It wasn't fair.

There finally came the sound of the back door clicking closed. Then the parlor door opened and Harriet came through. Her usually pale face was flushed and pretty. If China noticed this change, she subconsciously blocked it out. Instead, she said petulantly, "Well, it took thee long enough to remember me."

Harriet stiffened slightly, but her voice remained gentle as she remonstrated, "Really, China. Was it necessary to be quite so blunt? Poor Obed." She crossed the room to where China stood and took her by the arm. "Come now," she said. "Come back into the kitchen and have something to eat. Then I'll help you to get into bed for a good, sound sleep. Things will look better tomorrow."

Even though these were the comforting words China had been waiting for, she allowed herself to become further enraged by Harriet's reference to Obed. She shook off her friend's hand and said, abruptly, "I am not one of thy broken-winged birds or one of thy stray puppy dogs. Don't pat me on the head and snuggle me into a nest, as if I were a brainless creature. Thee can save such ministrations for 'poor Obed.'"

Harriet stared at China, a look of hurt and puzzlement replacing her contented flush. Without saying a further word, she went back into the kitchen, caught up her cloak and left, quietly closing the door after her.

"Nay," China said behind her, her tantrum instantly and entirely spent. "Nay, I didn't mean it. Oh Harriet, I'm sorry."

Those were her first words, the next morning, standing in the Swains' well-furnished front parlor facing her friend. After Harriet had left last night, she had forced the bread pudding, no longer steamy and succulent but cold and gluey, down her throat and had trudged upstairs to her bed. Sleep had been immediate and deep, and she had woken this morning feeling refreshed, though remorseful.

"Can thee ever forgive me?" she asked, mournfully. "Aunt Judith was always telling me to put a furl on my temper. 'Tis like a South Seas typhoon: sudden and destructive."

"Nonsense," Harriet said, plumping down on the overstuffed sofa and patting the seat next to her in invitation. "I know you didn't mean anything by your outburst. 'Tis already forgotten. You were hungry and tired and I can see a burn on the back of your hand. You must have had a wretched day. Come tell me every horrid detail so I can bring you hot chocolate and biscuits and convince you to come live with us."

Relief and gratitude flooded through China. It seemed impossible to her that anyone could continue to be as good and kind as Harriet. "I'll gladly sob on thy shoulder and drink thy confections," she said, crossing the room to join her friend on the sofa, "though why thee should encourage my peevish company is a mystery."

Just as she was about to sit down, the Swains' heavy brass knocker banged on the door. Since she was still standing, she peered out the window to see who was calling. A delighted grin broke out on her face. "'Tis Obed Hussey," she said, in immense amusement. "And he's wearing his best suit and carrying what looks like a sack of peppermint drops." She turned in time to see Harriet's hands flying to her flushed cheeks and shy excitement lighting up her brown eyes.

"Well, well, well," China murmured, speculatively. She still hadn't sat down. "I guess my sad story will have to wait again. 'Tis doomed to interruption by Obed, I can see. I'll let myself out through the kitchen, Harriet, while thee tends to thy caller." When Harriet only looked distracted in reply, China chuckled, bent over to place an affectionate kiss on her friend's forehead and walked out the back entrance to the parlor remarking, "There is a silver lining to my thundercloud of anger, after all."

China felt decidedly lighthearted as she made her way through the Swains' backyard and circled Elijah Howard's big barn to come out, again, on Main Street. She was relieved and happy that Obed had finally directed his attention away from her and toward Harriet, who was a willing recipient. Some things work out well in the end, she thought.

With a sigh, she set her mind back on the situation at hand. Though she had almost succumbed to Harriet's offer of cake and security a little while ago, she was glad Obed had arrived before she could commit herself. She felt fresh determination to make her way on her own. Not all jobs could be as onerous as the one at the Silk Factory, she reasoned. It was simply a matter of finding one.

China headed for Centre Street, commonly called Petticoat Row because its series of shops were mostly owned and operated by women whose husbands were away at sea. They ran the businesses for occupation and for income, courageous, efficient women who had learned to cope with their husbands' long absences. China hoped that one of these women would be sympathetic to her situation.

She went to one shop after another, a millinery, a dry goods, a dressmaker. Each proprietress did, indeed, commiserate with China's predicament, but none was able to offer her employment. At the fourth shop, Mitchell's

General Emporium, China found less compassion, but a paying position.

Mrs. Eulalia Mitchell was a large, brisk woman whose stiffly wound Grecian ringlets seemed completely incongruous against her hawkish face. She had small, shrewd, faded blue eyes that looked China up and down, measuringly. China felt a moment's panic under the scrutiny, doing a mental check to make sure her bonnet was properly in place. For once, it was demurely tied beneath her firm chin, almost hiding her silky bangs and straight, short hair.

Mrs. Mitchell's gaze traveled the long, slim length of China's body, seeming to nod approval at the neat gray gown and the snowy white neckcloth. It lingered longer on China's face, as if deciding whether her great, gray eyes, so strikingly outlined in charcoal, and set against porcelain white skin, would create envy, outrage or admiration among her customers. Apparently she decided that China's unusual beauty was no threat to the shop's reputation.

"There is a position," she finally announced. "Elizabeth, my clerk, is leaving to be married next month. She can teach you her job until she goes, for which you will be paid half wages." She waited for China to nod her agreement.

"I'll expect you to start promptly at eight every morning and work until six in the evening. I dislike tardiness and sloth. You'll be allowed half an hour at midday, but you must bring your meal here and eat in the storeroom. I look upon myself as the guardian of my employees' morals, especially in your case, with no one else to care for you. Young people have a tendency to stray."

China felt herself fill with dismay. This was a fine sort of torture, an affront to her proudly proclaimed independence. To be under this pompous woman's surveillance was almost worse than the ear-splitting din at the silk factory.

An image of Aunt Judith's wise face passed, suddenly, through China's mind. She could almost hear the elderly woman intoning, ''Thee has much to learn about life. Thee must learn to compromise.'' Aye, thought China, wryly. And this is my first lesson.

''Thee needn't fear for my behavior,'' she promised, solemnly. ''Nor for my work habits. I accept thy terms. Shall I start tomorrow?''

Mrs. Mitchell squinted her eyes as if she were having second thoughts. She studied China again, then nodded reluctantly. ''Aye. Tomorrow at eight.''

By the end of her first day at Mitchell's General Emporium, China was exhausted. By the end of her first month, she thoroughly loathed the job. When she wasn't waiting on a customer, she was sweeping the floor or endlessly dusting the shelves, piled to the ceiling with cans of tea from the Orient, boxes of spices from the Dutch East Indies, sacks of sugar from New Orleans and Havana, bolts of American calico, Egyptian cotton, Swiss muslin, and French silk, jars of English nuts, canisters of Puerto Rican coffee, bottles of elixirs, bars of scented soap, parasols, andirons, lanterns, washboards, buttons and crockery ware. There was even a case of jewelry containing gold and silver watches, ivory and shell combs, coral beads, jet ear bobs, filigreed brooches and pearl pendants.

Although China enjoyed sorting through the incredible inventory, she hated the feeling of confinement. Not only was Mrs. Mitchell constantly hovering, casting a critical eye at China's work, but Elizabeth, the thin, nasal girl whose place she was taking, was continually, and condescendingly, correcting China's ways. And although it was not unbearable to be indoors during the damp, gray days of March and early April, when the balmy breezes and bright sunshine of spring appeared, China felt like a prisoner.

There was no silent truce, no unspoken accord, with Mrs. Mitchell as there had been with Aunt Judith. She could not hurry through her chores, then disappear across the commons, breathing clean air and stretching her long legs. She was trapped in a long, narrow shop on Centre Street, dusting and sweeping and subject to scrutiny. She often reflected, ironically, as she walked home at dusk, that this was what it was like to be independent.

When Elizabeth finally left, China's job became more interesting. Moving into the clerk's slot, she helped Mrs. Mitchell to make up the lists of merchandise to be ordered from the mainland, and to select from shipments arriving on the island from abroad. She had a keen eye for quality and an exquisite sense of style. She quickly learned the basic elements of buying, and was soon confidently offering suggestions on which goods to purchase.

Mrs. Mitchell was skeptical of China's opinion, at first, but she had sound entrepreneurial instincts, even if she had dreadfully bad taste. When one or two of her clerk's ideas proved perceptive and profitable, she tentatively tried others. It wasn't long before she was relying heavily on China's judgment, though rarely giving her any credit.

"Here, China," she would say, nodding toward a bolt of cloth, her girlish curls bobbing. "Captain Folger has just brought this in from Boston. Did you see it?"

"Aye," China would answer, "I saw him bring it in, but I thought the color was too muddy and the weaving rather poor."

"Just what I was thinking," Mrs. Mitchell would say vigorously. "Let this be a lesson for you, China. You see how it is in business? It takes years of experience to make wise purchases."

Though China felt chagrined that her employer refused to acknowledge her contributions, she still found satisfaction in thumbing through catalogs and order lists and in talking with the packet captains who did their shopping. She daydreamed about owning her own business, about going to Boston and New York to rummage around warehouses. Even better, to have her own ship and sail around the world finding Chinese tea sets and Turkish carpets, French wines and Italian marbles; as long as she was daydreaming, she might as well do it right. She would laugh at herself for such unrealistic expectations, but her secret ambition wouldn't recede.

As often as she fantasized about having her own ship, China would think back to the day at Miacomet beach when she had confessed that desire to Jake. Against her will she would remember the warmth of the sand on her bare toes, the salty, sweet smell of wild roses and the sea, and the long, strong body of Jake stretched out next to her. She would see the sun glinting off his little gold hoop, the breeze ruffling his unruly dark curls and stretching the shirt across his back, and the teasing glint in his sharp blue eyes.

She would try to push those thoughts away, to sternly remind herself that she had decided to forget about him because he caused her too much anguish. Instead of retreating, however, the memories would multiply. She would see him, sleek as a seal, in the ocean off Coatue, naked in the pine needles, his eyelids heavy with desire, pressed against her in the rain. She would feel his heart pounding against her cheek, feel his fingers circling her ear and trailing down her neck, feel his lips, moist and warm, covering hers. She would hear his rich laugh, his infuriating mocking, his urgent insistence when he said, "We were always meant for each other. Nothing can keep us apart. In our souls we are already united." Oh Jake, she would think, in despair, what has thee done to me?

Mostly, though, she would just sweep and dust and measure out packets of tea and yards of cloth. By the time she arrived home in the evening, she was too tired to do more than eat a quick supper and to prepare for the next day. On Sundays, her one free day, she washed her clothes and cleaned her house and stole a few hours alone on the moors.

She rarely saw Harriet anymore, except when her friend came into the shop to buy something. Since Mrs. Mitchell discouraged idle conversation, it was impossible to exchange an intimate word. Harriet always asked her to come home for supper, but China knew that Obed called almost every evening, and she felt awkward about accepting the invitations.

China got up, went to work, came home and went to sleep, day after day after day. Except for those few moments when she was enjoyably occupied with contemplating new purchases, or when memories of Jake haunted her heart, she felt leaden and alone. In the back of her mind was the ever dimming hope that the *China Maid* would come sailing home with her father and Zacch, their pockets bulging with oil money, to rescue her from this calico and crockery jail. In the meantime, it seemed she was suspended, in limbo. Life went by without her.

11

SOUTH PACIFIC
June 1844

"BLOOOWS! THERE SHE BLOOOWS!" Jake was standing by the rail, scanning the horizon with his glass, when the cry went out. For once, he was not looking for whales but for the low, green shape of Rarua, the small island that was John James Henry's home. They were only hours from dropping anchor in its deep, protected bay, hours away from returning the big Polynesian to his people, and from enjoying the revelry that was sure to follow. Every man on board needed that spree ashore; they needed to feel solid land under their feet, to immerse themselves in clear, sweet water, to eat fresh foods, and to forget about the brutal life at sea in the arms of warm and willing wahines.

"Blooows! Two points off the larboard bow!" With a sigh, Jake turned his back to Rarua and resighted his glass in the indicated direction. A single geyser spewed into the empty blue sky.

"I see one spout. Do you see more?"

Jake brought his glass back to the deck and to Zacch, who had appeared beside him. "Nay, 'tis only the one," he answered, handing the telescope over. As Zacch brought it to his eye and fiddled with the focus, he added, "'Tis sperm. And judging from the size, I'd say it was a bull. Probably an old one."

"Aye," Zacch said, slowly, finally finding the immense gray shape floating in the ocean. A flock of birds hovered above it, occasionally dipping down to snatch tidbits from the thick, wrinkled skin. He lowered the glass and turned to Jake, who was standing with his arms across his chest and a scowl across his face.

"He ought to make ninety barrels," Zacch said, reluctantly. He, too, was looking forward to their arrival in Rarua, not only for his own sake, but also for John James Henry's.

"Aye, he should." Jake continued to glare in the direction of the whale.

"'Tis a good bet, being on his own, he's sick or dying," Zacch added, still hesitant. "That could mean ambergris." He was referring to the yellowish brown substance found occasionally in the intestines of diseased whales. Soft and malodorous on extraction, it turned hard and fragrant when exposed to sun, air and saltwater. Full of squid beaks and cuttlebones, the mainstay of the leviathan's diet, it was, incredibly, a precious ingredient in the world's finest perfumes. A good-sized lump of ambergris was a valuable bonus.

Jake sighed again, and postponed thoughts of roast wild boar on the beach. "'Tis what I was thinking as well," he admitted. "Though I can't say I favor poking around in a whale's gizzard over quaffing green coconuts, 'tis too rare an opportunity to pass by."

Resigned, now, his good humor returned. "We'll lower the two larboard boats only," he said, shooting a grin at Zacch. "If we can't fasten on that sperm, just you and me, we'd better hand in our lances for a pair of hoes and head for the nearest patch of potatoes."

"I doubt things are that drastic, yet," Zacch replied, giving back the grin. For a moment they shared a feeling of fraternal warmth, of total rapport. Then they split apart to prepare for the chase and to give orders to the less-than-enthusiastic crew.

Despite Jake's confident comment, both men knew that hunting a sixty-five-foot beast from a twenty-five-foot boat was never a sure thing. Jake was delighted, therefore, when both boats got irons in immediately. After a perfunctory sleigh ride and a half-hearted flurry, the giant whale turned fin up. As they towed their prize back to the *China Maid*, Jake felt pleased. This delay wouldn't cost them that much extra time, after all, and it would immeasurably add to the contents of the hold. It could almost be considered lucky.

The crew seemed to catch the same spirit. Like horses sensing they were heading for the barn, they picked up their pace, eager to get this whale below decks and get on to Ra-rua. The huge carcass was nearly stripped of its blubber when Zacch's voice suddenly cut through their concentrated work. "Squall," he said, tensely. "'Tis heading this way."

The tone of Zacch's voice filled Jake with dread, even before he lowered his cutting spade to look. An ominous sheet of gray clouds and blinding rain was traveling swiftly toward them. "Damn!" Jake muttered. "So much for luck." Then grimly, he ordered, "Look lively! Stop gaping at the sky. You've all seen squalls before and you're about to see one on top of us, now. Get those blanket pieces in the blubber room and get the head on board. Cut loose the carcass. We haven't time to go digging around in whale guts, now. Move! Before that squall hits."

They redoubled their efforts, but it wasn't fast enough. They had halfway severed the head when the squall struck with the suddenness of most tropical weather. One minute the sea was smooth and the sky was blue; the next minute thunderous black clouds and rain blotted out the light and strong winds whipped up angry swells.

With the first fierce gust, the *China Maid* listed sharply, almost burying the rail under the heavy drag of the whale. "Cut her loose!" Jake shouted above the howling wind. He seized the helm from the hands of the confused and frightened cabin boy, who never handled it except when they were hove to, trying out.

Under Jake's expert guidance, the old whaler righted herself. Before he could take a breath of relief, however, an earsplitting crack made his heart freeze. He knew instantly what had happened, even as he struggled with the huge wheel. Stressed by the erratic yanks of the weighty whale suspended from it, the mainmast had snapped. Almost simultaneously, the half-severed head, a full twenty feet long, ripped free of the carcass. Swinging crazily from tangled halyards on the broken mast, propelled by the force of the frenzied sea, the bloody, broken head slammed into the side of the *China Maid* with a shriek of shattered planks.

"Cut line! Cut line!" Jake yelled, helplessly fighting to control the helm. Zacch and John James Henry were already wielding razor-sharp cutting spades, slicing through the web of heavy lines as they tried to keep their balance on the wet, pitching deck. In minutes, the whale was loose and Jake had maneuvered away from the bobbing bulk. By now the storm was subsiding, just another quixotic South Seas gale.

"Zacch, go below and assess the damages," Jake ordered from his position at the wheel. "Get some men on pumps, if need be." He didn't doubt that there would be a need—the sound of splintering wood had been all too clear. He only hoped the need wasn't too great. "Samuel," he yelled to the second mate, "get that mess of line cleared off the deck." To no one in particular he said, "Thank God we're as close as we are to a friendly port."

John James Henry was hard on Zacch's heels as he clambered below. Water was seeping into the blubber room, nudging at the blanket pieces, which were all that now remained of their once rich prize. The hold, however, was another story. A huge hole had been bashed in the side and green water was flooding in everywhere.

"Poor old *Maid*," Zacch exclaimed, wading through the churning water to examine the smashed planks. "She's really taken a beating this time." He staggered and swayed with the agitated sea.

"Ummm," John James Henry said. "Time for pumps."

As he turned to go topside for the required equipment and men, he saw, out of the corner of his eye, a cask full of oil loosened from its place with the lurch of the ship. It rolled with the wave and caught Zacch between it and the bulwark. John James Henry saw Zacch's eyes go wide in astonishment, before the enormous cask blocked him from sight. Then the *China Maid* crested the swell, and the cask rolled back again. Zacch slid, unconscious, into the waist-deep bilge.

Alarm filled John James Henry's broad features. "Za-Zacch, ho, Za-Zacch," he called anxiously, reaching Zacch just as his head was about to go underwater. "Nay, Za-Zacch," he crooned, scooping the limp young man into his muscular arms.

When he emerged on deck with his burden, moments later, Jake went sick with fear. An awful premonition turned his stomach cold. "Oh Christ," he whispered, his throat suddenly dry. "Please don't let him be dead," he prayed, instantly and intensely. He was transfixed with dread by the sight of John James Henry moving slowly toward him with Zacch, white-faced and still, in his arms.

"Samuel!" he shouted hoarsely, rousing himself. "Come take this goddamned wheel!"

Blond, bearded Samuel Easton took the helm, just as John James Henry gently set Zacch down, almost like a tribute, at Jake's feet. The storm was completely past now, and the sun was peering around fleeing gray clouds. In the fresh light, Zacch seemed like a marble statue. Despite his tropical tan, his skin was pale and smooth, and stretched over finely cut features. A hank of straight, black hair, soaked from the rain, hung across his clear forehead; the black fringes of his lashes lay against his cheeks. Kneeling next to him, he reminded Jake as never before of China, his twin. The thought deepened the pain gripping Jake's heart.

"'Tis bad, Ja-Jake," John James Henry said, mournfully. "Sea came in like a waterfall and pushed a cask into Za-Zacch. Bam. Bam. Push him here." His huge hand hovered over Zacch's chest, imperceptibly rising and falling.

Relief flooded through Jake at the sign of life. The next moment, though, Zacch gave a feeble cough and a dribble of blood trailed down the corner of his mouth. Jake's fear returned, along with a sense of helplessness. He wiped away the trickle of blood, then gripped one of Zacch's cold hands. "Aye," he agreed, "'tis bad."

"When we make port in Rarua, there is a man there who can talk to the spirits, make medicines. Maybe he can mend Za-Zacch," John James Henry said, doubtfully. It wasn't that he had ceased to believe in his native ways, he was simply overwhelmed by Zacch's ashen face.

"Perhaps so," Jake said, seizing on the hope. If there had been a broken limb, or a visible wound, he would have been better able to deal with it. He would have splinted it with barrel staves or sewn it up with sail twine, but this invisible injury frightened him. He not only couldn't see it, he didn't know how serious it was.

"Aye," he said, in a stronger tone. "That's what we'll do. We'll bring him to your medicine man. In the meantime, let's get these wet clothes off him and set a pillow under his head." As he started to tug on Zacch's sopping shirt, another thought struck him. "Damn!" he swore. "The hold!"

Jake jumped up and scanned the deck, seeking Henry Easton, Samuel's younger brother and newly appointed fourth mate. Finding him by the snapped-off mainm'st, folding up yards of useless sails, he bellowed, "Henry! Belay that! Take some men and jump below. Set up both pumps and go like hell!" When Henry dropped the sail in midfold and leaped to follow orders, Jake returned to Zacch's side.

John James Henry had pulled off all of Zacch's clothes and had gone to fetch dry ones. Zacch seemed particularly vulnerable, lying naked and quiet on the wooden deck. Another spot of blood had appeared at the corner of his mouth, otherwise there was not a trace of trouble. Jake slid his hand under Zacch's head to cushion it from the hard deck. Even wet, the thick, silky hair reminded him of China's.

"Come on, little brother," he murmured. "Wake up and tell us you just banged your noggin." But as he tenderly dabbed at the bright red blood, he knew that was not going to happen.

It was sunset when they dropped anchor in the deep, blue harbor of Rarua. Canoes full of curious islanders came paddling out to meet them. John James Henry, torn between his anxiety over Zacch and his excitement at coming home, stood by the rail, alternately shouting to his friends and relatives and darting concerned glances over his shoulder.

When the startled natives realized who was calling to them in their own language, roars of welcome and peals of laughter filled the air. The canoes swarmed around the ship, seemingly heedless of the numerous women, coarse black hair streaming, who had swum out from shore. John James Henry carried on animated conversations with ten people at once. His arms waved wildly, his huge hands pointed.

While Jake watched, with increasing impatience, John James Henry gradually narrowed his attention to one important-looking gentleman seated in the center of the largest canoe. An enormous brown belly hung over a slender string and scrap of cloth, barely covering his loin. Pointed teeth gleamed between full lips, split in a happy grin.

"My uncle," John James Henry explained at last to Jake. "He is head man in Rarua. He say to fetch Za-Zacch to his house."

Jake nodded. "We'll set him in the larboard stern boat, then lower it," he instructed. "You and I can row it to shore." He swung around to face Samuel Easton, who was now next in command. "Samuel, keep two men on the pumps. There shouldn't be much trouble keeping afloat in this calm harbor. Then get the tryworks fired up. There'll be no shore leave until that oil is stowed below. Is that understood?" His blue eyes, hard and sharp, swept the length of the deck, encompassing the entire crew. They were wistfully watching the laughing women, with hibiscus flowers in their long hair, playing like porpoises in the sea.

"Aye, sir, 'tis quite clear," Samuel Easton responded. He was a conscientious officer and a sober man who could never get used to the casual, but complete, control with which Jake ran the ship. At his answer, and at the looks of glum resignation among the men, Jake nodded again and followed the larboard stern boat over the side.

On the beach, John James Henry gathered Zacch into his arms and carried him down the palm-tree-lined track to the village. At an open-sided house, sitting higher and larger than the rest, he entered. The only furnishings were a low table made from a single slab of a hardwood tree and a variety of mats, either spread out on the floor or rolled in a corner. John James Henry carefully set Zacch on one, then rocked back on his heels to gaze worriedly at the still-unconscious young man. A group of women and children gathered around to stare in curiosity. John James Henry sent them scattering with a wave of his hand.

"My uncle send for man with medicines," he told Jake, who was crouched by Zacch's side. "He'll come along in jig time. Talk to gods."

Jake accepted his statement without comment. His face was grim as he contemplated Zacch's quiet body. He was talking to God himself, alternately praying to Him, as he never had before, to preserve Zacch's life, and cursing Him for allowing this to happen to such a fine person. He doubted his unspoken words had any effect, one way or another; he only hoped John James Henry's medicine man had better connections than he. He couldn't ease the feeling of deep foreboding that filled him.

At length, the local doctor arrived. He was a wizened old man whose sparse hair was long and white. Almost all his teeth were worn away, though from his gaunt frame it looked as though he hardly ever ate. He carried with him a bag made from woven palm fronds from which he extracted, even before examining Zacch, an array of carved wood and bone figures. These he calmly placed in a line at the foot of the mat. Then he turned his watery brown eyes on his patient.

He listened, and lightly poked, while John James Henry explained what had happened. Jake watched, both apprehensive and hopeful. The old man shook his head dolefully. Ice formed again in Jake's guts as the last of his hope faded. There was nothing this man could do. No island magic he could perform to waken Zacch, gray eyes laughing and alert, from his unnatural sleep. He hardly noticed when the old man shuffled out.

"He go talk to gods," John James Henry explained. "Maybe give them something. Pig, maybe. Dog, maybe."

Jake looked up, somewhat shocked. "A sacrifice, you mean? Is he going to make a sacrifice?"

John James Henry's big brows knit together as he puzzled over this new word. "What is a sacrifice?" he asked. "Some kind of animal?"

"Nay," Jake answered, half smiling. "'Tis when you kill something alive to gain a favor from the gods. Or sometimes it is to pay them back for something they have already done."

For a few minutes both men studied Zacch's still form, each absorbed with his own sense of guilt and helplessness. For the hundredth time since the accident occurred so many long hours ago, Jake thought, if only I hadn't sent him below. But he knew that was foolish. Zacch was the owner and the first mate. Who better than he should have gone to assess the situation? His agonized musings were interrupted by John James Henry.

"'Tis my fault," the big man said, sorrowfully. "Poor Za-Zacch is sacrifice for me."

"What the hell are you talking about?" Jake barked, appalled by John James Henry's statement.

"'Twas sixteen years ago," John James Henry explained. "Same place, southeast of Rarua, same fast, fast squall as this morning. I was hunting dolphin all by myself

235

when, whoosh, came the gale and stove in my canoe. I was holding on to one little piece, staying afloat, ten, maybe twelve hours, when Captain Zaccheus came and made rescue. The gods were good. They saved my life. Now they take Za-Zacch for sacrifice." He stared stonily at his huge hands.

A chill ran down Jake's spine. "That's bilge!" he said, emphatically, as much to convince himself as to convince John James Henry. "'Twas a freakish accident, is all. 'Twas no one's fault." When the big man looked unpersuaded, he added, "Anyway, the gods already have Captain Zaccheus. That should satisfy them."

A glimmer of relief lit John James Henry's brown eyes. "You think 'tis true?" he asked.

"Aye, 'tis true," Jake replied, more firmly than he felt. He hoped it was true. He hoped the gods were satisfied with only one Zaccheus Joy.

"Ja-Jake?"

"John James Henry?"

"Be all right if I go gam with uncle and friends?"

"Of course, 'tis fine."

All night long Jake remained crouched by Zacch's side, straining into the darkness for some sight or sign of returning consciousness. The only thing he saw or heard was the distant flicker of a bonfire on the beach and the muffled sounds of drums and laughter as the islanders celebrated John James Henry's return. Just beyond the open walls were the shadowy shapes of other huts, the rustling trees and the unfamiliar stirrings of life on land.

Dawn finally came on the village, lighting well-trodden dirt streets running neatly among the thatch-roofed houses. Except for a few dogs, their tails wagging aimlessly, and some bright parrots up in the trees, no one else was awake. With a suddenly sinking feeling, Jake noticed that Zacch's cheeks were no longer chalky white, but were suspiciously flushed. He laid his hand on Zacch's forehead and was alarmed at how hot he felt.

At his touch, Zacch's eyelids fluttered open. For a moment, his large, gray eyes, clouded with pain, stared uncomprehendingly at the palm frond ceiling. Then he moved his head slightly and focused, with difficulty, on Jake. "Ah, 'tis you, Jake," he murmured. His voice was barely audible, yet the effort those few words cost him was obvious. Deep lines etched on his handsome face and a bubble of blood blew between his lips, impeding his shallow breathing.

Jake's heart froze in anguish at the sight, but he forced himself to reply steadily. "Aye, 'tis me," he said, wiping the bubble of blood out of Zacch's mouth with the corner of his shirttail. "But don't gally yourself. Just lie still. You're in John James Henry's house in Rarua, and you're pretty well stove in. You need to stay quiet and rest, so you'll heal up fast. Understand? No hula dancing for you just now."

Zacch's mouth twitched in an attempt to smile, but it came across as an agonized grimace, instead. His eyelids dropped shut, again, and he drifted into an uneasy sleep. All morning long he rolled restlessly, occasionally moaning or coughing up more bright blood. His fever seemed to mount as the sun grew higher in the sky.

Jake never moved from his position by Zacch's side. Though he tenderly cleaned the blood off Zacch's lips and chin, and patiently dipped cooling strips of his shirt in a gourd full of fresh water to lay on Zacch's forehead, he felt impotent. He knew that neither his ministrations nor his prayers were making any difference. He was tense with despair.

Around midmorning, as the village streets gradually filled with wakening people, John James Henry came in carrying a basket of fruit. "So sorry, Ja-Jake," he said, squatting down beside him and anxiously scrutinizing Zacch's fevered face. "Too much welcome home last night." He patted Zacch's hand. "Poor Za-Zacch. He don't look so very shipshape."

Jake wearily rubbed his eyes. "Nay," he replied. "He's not doing so very well."

John James Henry stared at Zacch for another minute and then turned to study Jake. "You too, Ja-Jake. I think you did not sleep at all," he said, reaching into the basket he had brought and pulling out a fragrant pineapple. Holding it by its plumed top, he began to trim away its horny skin with the bone-handled knife he kept tucked in his belt. When it was peeled and juicy, he handed it to Jake. "Here. Must eat," he said.

Jake hesitated, then, when John James Henry thrust it farther forward, he accepted it. Even though he had very little appetite, he saw the sense in the big man's words. Two days ago his mouth would have watered just thinking about this succulent treat; now he chewed the sweet fruit mechanically, hardly tasting it.

"Ja-Jake," John James Henry said, rocking back on his heels and resting his forearms across his knees. "What you want me to do?"

"I don't know," Jake said, wiping his fingers on what remained of his shirt. He looked at Zacch, tossing fitfully in his sleep. "I don't know," he repeated, softly. His sense of helplessness was overwhelming.

"Maybe I can fetch some medicine from the *China Maid*?" John James Henry asked, hopefully. "Maybe you got something in slop chest?"

Jake shook his head. "Nay, there's nothing there save paregoric and liniment," he said, dully.

"What we going to do, then, Ja-Jake?" John James Henry's voice was more desperate now. It was as if he were demanding an answer from Jake.

The tone of distress roused Jake somewhat. "All we can do is wait and pray," he said. Then, realizing that answer left John James Henry dissatisfied and uncomfortable, he added, "Look, why don't you go out to the *Maid*, anyway. Find out how they are coming with the pumping and the trying out."

"Good, good, good," John James Henry said, rising at once. He sounded happier with a specific task to perform. "I'll get news on everything and even pray as I go, too."

When John James Henry left, Jake picked up the limp hand he had patted. "Come on," he urged, holding Zacch's fingers to his lips. "Get better." He sat like that, oblivious to the village life going on around him. People laughed and called to each other. Women swished by with baskets or water gourds on their heads. Naked children played with puppies. Men sat under shady trees, sharpening spears or swapping stories. Jake saw none of it.

It was almost noon when Zacch opened his eyes again. His face, now covered in stubble, was still flushed with fever, but his eyes were less confused than before. Without turning his head, he whispered, "Jake?"

Jake, still clutching his hand, bent over him immediately. "I'm right here," he managed to say. His throat seemed closed and tight.

A spasm of pain made Zacch's eyes screw shut for a moment. When it passed, he said, "It doesn't seem as though I'll see Nantucket, again." Another bubble of blood formed with his words.

Tears were rolling down Jake's cheeks as he tenderly dabbed at Zacch's lips. "Nay," he admitted. "It doesn't seem so. You're sailing in shoal waters, now."

"Tell Sarah," Zacch started to say, then had to pause to gain strength. "Tell Sarah to forget about me. Marry someone else and live a happy life. Tell her, Jake." His eyes shut again. He was exhausted by the long speech.

"I will, Zacch. I will." Jake's voice was hoarse.

After a minute, Zacch's eyes struggled open, again. In an even fainter voice, he said, "Tell China..." He hesitated once more, this time to reshape his thought. "Nay, 'tis not necessary to tell her anything. She knows." He coughed up more blood.

As Jake wiped away the bright red trail, Zacch suddenly rolled his head toward Jake and weakly gripped his wrist. "Take care of her, Jake," he said, urgently. "She needs you."

Jake covered the fingers clutching him, with his free hand. "Don't fret," he said. "I'll take care of her. Always. I promise you that."

This time, Zacch could not summon the strength to speak. He simply nodded and attempted to smile. Worn out, his eyes closed again. After a moment, his shallow breathing stopped.

Jake saw Zacch's chest cease its imperceptible rise and fall. He felt the life slip out of the hand he was holding in his own. Yet he couldn't believe it. It seemed impossible that Zacch was gone. Outside the hut, a mother scolded her child, a young girl giggled. Nothing in the world had changed. Nothing save Zacch.

Jake dropped his face into the lifeless hand he was still clasping. Grief knotted his heart, torturing him. Never before had he felt so anguished, so all alone. Tears streamed down his face now, but even they couldn't relieve the sorrow that choked him.

HALF A WORLD AWAY, China sat up in her bed screaming. As the hysterical sound penetrated her sleep, she woke, though the images in her mind remained vivid. She had been dreaming. She had dreamed that an enraged whale, its tough hide bristling with lances, had come alongside the *China Maid*. With a flip of its powerful flukes, it had swept Zacch from the deck. As he had struggled in the churning sea, red with blood and snapping with sharks, the whale's flukes had found him again. With another flip, Zacch had catapulted into the air and had fallen, fallen, fallen, into the wide open mouth of the whale. It had clamped shut its mighty jaws and Zacch was gone.

China fell back against her pillow, sobbing brokenheartedly. This was the sign she had been waiting for. The sign she had been dreading. Zacch was dead.

12

NANTUCKET
June 1844

"I NEED HALF A POUND of sultanas, today, dear," Mrs. Coleman announced, as she waddled over to the counter. China sighed and reached for the jar of sultanas. Mrs. Coleman, in addition to being extremely broad abeam, was an incessant talker. China knew she'd hear about the entire Coleman clan before this purchase was completed. She cast an envious glance out the bay window in front, just catching a glimpse of June blue sky through the merchandise piled on display.

"Not the ones on top, dear," Mrs. Coleman instructed, while China shook some golden sultanas into the brass bowl of the scale. "They tend to be more dried out. The ones underneath are plumper. Mr. C likes them plump. I make a nice sweet bread for his Sunday dinner and he always comments if the sultanas aren't plump enough.

"Elspeth, on the other hand (that's my youngest who's just gotten betrothed to Seth Folger who works at the Pacific Bank), Elspeth likes them drier and chewier, but we have to please her papa. When she's running her own house, she can make her cakes as she wishes. My boys, though, David and Nathaniel, neither of them like sultanas at all. Why, every time I set a slice of sweet bread in front of either one, I get back a plate with all the sultanas sitting in a little pile.''

Her hand, rather plump itself, reached into the brass bowl to snatch a few treats. China resisted the urge to slap the fat fingers. ''They're all quite good, Mrs. Coleman,'' she said, evenly. ''This shipment has just arrived from Spain.''

''Of course, dear, I'm sure you are right,'' Mrs. Coleman said, wedging the sultanas into her mouth between words. ''My oldest girl, Abagail . . .'' Abagail's preference in dried fruit was drowned out by the tremendous pealing of the Lisbon bell and excited shouts from the sidewalk outside.

China's heart stopped, then started thumping wildly. There was a ship at the Bar! Despite herself, hope pounded through her. She wanted to drop the big jar she was holding and race for the wharves, exhilarated with anticipation, eager to welcome home her father and brother. Then she remembered the dream she had had, and her waking realization that Zacch would never return again. She would never see her tall, handsome twin striding down the lane, his sea chest on his shoulder, a glad grin on his face.

The grief that had sickened her that early morning now stuck in her throat. Zacch was dead. Probably buried at sea. Gone, like her mother, like Aunt Judith, resting forever in an unmarked grave. With her certainty of Zacch's death came her assumption that the *China Maid* was lost, too, that the sea had claimed her childhood home, had taken her father.

Her hope faltered and faded. The clamor of the Lisbon bell, ebulliently announcing a returning whaler, had no more meaning for her. Her eternal waiting and wondering was over; her ship would not be coming in. She forced her mind back to the half pound of sultanas, sitting partially wrapped on the counter. With numb, fumbling fingers, she twirled the brown paper into a cone and folded over the top. She took Mrs. Coleman's money and counted out the change, nodding her acknowledgment of the woman's unheard chatter.

When the shop was empty again, China just stood behind the counter, feather duster and broom untouched. Mrs. Mitchell looked over from the shelf of shawls she was rearranging, ready to prompt her employee into action. When she saw the bereft look on China's face, however, she refrained. She was not an imaginative woman, nor one to waste time on sentiment, but she was the wife and mother of whalers.

"'Tis a hard thing to hear the Lisbon bell welcoming home a ship, when you've still one at sea," she commented to no one in particular. "'Tis even harder when yours is overdue." China finally registered the remarks and turned to face Mrs. Mitchell, her gray eyes somber.

"My husband was once fourteen months overdue," the shopkeeper said. This was the most personal statement she had ever made to China, her own brisk way of expressing compassion. "He returned with a good lay, though. Daniel, my second son, on the other hand, was drowned when a whale stove his boat. His captain gave me half a lay."

China was astonished, as much by this intimate exchange as by Mrs. Mitchell's matter-of-fact way of recounting her loss. She couldn't imagine that there would ever come a time when she would be able to speak so casually about Zacch or her father. "Wasn't thee heartbroken?" she asked, incredulously.

Mrs. Mitchell regarded her in puzzlement. She wasn't sure what China meant. "Of course I was saddened," she finally said, "but life goes on." She turned back to the summer shawls, effectively ending the conversation.

WHEN CHINA LEFT THE SHOP at six that evening, the sky was still blue and the sun was still making pretty patterns on the cobblestones. She walked up Centre Street, then stopped at the corner. Against her will, she looked down Main Street to Straight Wharf. A throng of people and the luffing lighter sails beckoned her. Resolutely, she looked the other way, toward home, toward her empty little house and her lonely bed.

"Life goes on," Mrs. Mitchell had said. And so it did. It was time she realized it. It was time for her to accept her life and make of it what she could, starting in Mitchell's General Emporium. It was time she stopped daydreaming about grand careers and concentrated on being a clerk. It was time she stopped regarding her employment as a temporary adventure in independence, albeit a dreary experience, and reconciled herself to the fact that neither Papa nor Zacch was going to rescue her. Most of all, it was time to stop being haunted by Jake. Whether living or dead, he had left her. She was alone. "Life goes on."

China moved firmly in the direction of her house, going not more than a dozen steps before her pace lagged. She came to an uncertain halt, then swore softly in the coal-scuttle brim of her bonnet. She turned around and started swiftly for the docks.

The lighter was just tying up to the pilings when China edged through the crowd. A tall, lean man with straight, dark hair and a stern expression was stepping ashore. He was no one China knew. Her disappointment was so sharp, tears came to her eyes. Angrily she chastised herself for expecting the impossible, calling herself a fool.

"What ship is this?" she asked a small boy next to her. He was balanced on a barrel, craning to see above the crowd.

He looked at her, only a little surprised to see a woman on the wharf. In any event, his pleasure at being able to impart important information overcame any amazement. "'Tis the bark *Sally Ann*," he announced, proudly. "She's been out three and a half years and has come home with twenty-seven hundred barrels of sperm below. That tall man is her master."

"Thank thee," China muttered, turning away. The boy's words had hit her like physical blows, driving home her dejection. She was almost at the head of the wharf before she stopped again. This time she sighed wearily, then turned and retraced her steps down the dock. She had one last hope.

She waited patiently behind the crowd of men pressing against the captain, all demanding news of the Pacific. As one man after another caught sight of China, their loud questions ceased, and they turned to stare. An aisle opened up, and China determinedly marched down it, halting a few paces from the *Sally Ann*'s master. On closer inspection he seemed more melancholy than grim; his deep brown eyes were almost gentle. And astonished.

"Can thee tell me, please, if thee bespoke the ship *China Maid* at any point during thy voyage?" she asked in a slightly quavering voice.

It took a moment for China's tremulous question to penetrate Shubael's shock at seeing a young woman, in undeniably decorous dress, unescorted on the dock. His surprise increased when she tilted her head up toward him and he peered down the long tunnel of her bonnet. The neat fringe of her shiny black bangs, the unusual charcoal accents of her large, gray eyes, the exotic cast of her creamy cheeks, all intrigued him, but the wistful expression on her lovely face stirred something in his heart.

He finally answered her with deep regret. "Nay, miss. We did not bespeak a ship by that name." He was about to ask her the *Maid*'s departure date, or the design of her pennant, just to detain her, but her great, gray eyes grew misty with tears and her firm chin quavered. She nodded her thanks and walked away, seemingly oblivious to the suggestive sounds and guffaws of the assembled sailors. Shubael gave an inward shrug and turned to answer the next inquiry.

THE EARLY SUMMER SUN felt mellow on Shubael's shoulders as he strode across the commons, his coat under his arm. It was Sunday, First Day, as the Quakers called it, and his mother had insisted he accompany her to Meeting this morning. As he had sat in the silent church, with hundreds of Friends piously pondering, it had not been spiritual enlightenment that had filled his mind, but images of Amedee. In all his months at sea, sailing ever farther from her, his longing for her had not diminished one whit. It was in moments like those in Meeting, when his body and thoughts were idle, that his memory of her was most vivid and his hunger most intense.

It had been impossible to spend the afternoon in his mother's parlor, listening to her self-righteous complaints and watching the sad face of Susannah, the last of his sisters left at home. The austerity and the gloom in that room had been an unbearable contrast to the lush, tropical sensations seething inside him. He had sought release in walking through the quiet streets and lanes of town and out onto the moors, green and fresh and fragrant with wild roses.

He alternately attempted to exorcise the memory of Amedee and to cherish it, telling himself that there was no way he could have her, yet unwilling to give her up. Somehow, the honorable reasons that had seemed so compelling, so all important, for leaving La Digue seemed fuzzy and out of focus here at home. His father's debt, though substantially reduced, still existed, his need to succeed still existed, but their significance was dimming. The only thing that seemed real anymore was Amedee; the interesting almond shape of her soft brown eyes, the three delicate dots on her cheek, the singsong lilt of her husky voice as she called to him in Creole.

Shubael stopped in midstride, shaking his head as if to unplug his ears, but the singing persisted. For a minute he thought he was losing his mind, that he was hallucinating. Then he realized that although the song sounded like the Seychelles, it was not in Creole, but in French. He caught his breath, aware only then that his heart had been racing and his spirit had soared in hope. In the aftermath came an ache of loneliness.

He followed the song to its source and was surprised to find the young Quaker woman from the wharf. Today, however, she did not appear so plain and proper as she bent to pick wild strawberries on a sunny, sloping meadow by Capaum Pond. She was barefoot and bareheaded, her short, silky hair ruffled by the light breeze. The sleeves of her gray muslin gown were rolled up above her elbows and its hem was knotted around her waist, exposing long, slim limbs with porcelain-white skin.

Despite the indecent manner of her dress, Shubael did not find her wanton. Perhaps it was the aura of naturalness surrounding her as she picked berries, unaware of his presence, or the sad timbre of her tone as she sang an old ballad. Or perhaps it was that somehow she reminded him of Amedee. Again Shubael shook his head, this time less vigorously, simply denying the resemblance.

She was way too tall, and certainly not the same rich, café-au-lait color. Her face was not nearly as round, and her eyes, though they were now turned down, were totally different. He remembered her gray eyes, with their unique charcoal circles, as they had clouded over with tears of disappointment. He shook his head again. There was nothing about this Nantucket woman that was similar to his Seychelloise beauty. And yet there was.

Moving as noisily as possible, to warn her he was there, Shubael descended the slope toward her. He was curious about her, strangely drawn to her. It was more than the French song she was singing; he sensed something else. He was no more than ten feet from her when she finally heard him scuffling through the brush. She looked up, startled, straddling her pail, her normally pink lips stained a remarkable red, her clear skin faintly flushed from the sun.

"Oh," she said. "'Tis thee."

"Aye," Shubael acknowledged.

They studied each other for a moment, then she loosened the knot of her skirt so it fell to her feet, not, it seemed, out of embarrassment or modesty, but out of a suddenly remembered sense that that was what she was supposed to do. The innocence of her gesture made him smile, the harshness of his expression vanishing as his dimples appeared. She looked startled again, then uncertainly bent back to the berries.

China was feeling more than usually lonely today. The *Sally Ann*'s failure to sight the *China Maid* somehow underscored her certainty that Zacch was dead, the ship lost at sea. She was feeling abandoned, both by fate and by her family, and, despite herself, especially by Jake. She had been desolately contemplating a future completely alone, when she had heard the swishing of meadow grass and had looked up to see the tall master of the *Sally Ann*.

She wondered what he was doing there, with his shirt unbuttoned, his sleeves rolled up and his hands shoved in his pockets. The casualness of his clothes reminded her of her own improper appearance and she grudgingly released her hitched-up skirt to wind around her legs and to get caught on the brush. When he smiled at her action, she was astounded at the change in his face. He looked young and untroubled, strangely appealing. She wasn't sure how to react to his sudden attractiveness, his intrusion on her solitude. She stooped to pick strawberries.

Shubael watched her for a few minutes, not knowing what to say, but not wanting to leave. He thought of a dozen polite phrases, but they all seemed absurd in this situation. In the end, he simply laid down his coat and began to pick berries by her side. When his first handful of strawberries dropped into her pail, she glanced sideways, around a shiny hank of hair. He was aware of her puzzled gaze, but he didn't return it, instead keeping his eyes on the ground while his long fingers searched among the low leaves for the tiny ripe fruit. He didn't want to alarm her.

China didn't know why this quiet captain was picking strawberries with her, but after a while, she found his presence comforting. They moved silently from patch to patch, neither making any demands, but each feeling a lessening of loneliness. When at last the pail was full, they sat down on the slope and watched the sun descending in the sky. The reeds around Capaum Pond, in front of them, seemed spun from gold. Beyond the pond rose the bluff and the small grove of pine trees where she had lain naked next to Jake. China tore her eyes away from the bluff and fastened them on some deep depressions near the pond.

"Did thee know that the first town on Nantucket was here?" she asked suddenly, attempting to divert her mind. "'Twas called Sherbourne."

"Aye, I knew it," Shubael replied. "The pond was open to the Sound in those days."

She pointed toward the depressions in the earth. "Did thee also know that those are the cellars of the first houses on Nantucket?" she asked. "When the town moved to the harbor in the early seventeen hundreds, people took everything with them but the cellars."

"Aye, Nantucketers have always been a very thrifty lot," Shubael said, dryly. When China looked at him sharply, he hastily added, "'Tis as it should be on a treeless island when all the lumber has to be brought over from the continent."

China looked down, amazed at the irony in his voice. When she had seen him on Straight Wharf, he had seemed the very essence of a correct Quaker captain. Now, as he idly snared a berry or two off the top of the pail to pop in his mouth, he seemed considerably less conservative. "If thee had lived here then, would thee have not moved thy house?" she asked.

Shubael shrugged. He stretched his long legs out and leaned back on his elbows, the late afternoon sun burnishing the deep tan on his angular face. "Perhaps not," he said. "'Tis rather peaceful here."

"*I* would not have moved," China declared, firmly. She sat with her forearms resting lightly on her upturned knees, her hands clasped loosely together. "'Tis too crowded in town. Why, at the last census there were over nine thousand people living on the island, to say nothing of those that come and go with the tide. And most of them clumped in town like mussels on a rock."

"But if they were all spread out, how would they know their neighbor's business?" The irony was back in Shubael's voice, tinged with bitterness. "Nantucketers like to have each other in their sights at all times. 'Tis quicker to condemn some unlucky person's transgressions that way."

China looked sharply sideways, again. She had often had similar feelings herself. She was always particularly annoyed by the meddling visits from committees of Friends or by the high moral tone of the community pillars. Now, however, she felt somewhat defensive. "The wind blows both ways," she said. "They are also quick to come to each other's aid."

Shubael lay back on the grass, his hands tucked behind his head. He was as surprised as she was by his cynical observations. Never before had he questioned the virtuous ways he had been brought up to believe in. He felt a twinge of guilt and sought to make amends. "Of course, thee is right," he said, by way of apology. "Even at sea, Nantucketers will sail for days out of their way to help another islander. 'Tis almost like a family."

Again China looked his way, this time suspicious of the sudden temperance of his tone. He didn't seem to notice her glance as he stared at the sky, chewing a shaft of grass. She turned back to look at the pond, perfectly reflecting the reeds around it. She set her elbows on her knees and rested her chin on her hands. For a while they sat in comfortable silence. Then, speculating again, she said, "Perhaps if the town had not moved to the harbor, Nantucket would still be an island of sheep farms. Perhaps no one would have thought to go off whaling."

A snort of disbelief escaped Shubael before he had time to think about it. "I doubt that," he said. "Nantucketers have always found their way to the ocean. And to the ocean beyond that one. They can no more do without the sea than the fish can. 'Tis why they moved the town to begin with."

"Thee seems to be quite an expert on Nantucketers," China said, tartly.

Shubael rolled his head toward her and grinned. His smile worked its usual magic and erased ten years and untold tension from his face. His teeth showed white and even around the blade of grass still clamped between them. "Nay, not an expert," he said, "Just a Nantucketer." He pulled the grass from his mouth and tossed it away. "But I'll wager thee is not. No Quaker miss who sings sad songs of love in French could be born here."

"Nay, I was not born here," China admitted, with a little reluctance. She was still feeling altruistic toward her adopted island. "But I'm half a Nantucketer, at least. Papa's family came here a hundred and fifty years ago, and I've lived here since I was nine years old."

"A veritable aeon," he said, teasingly, his smile coming back. "It must be thy other half, then, that taught thee French ballads."

China cocked her head in his direction, afraid he was making fun of her. Her mistrust melted when confronted by his engaging grin. "Aye. I spoke French before I spoke English," she said cautiously. Then gaining confidence, she continued, "My mother was French. She was a laundress near Le Havre when Papa went to France to go whaling. She met him on the beach and married him four years later. My brother and I were born there, while he was away at sea."

Shubael turned on his side and propped himself up on his elbow. "'Tis a good thing, then, that the town of Sherbourne moved to the harbor," he said, still smiling, "and that the men of Nantucket decided to go whaling. If there were no whaling, thee would not be here picking strawberries, but in France washing clothes."

She laughed, suddenly realizing it was the first time in months she'd felt that tickling sound in her throat. It felt good. "If it were not for whaling, I'd not be on earth at all," she said. "I would not be me, but someone totally different. Perhaps I would have been a Nantucketer like Papa, or perhaps I would have been French like Maman. But thy tie to whaling is far more direct. Where would thee be if there was no whaling in Nantucket?''

Shubael's face became thoughtful and he turned his gaze toward the ground. He absently picked at a piece of heather while he pondered her question. Whaling was his salvation as much as his private prison. Without whaling he would never be able to repay his father's debt, never escape the severity of his mother's home and philosophy. Without whaling he would never have met Amedee, and his life would have been meaningless. Despite the fact that his enormous love for her caused him his greatest grief, it had also given him unaccountable happiness.

He looked up at China. Her head still rested on her hands, one strand of shiny hair falling carelessly across a creamy cheek, amusement giving her unusual gray eyes an inviting warmth. He forced himself to respond with appropriate lightness.

"'Tis hard to say where I'd be," he said. "I presume it likely I'd be in Ohio, like so many other nonwhaling Nantucketers, ploughing fields and feeding pigs." Before she could probe any deeper, he turned the conversation back to her. "But what of thy whaling Papa? Is it he thee was inquiring for when thee asked about the *China Maid*?''

The humorous expression faded from China's face. She looked back at the pond as she carefully answered, "The *China Maid* is my father's ship. He is the owner and the captain. My brother is also on board." And so is Jake, she thought, but she didn't say it out loud. She didn't want to acknowledge his existence, to make it any easier for him to creep into her consciousness. She didn't want to admit that though she grieved for Zacch and sorely missed Papa, she was desperately frightened of a future without Jake. "'Tis fifteen months overdue," she added, brokenly.

Shubael sat up, stricken by the sorrow in her voice. "Fifteen months is not so very long," he said, inexplicably wanting to soothe her. "Any number of things could cause the delay. Thy papa could have decided to cruise one more season to fill the hold. Or a storm could have blown them off course. Or they could be in some snug port making repairs." Like La Digue, he thought.

China looked back to Shubael, resentment flaring in her eyes. "Fifteen months may not seem so long if thee is sitting on a ship, but 'tis much longer when thee is waiting on shore," she said, roughly.

Impressed by the intensity of her emotions, Shubael quietly said, "Aye, thee is right." He could hear the distress in her voice, could sense the pain she was feeling. For the first time he realized that this was how Amedee must be suffering, waiting futilely for him to return. A wave of guilt washed over him, making him feel sick and sodden. "'Tis a miserable occupation," he muttered.

"Then why does thee do it?" China cried, both enraged and amazed. She sat upright. She had never heard a whaling man say that before.

Shubael dropped his face into his hands, rubbing his forehead with his fingers. Why indeed? He struggled again to bring his reasons into focus, to rediscover the clarity, the certainty, with which he had made his decisions. It evaded him. He only knew that he had to doggedly pursue his current course, to do his duty. He shook his head, peering at her through his fingers. "I don't know," he admitted. "Perhaps because I'm not ploughing fields and feeding pigs in Ohio."

China swallowed. She sat for a while, snapping twigs and dried weeds, her anger abating. She couldn't sustain her usual sense of outrage and injustice. Perhaps it was because the *Sally Ann*'s captain had such a beguiling grin, or perhaps it was because he seemed as much a victim of whaling as she. They both owed their existences to the industry that lit the lamps of civilized cities all over the world, but neither one could easily accept it, each obviously suffered from it.

They sat for a long while, neither one saying anything, but both finding solace in the other's presence. When the sun settled just on top of the pine grove on the bluff, and the sky turned pink and lavender and gray, China rose, brushing the leaves from her skirt. "'Tis late," she said, a little regretfully. "I must go home."

As she jammed her feet into her shoes and gathered up her bonnet and scarf, Shubael rose, too. "Let me see thee home," he offered. "I can carry thy pail of berries." He reached for the wooden handle at the same moment she did.

For an instant they stood head to head, hands touching, then China backed away, her heart suddenly beating rapidly. "I have no wish to take thee out of thy way," she said, somewhat uncertainly.

Once again, the appealing smile spread across Shubael's face. "On the contrary," he said, with total honesty, "thee would be doing me a favor. Nothing I look forward to is nearly so agreeable as the afternoon I have passed in thy company. 'Twould be a kindness to prolong it."

China stared at him, her wide eyes reflecting both her fascination with his smile and her pleasure with his words. "Very well," she willingly consented. Her heart returned to normal, her nervousness ceased.

They said very little else on the long walk home, only once commenting on a brilliant cock pheasant that flew out of a thicket of bayberry in front of them. It was a companionable silence, though, each finding a respite from the separate memories that haunted them. When they arrived at China's gate, she took the pail of strawberries from him, but continued to stand with one hand on the latch. Oddly, she didn't want the afternoon to end, either.

"There's a great pot of mutton stew simmering since this morning," she said, shyly. "And I can make beaten biscuits or soda bread. And I think there is a bit of cheese still, in the cupboard. And strawberries." She held the pail up for his inspection as if he disbelieved her. "Would thee care to stay for supper?"

"I would," Shubael answered immediately. Then, as a thought struck him, he added, "Perhaps I should tell thee my name and ask thee thine. I am Shubael Brown."

China laughed for the second time that day, enjoying it as much as before. The laughter wiped away any temporary bashfulness. "We're a fine pair," she remarked. "Between us we've not even enough social grace to make proper introductions.

"Well, Shubael Brown, I am China Joy, and now that we are such old friends, thee can come in the kitchen door instead of through the parlor."

She opened the gate and held it for him, but he grinned, gave a mock bow and said, "My manners are not altogether absent. After thee." China returned his bow with an exaggerated curtsey, then swept through the white picket gate in front of him. Both felt completely at ease.

Inside the house, China set the pail of strawberries on the table and hung her bonnet on its peg. "Thee can hang thy coat here," she said, as she went to the stove to stoke up the fire. When the embers came alive and snapped at the new wood she'd slid in, she shut the door and turned her attention to the kettle on top. She lifted the lid to stir the stew, and its aroma, redolent of spring onions and rosemary, filled the room.

"It should be good," she said, glancing toward Shubael. "What is it? What happened?" she asked, alarmed.

"Thee looks like the wind has blown out thy sails." Shubael was standing in the doorway, a puzzled expression on his face.

"But where is thy mother?" he asked. "And the rest of thy family?"

"Ah." China understood the cause of his bewilderment. She set the lid back on the kettle and turned to face him. "My mother died when I was nine," she explained. "After that, Papa brought me here to live with my great aunt Judith, but she died, too, last year. I've only one brother and he is at sea with Papa, so I live here all alone. Does thee feel uncomfortable? Would thee rather not stay to supper? 'Tis no matter to me." She was not entirely truthful about that last statement.

Shubael looked at her squarely. "Nay, China," he said. "I do not feel uncomfortable, and I would rather not leave." He continued to study her until a flush of embarrassment crept across her creamy cheeks and her lovely eyes lowered, showing only a fringe of lashes. He realized now just how desperately she wanted the *China Maid* to return. On board were her only living relatives; without them she was completely alone. "Thee is a remarkable woman, China Joy," he said softly.

Her blush deepened and her eyes shot briefly toward his before she turned back to the stew. "Thee can sit on one of these chairs or pull the rocker from the parlor, while I fix the biscuits," she said over her shoulder. She rummaged in the cupboard for all the equipment and ingredients.

While she worked, Shubael sat in a kitchen chair, tilted back against the wall. He enjoyed watching her sure, graceful movements, the swing of her straight-cut hair and shiny bangs as she beat the biscuit batter. He liked seeing her lay out two plates and two forks and fill two cups with water. A feeling of tranquillity pervaded his senses, a feeling of comfort and calm. If it wasn't as wonderful as watching Amedee pound peppercorns and ginger in her mortar and pestle, or set coconut-shell bowls in the sand, it soothed the ache of not having her.

China, too, felt a sense of contentment. It was satisfying to be preparing food for someone else's appreciation, to be sharing a meal instead of eating in solitude. Shubael, with his irresistible smile and his imperturbable manner, acted as a balm for her gnawing loneliness. He might not excite the same spirit in her as Jake, but he seemed to accept her without question. She was glad he was here.

The mutton stew was hot and savory; the biscuits were light and smooth. They ate with little conversation, but with great enjoyment. It had been a long time since either had had a good meal in sympathetic company. When the June dusk finally diminished, China lit a candle and they sat in its soft light, sated. "Would thee like more berries? Or a cup of tea?" China asked, anxious to extend the mellow atmosphere.

Shubael shook his head and leaned back in his chair. "Supper was excellent," he said, quietly. "Thee has given me a great pleasure."

For some reason, his kind words and subdued tone sent a stir through China. She rose quickly, to cover her confusion, and cleared the table. As she was stacking the dishes in the sink, she heard Shubael's chair scraping back and his steady footsteps toward her. Involuntarily, she closed her eyes, waiting, suddenly longing for him to touch her. Every nerve in her body was alive, remembering his hands next to hers on the berry bucket, anticipating the thrill of contact.

When his long fingers combed through her hair and gently traced the curve of her neck, a shock ran through her, electrifying her with need. She turned toward him as his arms formed a circle around her, lifted her face as his lowered to hers. She felt the strength of his lean, hard body, felt the heat of his sunbronzed skin. She felt her breasts, suddenly swollen and sensitive, pressed against his chest, felt herself seeking, needing, wanting. Then his lips covered hers with a tender kiss.

The desire drained out of her. The tension, the tremors, the tantalizing sensations ceased. He was not Jake. It was Jake she sought, Jake she wanted. Jake whose kisses filled her needs. Shubael was not the same. She turned her face away, even as Shubael raised his head. She was grateful he did not pursue his course, only peripherally aware that he seemed suddenly withdrawn himself. His arms fell from her and they moved apart.

"I think I'd best go home," Shubael said. There was neither embarrassment nor shame in his voice, only a deep sadness. He had thought he could lose himself with China, but he was wrong. Her silky black hair was not the same as Amedee's thick curls, her creamy white skin did not smell like cinnamon. She could not make him forget Amedee.

China did not attempt to detain him now. "Aye, 'tis late," she said.

"Thank thee very much for supper," Shubael said, politely. "And for the pleasant afternoon." His tone grew more sincere as he remembered their easy companionship.

"Aye, 'twas most enjoyable." China was equally polite.

"I shall call on thee again," Shubael said. He was more questioning than declaring, more courteous than enthusiastic.

"I am employed at Mrs. Mitchell's Emporium all week," China said, by way of an answer. "I truly have no free time."

"Ahh, I see." For a moment Shubael's preoccupation was pierced by his renewed admiration for China's courage as he thought of her earning her way alone in the world. Then his own memories overwhelmed him again. "Perhaps next First Day, then," he concluded.

"Aye, perhaps." China was as indifferent as he.

They went their ways that evening and the following week, hardly thinking about Shubael's vague promise. As China swept and dusted and waited on customers, and as Shubael sorted through the final details of his trip, they coped with their freshly opened wounds. That brief moment of aroused desire had taunted them. It had offered them an ecstatic release from the voices and faces that haunted them, an opportunity to resume lives suspended by impossible yearnings. But in the end, the offer was unfulfilled. Instead, it stirred up the pain they had long been suppressing.

By the end of the week, however, the hurt subsided again and the monotony of their lonely lives reasserted itself. It was then that they remembered the pleasure they had felt just being in each other's presence. On Sunday, China flew about her chores, wondering if Shubael really would show up, frequently peering out a window to look for him in the lane. She had almost given up on him, unwilling to admit how disappointed she was, when he appeared at the kitchen door.

A smile of relief and welcome lit up China's lovely face. "I thought that thee had forgotten," she said, happy that he hadn't.

"Thee is not that easy to forget, China Joy," Shubael replied, honestly. "But it looks as if I have come at the wrong moment. It seems that thee is going out. Perhaps I should call some other time."

"Nay, 'tis perfectly fine," China said, hastily. "I had thought to walk to Abiah Macy's, by Macy's Pond. He keeps bees and will always sell me a jar of honey. But 'tis not necessary. Shall I make tea?'' She went to fill the kettle at the pump in the sink.

"I know Abiah," Shubael said, leaning casually against the door frame. "And I know he sells his honey in town. Would it not be easier to buy it there?"

China laughed and answered, "Of course, it would be much easier, but then I wouldn't have a walk." She set the kettle on the stove and reached into the box for firewood.

"Wait then," Shubael said. He straightened up, reaching to stay her hand. This time his touch did not send a thrill through her, this time it was just a friendly grip, warm contact. "I'm not desperate to drink tea and I could do with a walk, as well. There's only so far I can stretch my legs on a hundred feet of deck. May I accompany thee?"

"Of course thee may," China said, delightedly dropping the firewood and reaching for her bonnet. "In truth, I hate to spend a fine afternoon such as this in the parlor. We've all winter to stay indoors, huddled by the hearth." She grabbed up the honey pot and stepped outside.

Shubael shut the door behind them then took the crock from China, stowing it easily under his arm. "I'm beginning to get to know thee," he said, as he followed her down the narrow path. "And I suspect that thee would prefer to sail around in a full typhoon than to ever sit huddled in thy parlor." He opened the gate and held it for her. "I also suspect," he said, passing through the gate and clicking it closed, "that thee would sooner tie a lead weight to thy hat and drop it in the deepest part of the harbor than to hoist it to thy head."

"Twice right," China said with a grin, tossing the long-brimmed bonnet in question over her shoulder by its ribbons. "Does that lead thee to think I'm a scandalous creature? Or simply one who is daft?"

"Neither," Shubael replied. His own face broke into an enchanting smile. "It leads me to think I would like to know more about thee, and how thee came about such sensible ideas."

China laughed. She laughed a long, contented time, flushing away all her gloomy feelings and heavyheartedness. Then she told him. She told him about toddling around the fields in France with Zacch and about living aboard the *China Maid*, about swimming and rowing and climbing the rigging, about arriving in Nantucket dressed in duck trousers and shark's teeth, about exploring every dune and cove on the island and being outcast from the other children her age.

"But thee can't mean it," Shubael protested. By now they were well beyond town and he was carrying his wool jacket the same way she had slung her hat. His long legs made easy work of the rutted road. "Just because thee had an unusual hairstyle and a bit of an accent is no reason to shun thee. Why, I should think that with thy beauty and thy whaling background, thee would have been a heroine among thy peers." He shook his head disgustedly. "They must have been jealous."

China laughed. "That's what Harriet always said, too. Aye," she answered when Shubael raised his eyebrows in question. "I did have one friend. I still do, though I haven't had a good gam with her in ages. Harriet Swain is the kindest person I've ever met."

Shubael stopped still in the road. The bright yellow petals of Scotch broom blossoms drifted in the breeze to his feet. "I know Harriet," he said, quietly. "Her father is the owner of the *Sally Ann*. I've made three trips for him."

"For Benjamin Swain?" China asked delightedly. "Then thee knows Harriet and can verify how good she is."

263

"Aye, I can," Shubael said, thoughtfully, slowly walking again. "And I've ample reason to know how good and generous her father is, as well."

For the rest of the way to Abiah Macy's beehives he told her about his childhood on the island, about the bad fortune and bankruptcy that hounded all his father's ventures, about how his lay always went to pay back the debt, about his querulous mother and each of his seven siblings. On the way back from Abiah's, with a jar full of dark, wildflower honey, he told her about his life at sea, how he had risen from cabin boy to captain. Unlike last week, when they had spent hours in silence, today they talked constantly.

That evening, over a supper of minted fresh pea soup and hot cornbread with honey, they talked some more. It was almost as if they were making up for the previous week, or as if they were letting their lonely feelings out with a rush. They told each other everything about themselves. Except the most important parts.

China told him about Zacch and the dream she had had, about Papa and Aunt Judith, even about Obed, but she never mentioned Jake. Shubael told her all about his father and his fear of failure, but he never said a word about Amedee. When they finally parted, late that night, Shubael held China's hands in his and pressed a kiss against her porcelain cheek. It was enough.

OVER THE FOLLOWING WEEKS, Shubael's visits became more regular. He had supper with China two or three nights during the week, in addition to every Sunday, often arriving home before she did, and always bringing some provisions, a ball of sweet butter and a slab of cheese, or a basket of new potatoes and a rasher of freshly smoked bacon. It satisfied some sense in him to set the food in her cupboard, just as it continually pleased him to watch her prepare it. He almost felt as if he belonged in this little house with this beautiful woman.

Shubael wasn't sure exactly when he formed the idea, or how it came to be, but he was suddenly conscious of his wish to ask China to marry him. He knew she wasn't Amedee, knew she would never claim him completely, but perhaps China could chase away those fierce longings he felt whenever he thought of the Seychelles.

It could work, he thought. It could mean contentment for both of them. China, despite the eccentric manner he admired, was nominally Quaker and almost a Nantucketer. She would make a respectable wife, an elegant asset to a successful man. She would keep him moored to this island where his duty and responsibility lay; she would anchor him with her seductive gray eyes and her clear creamy skin, with her sense of humor and her courage. Her unique ability to be both bold and tender would make him forget the Seychelles, in time, would give him reason to return to Nantucket, as he should.

Not a small part of his decision revolved around the satisfaction he found in giving to China. He wanted to do more than bring her a pail of oysters or a quart of cream. He wanted to fill a gap in her life, to lessen her loneliness, even as he was easing his own. He felt the urge to provide for her so she could leave that store, where the sunlight rarely found its way past the piles of merchandise. She belonged in the fresh air, and it would give him pleasure to put her there.

Shubael went over and over the idea in his mind. Though something in his heart lurched every time he imagined being married to China, irrevocably severed from Amedee, from his sweet, sensuous beauty with three delicious dots on her round cheek, he told himself it was a wise course, it would be clear sailing. He and China were already good friends; they would overcome their obvious lack of desire. It would be a placid marriage. Shubael ignored the fact that neither he nor China was complacent by nature; he ignored the fact that he was plotting a marriage without love.

Having decided to make a proper marriage, he further decided to make a proper proposal. He felt that decency demanded that China meet his mother first. Accordingly, he got Prudence to write a grudging invitation to supper on Sixth Day, then delivered it to China, himself.

"But why should thy mother want me to come to her home?" China asked, perplexed. She stood with her hip cocked against the cupboard, one hand stirring the corn cakes batter, the other holding the meager message.

Shubael tilted his chair against the wall and folded his arms across his chest. "Because I would like thee to meet her," he answered. "I can promise thee that it will not be enjoyable, for she has a narrow and gloomy sight on life, nonetheless, it would be a favor to me if thee accepts."

"Of course I shall," China agreed, still puzzled. "But it can't be as unpleasant as thee pretends."

BY EIGHT O'CLOCK Saturday evening, China readily admitted how mistaken she had been. The evening was worse than Shubael had predicted. Not only was his mother overbearing and critical, and his sister pathetic, but Shubael seemed to withdraw inside himself. The smile that magically made his lean face so handsome was nowhere in evidence. Instead, he wore the harsh, haunted expression that China had seen that day on the dock.

While she struggled valiantly to make conversation in the face of Mrs. Brown's self-righteous remarks and Susannah's nervous monosyllables, Shubael remained silent. It was almost as if he were not in the room. Although China could well understand his wish to absent himself from such an oppressive atmosphere, she began to feel annoyed that he was not coming to her aid. Still, she tried her utmost.

Remembering everything Aunt Judith had ever drilled into her, China sat with her back straight, her feet on the floor, her hands in her lap, and her tone refined and respectful. By the time the roast was served, a pain was searing between her shoulder blades, a result of her rigid posture and the unremitting tension. By the time the plates were cleared, the pain had transferred itself to her head. Sorrowfully, she compared this miserable tableau to the warm, happy suppers she had shared with her family. By the time Shubael mercifully ended the evening by rising to walk China home, her nerves were frayed raw.

They said very little on the way home, though once, when China hunched her shoulders to relieve the pain, Shubael stopped her in a shadow and kneaded her neck as if he knew all about that knot of tension. When they arrived at her house, China tried to say good-night at the gate, envisioning the comfort of her feather bed, but Shubael came into the kitchen with her. "Would thee like tea?" she asked, weakly, hoping that he wouldn't.

"Nay, 'tis too much trouble to light the fire on a warm evening like this," Shubael answered. He waited until China sank into a chair, her shoulders slouched and her legs crossed, before he sat down opposite her. He rested his arms on the intervening oak table and leaned toward her. He could tell that she was tired and upset, and he himself felt edgy, still he meant to pursue his plan before he could succumb to any excuses.

"I've something to ask thee, China," he said, slowly.

"Aye, ask away." China rubbed her eyes wearily. She was imagining climbing up to her room, stripping off all her clothes and sliding between cool, crisp sheets.

"I would like thee to become my wife."

Shubael's quiet words seemed to fill the kitchen. China's eyes shot open, wide with shock. "What is thee saying?" she asked, incredulous, all thoughts of sleep suddenly gone.

"I am saying I would like to marry thee," Shubael answered. "What does *thee* say?"

"Nay, I cannot," China said immediately, shaking her head emphatically, still stunned.

Now it was Shubael's turn to be shocked. It had never occurred to him that China might refuse his offer. He had been concentrating so hard on convincing himself of the advantages to their marriage, he had neglected to consider her possible reaction. "I see," he said, soberly. "Forgive me for presuming. I had thought thee bore me some affection."

"Oh, but I do," China assured him. "I am extremely fond of thee." Her mind was still dazed.

"Then why does thee refuse my offer of marriage?" He leaned farther across the table as if he could physically glean understanding from her. "Is it my mother? Does her severity discourage thee? If that is the case, thee need not worry. Thee shall not have to spend very much time with her."

"She is a difficult woman to please," China admitted. "But I was not thinking of her when I made my answer."

"Of what were thee thinking, then?" Shubael probed. "Does my debt to Benjamin Swain cause thee concern? Does thee think I shan't be able to support thee properly? I would always allow enough for thee to live comfortably, China, and someday, I shall be successful and prosperous."

When China started to shake her head, Shubael spread his hands in exasperation and demanded, "Why, then? Why?"

China's answer did not come so quickly this time. Under his questioning gaze, her own eyes dropped and she studied her hands, now twisting nervously in her lap. Why indeed had she refused him? It seemed a sensible solution to her problems. She would be financially secure and reasonably content. It wasn't as if he were Obed, whose stolid ways and stumbling speech had made her yawn. She hadn't lied when she had said she was extremely fond of Shubael. But she didn't love him.

Again she rubbed her face, this time not in fatigue but in frustration. Why wouldn't Jake leave her alone? He had left her, he had sailed away almost five years ago and would probably never return. Why couldn't he release her, let her live her life? Determinedly she pushed him from her mind, pushed away the memory of his rich voice saying, "In our souls we are already united."

China's hands dropped and she looked steadily at Shubael. His face reflected disappointment and bewilderment, and, oddly, a hint of relief. "Thee is a kind and thoughtful man, Shubael," she said. "But I long ago vowed that I would never marry a man who goes whaling. 'Tis a fearful life, both at sea and on shore. It does not suit me to wait at home and worry. I have done enough of that all my life and I have suffered enough grief. I am honored by thy offer, but I must tell thee I cannot accept it."

Shubael sat up, slowly digesting China's words. In a way he did feel relieved, because as much as he told himself that China would be his anchor to Nantucket, his heart was already anchored somewhere else. But he couldn't return to the Seychelles, he couldn't have Amedee. He had to maintain his sense of discipline, perform his duty. He had a debt to repay, obligations to meet, and, most of all, a legacy of failure to overcome. With China, such a life would be less onerous.

"I understand thy objections," he said, sincerely. "Long absences are easy for neither husband nor wife. But just yesterday I had a talk with Benjamin Swain." He reached across the table and took China's hand in his. Her eyes lowered again, a dark fringe of lashes resting against her cheek.

"I asked him for a berth on one of his smaller ships. I thought to make a trip to the Western Islands, or to cruise on Brazil. 'Twould be a short voyage. Trips in the Atlantic are rarely more than a year." He did not add that his request was motivated more by his memory of Amedee than by his concern for China. He did not want the temptation of rounding the Horn, or being cut off from his home ocean and of being enticed into Amedee's.

"By chance, Benjamin is just fitting out a small schooner he bought five years ago. 'Tis called the *Justice*. He means to send it to the Antarctic for some whales, but mostly for seals. He agreed to make me master. I wouldn't be gone more than a year, China. Most probably only nine months. We have to leave the Antarctic before July or risk being frozen in. 'Tis not so very long."

China withdrew her hand and looked up at him. Her gray eyes were beginning to look smoky. "'Tis long enough," she said, briskly. "Nine months is long enough to wonder if thee is sound or sick, alive or dead. 'Tis long enough to imagine thy schooner being blown about by hurricanes at the Horn, or being dashed upon icebergs. Why, a wave could sweep thee overboard in one of those terrifying storms. Even if the sea were calm, as cold as it is in the Antarctic, thee would perish instantly. Nay, Shubael, the man I make my husband shall not torture me so."

"Thee is not being reasonable, China," Shubael protested. "I could just as easily drown in the Mill Pond on a sunny day in May. Or be hit by a runaway horse and wagon. There is a risk involved in all aspects of living. Besides, there is no way I can earn so much money staying on land. Thee knows I have a debt to repay and my mother to support. Would thee have me ignore those responsibilities?"

"I do not ask thee to change thy ways," China snapped, irritated at being called unreasonable. Jake had said the same thing when she hadn't agreed with him. "But do not ask me to change mine. Thee must do what is right for thee, just as I must do what is right for me."

"How can being stowed in that store, like a barrel of sperm in the hold, be what is right for thee?" Shubael demanded, angry, now, himself. "'Tis dreary and dark in there and that woman is a Trojan. I can give thee a life in the sunshine and the air. Long hikes on the beach, shooling around the commons. That is what thee thrives on."

China's nerves, already sorely frayed by supper with Prudence, flew apart. She rose to her feet shouting, "Surely thee will grant that I am the best judge of what I thrive on! Of what I need for my life!" For an instant, following her outburst, the room was silent. In that moment, she saw Jake's face in her mind, grinning triumphantly, goading her on, smug in his assurance that no one but he could satisfy her. She sank back in her chair, exhausted, her fury spent.

Now Shubael rose, also drained of anger. China's words had been like someone shaking his shoulders. An image of Amedee came to him, her lovely almond eyes hurt and puzzled by his actions this evening. "Of course thee is the best judge of thy life," he said, stiffly. "Please forgive my presumption." He left before China could respond.

SHUBAEL RETURNED the next day, because he had promised to help China gather rosehips. Although the late August afternoon was lovely and crisp, with a promise of autumn, neither seemed to notice. They plucked the plump orange rosehips in virtual silence. It was not the comfortable, and comforting, quiet of their first meeting, but a strained uneasiness.

In the two months that remained before Shubael set sail for the Antarctic, they saw each other less often than before. Gradually, some of the tension faded, but they never wholly returned to their previous peaceful relationship. Neither of them ever mentioned Shubael's proposal, but it lay between them, hindering the flow of solace and sympathy.

It was only after Shubael departed that China realized how much she depended on his companionship, however imperfect it might be. For the first few weeks, she was almost frantic with loneliness, again having no one with whom to share her daily thoughts and observations, no one who provoked a laugh or a grin, no one sitting on the other side of the table.

She half regretted having refused Shubael's offer of marriage, her solitude weighing heavily. Although her logic told her that marriage to a man absent at sea was the same as being alone, she sometimes wondered if it might not be different, after all. In any event, she always concluded, with a shrug, it was a futile debate. Shubael was gone, just like Papa and Zacch. And Jake. The skies turned leaden in late November, and so did her spirits as she regained her stoic composure.

13

RARUA
October 1844

JAKE CROUCHED IN THE MAIN HOLD of the *China Maid*, alternately running his hands over the scarfed ribs and patched planks, and wiping the sweat from his face. The repairs were finally finished. "She looks good as new, Samuel," he said, in satisfaction. "Even old Ezra Barnard, down at Brant Point, couldn't have done it better, given the tools and wood we had to work with."

Samuel Easton, leaning over Jake's shoulder, drew the back of his hand across his beard. "Perhaps he couldn't have done it better," he said loyally, "but I'll wager he could have done it a sight faster."

Jake laughed and rose. He slapped Samuel on the shoulder. "'Tis true," he admitted. "Though this infernal heat would have slowed even Ezra, I'm sure. 'Tis like the inside of the tryworks, down here. Now that we're high and dry on the beach, we haven't the sea to insulate us from the sun and heat. 'Twas impossible to work more than a few hours a day."

"Aye," Samuel said, pursing his lips, "or more than a few days a week."

Jake laughed again. "I'll officially enter your disapproval in the log, Samuel," he said, dryly. "Though I don't see how we could have done it any different, without insulting our hosts on Rarua. For the sake of progress, 'tis a bit unfortunate they are such a festive race. If they haven't got a good excuse for a two-day feast, they'll invent one. I've lost count of how many times we were the guests of honor.''

"Eleven times," Samuel said, primly. "Four times with John James Henry, and seven times on our own. Plus one feast for his uncle and once for the birth of his uncle's grandson."

"'Tis a good job you were sober enough to keep a tally," Jake said, sardonically. "Well, you won't be plagued by merrymaking much longer. John James Henry has organized a towing party for tonight. 'Tis a full moon and we'll be afloat again easily. Then 'tis back to butchering whales and drinking brackish water. But come. Why are we standing in this hellhole gamming, when we could be in the shade of a palm?''

As he led the way topsides, he caught a glimpse of Samuel's face, boiled red from heat and suppressed vexation. Jake sighed. Not for the first time, he felt the sharp pain of missing Zacch. He missed Zacch's good-natured grin and his sense of humor. He missed his perceptive comments, his appreciation of life and his unequivocal companionship. Zacch had grown over the years from affectionate kid brother to full-fledged friend. And now he was gone.

When they reached the deck, Samuel went aft to double-check with the cook about provisions. Jake vaulted over the rail and lowered himself along the sideboards in waist-deep water. He half floated, half waded ashore, immersed in thought. He'd done a lot of thinking since Zacch's death, despite Samuel's unspoken conviction that all he had done was eat and drink.

In the agonizing days immediately following the tragedy, he had bitterly blamed himself for the accident. He had jeered at his smug presumption of being head of the family, at his self-righteous acceptance of responsibility. He was more like a jinx, a Judas. As his natural tendencies had overcome his intense grief, though, Jake had ceased to be so hard on himself. He now recognized that what happened to Zacch was one of the hazards of whaling, a tough, risky business that could bring great rewards or devastating loss. With the passage of time, and the calming effect of laughter and luaus, Jake realized he could not brood forever, punishing himself with "if only..."

He fastened his attention now on the living, on China. He hardly needed his promise to Zacch to remind him of China. Scarcely a day went by that he didn't think of her, long for her to be near him. With Zacch gone, he missed her more than ever. Even the languid island life, and its beguiling tropical maidens, couldn't blunt the ache of being without her. He didn't need Zacch's urging, he would take care of her always.

And yet, he decided to cruise for one more season in the South Pacific before rounding the Horn and heading for Nantucket. Floating on his back in the bathtub-warm, blue water, Jake grinned ruefully. It was the coward's way out, he admitted to himself, but he knew of no other course. He had to bring home a rich cargo. He couldn't sail around Great Round Shoal in a tattered ship and tell China that her father and her brother had died for the sake of half a hold of sperm. There had to be some recompense, some return for the high price they had paid.

In his mind, Jake could see the flush on her porcelain cheeks, the smoke in her gray eyes, as she argued with him about whaling. He knew her already stubborn stand would become more obdurate when she heard the sad news he bore. His only hope of softening her views lay in a successful trip. There was no way he could bring back Zaccheus and Zacch, but at least he could bring her an abundance of the oil they had sought. It wasn't much, but it was better than running home whimpering.

Jake ducked briefly under the water to cool himself off before standing up and slogging to shore. He was surprised to see John James Henry, hunkered in the shade, waiting for him. As Jake emerged from the water, the big islander rose and hurried toward him, an excited look on his broad face.

"What's happening?" Jake asked, raking the wet curls off his forehead with his fingers. "You look like you just discovered gold in the bilge."

"Nay, Ja-Jake," John James Henry said, grinning. "Much better. I have a dream last night."

"Oh?" Jake said, cautiously. He knew about John James Henry's dreams. They were full of talking tortoises and laughing lobsters, all giving him indisputable directions in life. "What did you dream this time?"

John James Henry spread his legs and settled himself into his story-telling stance. "I was walking out on the reef," he began, gesturing to the coralline barrier at the edge of the bay. "I was carrying big stick. To clobber octopus for supper. All of a sudden, big shark comes swimming up to me and opens his mouth. I almost bam, bam, bam him with my stick, but he speaks to me. You know what voice he have, Ja-Jake?"

"Nay, John James Henry. What voice did he have?"

"Voice of Captain Zaccheus," John James Henry said, solemnly. "You know what he say, Ja-Jake?"

"Nay, John James Henry. What did he say?"

"He say, 'John James Henry, 'tis not time to retire yet. Please go back to *China Maid*. Ja-Jake still needs you. One more trip. When he sails from Rarua, go with him.' That's what he says, Ja-Jake. Then he swims back into the sea."

He crossed his arms against his massive chest and grinned triumphantly. "I'm coming along, Ja-Jake."

"'Tis not necessary," Jake protested. "This is your home. You've been waiting years to return. I can't ask you to leave again."

"You didn't ask, Ja-Jake. Captain Zaccheus did. I'm coming along," he repeated, tenaciously, a scowl forming on his face.

Jake sighed. In truth, he was glad John James Henry wanted to continue on board. Aside from being an outstanding harpooner with an unerring aim, he was part of the family. It would be a comfort to have him around. He would also, Jake admitted wryly, be a great relief from the company of the earnest, but humorless, Easton brothers. Still, he felt guilty about taking John James Henry so far from his home. "Are you really sure you want to?" he asked.

"Sure, sure, sure," John James Henry answered, the scowl dissolving again in a grin. He stretched out his arms and captured Jake, astonished, in a rib-crushing hug. "Anyway," he said, setting him back down on the beach, "I've had enough being at home. Too much celebration. Get too fat."

"Aye," Jake mumbled, stumbling in the sand and struggling to catch his breath.

A week later, with the *China Maid* floating easily again, Jake and John James Henry hauled themselves aboard from his uncle's canoe. There had been one last load of fresh food ferried out, one last round of uninhibited feasting. Now Jake ordered all hands to turn out and he counted noses, to make sure that no one was left behind. Then the anchor was upped, the newly mended sails were raised, and the *China Maid* sailed gracefully away, her wake strewn with flowers tossed from the canoes.

14

NANTUCKET
September 1845

"BE DAMNED!" CHINA SWORE. Already late to work and upset, she dodged a loaded dray rumbling unyieldingly down the narrow dirt road and was forced, ankle deep, into a mud puddle. Cold water soaked through to her stockings almost instantly. The unladylike oath, learned during her youth at sea, adequately expressed her displeasure with her wet feet, with the gray, drizzly day and with the tax collector from whom she had just come.

"Let me see," Mr. Hawkins had said, alternately peering over the edge of his half glasses at China, and elaborately studying the ledger page. "Hmmm. According to my records, thee has not yet paid last year's tax on thy house, and this year's tax is also overdue. 'Tis all here in black and white. We can't have that, Miss Joy." He had slapped shut the book and had sat up straight, his hands folded in front of him, a sanctimonious look on his pasty face.

"But thee knows that my father is away at sea," China had replied, pleadingly. "He's been a bit delayed, but as soon as he returns I'm sure he will settle the bill, immediately, even paying any interest that accrues. Thee knows he has always paid promptly in the past."

"I'm afraid I can't concern myself with the past," Mr. Hawkins had said, with exaggerated patience. "'Tis the

278

present I must attend to. I have been charged by the town to collect the monies owed it by property owners. It would be a dereliction of my duties if I were to allow thee to eschew payment.

"And let us be frank, Miss Joy," he had said, leaning forward with a patronizing display of confidentiality. "Thy father is more than 'a bit delayed.' There is a good possibility he may be lost at sea, in which case it would be impossible for him to attend to this matter. The longer that I allow thee to wait, the larger thy debt will grow, and the greater thy difficulty in meeting it. I'm sorry, but I must ask thee to pay thy taxes within ten days or have a lien put on the house." He had sat back and had cast a smile at her, presumably meant to be benevolent, but, in fact, highly offensive.

The tax collector's condescending manner, as well as his ultimatum, had angered China. "Thee needn't tell me thee is sorry," she had snapped, "for it obviously gives thee great pleasure to steal people's homes in the name of duty. Don't worry, I'll get thee thy miserable money!"

Now, emerging from the puddle and shaking the mud from the hem of her skirt, her expression was more despairing. 'Tis a good thing this dress is a dingy color to begin with, she thought dully, avoiding her main problem. Where was she going to find money to pay the taxes? As she turned onto Centre Street and the sign over Mrs. Mitchell's door came into view, she half formed the idea of asking her employer for a loan. Perhaps she could pay it back by deducting a small portion of her wages every week.

The idea never had a chance to develop. As soon as she opened the door to the shop, she knew something was wrong. The store was empty of customers, but Lucinda Mitchell, the owner's niece and newest employee, was standing behind the counter with a malicious smirk on her face. Lucinda was a small, slight girl with a sallow complexion and a selfish nature. She resented her aunt's reliance on China's taste and opinions, feeling that China was usurping a position that belonged, by virtue of blood, to her.

She never tired of trying to order China about, pointing out crockery that needed dusting or a stack of collars that needed straightening. Naturally, she didn't do it within her aunt's hearing, as Mrs. Mitchell had her own definite idea of who was solely in charge. Normally, China put a furl on her temper and totally ignored Lucinda, to the girl's ever increasing chagrin. Today, though, there was something about the leer on Lucinda's face that made China uneasy.

She had barely taken two steps into the shop when Mrs. Mitchell swept in from the back room. "You needn't bother to take off your cloak," she said ominously. "I do not require your services any longer, nor do I wish to see you in my shop again. I have prepared your wages to date, though heaven knows, 'tis far more than you deserve." She held out the envelope, her large face utterly cold.

China's jaw dropped in astonishment. If she hadn't known Mrs. Mitchell to be humorless, she might have hoped this were a joke. Between the finality in Mrs. Mitchell's words and the frigidness of her tone, China's mind was in a state of total confusion. "But..." was all she managed to say.

"You needn't pretend to be so surprised, young lady," Mrs. Mitchell said austerely. "I'm not a stupid woman. It was only a matter of time before I found out."

China struggled to make some sense of what was happening. She could only suppose that her employer had somehow learned of her delinquent taxes and had guessed that China meant to ask for a loan. Grasping that unlikely explanation, she hastened to reassure Mrs. Mitchell.

"Please do not fret," she said. "I will not ask to borrow any money from thee. I..."

"Gracious heavens!" Mrs. Mitchell interrupted, almost shouting. "I should hope you wouldn't ask to borrow any money from me, since you've already stolen it!"

This time China was truly speechless with shock. She couldn't imagine what Mrs. Mitchell was talking about. Nor had she ever before been accused of any form of dishonesty. Horror and hurt closed off her throat.

"You can save your fancy play-acting for someone else," Mrs. Mitchell thundered, wound up in her rage. "I've been watching you for some time now. I first noticed some money missing from the till two months ago. And then small pieces of jewelry and a watch disappeared. You thought I wouldn't miss them, didn't you? Well, you were very wrong, young lady."

Angrily, she shook the pay envelope she was still holding out. "Come on. You'd better take this. 'Tis the last penny you'll ever get out of me. Never let it be said I am anything but fair. Even to those who would take advantage of my fairness."

"But why does thee think I took the jewelry?" China asked. Her voice was weak and hoarse. She didn't move from where she stood or attempt to take the envelope. She felt as though she were groggily gaining comprehension of what was happening, like slowly awakening from a bad dream. She half hoped she would find herself sweaty and safe in her feather bed any moment.

"Oh, you want to know how I finally caught you out, do you?" Mrs. Mitchell pulled in her arm and placed her hands on her ample hips. "You got a little careless yesterday, as if you didn't know. You probably arrived home and searched your pockets high and low, wondering where those jade ear bobs you stole got to. Maybe you were even searching for them this morning, which is why you are late. Well, you dropped them out of your lunch sack and they were lying right there on the shelf in the back room where you have kept your things for the more than two years you have worked here. It said to me as clear as day that my suspicions about you were true." She sounded very pleased with her clever detective work.

China's head started clearing as the story was unfolded. Now that she understood the facts, she felt better able to refute them. "Thee must be mistaken," she began, with every effort to be reasonable.

"I am not mistaken!" Mrs. Mitchell shrieked, her large face turning red, her ringlets bobbing foolishly. "Don't seek to flummox me, girl. Imagine the impertinence! Telling me that I am mistaken."

She shook her meaty finger menacingly. "The only thing I was mistaken about was hiring you in the first place. I should have known better than to take a foreigner into my shop. You can never trust foreigners. They're all alike, oily liars and thieving sneaks. You have to keep your eyes on them every minute, or they'll steal the canvas right off the spars!"

For a moment China had an image of her mother, gracious and graceful, delicately beautiful, laughing, alive and radiating innocence. She compared her with the hulking woman before her whose eyes were bulging with spleen. A wave of pure anger washed away any lingering confusion, any attempt at reasonableness. She had been badgered and insulted enough for one day.

"If thee is an example of what it is to be a native, I count my blessings I am not!" she shouted back. "I would die of shame if I possessed such a narrow view of the world as thee. 'Tis a low and mean-spirited way to behave. 'Tis a sign of abysmal ignorance to be always cowering in fear, to be isolating thyself from people and customs that are different from thy own.

"And I *will* tell thee that thee is mistaken. 'Tis not the least bit impertinent of me to tell the truth. I never stole thy money nor the jewelry, Mrs. Mitchell. I never stole so much as an ounce of tea nor took an extra cup of flour. I always paid thee every penny I owed for purchases and I did all my provisioning here, despite the fact that thy prices are often higher than others about town. Except for my loyalty to thee, I might have made much wiser use of the paltry wage thee pays me."

Now China really warmed to the subject, as two years' buildup of petty grievances finally found a vent. While Mrs. Mitchell's face grew progressively redder, China continued heatedly, "If we want to talk about thievery, there is a good place to start, with the miserly stipend thee doles out every week. For over two years thee has stolen from me. Thee has stolen my ideas, my advice, my knowledge of goods. I have acted as a purchasing agent for thee, yet thee pays me as thee would a char. Despite all the service I have given thee, from which thee has profited and prospered, thee has not raised my wage so much as a cent since the day I started. If that is not oily and sneaky, I don't know what is!"

"Out!" Mrs. Mitchell roared, practically spitting with ire. She pointed to the door with the hand that still clutched China's pay envelope, now crumpled and twisted.

"With pleasure!" China retorted, twirling to leave. She just caught a glimpse of Lucinda's face, alight with triumph, before she roughly pushed past round Mrs. Coleman, who was entering the shop. She was on the sidewalk before Lucinda's expression registered in her churning mind. She did a quick turnaround and marched back into Mrs. Mitchell's General Emporium.

Standing just inside the door, her hand still on the knob, she said, fiercely, "If thee is so proud of thy fairness and so pleased with thy deducing, thee might ponder why these thefts have occurred only in the past two months and never once during the years that I was thy sole employee."

"Get out of my shop!" Mrs. Mitchell screamed.

China paused long enough to see a worried look creep across Lucinda's sly features and to note Mrs. Coleman's open mouth as she looked excitedly from one woman to the other. Then, chin high, gray eyes gleaming with dignity, she turned again and left. As she was shutting the door behind her, she heard Mrs. Coleman saying, "I always did think she was a queer one, Eulalia. And more than once I caught her with her finger on the scale, though it never crossed my mind to mention it. Still..."

As in most times of emotional turmoil, China felt the need to stalk the moors. She left the shop and headed instinctively for the field by Capaum Pond, desiring fresh air and open spaces in which to discharge her overwrought nerves. She couldn't remember ever being so angry in her life. Even during her worst quarrel with Jake, she had somehow known, underneath it all, that they still loved each other.

There was something unclean about the argument she had just had with Mrs. Mitchell. Despite her indignant words, she felt essentially powerless against the look of loathing Mrs. Mitchell had directed at her, against the unfair accusations, and against the ingrained prejudices. No matter how she turned the events over in her mind, the end result was always as infuriating, always as humiliating.

China walked for hours, oblivious to the steady drizzle of rain until a cold trail of water wound around her neck and down between her breasts. She realized then that she was soaked, and she looked up at the sky, surprised. As she headed for home, her fury and frustration expanded to include the uncooperative weather, then, remembering the day's beginning, it also encompassed Mr. Hawkins and his infernal ledger.

It wasn't until she entered her kitchen, thinking herself safe, that the protective shield of her anger fell away and she saw the situation as it really was. The cottage was damp and cold, the fire was only embers. The pine door of the cupboard stood ajar, revealing shelves scantily stocked with food. She had no money, no employment, the taxes were overdue. With a moan, she collapsed into a chair, suddenly aware of her sopping shoes.

"Oh, Jake," she said aloud, "why did thee do this to me? If thee had not left me, this never would have happened. I've lost everyone I've ever loved, and now I am to lose my house and my reputation, as well."

After a long while, she stood again, shivering in her wet clothes. She hung the soggy cloak by the stove and set her shoes underneath. With her impending destitution as a guide, she fed a frugal amount of fuel into the fire, and, later, dressed in a dry gown as drab as her hopes, she made a meager meal. The boiled egg and cheese toast wasn't very filling, but at least it felt warm inside her. In any event, it revived her enough to remark, defiantly, to the plate she was scrubbing, "'Tis not the only job on the island. Tomorrow I'll have to find another one."

She set the single dish in the drainer, enormously depressed. "Now I'm even talking to myself," she said. Long before night fell, China went to bed, chilled, weary and emotionally spent.

The next day was gray and windy, and although the rain had stopped, it still felt damp. China dragged herself out from under her quilts with great reluctance. She felt heavy-headed and achy, the signals that a proper cold was on its way. Nonetheless, she was in no position to pamper herself; she couldn't afford to sit around, steeped in self-pity, and wasting firewood.

After a comfortless cold breakfast, she set out for town. Her cloak and boots, left overnight by the barely lit stove, hadn't completely dried, adding to her shivery feeling. She made her first stop Rebecca Coffin's Dry Goods, a shop she had always admired because its buxom proprietress was so good-natured. It was three doors down from Mrs. Mitchell's on Petticoat Row. Its sign swung without creaking from a wrought-iron bracket and its wooden front was freshly painted, a testimony to the devotion of Mrs. Coffin's many sons.

China found herself pausing outside to gather courage and to glance nervously along the board sidewalk toward the less pristine front of her former place of employment. When she finally pushed open the door and forced herself to calmly state her business, she realized she had had reason to be nervous about Mrs. Mitchell.

Pressing her usually smiling lips into a scowl, Mrs. Coffin answered China's request for a job. "I have no need for thee here," she said. "This is a *nice* shop."

A flush of mortification colored China's pale cheeks and her stomach lurched to her throat. Though she held her head high as she left, she felt like a kicked dog, slinking away. It didn't do any good to remind herself that she was in the right. Mrs. Coffin's harsh rejection still stung, her look of distaste made China cringe.

She forced herself to inquire at three other shops on Centre Street before she finally allowed herself to admit that Mrs. Mitchell had preceded her along the whole commercial block. Mrs. Mitchell and Mrs. Coleman. Miserably, China remembered the vulturelike look on Mrs. Coleman's puffy face as she had overheard the end of their argument. Rumors and gossip ran the length of Petticoat Row as contiguously as the clapboarded and bow-windowed buildings.

Desperate, and beginning to cough and feel feverish, China thought ruefully of the pay envelope she had been too angry and proud to accept yesterday. It wasn't much, but it was better than an empty pocket, and, after all, she had earned it. She wandered closer to the wharves, asking for employment in stores she probably shouldn't even have entered. One was a ship's chandler, another specialized in seamen's clothing, a third carried nothing but kegs of paint and barrels of dye. In each establishment the answer was an astonished no, delivered with a tsk and a shake of the head.

As China was dejectedly leaving S.B. Tuck's Paint Store, careful not to get any powdered verdigris on the folds of her cloak, a weatherbeaten man, with moth-eaten mutton-chop whiskers, planted himself in front of her. He was wearing tall boots and a tattered oilskin coat.

"Here now," he said, in a growly voice, "if ye really need money, I've work enough for one day. I'll pay ye one dollar. What do ye say?"

"Aye, I accept," China responded, eagerly. She caught sight of the incredulous expression on the face of the man behind the counter. It made her realize, with embarrassment, how shameless she sounded. More cautiously, she asked, "What is the job?"

"Cuttin' cod for saltin'," he replied. "About three thousand pounds. 'Tis the second shanty from the end on the harbor side of Washington Street, right next to the Creeks. Seven in the morning."

"I'll be there," China said, quietly, suddenly caring very little what a paint clerk thought was respectable.

WHEN CHINA WOKE the next morning, her face felt flushed and hot and her legs felt shaky. While she pulled her petticoats on, with awkward, disjointed movements, she thought about Aunt Judith. She could almost hear her say, "A hot garlic poultice and some hyssop tea is what thee needs. Scud! Back into bed."

But Aunt Judith was dead. There was no one to make her tisanes or to wipe away her worries. Sour Silas Ray, who sold her firewood, didn't care about her fever. Coffin and Macy's on Main Street, where she always used to shop for supplies, wasn't interested in her health either. Certainly Mr. Hawkins wouldn't accept that excuse. The only thing that mattered to any of them was money, and the only way China was going to get some was by working, sick or sound. She couldn't afford to pass up this opportunity.

The day was clear and almost sunny when China set off for the shanty, but the chill in the air and the strong breeze from the east reminded her that summer was over and there was a long winter ahead. The twenty-minute walk, which would normally have been a pleasure, seemed endless. She hardly noticed the harbor, chockablock with schooners and ships and innumerable lighters, as she trudged along Washington Street. Even the tooting of the steam ferry *Telegraph*, a sight that always fascinated her, failed to change the downward glance of her glazed, gray eyes.

It was little better inside the shanty. The rough-hewn boards and weathered gray shingles of the beach shack kept out the sunshine, but didn't work as well on the wind. Despite her ever-hotter forehead, China shivered in the chill and dampness. Somehow she must manage to last the day.

With a full-length oilskin apron protecting her dress, she stood at a bench between a twelve-year-old boy and a peg-legged sailor, wielding a razor-sharp filleting knife. Though it seemed as if she were continually swaying, and she often saw double, she steadily slashed, slashed, slashed, slicing the firm white flesh from the symmetrical fish bones, tossing the fillets in one pile for salting, the head in another for soup and the carcass in a third for sea gull fodder. She couldn't think of anything but the codfish in front of her, its horrified expression frozen in place. It required all her concentration not to cut off her fingers, not to slide to the floor in a faint.

By the end of the day, China was alternately burning up and shaking with cold, her vision was blurred. The boy edged suspiciously away from her, but the one-legged sailor advised her to down a tot of hot rum and turn into a snug berth. China nodded numbly, collected her dollar and staggered home. She had forgotten his well-meant words before she was halfway there; she had almost forgotten which direction to take, she was so befuddled.

When the familiar cottage finally hove into sight, relief gave China a momentary lift. She dropped her cloak and bonnet to the floor as she passed through the parlor on her way to the stairs. She hadn't paused in the kitchen; there was little enough to eat even if she had an appetite. Her legs grew more trembly as she mounted the steps, steeper than they had ever been before. The top step seemed to ripple and recede, and she had to hold it down with her hands while she crawled over the top.

Still seated on the floor, she tried to remove her clothes. Tears of frustration rolled down her cheeks as her fingers fumbled over buttons and knotted-up laces. When finally, after many attempts, she pulled off her boots, she heard a button pop and roll away, but she was past caring. With the utmost effort, China shed her cod-scented dress and underpinnings, donned her flannel nightgown and slid between her clammy sheets, unconscious.

The next thing she was aware of was someone piling another quilt over her icy body, tucking the edge under her chattering chin. It must be Maman, she thought, too weak to open her eyes. No one else had such a gentle touch. Of course it was Maman. She could hear the creaking of the *China Maid*'s masts, the snapping of wind in her sails. Zacch must be topsides, practicing knot tying with John James Henry, or reciting southern constellations for Papa. Why did he go on deck without her?

"Où es-tu?" she called. "Where are you, Zacch?"

"Ici," he replied. "I'm right here." He took her frigid hand when she extended it searchingly. The warmth of his grasp made her smile between shivers. She returned to the dark, silent world where she had been.

Raging thirst brought her around again. She stood helplessly on the hot sand watching Jake swim toward her. The sunlight gleamed off his bronzed, wet body, it sparkled on the gold hoop in his ear. Water splashed over his head, plastering his unruly dark curls to his brow, making him blink his brilliant blue eyes, bringing a gleeful grin to his face. He swam toward her, yet he never got nearer, he just stroked through the sea, tossing his handsome head and grinning. Nor could she dive through the waves to join him. She was stuck in the hot sand, the sun blazing down on her, burning, drying.

"Please come, Jake," she begged him. "Please come. I need thee. Thee promised me thee would return. I'm so thirsty, Jake. Please help me."

A strong hand held her head, and a cup with refreshing, sweet water was placed at her parched lips. Greedily China swallowed the drink and allowed her head to sink back on the pillow. A cool compress was spread across her forehead, dousing some of the fire burning her skin. "Thee did come back, Jake," she murmured happily. "Thee kept thy promise."

"I did," he said.

"I love thee," she said. "I always have and I always shall."

China drifted into an uneasy sleep. She was unbearably hot. Even the cool cloths and cups of barley water didn't help. Then she was shivering again. The gentle hands tucked blankets and quilts around her. Gradually the spasms of cold ceased and she slept more soundly.

She was safe and secure on a stormy day. Rain beat at the shingles on the roof and fogged the panes of glass in the windows, but there was a fire crackling in the grate and Shubael was slowly rocking in Zaccheus's chair, a copy of the *Inquirer* on his knee. His elbow rested on the arm of the chair, his chin set on his hand. His brown eyes, often so melancholy, were meditatively watching the fire.

China studied the strong, lean lines of his face for a long time until she slowly became aware that he was real, that she was awake, not dreaming. "Shubael?" she asked, dimly surprised that her voice was barely a whisper.

"Aye?" he answered, turning his head toward her. For a brief moment China could see the fatigue and anxiety etched beneath his eyes, then his radiant smile appeared, transforming his face. "I do believe thee is back among us, at last," he said, rising and crossing to where she lay. He put his hand on her forehead and nodded happily. "Thy temperature is down and thy lovely eyes look clear and bright."

"What does thee mean, Shubael?" China was confused. Her thoughts came as weakly as her words. It almost seemed like more effort than it was worth to sort out what was happening. All she wanted to do was slip off to sleep; she couldn't understand why Shubael should be here. She struggled to comprehend. "Why is thee in my bedroom?" she asked, her fingers creeping cautiously from under the covers as if to ascertain that it was, indeed, her bedroom. "And what is thee doing with Papa's chair?"

Shubael laughed, relieved to hear her asking such normal questions, even if her tone were so frail. He gently enclosed her exposed fingers in his own hand and explained, "I brought thy papa's chair upstairs because 'tis far more comfortable than the mean little stool that is here. Thee has been sick and I have stayed here to tend thee."

His words jogged China's memory, somewhat. "Aye," she said, hazily, "I must have caught a good chill cutting codfish in that damp shanty yesterday. I went to bed without supper."

"'Tis more than one supper thee's missed," Shubael said, gravely, squeezing her fingers. "I've been here three nights already and the Lord knows how many more thee tossed about before I arrived."

"Three nights?" China was astonished. "Thee has been here three nights?"

"Aye. I came to call on thee the evening I returned. There was no fire lit when I came, nor any sign of life. At first I thought thee was away, or..." He paused. At first he thought she had found someone to marry and had moved away from the cozy cottage. The thought had depressed him tremendously, and he had almost turned to go. Although he knew he did not love her, not the way he loved Amedee, nonetheless, China was the only reason he looked forward to coming home. Without her wit and spirit to offer him a refuge, his life was totally empty and dismal.

"Or out visiting," he finished. "But then I thought that perhaps thee stayed late at the store, so I decided to come in and wait. That was when I noticed thy cloak and bonnet in a heap in the parlor. When I called out to thee, I heard a faint thrashing from up above. I called again and again, and even stood at the bottom of the stairs and waited for thee to respond. I did not want to intrude where I was not welcome, yet I was beginning to worry. Finally I came upstairs and found thee raging with fever and tossing wildly about.

"But thee is asleep again, peacefully this time, I hope," he said, noting her closed eyelashes. Her cheeks seemed so white with her thick black lashes lying against them. "I shall finish this account some other time."

"Nay, Shubael, I hear thee," China said faintly. She could scarcely concentrate on what he was saying. It seemed like so much trouble to keep her eyes open. "Let me rest a minute, then I'll make tea."

Shubael chuckled. "Thee shall do no such thing," he said, leaning over to plant a tender kiss on her forehead. "Thee shall allow me to take care of thee. Thee needs to rest or the fever might come back." This time, however, his words did fall on deaf ears. China was sound asleep.

It was a while before he released the hand still lying, trustingly, in his own. He softly stroked the pale skin of her cheek, smoothed the silky black hair strewn around the pillow. She was so beautiful and so vulnerable. She needed him. A feeling of tranquillity flowed through him, keeping rhythm with her slow, regular breathing.

The first thing that registered in China's mind when she drifted awake was that the rain had stopped beating on the roof. As her eyes fluttered open, she could see bright blue sky through the windowpanes in the background. In the foreground, Harriet's face slowly came into focus. Tears were streaming down Harriet's cheeks as she stood clutching her hands in front of her.

"What has happened, Harriet?" she asked, concerned about her friend's expression of despair. Her voice was stronger today. Indeed, she felt somewhat stronger, less groggy and confused.

Harriet flung herself to her knees by the bed. "Oh, China," she wailed, "can you ever forgive me? I have been so selfish, so preoccupied with my own pleasures these past months that I've not kept in touch with you as I should have.

"For a whole week I have been wanting to visit you at Mrs. Mitchell's, even if I could only say hello without that dragon breathing down my neck. But I kept allowing one excuse after another to prevent me from calling in on you, until, finally, this morning I was determined to see you. We were seven yards short of blue ribbon for my wedding quilt, so I told Mama I would get it at Mrs. Mitchell's and invite you to supper at the same time." She paused to swipe the palms of her hands over her tear-streaked cheeks.

"I sailed into her shop as pleased as can be," Harriet continued, shaking her head in recollection, "and even though you weren't in sight, I was sure that you were only in the storeroom or the cellar or somewhere close by. I even allowed that weasely little Lucinda Mitchell to measure out my ribbon before I asked when you would return. China, her face was positively *aglow* with pleasure when she told me you were no longer employed there. Honestly, I could have slapped her, she was that unpleasant." Angry bright spots appeared on Harriet's still-damp cheeks, her warm brown eyes snapped.

"And then that Mrs. Mitchell began to tell the most dreadful lies about you," Harriet continued, her voice trembling with indignation. "She said that you were a thief and that you couldn't be trusted. I was outraged. How dare that terrible woman say such things? I only wish I had your knack with words, China. You are always so quick. All I could do was stand there sputtering, and finally I said I didn't believe a word of it, and I walked out of her shop without buying the ribbon, even though she had already cut it!''

China blinked at Harriet's breathless recitation of events. Laughter welled up inside her at the thought of her mild and kind friend stirred to such acts of anger, but it turned to a cough somewhere in her chest.

''Perhaps thee had best speak of other matters,'' came Shubael's quiet voice from the other side of the room. ''China is still very weak and probably should not be excited.''

China rolled her head to see Shubael standing by the fire, his hands clasped behind his straight back, a hank of dark hair across his forehead. She vaguely remembered, then, what he had said last night, that he had been here for three, now four, days, taking care of her. She was touched by his solicitude.

Beside her, Harriet gulped and said, ''Of course, I'm so sorry. I came directly here from town and Captain Brown told me how frighteningly ill you've been. 'Tis all my fault, I'm sure. If I hadn't neglected you so badly, you never would have fallen into such straits.'' She took out her handkerchief and blew her nose vigorously.

'''Tis most surely *not* thy fault,'' China replied, stretching out her arm and patting Harriet's shoulder. She was surprised by how much effort it took. Shubael was right, she was still very weak. ''Thee is busy with Obed and with thy wedding plans, which is as it should be. If there's fault to be found, 'tis with Mrs. Mitchell for her small-mindedness and with me for my stubbornness and, oh dear, with Mr. Hawkins.'' She struggled to sit up, suddenly remembering the delinquent taxes.

Shubael was across the room in an instant, gently pressing her back against the pillow. Harriet, an alarmed look on her face, fussed with the edge of the sheet. "Oh nay, China," she pleaded, "you must not get up yet."

"But Mr. Hawkins," China said, exhausted from her attempt to rise. "I must pay him the taxes or he will take my house."

"Thee needn't fret, China," Shubael said, softly. "He came around two days back and I gave him the money. He won't take thy home."

China stared at Shubael, amazed and grateful. "I don't know what to say," she said, wonderingly.

Shubael only smiled, but Harriet, who was unfamiliar with financial worry, swept the matter aside. "There is nothing for you to say, right now," she said stoutly. "You need only lie here and rest. Captain Brown has been taking splendid care of you, and I am going to come stay with you until you are better. Between us, we shall see to all your needs, so let us hear no speeches. I am also going to have Papa go talk to Mrs. Mitchell and make her stop spreading those disgraceful lies about you."

While Harriet rose and started smoothing her covers, China just nodded. For once, her common sense overcame her pride. She knew she was in no condition to protest this special treatment. Besides, she had to admit, looking from Shubael, standing staunchly on one side of the bed, to Harriet, hovering loyally on the other, that she liked it. Despite feeling weak and worn, she felt loved and wanted. It was such a long time since she had felt anything but alone.

Just as Harriet predicted, all of China's needs and wishes were attended to. That afternoon, Harriet moved into Zacch's room, relieving Shubael of his position as full-time nurse. Though Shubael relinquished the role somewhat reluctantly, he realized it was a far more practical, not to mention respectable, course as he had business to do. He still came every noontime and spent the evenings at her bedside, so Harriet could go strolling with Obed. Providing comfort and care for China gave Shubael's life purpose.

Harriet outdid herself with her ministrations. She put color back in China's cheeks with an endless procession of freshly made custards and soups, toasts, muffins and jam. She kept China's bed linen immaculate and her nightgowns clean and pressed. She entertained her with chatter about her upcoming wedding, aided her for initial walks around the room, and insisted that she take long, lazy naps every afternoon. True to her word, Harriet had her father roundly chastise Mrs. Mitchell for her unfair accusations.

China was reclining on the parlor sofa one evening, having recovered enough to make a daily trip downstairs. Shubael had swathed her in quilts and was sitting in Zaccheus's rocker reading her poetry in French. She never asked him how he came to read it with such a strange accent, somehow sensing that he didn't care to discuss it. Instead, she just leaned back and looked into the fire, mesmerized by physical and spiritual warmth.

A knock on the front door shattered the peaceful spell. Both Shubael and China were startled, simply staring at each other. Then Shubael gave a little shrug, set the book aside and went to answer the abrupt summons. Mrs. Mitchell marched in.

"Here you are, China," she said, as matter-of-factly as if China had just stepped into the storeroom for a minute. She pulled Aunt Judith's ladder-backed chair from its place by the hearth and sat down without invitation.

China could feel anger rising in her as she pushed herself into a sitting position, all the better to do battle from. It had been several weeks since she had been so wary, so dependent on her own wits for survival. It wasn't a totally welcome sensation. She felt a hand on her shoulder and looked up to see Shubael standing behind the sofa, his eyes fixed sternly on their intruder, while his fingers conveyed reassurance and support. Not for the first time, recently, China felt a flood of gratitude and relief. She wanted to lay her cheek against his hand, accepting his solace, but she faced Mrs. Mitchell squarely instead.

"Of course I am here," she said, flatly. "'Tis my home. More surprising is that *thee* is here."

"Oh, 'tis not so surprising," Mrs. Mitchell said, with a wave of her hand. "I've come to tell you that a mistake has been made about the ear bobs and the other missing merchandise. 'Twas not you who took them after all."

China did not know whether to laugh or to spit. Mrs. Mitchell seemed unembarrassed by the admission. Rather, she related the news as if she were uninvolved in the incident. "There was no need to come here to tell me that," China said, ironically. "*I* already knew that. In fact, I told thee as much."

"So you did," Mrs. Mitchell said, calmly, the irony completely lost on her. "But I didn't believe you at the time. I have since realized that it was Lucinda who made the mischief. My brother's wife has always been inclined to spoil her and give her her way. Besides which, she grew up the only girl in a gang of boys who were all given to practical jokes. She is still young and will have her fun."

China's anger returned, despite Shubael's pressure on her shoulder. "How is it that when Lucinda steals from thee it is 'fun' and 'mischief,' but for the same act thee would brand me a sneak and a thief?" she demanded. "Stealing is stealing."

"She said she was sorry," Mrs. Mitchell retorted, sharply. "And she gave the goods back." Her tone moderated as she added, "I'm afraid I may have to let her go, anyway. She can be a bit surly with the customers, and she's not very good at keeping the stock neat and tidy. And I've had nothing but complaints about the cloth she advised me to buy last week. The dye job is cheap and bleeds all over everything that it touches.'' She shook her head in memory of how much that had cost her.

"Well, China," she continued, bringing herself back to the present situation, "I know we parted on bad terms, but that's in the past and I'd like you to return to work.'' For the first time she seemed to realize that China was dressed in her nightclothes. "When you are well again, that is,'' she added. "Mr. Swain told me you'd taken a chill. You should be more careful.''

China's temper exploded. She resented the way Mrs. Mitchell removed herself from any possible blame, the way she conveniently forgot the poisonous accusations she had made. "How dare thee come here expecting me to return to thy shop!'' she shouted. "'Tis only thy damned merchandise that thee cares about. When thee thinks one of thy precious geegaws is missing, thee will think nothing of blaming its disappearance on me. Thee will call me an 'oily foreigner' and a 'thief.' But let thee need my advice on a purchase and 'tis 'all in the past.' Thee has ruined my reputation and thee doesn't even offer so much as an apology. Nay, Mrs. Mitchell, thee has set thy course, thee can sail it without me aboard.''

Mrs. Mitchell stared hard at China. Her fierce glower had always worked well at bringing truculent children and employees into line, but China stared back, her gray eyes defiant and irate. "Well then,'' she said, rising abruptly. "I did my best. I'll show myself out.''

"Please do,'' China snapped.

When the door closed behind Mrs. Mitchell's broad back, China felt the anger drain out of her. "Oh dear,'' she said, with a sigh. "Aunt Judith always said my temper was the rotten timber in the hull of my spirit. I should not have shouted like that. I think 'twas probably foolish and impractical.''

"Why does thee say that?" Shubael asked. He placed his other hand on China's shoulder and began to gently knead the tensed muscles. "Aside from stressing thyself, I think thee put that woman in her place, as well as can be done. She is singularly insensitive and concerned only with herself.''

"Aye, that may be so, but she did offer me employment. 'Tis not so easy to come by. Even if the word gets around that I did not steal her baubles, I could never go back to those shops on Petticoat Row and ask for work. Not after the way the owners looked at me the last time." She shivered at the memory of the humiliation she had felt.

Shubael's massaging stopped, though his hands remained, resting lightly on China's shoulders. "I wish thee would forget about finding a job and let me take care of thee," he said softly.

"But thee is, Shubael," she replied, suddenly feeling very tired from her confrontation with Mrs. Mitchell. She shut her eyes and set her head back.

"I mean all the time. Forever."

China's eyes opened, but she didn't answer. Instead, she yielded to her previous impulse and laid her cheek against the strong hand on her shoulder. Shubael slowly turned his hand palm up and cradled her chin. With his thumb, he stroked the porcelain skin on her cheek, still slightly flushed from the heat of the fight, ran it lightly over the silky fringe of her lashes. Then he bent over the back of the sofa and placed a kiss on her lips.

It was a brief embrace, a sweet, satisfying caress that meant only that he cared for her. China accepted it as such, letting its intimacy wash over her, touching her heart but only vaguely arousing her body. She raised her hand toward his and turned her face toward his palm.

Holding her hand, Shubael came around to the front of the sofa, seated himself next to China and pulled her into his arms. She snuggled unresistingly against his lean body, basking in the tender touch of his lips rubbing through her hair. It felt so good to have someone hold her, to shut out the lonely world. Forever, he had said.

"Shubael?" China asked suddenly.

"Aye?" He rested his chin, eyes closed, on the top of her head, luxuriating in the warmth and softness of her body next to his.

"When I was sick, in the fever, it seems to me that I had very vivid dreams. At the time I thought they were real, but now I can't remember them. Did I . . ." she hesitated. She had to know the answer. "Did I speak of anyone?" she finished.

Shubael's eyes opened. He felt some of the peacefulness leave him, but he didn't move. "Aye, thee did," he replied quietly.

"Of whom?" She was tense in his arms.

He removed his chin from her head and leaned back against the hard horsehair sofa. He absently ran his fingers through her silky hair while he answered. "Thee spoke of people from thy past, of people long gone."

"I see."

They were silent for a few minutes as they listened to the grandfather clock tick and the fire pop, each with their own thoughts, grateful for each other's presence.

"China?"

"Aye?"

"Will thee marry me?"

"Aye, Shubael, I will."

It was done. They had severed themselves from their haunting memories. Shubael pulled China closer to him and pressed another kiss on her lips. She was warm and alive. If she didn't stir his senses as did Amedee, if she didn't set his blood pounding and fill him with excitement, at least she brought him contentment and companionship. In a way, he was glad he knew about China's feelings for Jake. It made him feel less guilty about not being able to love her.

It would be a good marriage, though, he thought. He would take the *Justice* on voyages to the frozen Antarctic in search of seals, then return to the comfortable company of this beautiful woman. He would pay off his debt, see that his mother was secure and build a future that was free of failure. With China he could do it; for China he could do it. She was his anchor, the center of his world. He kissed her again, well pleased.

China, too, was serene. She felt she had finally found the inner peace Aunt Judith had always talked about. Even though Shubael knew she couldn't love him, not completely and passionately, he wanted to marry her. She sensed that his feelings for her were similar, and that, yet, he still needed her. She owed him so much: he had saved her life and her home. She was glad she could somehow repay him.

Not that it was so onerous an obligation, she told herself. He was a kind and decent man who was offering her an honorable match. He respected her, he appreciated her. If he wasn't madly in love with her, perhaps it was just as well. Perhaps this feeling of fondness was more mature and enduring, perhaps it would protect her from the devastating grief, which her father had felt when Josephine had died.

She refused to consider Jake. As Shubael had said, he was a person from her past, long gone. Probably dead. Besides, if she thought of Jake, she would never marry Shubael, and she must, for his sake and for hers. She knew he needed her, and, after all, she acknowledged with a touch of resignation, what other choice did she have?

THEY MODESTLY MADE their announcement at Harriet and Obed's wedding supper in mid-November. Although the combined popularity and prominence of Benjamin Swain and Gideon Hussey had meant a huge reception in the afternoon after the ceremony at the South Church, by suppertime the party had dwindled to just those closest to the newlyweds.

Harriet sat at the center of the Swains' large mahogany table. She hadn't stopped smiling and blushing since early morning. It was very becoming, especially in the glow of the spermaceti candles, burning in the silver candelabras. Her white satin gown, scattered with pale pink embroidered rosebuds, fit gracefully on her small frame. Her white lace veil, held in place by a wreath of silk roses, made her warm brown eyes seem particularly large. Harriet would never be beautiful, but today she looked pretty.

On one side of her sat Obed, the object of her devotion, looking sheepish and slightly choked in his high, starched collar. By contrast, on Harriet's other side sat her brother Zenas, only lately returned from his long sojourn in England. Zenas, always slender and fair, with fine, regular features, had acquired a great deal of polish abroad. His accent and manners, though not overly British, were, nonetheless, slightly cultured; his suit had been superbly tailored on Savile Row.

China was sitting on the opposite side of the table and watched all three faces drop with their separate disappointments when Shubael quietly announced their intentions. Two of the reactions she greeted with amusement, one with grim dismay. She could tell that Obed felt somewhat slighted. Even though he no longer wanted her, he apparently felt offended that she should choose someone other than he. As if to prove his desirability, he leaned over and loudly bussed Harriet's cheek, then turned bright red.

The flash of frustration on Zenas's smooth face also tickled China. She knew he had been delighted to renew his acquaintance with his sister's long-legged and eccentric best friend. She sensed that he was surprised and enchanted by the graceful and dignified woman she had become. Now, even before he could pursue his interest, she was being snatched from his reach. Zenas studied Shubael with suspicion. He would never have picked this taciturn Quaker captain as the man China would marry.

Harriet's tight-lipped expression, Obed's kiss notwithstanding, was the one that caused China the most distress. Disapproval was plain on her face and China knew why. It wasn't because she disliked Shubael or because she felt that China shouldn't marry. It was because she felt that the only man who could make China happy was Jake. And to this day, she stubbornly refused to believe that Jake would not return. Though she readily accepted the probability that the *China Maid* was lost at sea, she felt that somehow Jake had not perished. In her good-hearted way, she wanted only happy endings. She was sure China's would come.

China's own lips pursed in response to Harriet's censure. Before she could mentally frame a reply, though, Benjamin's voice blotted out all other comment. "Well, that's fine!" he boomed. Obviously he wasn't aware of his children's opinions. "'Tis wonderful news. And 'tis coming on such a special day. Happiness begets happiness, I say. Well, well, well. Let me propose a toast." While everyone dutifully took up their flutes of champagne, Benjamin stood and beamed at his family and guests. "To China, who is like my second daughter, and to Shubael, who is my favorite shipmaster. Smooth sailing and greasy luck."

The words were echoed up and down the table. China attempted to hide her unexpected embarrassment by burying her face in the champagne, but the bubbles bothered her nose and she wound up sputtering.

"Easy, girl, easy," Benjamin cautioned from the head of the table. "We want you fine and fit for your wedding. Have you decided when it will be?"

China nodded while she regained her breath. "Aye. We've picked the eleventh day of Twelfth Month. By then, Harriet and Obed will be back from their wedding trip to Boston and settled in on Trader's Lane." She paused for a moment before continuing her explanation. For some reason, this just didn't seem real. "'Tis to be a small enough wedding, but it wouldn't be right if they weren't there."

"Well, that's fine," Benjamin said, again. "Shubael, come to see me in the study after supper. I have a special wedding present for you."

Shubael raised his eyebrows in surprise, but disappeared with Benjamin when the last of the roast pheasant and rice, the quahog pie, the saddle of venison, the scalloped potatoes, the relishes of cranberries, green tomatoes, and strawberries and rhubarb, the smoked eels, the onion bread, the squash rolls and the sugary sweet wedding cake were cleared from the table. While he was gone, China pulled Harriet aside and hugged her affectionately.

"I wish thee every happiness, Harriet," she said. "If ever a person deserved it, 'tis thee."

"Oh, China," Harriet replied, returning the embrace, "I wish the same for you, my dear, dear friend." It sounded more like a plea than a felicitation. At the sight of China's chin, stubbornly stiffening, however, she wisely said no more.

Walking home afterward, Shubael seemed preoccupied, puzzled. "Is something troubling thee?" China asked in concern. "Is it something Benjamin said to thee?" She felt slightly awkward, as if it were none of her affair.

Shubael brought himself back to the present. "'Tis not troubling," he said. "At least, it shouldn't be. Benjamin took me into his study and poured me a stiff tot of rum, all the time saying, over and over, how pleased he was that we were to wed. Then he said that two fine people like us should start our life together with a clean slate, so he was forgiving the remainder of my father's debt."

China gasped. "But that's splendid. 'Tis almost too generous."

"That's what I told him, but he said nay. He said 'twas a long time ago and that I had been most diligent and shown my good faith. That the service I have given him is enough, and that I should not spend my life paying for my father's mistakes. He said that it would make him happier if I spent my money on thee."

Again, China felt an unexpected wave of embarrassment, as if she didn't deserve such sentiments. "Thee must be most pleased," she said.

"Aye," Shubael said, thoughtfully. "I presume it likely that I am." Actually he wasn't quite sure how pleased he was. The repayment of his father's debt had hung before him for so long, it had taken a significant role in the shaping of his life. Now he felt adrift without it. "You can't spend the rest of your life paying for your father's mistakes," Benjamin had said. But he had. He was. Take that away and, like the mast and yardarms holding aloft the sails, everything collapsed.

He looked across at China. She was walking along beside him, long-sparred and lovely. Her good health had returned and with it some color on her porcelain cheeks, heightened now by the brisk breeze. She turned to meet his glance, gray eyes wide and ever intriguing with their charcoal accents and their outlines of dark, thick lashes. He pulled himself together. He still had China. She was his anchor.

15

NANTUCKET SOUND
December 11, 1845

"GET THOSE ANCHOR CHAINS stowed below, Mr. Myrick," Shubael said. "We'll not be needing them for a good while." He wrapped his wool muffler tighter around his neck, then thrust his hands deep into his pockets, seeking relief from the raw wind. He watched glumly as the massive anchor, still encrusted with sand from the Bar, was catted to the bow of the *Justice*, and as its thirty fathoms of chains were slid down the hatch for storage in the hold. It was just the beginning of a voyage.

The screech of sea gulls distracted him and he turned to stare behind him, to see the low, lumpy shape of Nantucket sitting between a cold, gray sky and a cold, gray sea. The solid, white brick silo of Great Point Light was still clearly visible; they weren't even an hour underway. He glanced at the sky to check the time, but the sun was hidden from view. He shrugged. He knew what time it was.

It was time for him to be standing in the Friends' Meeting House, joining his life with China's. At this very moment, he was meant to be marrying her, to be tying himself to a respectable, successful future. He was meant to be sailing this afternoon, not for the icy extremities of the Antarctic to hunt whales and seals, but for the civilized pleasures of Boston to celebrate his wedding. He was meant to miss this trip, to spend a whole year on land adjusting to married life. He shrugged again, burying his face farther in the folds of his muffler.

Benjamin had approached him four days ago, wringing his hands in apology. "I've a huge favor to beg of you," he had said, a sincere expression on his homely face. "'Tis my schooner the *Justice*. I know we agreed you would sit this voyage out, but she's all fitted and ready to sail. Josiah Folger was to take her. Then yesterday morning, he went out to the woodpile to grab a few sticks of firewood, and, what do you know, but he slipped on the early morning ice on his back porch, fell down the stairs and broke his leg. Thank heavens it wasn't worse, but he'll not be going anywhere for a good six months.

"I'm in a pinch, Shubael," he had said, rubbing his chin. "I've got to send the *Justice*, but have no one to be her master. Ephraim Myrick is a capable mate, but I don't think he's old enough yet for command. I'm asking you to take her on this trip. I'll try to make it up to you somehow. What do you say?" He had looked at Shubael anxiously.

Under the circumstances, Shubael could hardly refuse. Not only had Benjamin been more than magnanimous with his wedding gift, but he had also been kind and thoughtful over many years. "Aye, of course I'll take her," he had replied. "We'll have the wedding when I return."

Resolutely, Shubael turned his back on Nantucket and faced forward. He saw a ship approaching from the south, making for the anchorage he had just left. Her battered sails and her deep gunnels showed her to be a heavily laden whaler returning to Nantucket after a long, and obviously greasy, voyage.

As he watched her coming, mildly wondering who she was, he speculated about the future. Perhaps it was just as well that he was going now, he thought. With any luck his lay would be great enough for him to put this business behind him for good. He could start some enterprise on land, or invest his money in other ships' voyages.

"Ship off the starboard bow, sir," the first mate said, interrupting his thoughts.

"Aye, Mr. Myrick, I have her well in my sights," he answered, dryly. The unknown whaler was only a few hundred yards off, now, and raising her owner's identifying flag.

"I don't recognize the pennant. Does thee, Mr. Myrick?" Shubael asked the ruddy-cheeked young man at his side.

"Nay, sir. Shall I fetch the pennant register?"

"Aye, Mr. Myrick. Please do."

The whaler was even with them now, stealing their wind and making their sails fall into a shuddering sag. Her crew crowded to the rail, scruffy, weather-beaten men in ragged clothes, all laughing and shouting in excitement. At the wheel of the homeward-bound ship was a tall, broad-shouldered man, no older than Shubael, with dark, curly hair carelessly exposed to the wind, and a roguish grin spread across his strong, handsome face. When he turned his head, Shubael could see a small, gold hoop gleaming in his ear.

"Godspeed!" the stranger shouted, raising his hand in salute. "And greasy luck!"

Shubael acknowledged the greeting with a nod of his head and a wave. "Welcome home!" he called in reply, suddenly envious of the shabby ship. He heartily wished it were he, weatherworn and threadbare, but heavily burdened with oil, who was only hours from home, from the comfort and contentment of China's cozy house.

Ephraim Myrick came up the companionway carrying the pennant register just as the whaler glided past them.

Following her course with his eyes, Shubael saw her transom and the faded legend it bore. *China Maid. Nantucket.*

For a moment it seemed as if Shubael's heart stopped beating, and then it began again with slow anguish. He knew instantly that the rakish stranger at the helm was Jake, and he knew in the same moment that he had lost China, forever. Oh, she might eventually marry him because she had promised to do so, and she was a fiercely loyal person, but she would no longer need him. She would no longer rely on him for solace and support, to contentedly stem the loneliness or to generously stock the cupboard. Now she had wealth and she had love. He had nothing. He had lost his anchor.

"Sir?" Ephraim Myrick's face was uncertain. The stocky first mate hesitated to interrupt the thoughts that had put a bitter, distant look in Shubael's eyes and had harshly pulled the lean, angular lines of his face. "The register, Captain Brown."

Shubael stared at the booklet he was holding out, as if he had no idea what it was. Then he held out his hand and Ephraim carefully set the register in it. Scarcely seeing, he found the flag and confirmed what he already knew. *China Maid. prop. Zaccheus Joy.* He handed the book back to the mate and turned his eyes south, toward the barren ice of the Antarctic, toward a future as empty and desolate as the frozen ocean for which he was heading.

16

NANTUCKET
December 11, 1845

TRYING TO PRETEND TO HERSELF that it was just an ordinary day, China went about her morning routine efficiently. Bare toes shivering on the frigid floorboards, she hurriedly pulled her petticoats and her gray gown over her head. Then, seated on the corner of her bed, she donned her stockings and thought, as she had thought every winter day since she had lived in Nantucket, how wonderful it would be to replace the itchy wool hose with smooth, slippery silk. She jammed her feet into her boots, grabbed a clean fichu from her drawer and ran downstairs. She would knot it around her neck after she had stoked up the fire and had washed her face with warm water.

Ablutions over, China made toast, tea and bacon, set a solitary place at the end of the oak table and ate her meal alone. It was only then that a hint of resentment edged against her determined composure. She shouldn't be frying a single rasher of bacon and brewing one cup of tea. She should, at this very moment, be setting the table with cakes and confections, with a whole baked ham, with Aunt Judith's Chinese tureen full of scallop stew. Today she should be marrying Shubael, she should be settling her life into a comfortable, sensible mode, not living silent and alone, moving mechanically through suspended time.

With a sigh, China pushed herself away from the table and pushed away her morose thoughts. None of that, she warned herself. She had a whole year to go, twelve months to wait. It was too long a time to be consumed by self-pity. She knew that Shubael would be leaving her sometime when she accepted his proposal. What difference did it make when? What difference did it make if she passed the time as Mrs. Brown or as China Joy? It was all the same. It was a compromise.

Besides, she rationalized, as she dumped a kettle full of hot water into the dishpan, it was not as long as it could be. At least it wasn't a voyage to the South Pacific that lasted three or four or five years. At least her memory of him would not fade before he finally returned. She consoled herself with that thought and resolved to remain strong and calm, to maintain the sense of peace and serenity that was the cornerstone of her relationship with Shubael.

It was not easy. By midmorning she was roaming from parlor to kitchen, at a loss for something to do. During her years at Mrs. Mitchell's she had learned to condense her chores, to execute them swiftly, with no wasted motion. She had swept the floor, emptied the ash bin, aired her bed linen, filled the woodbox and even dusted the shelves of books, shells and South Pacific souvenirs that stood next to the grandfather clock.

Feeling restless and out of sorts, China slumped on the horsehair sofa and considered her options. She could, of course, clean Aunt Judith's room, opposite the parlor, or her father's, in the wart off the kitchen. She had closed the doors on both more than two years ago, promising to attend to them when she had time. Now she had the time, but not the desire. Today was not the day to be sifting through remembrances of the past.

Nor was it a day to pay a visit to Harriet. As much as she enjoyed her friend's company, she didn't feel she could face, with equanimity, Harriet's glow of newlywed bliss. She felt vaguely jealous when Harriet spoke of Obed in utter adoration, or when she blushingly recounted incidents of their wedding trip to Boston. It was more than Harriet's being married that China envied, it was her being in love.

She stood up quickly, anxious to end this train of thought before it, too, led to dangerous memories. Maybe she would take Zenas Swain up on his offer to show her around the offices of Swain & Son. He had made the suggestion the other evening, at supper on Gardner Street, ostensibly to give her a better understanding of the company for which her future husband worked, but actually because he was extremely attracted to her, despite her engagement. China knew she shouldn't encourage his attention, even though she found him to be an agreeable person. And, after fifteen years of friendship with Harriet, she was quite familiar with Benjamin's office above the bank, but she couldn't bear to be alone today.

Zenas was delighted to see China a short time later. He was fascinated by her exotic beauty and by her unusual poise. During his years in Europe, he had acquired an appreciation for sophistication, and no woman he had met since he came back seemed to possess quite so much as China. He measured sophistication by breadth of knowledge and experience, and despite her plain clothes and unaffected manner, he found China to have an ample share of both.

"I'm glad you decided to accept my invitation," he said, holding out both hands in welcome. "I was afraid you might think I was merely being polite."

"I've known thee too long, Zenas, to think such a thing," China answered. She undid her cloak and draped it across

Zenas's extended hands, deliberately misconstruing his gesture and avoiding contact. She softened her action with a smile and a mischievous wink.

"Besides," she added in all honesty, "I need to be distracted today, and to be in company other than my own. Thee can tell me tales of thy ships and shipping to occupy my mind and to keep me from moping. Perhaps thee even has an old newspaper or two from Paris, as thee used to."

Zenas hung her cloak on the rack by the door and gave her a mock bow. "It will be my pleasure to divert and amuse you, Miss Joy," he said, taking the hint. "We can start with a tour of the half models of the Swain fleet and proceed from there." With exaggerated decorum, he offered her his crooked elbow, and China slipped her hand delicately through it. He was only an inch taller than she, slender and elegantly built. For a moment they stood facing each other, then they both broke out in grins. The tension eased and they became old friends again.

For the next hour, true to his promise, Zenas very ably entertained China. She studied the intricate ship models, tracked their real-life counterparts' routes around a floor-standing globe, and listened with absorption as Zenas proudly explained the practical, and profitable, system they had for relaying cargo around the world. While most of the ships the Swains owned or had an interest in were whalers, some of the vessels served only to carry oil to England or seal skins to the Orient, returning with fine cloths and foods. It reinforced China's long-suppressed desire to have a merchant business of her own, to deal in interesting goods and with international commerce.

"We've just sent a ship to England," Zenas was saying, when the ringing of the Lisbon bell drowned him out. Only a block away, the peal was loud and insistent. Reflex excitement rose in China as she raced to the window, along with everyone else in the office. They were high enough up to see over the rooftops, beyond the wharves and the warehouses, around the lighthouse at Brant Point, to the Bar at the Chord of the Bay, where a whaler was setting her anchor and lowering her sails.

"Who is she?"

"Any sign of her pennant?"

"She's sitting deep...."

China heard the buzz of voices around her, felt the curious office staff crowding against her. Then, suddenly, she seemed all alone, the voices and people were far away. There was something familiar about that ship. Even at this distance, she recognized the rake of the foremast, the set of the bow. Shivers ran down China's spine; she had trouble drawing breath.

"May I see thy glass?" she heard herself asking Zenas. She held out her hand without ever removing her eyes from the whaler.

Zenas hesitated a moment, puzzled by the peculiar flatness of her tone and by the intent look in her gray eyes as they stared out the window. "Of course," he finally said, his politeness overcoming his sense of propriety. He laid the brass telescope in her hand.

Silently, China focused the glass on the shape of the ship. Her throat was very dry. She let her magnified view sweep along the bowsprit, over the deck and up the halyard to where the battered pennant was standing almost straight out in the December wind. Her heart started beating very fast. It was her father's pennant.

"'Tis the *China Maid*," she whispered.

"What's that you say?" Zenas asked, bending closer to her. He thought he had heard China's soft announcement, but he must have misunderstood.

"'Tis the *China Maid*," she repeated, her voice stronger now, gathering excitement after the initial shock. She squinted through the telescope, checking and double-checking the design of the pennant. It was her father's. She had stitched it herself six years ago.

"The *China Maid*?" Zenas said, disbelieving. "You must be mistaken. Here, let me see."

China tore her gaze away from the whaler and turned toward Zenas, handing him the telescope. Her gray eyes were shining with happiness, her clear white skin was aglow. "Nay, Zenas," she said, "I'm not mistaken. 'Tis the *China Maid*. 'Tis Papa's pennant. Oh, Zenas, she's come home at last!" Her voice was not dull and monotonal now, it was vibrant and alive. Every person in the room sensed her exhilaration.

"Are you sure?" Zenas questioned, again, as he started to refocus the glass. "No, wait, China!" he said, suddenly thrusting the instrument at a clerk by his side. Out of the corner of his eye he had seen China bolt for the door. "Where are you going?" he asked, racing after her.

"To the wharf," China answered, happily, grabbing her cloak off the rack and swirling it to her shoulders. She had ceased to bother with a bonnet.

"You mustn't," Zenas said, seizing her by the arms just as she had her fingers on the doorknob. He covered her hand with his and pulled her away. Still holding her hand, he led her back into the office.

"In the first place, you know very well the wharves are no place for a lady," he said. As China started to shrug in disdain, he hastily added, "And in the second place, it might be hours before they actually arrive on shore. This is no weather in which to be passing that time at the end of a windy wharf. You can see what is happening just as well, if not better, from here. And when the time comes," he finished wryly, "if I have failed to convince you, in the meanwhile, of the impropriety, I shall accompany you myself."

Buoyed up though she was with eagerness, China grudgingly conceded Zenas's point. His latter point. "'Tis a bit chilly," she admitted. "Aye, I presume it likely thee is right. I'll wait a while here." She refused to take off her cloak again, however, lest she waste time later pelting out the door.

Now not even noticing the ships' models or the intriguing maps, the imposing portrait of Benjamin, the stacks of foreign newspapers or the air of solidity and success created by the oak paneling and the Persian carpet, China paced in agitation. She interspersed her restless circuits of the room with short spells of sitting at the very edge of a polished Windsor chair, then frantic sprints to the window to follow the agonizingly slow progress of the lighter.

Though she nodded and smiled at Zenas in response to his attempts at calming her, she had no idea what he was saying. Her mind was racing even faster than her heart. She was alternately exultant with anticipation and overcome with chagrin for having given up hope. How could she think Zacch was dead? What did a silly dream mean, anyway? She was beginning to sound like John James Henry. She should have known that an overdue ship didn't necessarily mean she was lost at sea. Any number of things could cause a delay in ten thousand miles of open ocean. Soon, very soon, she would hear Zacch and Papa recount all of them.

Subconsciously, she excluded Jake from her thoughts. The suddenness with which the *China Maid* had reappeared was confusing enough to the new order of her life. She was still too stunned to sift through any emotions other than enormous relief and utter elation, especially since she had kissed Shubael goodbye only the night before.

318

"They're almost at the wharf, Zenas!" she finally cried, whirling away from the window. "I'm going to meet them."

"I'm coming with you," Zenas said, firmly. Even if he weren't concerned about China's safety, he had, by now, caught her excitement. "Just wait one minute while I get my coat and hat. Wait, China, you shan't miss them, I know. They've barely rounded the Point. I'll warrant you'll be shivering long before they tie up." Still buttoning his finely tailored coat, he followed China out the door and down the stairs. Only by taking a firm grasp on her arm was he able to restrain her from catching up her skirt and running to the dock.

As Zenas predicted, they reached the end of Straight Wharf while the lighter was still a few minutes off. He was wrong, however, about the effect the weather had on China. Far from being pinched with the cold, she looked positively radiant. Her silky black hair was flying in the wind, her cheeks were rosy. And her eyes, gray as the fog hanging over the island, were sparkling, joyous. Zenas held her arm tighter, warmed by her nearness, even though he knew she was oblivious to him.

China's gaze was fixed on the lighter, trying to pick out familiar faces, frustrated by the shadow and the set of the sail. Her stomach was knotted, but fluttering. Her mouth was dry. Every nerve in her body was clenched in anticipation, waiting. Waiting to catch sight of beloved faces almost lost to her memory. Waiting for familiar voices and laughs. Waiting for strong arms to scoop her high and hug her hard, bristly sunburned cheeks pressed against hers, to blot out the cold and the loneliness of six long years. Waiting for her family to finally come home.

Peering around the edge of the big mainsail, Jake saw China before she could see him. He caught his breath sharply. He thought he was prepared for this moment. He thought he had remembered her perfectly. But he hadn't. He had forgotten just how beautiful she was, how unusual, how graceful. He had forgotten how smooth and creamy her skin was, how her thick, straight hair shone. He felt desire spread through him, aching, arousing.

Shifting impatiently, he willed the lighter to go faster. He couldn't wait to wrap his arms around her, to fill his senses with her, to tell her how much he loved her. Jake was so immersed in his expectations, he almost didn't hear the natter of the lighter pilot, who had been alternately prying for Pacific news and giving out local gossip since he had come alongside. Almost.

"What did you say?" Jake asked quickly, spinning to face the skinny little man whose red nose was dripping.

For a moment he looked confused. He had said so much. "I presume it likely I was talking about her." He lifted his thumb off the halyard he was holding and pointed at China. "I was just sayin' ain't it somethin' what a real Nantucketer she is. Her lookin' so furrin' and all. But nay, she's the daughter of a whalin' cap'n, she's as good as married to a whalin' cap'n, and now she owns a whalin' ship to boot. There's no tellin'." He shook his head at the ways of the world.

"What do you mean, she's as good as married to a whaling captain?" Jake demanded. His stomach was growing cold in fear. He dimly hoped the scrawny man was referring to him, but that seemed unlikely. Even if China had announced their intentions, when he had left he was not a captain but a first mate.

"Just what I said," the pilot said, staunchly. "She's betrothed to Cap'n Brown. Brought him out to the *Justice* just last evening. The way I heared it, if Cap'n Joe Folger hadn't gone and broke his leg, and if Cap'n Brown hadn't shipped in his place, he'd be marrying that gal today. That's what they say." He brought the lighter expertly alongside the dock and dropped the sail. "Ho," he said, as an afterthought, "you must have gone bulwark to bulwark with him in the Sound."

But Jake didn't hear him. He had lost interest in the conversation. The particulars of China's betrothal didn't interest him. He was too devastated by her betrayal. How could she have forgotten him so easily? He thought he knew her better than that, he thought she had more faith. Obviously he was wrong, he thought bitterly. She must have changed tremendously since he saw her last. Why, her future husband was hardly over the horizon, and she was already arm in arm with yet another man. His fair, slim face looked vaguely familiar, but Jake was too outraged to wonder who he was. Grimly, he seized the top rung of the ladder and hauled himself to shore.

The instant that Jake set foot on the dock, China's heart swelled. Her head felt light. Almost in a trance, she found herself moving toward him, mesmerized. All other thoughts fled from her mind; the subconscious dam she had been building, to keep her feelings for him at a safe distance, burst in a sudden flood of emotion. For that first instant, that first moment when he stood before her, tall and rugged, his dark, unruly hair whipped by the wind, his strong, straight features burnished and browned by the South Pacific sun, the collar of his coat turned up against the cold with characteristic insouciance, that first moment, all China could think was that here was the man she loved, home to her at last.

Then she saw his expression. His deep blue eyes, so distinctive and commanding, were cold with disapproval. Under the force of his harsh stare, she faltered, and the spell was broken. Other thoughts came rushing back. She looked beyond him, straining once more to see her father and her brother. Samuel Easton came up the ladder behind Jake, and Henry came up behind him. Five grinning seamen set swaying legs on land and the cooper appeared shouldering his box of spoke shaves. China felt a flicker of anxiety, a little stab of fear, but she kept waiting. Four more sailors, the blacksmith, and Charlie Jones, the fourth mate, grown three inches since he left home. Then the skinny pilot struggled up the ladder and looped his bowline around a piling. The lighter was empty.

China turned disbelieving eyes back toward Jake. "Where's Zacch?" she asked in a small voice. "And Papa?"

Jake's hostility dissolved. Those enormous gray eyes, capable of such seduction, now seemed so vulnerable. Sympathy and sadness filled him as he felt the losses of Zaccheus and Zacch all over again, already grieving for her. In two rolling strides he closed the gap between them. He pulled his bare brown hand from his pocket and clamped it around her arm. "Come, China," he said. "Let's go home and I'll tell you." He glanced around at the crowd of curious townsmen, all pressing for news of the Pacific.

Panic suddenly swept through China. She wrenched free from Jake's grip. "Nay, Jake," she said, wildly. "Tell me now. Where are they? Where's Zacch? Tell me!"

"Hush, China, 'tis not the place," he placated, again taking her arm. "Let me take you home. We can talk there."

"I don't want to go home! I want my father and my brother," China cried. Tears were starting to roll down her cheeks, making wet trails on the luscious skin. "What has thee done with them? Where are they?"

Jake started to feel desperate. The onlookers were quiet now, intrigued by this drama. He wanted to get China off this public stage, to tell her the tragic news in private. He reached for her other arm and tried to steer her toward the head of the wharf. "Please, China," he said. "There's John Baker's hack. Let me help you in it and we can go home."

China pushed away his hands and took a step back. "Why won't thee tell me?" she asked, hysterically. She was incapable of gathering her wits. Fear and horror poured out of her. She knew the answer, but she had to hear him say it. "Where are they? Where are Zacch and Papa?"

Jake stepped after her, ready to reach for her, to attempt to soothe her, when Zenas appeared at her side, concern on his delicate face. "Really," he said to Jake, "you are frightening her." He looked pale and fragile in contrast to the broad-shouldered and sunburnt Jake. "Why can't you just answer her questions? It's your duty to give her a full report."

Jake's blue eyes narrowed in instant dislike. Irritation at this man rose in him. He had no business intruding in a family matter, no business treating Jake like an out-of-line employee. What was China doing with him anyway?

"Answer me!" China screamed, suddenly pounding her fist against Jake's chest. "Where are they? Why aren't Zacch and Papa here?"

"Because they're dead," Jake said, bluntly, not at all in the tender, gentle way he had practiced for the past two years. He instantly regretted his abrupt tone, regretted having allowed the polished, blond man to get the better of him. But it was too late.

For a moment China went totally still. Her clenched fist fell to her side. Her gray eyes grew wider, more horrified. Tears plastered her magnificent lashes to her cheeks. "China, let me tell you what happened," Jake started to say, trying to retract. She gasped, almost gagged. Both hands came up again, clutching her face. A great sob racked her body, buckling her knees. She collapsed on the splintery wooden planks of the walk, weeping uncontrollably.

That was it. It was final now. No more guessing, or supposing, or gradually dulling desires. Six years of waiting in vain welled up in China and overflowed. Six years of pent-up emotions, of frustrated longing, of heartbreaking loneliness were released in gushing, choking sobs.

Jake knelt down next to her, awed by the enormity of her grief. He wanted to cradle her in his arms, to relieve her of her pain. He put a hand on her shaking shoulder. "Let me carry you over to John Baker's hack," he said, softly. "I'll take you home."

"Don't touch me!" China shrieked, flinching away. Her anguish heightened her confusion, muddled her senses. "'Tis all thy fault!" she cried, unreasonably. She hardly knew what she was blaming him for, except for not being there when she needed him.

"You don't mean it," Jake said, reaching for her again. "You're distraught. I'm going to lift you into that hack."

"Leave her alone," Zenas said quietly. "Haven't you already done enough?" He, too, knelt by China and she sank into his arms, grateful for the comfort. Here was a man who was safe, a man who didn't go to sea, who wasn't a constant torture to the women who loved him. Weak and weeping, she allowed him to help her to her feet and to lead her, shakily, to the waiting carriage.

Jake sat back on his heels, astonished. As he watched them depart, he felt a mixture of jealousy and contempt. How dare this pallid young man in a prissy suit, with ink in his veins where red blood should be, claim a woman as vibrant as China? He was too fragile even to pick her up, to properly hold her. She didn't belong with such a watered-down, washed-out dandy. She belonged with him.

He stood up. "Samuel!" he barked. There was a savage tone in his voice. "Get a shipkeeping crew on board and get the rest of the men ashore." He glared across the wharf long enough to make sure his conscientious mate had heard him, then spun away and plunged through the throng of onlookers, intent on finding the nearest tavern and getting drunk.

BY EVENING, Jake had consumed a fair amount of rum, to no avail. The liquor did not blunt the sharpness of his pain, or ease the ache of his bitter disappointment. Even as he downed tot after tot, in an attempt to drown his old, cherished memories of China, a fresh image of her burned in his mind. He saw her as she had stood on the dock, with the wind tossing her silky hair and wrapping her cloak tightly around her tall, graceful body. He saw that brief moment when her eyes had looked only at him, filled with love and desire.

Mumbling an oath, Jake slammed down his glass and slapped some coins on the table to pay for his drinks. He decided to go see her right away, no matter the hour. He would do as her pale-faced escort had demanded, he would give her a full report of the trip, he would discharge his duty and deliver the *China Maid* into her hands. He would be done. When the next packet sailed for New Bedford, he would be on it. He wanted nothing more to do with Nantucket and the deep grief it had caused him.

Swaying slightly, more from the unaccustomed feel of firm ground under his feet than from the effect of the rum he had swigged, Jake arrived at China's cottage just as Harriet was closing the gate behind her. A full moon, hiding in the fog, lightened the December night. Despite the fact that her lantern remained unlit, Jake could clearly see the smile of relief and welcome on Harriet's plain face. He regarded her suspiciously.

"I'm so glad you're here, Jake," she said, holding out her hand. "I knew you would come home." It was true. Over all the years she had remained unrealistically optimistic about Jake's return. And although China had steadfastly refused to admit it, Harriet had remained convinced of her friend's powerful love for him. She approved. Knowing China better than anyone else in Nantucket did, she was sure that Jake, with his roguish grin and his rock-hard strength, was a perfect match for China's spirit and vitality.

It had never seemed right that China should consent to marry sober Shubael. In fact, it had been Harriet, anxious to prevent her friend from making a mistake, who had insisted that her father ask Shubael to ship out on the *Justice* this trip. While she had felt badly for Josiah Folger, she had almost considered his accident a stroke of fortune. Now she was sure of it.

"Thank you, Harriet," Jake said, stiffly, shaking her hand. "Though you seem to be sailing single-handed in your views."

Harriet's face fell a little. "Please don't be cross," she begged. "Zenas told me what happened this morning on Straight Wharf. I think, perhaps, he was impolite, even though he didn't mean to be."

"Ahh," Jake said, as the pieces suddenly fit. "That was your brother." Some of his jealousy eased.

"Aye, that was Zenas. He's only recently returned from England and I fear he's acquired a certain, um..." she paused, searching for a word that wasn't too unkind, "a certain aloofness of tone," she finished. "But he really meant no harm," she hastened to add. "He was just being protective of China. 'Twas a shock for her. Times have been bad for her.''

"Oh?" Jake said, hardening again, sarcastic. "They couldn't have been too bad if she's about to be wed. Or is she fretting because the marriage party had to be postponed?"

"Don't, Jake," Harriet chided softly. "China truly hit a patch of rough water. She nearly died, all alone and penniless, and no one even knew it."

Jake felt fear grip his stomach. "What do you mean?" he asked hoarsely. "How could that be? Where was Aunt Judith?"

"Oh, Jake," Harriet said, sadly. She took hold of his hand again and held it close to her heart. "Aunt Judith died almost three years ago, and China's lived here by herself ever since." She paused to shake her head sympathetically.

"It has been an awful time for her, but she wouldn't tell anybody. Her money ran out and the taxes were overdue and she had to work in a shop on Petticoat Row until Mrs. Mitchell made up some terrible lies about her. And then she got dreadfully ill and almost died."

"My God," Jake said in awe. He was stunned as much by the thought of such calamity as by Harriet's breathless recitation.

"She's quite recovered her health, now, though," Harriet quickly reassured him. "But you can see how wretched it's been for her. If she said some harsh things this morning, 'tis only because she has had more misfortune than she can bear. You understand, don't you, Jake? You will be gentle, won't you?"

It was on the tip of Jake's tongue to say he couldn't be anything else but gentle and tender, that he would fold China in his arms and soothe her, that he would kiss her until the sorrow subsided, that he would fill her empty life with love, but then he remembered that China had chosen someone else for that role. His own pain returned.

"You needn't fret," he said, in a cool, correct tone, extracting his hand from Harriet's grasp. "I'll do nothing to deliberately gally her. I mean only to discharge my responsibility, to give her my report."

"Oh, Jake," Harriet said again, in exasperation this time.

"Oh, Harriet," Jake mocked back. For a moment his mischievous grin broke across his face. "I see there is a band on your wedding finger," he said, trying to divert her attention. "I hope 'tis Obed Hussey you've finally got your iron in."

Harriet blushed. "Aye," she said, happily. "We've been married for almost a month."

"Well, I give you both my felicitations," Jake said sincerely, bending over to peck Harriet's cheek. Then he moved past her and through the gate.

"Jake," Harriet said, not wholly distracted.

"Aye?" Jake paused and turned back to regard her.

"Be patient."

"Good night, Harriet." He turned again and made his way purposefully down the path. Harriet sighed and headed for home.

Jake tapped softly, then let himself in through the front door. Despite his cold resolve, being in the little cottage again affected him unexpectedly. The steep staircase, rising in front of him, reminded him of all the evenings he'd spent upstairs, listening to Zacch's easy breathing and speculating on whether China was awake on the other side of the chimney. He walked quietly into the parlor, half expecting to see Aunt Judith in her ladder-backed chair by the hearth and Zaccheus in his rocker, the chess board set up and ready on the small pine table beside him. Except for the simple furniture, the well-worn rag rugs and the grandfather clock, though, the room was empty. A heaviness at the back of his throat melted some of his icy resentment.

When Jake walked through to the kitchen, the sight of China thawed him completely. She was leaning against the cupboard, gazing out the window, across the moonlit moor. With a wrench, he remembered the last time he had discovered her in that position, at dawn so many summers ago. Hours later he had tracked her down in the thickets by Hummock Pond, asleep against a log, her lush lips stained purple from blueberries. He had kissed those lips for the first time that day, a hard, hot kiss, intensified by the driving rain against their bodies.

Jake went to stand silently next to her, studying her profile. She wasn't weeping now, nor did her eyes show any sign of redness or recent tears. They were only deeply, profoundly, sad. The somberness on her beautiful face, even more than his own haunting memories, made Jake mourn anew. He put his shoulder against the wall, leaning his long, strong body at an angle to China's. He reached across and took her hand. "Shall I tell you about it?" he asked, quietly.

For the first time, China turned her head to look at him. She did not remove her hand from his, but she did not return the pressure, either. "Please do," she said, her voice calm, but remote.

Jake took a deep breath and began. "'Twas March seventh, eighteen forty-three that your papa passed away. He had caught a tropical fever in Valparaiso that he had never been able to totally shake. He would seem to recover, and then the fever would come on him again. Each time it took

329

a little more out of him. Then he got caught out overnight when a whale gave his boat a sleigh ride out of sight.''

"He ought not have gone," China reproved mildly, tears rising in her eyes again, but not flowing down her cheeks.

"Zacch tried to stop him," Jake explained. His deep voice was slightly husky as he relived the incident in his mind. "But Zaccheus wouldn't hear of it. We'd been plagued by bad luck and the hold was still nearly empty. He was determined not to waste any opportunity.

"When we came on him the next morning, he had the fever again. He died the next day." He hesitated a moment, squeezing her hand. "He looked very peaceful. He was with his Josephine at last."

China nodded noncommittally and turned back to stare out the window. This all seemed so unreal, as if she were replaying the past, reburying her family. Only now she had dates and causes, she had certainties.

"And Zacch," she said, softly, her head still lolled against the cupboard, her eyes still probing the moonlit shadows on the moors. "It was in June the following year, wasn't it?" She blinked on a tear as she remembered her horrifying dream. "The sixteenth."

"Aye, it was," Jake said, astonished. "How did you know? I had no chance to write you. We never bespoke a homeward-bound ship till we were on course for Nantucket ourselves."

China just shrugged in reply. She was too choked to speak.

"He said so," Jake said, slowly, remembering. "He said you'd know." He hadn't realized that this was what Zacch had meant. He hadn't realized that the bond between the twins was quite this powerful. It seemed doubly devastating that such a tie should be severed. "I'm sorry, China."

Again China did not reply. She withdrew her hand from his and held it against her slender, white throat, as if trying to push down the tears gathered there. She didn't want to hear any more. It didn't make any difference how Zacch had died. He was gone. She would never see him again. It had happened a long time ago and it didn't change the way she felt now.

Sensing her mood, Jake refrained from describing the careening cask and the bubbles of blood on Zacch's waxen lips. Instead, he quietly began to relate the other details of the voyage. It was not the cut-and-dry report that he had originally intended, but a concerned account, chronicling their early misfortunes and the greasy luck that had favored them at last.

"We brought home thirty-three hundred barrels," he concluded, hoping to coax some sign of interest into her increasingly withdrawn expression. "You are a wealthy woman. You never have to worry about money again."

When only a flicker of her lovely lashes indicated that she had even heard what he was saying, Jake changed the subject again. "I've heard that you are betrothed," he said. He tried to keep his tone dispassionate, level, but his voice rasped with uncontrollable resentment. "I suppose I should offer my congratulations." Still leaning against the wall, he crossed his arms on his chest and fixed his blue eyes on her. "Who is he, China?" he demanded.

China darted a glance at him, then quickly looked away. She was expecting his question, but she was still unprepared to answer it. She felt bruised and weak, worn out with emotions. She could scarcely straighten one from the other, sorrow from relief, anguish from amazement, love from loyalty. "He is Shubael Brown," she said at last. "He is master of the *Justice*."

"I know his name," Jake said, bitterly. "Who is he?"

China knew what he meant, but her mind seemed blank, washed empty by her tears. She squeezed shut her eyes and rubbed her brow, as if to conjure up an image of Shubael that could help her explain who he was in her life. She shrugged her shoulders. "He's Shubael," she repeated, lamely.

Angrily, Jake straightened up and seized China by the arms, wheeling her around to face him. "Is that all you can say?" he asked, fiercely. He made no effort to control his rancor now. Set against his sun-darkened face, his cold blue eyes seemed unusually startling. "Have you decided to marry him because you've taken a fancy to his name? Has he no other attributes?"

"Nay, he has many good qualities," China answered, defensively, struggling to free herself from Jake's clutches. His touch, no matter how rough, seemed to stir the life in her again. "He's kind and considerate and always respectful," she said, her own temper starting to rise.

"That could be Harriet you are describing," he snapped, giving her an ungentle shake. "Or old Asa Harkens, or three dozen other people. That's a reason to pay someone a call on a Saturday afternoon, not to get married. Why, China, why? I thought you were going to marry me."

"Thee?" China said, scornfully, pushing her palms against his hard chest. She was angry now. Angry at the way he was imprisoning her with his iron grip, and angry at the accusation in his voice. "How could I marry thee? Thee wasn't here. Thee was too busy sailing around the world hunting whales, or whatever it was that occupied thee for so many years. I could as easily have married the smoke from my chimney or my breath on a cold morning as I could have married thee. 'Twould be the same thing. Thee all disappear into thin air, without a word or a warning...."

"I wrote to you," Jake said, exasperated. He ignored the pressure of her pushing hands. "I told you why we were delayed."

"Ha!" China snorted. "Does thee mean that scanty little note thee sent with that gaudy shawl? Thee wrote that not even a year after thee departed, and for all the news it gave, thee needn't have bothered."

"I wrote more than that," Jake said. "I left half a dozen letters to be picked up by ships heading home. Long letters, detailing our voyage and telling you why we were delayed. Zacch wrote you, too. And your papa."

China gulped. She felt another wave of grief at the thought of Zacch's last words to her also lost somewhere in the vast oceans of the world. "I never received them, if that is so," she said in a smaller voice, her anger slackened by this new sorrow.

Jake gave her another shake, less harsh this time. "You should have known, China," he said, reprovingly. "You should have known that there are hundreds of problems that can delay a whaler: sickness, repairs, poor luck, bad weather. You were out over five years, yourself. 'Tis not unusual, though we might wish it to be different. And 'tis half a world away, with no reliable postal system. You should have known."

Her moment of grief gave way to renewed wrath. "The only thing I knew," she said, fighting to free herself, again, "is that thee didn't come back. Thee sailed blithely off in pursuit of whales, and save that one insulting shawl, 'twas the last I heard of thee until this day. Now let go of my arms."

Jake disregarded her demand and tightened his fingers around her soft flesh. "How is it that you can marry a whaling captain," he asked, acidly, "when you are so contemptuous of the whaling industry? Or does your Shubael have some secret methods that the rest of us don't know about? Perhaps he is able to fill his hold in the harbor, going out in the morning and coming home for supper. You might even pack him his noontime dinner.

"Or perhaps he raises whales, the way some people raise sheep. Does he have a whale farm off of Tuckernuck? When the day is fair and he feels the need, does he cruise out of Madaket and fasten on a few? Is that how he does it, China?" He shook her again. "Does he have a nice, clean, safe job? Is that why you agreed to marry a whaler?"

"Stop it!" China screamed. "Thee is being unfair. Thee has no right to say such things about him. For that matter, thee has no right to say anything about me. Thee went away. Thee left me alone for six years. How long did thee expect me to wait? To keep faith? Six years, Jake! Thee has been gone for six years."

As she shouted, her fists balled up and beat against the arms trapping her so close to him. She could smell the rum on his breath and the scent of the sea on his skin. She felt dizzy. Suddenly she ceased pounding against his steely arms. Her clenched fists opened. With a moan, she buried her face in her hands.

"He was there when I was all alone," she sobbed. "He was there when thee wasn't. He's a good man. He'll never break my heart."

China's woebegone words hit Jake harder than her blows had. His bitterness dissolved, and his bruising grip on her eased. Now he understood. She hadn't forgotten him, hadn't tossed him away like a book she'd grown bored with. Nor did she love Shubael. If he couldn't break her heart it was only because she hadn't given it to him. She had been lonely, and, what had Harriet said? She'd been penniless and ill. Shubael had been here when he hadn't, but she still loved him. He was sure of it.

With one hand he pried her fingers away from her tear-streaked face and turned it up toward his. With the other he cradled the back of her head. "Don't cry," he whispered, placing the breath of a kiss on her wet, reddened cheek. "Please don't cry." His lips trailed down her satiny skin until, salty with her tears, they brushed over her mouth.

Heat surged through China, even as she shivered. "Nay, Jake," she said weakly, fighting with herself as much as with him. "Nay, 'tis too late."

"'Tis not too late, China," he said, softly, bringing both hands around to hold her face. With his thumbs he gently wiped away the teardrops clinging to her thick lashes. He set another gossamer kiss on her lips, then traced its imprint with the tip of his tongue.

"I love you," he said, his sea-blue eyes fathoms deep with desire. "You are part of my life." He lowered his face again, touching his lips to hers, lightly at first, tasting, tender, then crushing, the hunger of six long years released by the clean scent and sweet flavor of her skin. His fingers twined through her hair, pressed down her back, following the lush curves of her body, remembering, reveling.

China hesitated. For a moment her entangled commitments, her facade of complacency, intruded upon her senses. Then she surrendered. She let his urgency, his insistence overwhelm her. She let the strong circle of his arms block out the world beyond, until the only things that existed were his lips laying sensuous kisses in the curve of her neck, his knowing hands stroking, tantalizing her sensitive flesh, and his hard, muscled body pressing against hers, spreading a delicious ache through her belly. She surrendered completely, with abandon, to her long-suppressed passion, to her love for Jake.

She arched closer, clutched his broad shoulders, buried her face in the salt spray of his curls. She wanted to fuse with him, melt into him, become part of his being and have him become part of hers. Her fingers ran a loop around his ear, her tongue chafed against his rugged, sun-scorched cheeks, her thighs strained toward him.

"I love thee, Jake," she said, slipping her hand under the frayed collar of his shirt, thrilling at the hot, tropical touch of his bare back. "I want thee," she said, responding to her body and to her heart. Jake swung her into his arms and carried her upstairs to the soft comfort of her feather bed.

BY THE NEXT MORNING, however, reality was as cold as the fire in the cookstove. China rose first, leaving her oblivious rapture in the warm bed with Jake. As she had done only yesterday, she quickly drew on her petticoats and dress, but dashed downstairs holding her boots and woolen stockings, her toes cringing from the icy floorboards. Sitting in a kitchen chair, she pulled on the itchy hose, stopping suddenly with her skirt heaped in her lap. She was a wealthy woman, now, Jake had said. She no longer had to dream about silk stockings, she could buy as many pairs as she wished. Somehow the thought was unsettling, anticlimactic, not as exciting as it should be.

Shivering in the December draft, China carried out the rest of her morning routine. She shaved kindling onto the barely lit embers, stuffed chunks of stove wood on the flames and set a kettle of water to warm so she could wash her face and thaw out the frozen pump. As she mechanically went about her chores, China reassessed the situation. Though her body still tingled from the effects of making love to Jake, her mind was bewildered.

Yesterday, a virtual pauper, she should have married Shubael. Instead, she became rich and slept naked next to

Jake. She should have been content, instead she was ecstatic. She should have become a wife, instead she became an orphan. She had meant to make it an ordinary day, instead her world turned upside down.

When Jake descended, a little while later, the kitchen was warm and cozy, but China was not. She was standing by the stove, stirring savory-smelling applesauce, as he entered the room. Delight filled him at the sight and the smell. In three strides he was across the kitchen, capturing her in an exuberant hug.

"Don't," she said, pulling away his arms and spinning out of reach, her hand still clutching the long-handled, wooden spoon.

"Don't?" Jake asked, advancing toward her. His blue eyes were lazy and laughing, a grin split his handsome face.

China backed away, thrusting the spoon in front of her. "Thee mustn't," she said, her voice trembling. "Thee mustn't touch me anymore."

"What?" Jake stopped still, his brow puckering in puzzlement. "What are you saying?" His tone was curious more than concerned.

Taking a deep, quivering breath, China said, "What happened last night was a mistake. Thee took me by surprise. It must not happen again."

Jake's eyes narrowed and the warm light in them cooled. He put his hands on his hips, saying, "If this is your idea of a joke, China, 'tis not very amusing."

"I am not making a joke," China said, more firmly. She shook her head for emphasis, sending shiny black hanks of hair flopping across her creamy cheeks. "I have thought this over and I have made some decisions." She lowered her spoon and looked him squarely in the eyes, magical, seductive gray meeting startling blue.

"And what are those momentous decisions?" Jake asked, a touch of sarcasm in his tone.

"I am going to sell the *China Maid* and I am going to marry Shubael."

"What!" Jake said again, this time stunned. A reflexive knot of fear tightened his stomach.

China turned to stir the applesauce again, though the aroma no longer seemed so tempting. Eyes fixed on the flecks of cinnamon swirling beneath her spoon, she explained, "I cannot live like this any longer, Jake. I cannot bear these high crests of elation that always end in troughs of terrible grief. The brief moments of happiness are not worth the high price I must pay." Suddenly disgusted by the applesauce, she pushed the pot to the back of the stove and turned to face Jake again.

Almost beseeching him to understand, she said, "I have, one by one, lost my whole family. I'm sailing single-handed through life. I must clear the decks and stow things neatly, or I'll capsize for sure. Can't thee see, Jake? The only course is to be rid of the *Maid* and to marry Shubael. It will bring order into my life."

Still too astonished to think straight, to remember that she was somewhat in shock, Jake demanded, "What kind of order is that? You love the *China Maid*. 'Tis your namesake and your home. And you love me. You know we belong with each other."

China shook her head again, pressing her pink lips together. "The *China Maid* is no longer my home," she said. "'Tis a place I lived with Maman and Papa and Zacch." She paused to swallow the lump suddenly rising in her throat. "They're gone now." She cleared her throat before continuing. "This is my home. This cottage. And I would have lost it if it were not for Shubael. He paid the taxes when Mr.

Hawkins would have taken it. Shubael saved my life and saved my home. I owe it to him to wed.''

Jake ran his fingers through his hair in exasperation. "Bilge!" he shouted. "You owe him *money*, you don't owe him marriage. 'Tis no reason to marry a man you do not love. You're rich now, you can pay him back the damned tax money. If it will ease your conscience, you can pay him back one hundred percent interest. Two hundred percent.

"For that matter," he said, whirling and smacking his palm on the oak table, "*I'll* pay him back. Hell, I'll *buy* him a whole house, if that's what he wants. I'll have a mansion built for him on the bluff on Orange Street, or I'll build a fourth brick house on Main Street like the three that Joseph Starbuck built for his sons. You can't trade your life for a pile of boards and a stack of shingles, China. You can't marry that man!"

"I can and I will," China retorted. She could respond more easily to Jake's anger than to his hurt and bewilderment. She allowed her own temper to explode as she said, contemptuously, "Thee can only think in terms of dollars and cents. 'Tis not money that I owe Shubael, but loyalty. He was here when I needed him. Now I must be here when he needs me. 'Tis as simple as that. There is more to life, and to marriage, than passionate fits of love. Thee must grow up, Jake. Thee must learn to recognize the true virtues in this world."

"Nay, China, 'tis you who must grow up," Jake thundered. "I told you once before that that sanctimonious prattle has no place in your mouth. Your mouth was made for smiling, for laughing, for turning purple from eating blueberries, for kissing, not for pursing up like a prune and spouting pious platitudes." He pointed his finger at her, furious. "There is precious little else in this world worth more than love. Especially for someone as full of life as you." He jabbed his finger through the air to reinforce his words.

"I've said it before, you were born a Joy. You were aptly named. Now you want to hide that joy, to become Mrs. Brown. Plain, decent, joyless Mrs. Brown. You want to become an old *corbeau* instead of a swan. Mrs. Swan. Beautiful, happy, vital Mrs. Swan."

"'Tis only a name, Jake," China snapped. "'Tis not a nursery riddle." Despite her heated reply, a chill ran down her spine at his words. Still, she stubbornly maintained her stance. She was too overloaded with emotions to analyze them. She had to cling to the constant facts of life, not grab for the shooting stars. She had to keep her promise to Shubael and to the calm existence he represented.

They stood glaring at each other, at a stalemate. Despite his fury, Jake recognized, by the grim set of China's delicate jaw, the futility of arguing any further. "Very well," he finally said, his eyes slitted in his harshly drawn face. "If this is the course you've charted, you must sail it." He lifted his coat from the back of the chair, where he had dropped it last night. Shrugging into it, he said, "I'll see to the off-loading of the *Maid* as my *final* duty. Then I'll oblige you by removing myself from the dreary prospect of your life."

He stalked to the door and lifted the latch, then turned for one parting remark. China's face followed him, pale and tense. "Where is he now, China?" he asked, bitingly. "When I leave here, you'll be all alone again. Where is your savior this time?" He didn't wait for an answer, but turned and went out, slamming the door behind him.

China stared at the closed door. She listened to the diminishing sound of his feet crunching against the shells in the path. She heard the gate being shut. Then there was silence. The kitchen was empty. With a sharp intake of breath, with a heartwrenching wail, China collapsed to the floor, weeping with renewed loss.

17

NANTUCKET
January-February 1846

WITH A TRIUMPHANT FLOURISH she didn't quite feel, China signed her name to the bill of sale. The *China Maid* was now the property of Jacob Swan. Although China could sense the eyes of Jake, and Benjamin and Zenas Swain, in whose offices they were sitting, watching her expectantly, she didn't look up. She pretended to be rereading the legalese, but the neatly scribed words were actually a blur before her. In her mind, she was seeing the *China Maid*.

She knew every timber and plank in the old ship, every halyard and sheet, every hatch, stanchion, deadeye and davit. She had spent the happiest years of her life roaming the whaler's beamy decks, secure in the warm presence of her family. The *China Maid* had been her home, but it had also been the source of her greatest sorrow. First, her beautiful, laughing mother had died, shivering and pitching in a treacherous storm off the Horn, then her father had succumbed to a debilitating fever in the very same berth. With a final vicious kick, the old whaler had let loose and killed her beloved twin. That was enough. China wanted nothing more to do with the ship. At last she looked up at Jake, a defiant gleam in her eye.

"'Tis thine," she said, pushing the paper toward him.

Equally as defiant, Jake seized the document and thrust it, roughly folded, into the pocket of his coat. He had half hoped China would renege on her promise to sell the *China Maid*, would begin to behave rationally again, but she had insisted on putting the old vessel on the market. And although he had scoffed at her motives, deeming her emotional purging melodramatic and superstitious, it was his own sentimentality that made him buy the old ship. With the money he had invested in New York, he could certainly afford to have a new one built; he could afford a whole fleet, for that matter, but he couldn't bear the thought of losing the *China Maid*.

Despite the arduous life at sea, he, too, had found great happiness and family warmth on board. The ship was alive with memories of the people he had loved the most in this world. Even its name was a constant reminder of the woman who was part of his soul. After his cold-tempered departure from Nantucket last month, it had taken only three days in New York for him to confess he couldn't just walk away and forget China. He couldn't give her up. When the next packet had sailed from South Street, he had been on it, determined to purchase the *China Maid*. China's namesake seemed somehow symbolic of his hold on her. If he kept the whaler, he felt he could also regain the woman; to lose one would be to lose both.

"It is," he responded. "I'm well pleased with my bargain. She's a trim, tight ship, who'll do me proud. We belong together." He stared pointedly at China, daring her to understand his double meanings, to acknowledge their love.

China's gaze faltered before Jake's intense blue eyes. Her thick lashes lowered and a pink blush tinged her cheeks as she murmured, "I wish thee greasy luck." She might have said more if it weren't for the presence of the Swains, especially Zenas. She might have broken down and admitted she had been miserable without him, that she had been enormously relieved when he had returned from New York insisting that she sell him the *China Maid*, that she invented errands to do in town in the hope she would catch sight of him. But instead, she just sat there, examining the pen she was still holding.

"Well, well, well," Benjamin said, rubbing his generous chin. "I think it has been a fair deal for both parties. Everyone profits. 'Tis the way I like to do business. And here's another business practice I like to indulge in." He rose from his chair and went to the oak cabinet behind his desk. When he opened the door, several cut crystal decanters were revealed.

"I always like to seal an agreement with a drink and a gam. What will you young folks have? China? How about a small glass of sherry? I know your Aunt Judith taught you not to drink, but this is a special occasion and it is a particularly nice cask from Spain. And 'tis so delicate and mild you'll scarcely believe you're imbibing wine." As he spoke, he poured some sherry into a tiny, stemmed glass, and handed it to China with a wink.

"Thank thee," she said, smiling. "'Tis a lovely amber color so I'm sure it can do no harm."

Benjamin rubbed his chin and nodded in approval, then he turned to Jake. "How about you, Shipowner?" he said, congenially. "I've an excellent rum that Peleg Gibbs brought up from Jamaica last year. Or a first-rate brandy Zenas brought home from Europe."

Jake cast an amused glance at Zenas at the mention of his name. It somehow seemed right that the young dandy would return from an ocean voyage with a barrel of brandy. Zenas stared coolly back at Jake, his stylish appearance and blond good looks in sharp contrast to Jake's comfortable clothes and rugged complexion.

"Thank you, Benjamin," Jake said, rising and turning his back on Zenas, "but I really can't stay. I'd enjoy downing a tot with you some other time, but at the moment I have many arrangements to make. I mean to sail again in April."

He turned toward China in time to catch a look of dismay flash across her face. It reassured him. Actually he was ambivalent about sailing again, but he wanted to prod China into some sort of reaction. He wanted to prove to her that she still loved him.

Holding his hand out to her, and grinning, he said, "I wish you luck, too, China. And don't let Benjamin teach you too many bad habits." He nodded toward the small glass on the mahogany table by her side. When she blushed again, but laid her slender hand in his, he squeezed it gently and added, in a more serious tone, "If you need any help at all, please let me know. I'll come at once."

For a moment it seemed as if she would accept immediately. It seemed as if she were going to succumb to the will of her heart instead of the discipline of her head. For one moment he could read the longing in her wonderful eyes, feel the desire in her grip. Then she gathered herself together and withdrew her hand. "Thank thee," she said, politely. "But I'm sure I'll manage. The Swains are always here when I'm in need. Besides, I am sure thee will be very busy before thee leaves."

Jake's grin turned bitter under the blow of her sweetly spoken, but sharply directed words. She was reminding him of his long absences, of her lonely waiting while he was occupied with whaling. She was telling him, once again, why she wanted nothing to do with him. Forcing himself to be civil, he shook hands with Benjamin and Zenas and strode out of the room, rigid with frustration.

When Jake left, deed to the *China Maid* stowed in his jacket, China felt something in her close. She had truly severed every tie to her past. Despite the fact that it was what she wanted, what she intended to accomplish when she had sent Jake away and had put her ship up for sale, she was, nonetheless, unprepared for the peculiar, desolate feeling it created. She had expected to feel liberated, instead she felt bereft, an orphan in all senses.

Even John James Henry, whose initial greeting had been boisterous, seemed cut off from her. Puzzled by the obvious tension between China and Jake, he had gradually ceased coming to see her. He wasn't sure to whom he owed his loyalty: to China who was the daughter of the man who saved his life, or to Jake who was the man who had taken his place. In the end, he opted for what was most familiar to him. He accompanied Jake to New York, calmly ignoring Jake's growls of dismissal, and, again, back to Nantucket. Another link to China's childhood was lost.

"Are you listening, China?" Zenas asked.

With an effort, China forced herself to focus on what Zenas was saying, to put her forlorn thoughts to one side. They were just mawkish reactions, she told herself sternly. After all, why did she need to hang on to these people and things that reminded her of a life long gone? For every happy memory, she had paid a thousand times over in misery. She was best rid of them, better off embarking on the future without carrying any cargo from the past.

"Aye, Zenas, I am listening," she responded, struggling to regain control. "Thee was saying something about Edwin Gardner. Isn't he the man who ran off to Portugal with the daughter of Jorge Cabral last summer? I remember it caused quite a scandal and the town elders went about shaking their heads solemnly. Is he the one thee refers to?"

"The very same," Zenas answered wryly, "although I wasn't talking about his personal life. It was his business interests that concerned me."

"I don't understand why there was so much fuss," China interrupted, involved in her own musings, now. "True, she is considerably younger than he, but she comes from a decent family and they say she is quite beautiful. As I heard it, he was very faithful to his first wife, though she was abed and ailing for years. This Serafina was a nurse and housekeeper who came to help with his wife during her last months. And when she died, Edwin fell in love with the girl and eloped. I think it is a perfectly lovely story and nowise immoral, so I don't see why people are whispering and pointing their fingers and saying he took leave of his senses."

"They are saying so for a great many reasons," Zenas said, rearranging the already neat stacks of papers on his desk. "Chief among them because most people are basically suspicious of anything out of the usual, but also, and perhaps more justifiably, because he left quite a financial muddle behind. Which is where you could benefit, China."

"I?" China asked, startled. "What possible connection could I have with Edwin Gardner?"

"I was starting to explain, but you weren't paying any attention. You didn't even hear Papa saying goodbye to you," Zenas said, with mock severity. "Are you listening now?"

"Aye," China answered, meekly.

"Edwin Gardner had a very respectable importing business established," Zenas began, leaning back in his chair and letting his slender fingers run along the gold watch chain suspended across his chest. "It wasn't a large operation, but he did well enough. He consigned his goods on the ships of others, and though it cost him more in cargo charges, he was spared the expense, and the risk, of owning his own ship. Then a year or so ago, he decided that was no longer enough.''

Zenas paused and rubbed his chin, an unconscious gesture copied from his father. ''Perhaps that was when he began to lose his grip on the helm,'' he said speculatively. Then he shook his head and sat up, smiling across at China. ''In any event, we shall leave that point for the public at large to debate, as I am sure they are better equipped than either you or I.''

China smiled back. ''Very probably,'' she agreed.

''So,'' Zenas resumed, leaning back again, ''he went to the Pacific Bank and managed to convince them to make him a loan covering the cost of his own ship, a smart-looking clipper he meant to build at Brant Point. He had John Hoskins design it specifically for fast trips across the Atlantic. Most of Gardner's trading was in Spain and Portugal. It is a beauty, I must admit. And it is sitting, half completed, and currently the property of the bank. I *know* they are most unwilling proprietors; they're in the banking business, not the shipping business. They are quite eager to dispose of it. This is where you come in.''

As Zenas's words sank in, China felt excitement growing in her, filling the empty hole where she had just been brooding. She remembered the daydreams she had had while dusting the shelves at Mrs. Mitchell's General Emporium. A merchant ship. To sail across the ocean in pursuit of exquisite silks and fine furniture, to hunt for perfumes and wines and elegant porcelains, instead of for whales. It had seemed like an impossible notion then, an unattainable wish, but all of a sudden, it was here in front of her. All she had to do was reach out and take it. The thought left her temporarily speechless.

"Well?" Zenas asked, teasingly. He could see by the glow in China's lovely gray eyes that she found the thought of owning Edwin Gardner's half-finished ship very appealing. "Didn't you mention to me that you were interested in investing your profits in the merchant trade? I could find several parties to buy shares with you on this venture. And I could be the ship's agent as well. It's one of the services our company does, you know."

"Nay, Zenas," China said, hunching forward in her chair, animated. Once she started talking, the words tripped over themselves rushing to be said. "I want to own the ship all by myself. And I want to run the business by myself, too. I don't want to sit at home knitting while thee makes all the decisions, and I only know what is happening when I receive thy quarterly reporting. Of course," she added, hastily, "I welcome thy advice and aid, especially at first, but I want to be an active owner."

"It is a great risk, China," Zenas said, cautiously. He hadn't expected quite such an outpouring of enthusiasm from her. "I would have to advise you to spread your investments over several ventures. In the long run, the profits will be greater because of the fluctuation in the market. I just mentioned this one to you today because I heard of it this morning. Other opportunities will come along, though, and it really is the wiser course to reserve some capital for those, too."

China shook her head, waiting impatiently for Zenas to finish talking. She wasn't interested in other investment opportunities or in enlarged profits. Here was her chance to fulfill her ambition, to prove to herself, and to everyone else, that she was capable of running a business, that she could combine her love of the sea with her dislike of whaling, that she could be successful. And that she could do it by herself. The thought thrilled her.

"I don't want to reserve capital, Zenas," she said, her excitement propelling her even farther forward in her seat. "I want to buy that ship. I've imagined this moment for so long, I know exactly how I shall proceed. I know much more than thee suspects, and where I lack knowledge, thee can guide me. Please, Zenas, don't sound stodgy and prudent. Please say that thee will help me get her."

Zenas regarded her for a long moment. His business sense told him to attempt to make China change her mind, to have her invest the funds more carefully, but there was something about the spirited expression on her face, something about the determined light in her magnificent eyes, that he found irresistible. His slender face broke into a grin of capitulation. "Very well," he said dryly, "but don't you think you should at least *see* her before you make a decision to purchase?"

China sat back and clapped her hands together in delight. "Of course I shall see the ship," she said, smiling. "But it shall make no matter. I already know that I want her. In fact, I have already named her. I shall call her the *Josephine*."

That afternoon, they drove down to Brant Point to inspect Edwin Gardner's unfinished ship. Three days later, the newly named *Josephine* belonged to China. She was ecstatic. Unable to contain her happiness, needing to share it with someone, she rushed to see Harriet.

"Thee must come at once," she insisted, pulling the shirt Harriet was mending out of her hands. "Thee must come and see my ship. She is beautiful. And she'll be fast, too. I'll wager she'll do twelve knots when she's done. Ezra Barnard promised he'd have her ready to sail by summer. I may even go along on her maiden voyage. Where's thy cloak, Harriet?" Having tugged the startled woman to her feet, China was now rummaging along the coat rack looking for Harriet's wrap. Finding an old, but sturdy, fur-trimmed cloak, she yanked it off its peg and held it out.

"This one should keep thee warm. There's a bit of a chilly breeze at the Point. Come, Harriet, step lively. Zenas is waiting with a carriage."

"I'm coming," Harriet said, laughing at China's almost childlike excitement. "Although I'm not sure why. For someone who has grown up surrounded by ships and shipping, I barely know the bow from the stern. I'll have to take your word that she's the pride of the fleet. Here, China, if you stop jiggling my cloak, it might be easier for me to put it on."

Harriet gently pried the pelisse from China's eager fingers and settled it on her shoulders. When she turned to face her friend, her tone was more serious. "How can you consider going on the maiden voyage?" she asked. "If you still mean to marry Shubael, as you claim, shouldn't you be here when he returns?"

A frown blotted out the bliss on China's face. In truth, she hadn't quite decided how Shubael figured into her new plans, and it made her feel somewhat guilty. She had trouble concentrating on that problem, though. In fact, she had trouble bringing Shubael to mind, at all. Her life had changed so dramatically in the month since he'd sailed, it seemed as though decades now separated them. Whenever she reached this point in her thinking, however, she stubbornly shut off any untoward ideas and staunchly reaffirmed her intentions of marrying him. She did as much now.

"Of course I mean to marry him," she said, adding more vaguely, "We shall see what happens. Things will work out."

Wisely, Harriet said no more. There was very little chance for her to say anything else, actually, since China and

Zenas did most of the talking on the carriage ride to the shipyard. They discussed building materials and local craftsmen, ship designs and sail set, they talked about sheers, strakes and spars. It was all gibberish to Harriet. She had been, basically, disinterested in such terms all her life, and though she dearly loved both her friend and her brother, there was little hope she would ever share their enthusiasm. She was content to sit back and enjoy China's exuberance.

When they reached the shipyard, China jumped down, almost before Zenas had halted the horses. She knew Zenas always liked to help her down and to hold her arm, but she couldn't be bothered waiting. "See, Harriet?" she exclaimed, waving one hand out from her cloak toward the huge hull perched on the ways and extending the other hand toward her friend to aid her descent. "Isn't she beautiful? Did I not tell thee? Don't look like that. Stop laughing. I know thee cares little for ships, but surely thee must see how pretty the *Josephine* is."

While Zenas joined them, Harriet did her best to stifle the mirth bubbling inside her. "Indeed, China," she said, as seriously as she could. "She's a lovely boat. I presume it likely she'll look even better when she's done. With masts or something."

"It is a ship, Harriet, not a boat," Zenas admonished, taking both women by their arms. "You should at least know that."

"Of course, I should," Harriet said, apologetically, struggling to find other compliments she could pay. "She seems, um, very well built."

"Come look at her from the stern," China said, pulling both Swains, in tandem, over the rough, rubble-strewn ground. "Look at those graceful lines," she said, proudly. China squinted down the side of the ship and Harriet, dutifully, did the same. "Can't thee just see her riding out a swell? She's like a beautiful bird. A heron or a swan."

"A swan?" came a deep, amused voice. "Not a crow?"

China straightened sharply at the familiar bantering and looked over to see Jake leaning casually against the *Josephine*'s scaffolding. The collar of his coat was turned up against the cold, meeting his wind-tousled curls. His hands were stuffed in his pockets, a mocking grin spread across his face and lit his blue eyes.

"What is thee doing here?" she hissed, her excitement interrupted.

"It seems we are neighbors," Jake answered, still grinning. He took one hand out of his pocket and jabbed his thumb in the air, over his shoulder.

China looked in that direction and saw the *China Maid*, looking old and battered, sitting on the ways next to the *Josephine*. What elation remained, deflated. A lump rose in her throat, involuntarily. She thought she had put the past behind her, especially now that she had her own ship and her own goals, but it was not that simple. The sight of the *China Maid* still evoked powerful memories. And so did Jake.

"Well," she said, tensely, "we must be going. We just came to show Harriet my ship, but I'm sure she has seen enough, now, and is feeling the cold." She tried to turn away, but it was not an easy operation when she was linked to two other people, one of whom wanted very much, suddenly, to stay.

"Nay, I'm not at all cold," Harriet protested, hurriedly. "And although I admit I don't know a trunnel from a gudgeon, I am finding this shipyard tour quite fascinating. Is that your boat, Jake? I mean, your *ship*?" She took a step toward him, hoping to pull the others along. While it was true she didn't find the ship so interesting, the emotional charge between China and Jake very much captured her attention.

"It is, Harriet," Jake said, standing upright. "'Tis China's namesake." He made a sweeping gesture with his hand. "May I show you around? I'm afraid she is not looking her best, just now, but with a little loving care, she'll soon be shining."

Harriet took another step forward, ready to accept his invitation, but China took a step back, annoyed by this intrusion on her happiness, which no longer seemed so perfect or so complete. It was Zenas, however, tugged in two different directions, who cast the deciding vote. "Perhaps some other day," he said, with cool politeness. "Right now, I must be getting back to my office."

"By all means," Jake said, levelly, though his deep blue eyes hardened in distaste. He resumed his casual stance against the scaffolding. "Some other day," he repeated.

The trio turned, awkwardly, and left, but for a long while Jake didn't move from his position. He had been surprised, but on the whole, pleased, when Ezra Barnard had cryptically informed him that China had bought the half-finished clipper beside him. He was glad she was finally fulfilling her long-cherished dream. He was sure she would do well. She had a canny mind and good common sense, and, he had to admit grudgingly, she would get sound advice from Swain & Son. Especially son.

That was what bothered him the most. He could give her equally as sound advice, if only she would let him. He not only knew about ships and the sea, but, after his years in New York, he also knew about business. It irritated him to see Zenas, pale and proper, taking the place that was rightfully his. He looked ridiculous hovering around a strong, vital woman like China. He was as out of place as an orchid on the moors. "Damn!" he muttered, straightening up and banging his clenched fist into the scaffolding. Why couldn't China see that?

If China couldn't see it, or, at least, wouldn't admit it, Harriet could. She saw the way China stalked back to the carriage, half a step ahead of Zenas. She saw the way she sat on the drive back to town, her arms folded grimly across her chest, her back erect, her gray eyes smoky and smoldering. And she also saw the way Zenas looked uneasy before China's fierce silence.

Harriet sighed. She had a sister's loving loyalty for Zenas, but even that had its limits. He was not the man for China. He might be able to share many a cozy gam with her about cargo and shipping routes, but he could never match the intensity of her emotions. Nor could the somber, respectable and absent Shubael. Jake could, though. Tall, strong, sea-seasoned Jake. If only China could see it. In her own quiet way, Harriet resolved to make her friend try.

CHINA WOUND HER MUFFLER more tightly around her neck, slung her wooden skates over her shoulder and set off for Washing Pond. It was a clear, crisp and very cold February afternoon. Dustings of snow were caught between the branches of bayberries and around the bases of the Scotch broom, otherwise the heath was brown, dry and crunchy underfoot.

As she walked, China wondered vaguely what had inspired Harriet to suddenly organize this skating party, especially when her brother had been called to Boston on business. She shrugged. It didn't puzzle her that much. Harriet had probably just wanted to take advantage of the thick ice and fair days, an unusual condition for Nantucket, where winter ran mostly to raw winds and gray skies, but not to severe cold. Some years there wasn't any ice on the ponds at all. Despite the cold, though, it was a pleasure to be outside today. She had refused Harriet's offer of a carriage ride, choosing instead to stretch her long legs and to let her mind drift.

Everything was happening so fast lately, China sometimes felt stunned. After all those years of waiting, suspended in time, this rapid pace, where every day brought something new and different—decisions to be made, plans to be laid—left China breathless. Although she found the activity stimulating, and the responsibility gratifying, she occasionally missed being able to just let her thoughts wander.

Today, however, instead of the soothing daydreams that used to accompany her across the commons, her mind filled with images of Jake. She saw him almost every day at the shipyard, and every day she would have to turn away from his taunting blue eyes and his roguish smile. She would have to turn back to Zenas, clinging, blue-lipped and shivering, to her side. Her stomach would be fluttering and her heart would be pounding and she would never quite hear what Zenas was explaining.

It was in a state of agitation, therefore, that China reached Washing Pond. Two carriage loads of young couples had already assembled, strapping on skates, calling out gaily, taking practice turns around the ice. Five red-cheeked young women, hands hiding inside of furry muffs, five robust young men, expelling white clouds of laughter. And Jake.

He was skating in slow, solo circles when China arrived. He lifted his hand in an insouciant salute, grinning at her obvious dismay. The gesture so annoyed China, on top of the irritation she had already been building on her walk across the moors, she would have turned around and left at once if Harriet hadn't detached herself from Obed and skated, inexpertly, her way.

"Here you are at last, China!" she cried, flailing her arms wide to halt herself at the edge of the pond. She would have crashed into the frozen reeds if China hadn't, automatically, held out a steadying hand.

"What is thee trying to do, Harriet?" China asked angrily. The reason for this impromptu party was suddenly clear.

"Um," Harriet said, nervously, "I'm trying to skate, but I'm afraid I'm too clumsy. Come, China, I know you shall do much better." Poor Harriet was as inept at social fibbing as she was at skating.

"Harriet," China said, menacingly.

"Oh, don't be grim," Harriet begged, abandoning her innocent pretense. "I only want you to be happy. Don't turn away, China. At least take a skate around the pond. 'Tis a lovely day for it and there may not be many more this winter. You can fume at me later."

"'Tis not like thee to meddle so," China began, furiously, when Jake skated up.

"Does she need some help with her skates?" he asked Harriet in a deliberately bland voice.

"Um," Harriet said, nervously, again, glancing from Jake's amused blue eyes to China's gray ones. This wasn't going as smoothly as she envisioned.

"What does thee mean, 'Does she need some help?'" China raged, plumping her hands on her hips. "I am neither deaf nor mute. Thee may direct thy questions at me, Mr. Swan."

"Certainly, *Mlle Corbeau*," Jake replied, flashing her another irreverent grin. He felt more confident when she confronted him head-on, her temper flaring, her spirit high. It was a China he knew how to tackle, not the cool, constrained stranger on Zenas's arm. "Do *you* need some help with *your* skates?"

"I don't need thy help with anything," China snapped. She was beginning to feel her fury was out of proportion to the situation, but she didn't know how to control it. Jake unleashed emotion in her and it had to have some vent. "I am perfectly capable..." she started to say, but she suddenly found herself sitting on the frozen bank next to Jake. With one swift stroke, he had skated forward, spun around and grabbed her by the waist, propelling them both to the ground.

"You are *very* capable," Jake said, with wicked calmness of tone. He unslung the skates from her shoulder and reached for her foot. "But I'm not sure that skating is one of your many specialties."

"And is it one of thine?" China asked, sharply, snatching the blades out of his hands and yanking her foot away. She started strapping them with quick, angry motions to her boots.

Having achieved his objective, which was to keep China from walking off, Jake leaned back on his elbow. "You forget, I grew up in Manhattan, where there are cold winters and a Dutch tradition. I spent January afternoons on the Harlem River, not cruising the Line in the South Pacific, the way you did."

"Well, as long as everything is settled, I should go back to Obed," Harriet interrupted, hoping the volatile mess she had made would somehow put itself to rights. She turned, awkwardly, and skated away.

"Everything is *not* settled," China shouted at her friend's back, but Harriet was concentrating too hard on staying upright to answer, even if she had known what to say.

"Nay, 'tis not, you're right," Jake said, directing China's attention, and wrath, back toward him. He appreciated Harriet's efforts on his behalf and did not want to see her suffer in recompense. "We still have to settle whether or not you can skate."

"*That* issue," China said, rising gracefully to her feet, "was settled years ago." With an easy stroke, she pushed away from the bank and slid across the slick ice. She skated smoothly past Harriet and Obed, ignoring their calls to join them. In a huff, she headed for the far end of the pond, meaning only to show Jake her prowess on skates, before ripping them off her feet and heading for home. As usual, she was churning with anger not only at Jake, but also at herself, for allowing him to manipulate her so.

Jake followed a few yards behind, his blue eyes bright with delight. He was enjoying himself immensely. China looked lovely gliding over the ice. Even in the dead of winter she refused to wear the blindering Quaker bonnet, preferring, instead, a wool knit beret that caught her shiny bangs and short black hair against her porcelain skin, tinged pink by the weather and emotion.

A loud crack, almost an explosion, interrupted Jake's leisurely pace. At the same moment, he saw China's slim body jerk off balance and her arms fly out in panic. The next instant she slid into the inky black water that opened up at her feet and disappeared from sight.

Jake's heart strangled in fear, but his mind didn't blink. He stopped where he was and shouted, "Obed, come quickly!" With the assurance of one who is used to giving orders, and to having them obeyed, he didn't wait to see if Obed had heard but went flat on his stomach and inched toward the ominous hole in the ice. Momentary relief flooded through him when he saw China's head break through the surface of the frigid water, her saucy beret no longer in place.

"Steady on, China!" he called. "I'm coming." He forced himself to move slowly, cautiously, though he wanted to race forward before her beautiful face and horrified gray eyes disappeared again.

China heard Jake's voice as if it were a hundred miles away. Somehow, though, it managed to cut through the shock, and mitigate the terror that had seized her when the icy water had closed over her head. Panic-stricken, she had fought for the surface, becoming more frantic as her heavy wool clothes had hampered her movements. Now, she focused on Jake's voice, struggling against the cold, painful paralysis overtaking her, against her diminishing strength, both mental and physical.

"Steady on," Jake called again, softly this time. He was afraid any loud noises might reverberate against the ice, causing it to crack further. His stomach was knotted with dread. He could see China's great, gray eyes, could see the consciousness fading from them. He had to reach her before she slipped away.

He felt, rather than heard, Obed skate up behind him, hovering ten feet away. "Stay back, Obed," he warned, then concentrated again on the frightened face in front of him. "Give me your hand, China," he said. "Reach your hand to me. Come, *corbeau*, I can't do it alone. I need your help. Give me your hand. Nay, China, don't close your eyes. For Christ's sake, keep those gray eyes open!"

His tone sharpened as his arm snaked over the open water. He was almost afraid to breathe, afraid that even the rise and fall of his chest would unsettle the fragile ice. "Think of Zacch, China," he coaxed. "He'd be upset if he thought you gave up. Open those eyes, dammit, and give me your hand."

Somewhere deep inside herself, China wished Jake would stop swearing at her. She was doing the best she could, didn't he know that? Her arm was stretched as far as it could go, her legs were tired from treading water. What was he saying about Zacch? She tried to look at him to find out, but it was so difficult. She felt herself sinking, felt the black water cutting against her mouth, covering her nose. She couldn't breathe. And then she felt something clamp around her wrist, and she was rising out of the water and sliding across the ice on her side. Cold, frosty air filled her lungs.

Jake dragged China slowly, steadily, back from the edge of the thin ice. For a moment he felt sick with fear; he thought he had lost her. Then she gave a splutter and began to gasp. He went weak, intensely grateful that she was still alive. It took all the self-control he could muster not to scoop her instantly into his arms, warming her, covering her with kisses. But the ice was still spidered with sinister black lines, and it was making dangerous-sounding creaks. He inched awkwardly backward.

"I'll give you some help," he heard Obed say, behind him, then felt himself seized by the ankles and drawn easily toward thicker ice.

"Good man," Jake muttered, pulling China closer to him as the frozen surface got safer. By the time Obed released his feet and skated up beside him, China was even with him. Her eyes were closed, the thick lashes lying wetly against white skin that was no longer tinged a fetching pink, but was unnaturally blue. An image of Zacch, lying in a grass hut in Rarua, dying, filled Jake's mind, as he came quickly to his knees. He had to save her. He ripped off his coat and wrapped it around her, instinctively knowing how little good it did.

"Obed, get the blankets from the horses," he said. "They won't be needing them anyway, since we're taking her home."

"Aye," Obed agreed, though he didn't immediately move. He remained, hands on his knees, bent over China's

361

still form. His brown eyes looked worried. "She looks bad," he said.

"She won't improve out here in the cold," Jake snapped, impatient with Obed's slowness. "Look lively. Get those blankets."

Obed seemed unoffended by Jake's sharp tone. He pulled the blue tasseled cap Harriet had knit for him off his head and tugged it clumsily over China's wet hair. Then he straightened. "I'll bring the carriage 'round to this side," he suggested. "You can fetch her to shore." Without waiting for Jake's nod of approval, he skated off across the pond.

"Oh, dear God," Harriet said, arriving almost simultaneously and falling at China's side. "What have I done now?" She clutched at the coat China was wrapped in and peered anxiously at her friend's marblelike face. Her own was distraught. She looked quickly at Jake. "Is she..." she started to ask, then her throat closed in apprehension.

"She's alive," Jake said, tersely, gathering China into his arms. He let his cheek press against hers. It was cold, very cold. He turned his head so his lips were against her skin and breathed softly, half kissing, half heating. A shiver ran through the body he was holding. He hugged her closer to him and rose.

"I'm going to carry her to the bank," he said to Harriet. "Obed will be coming in a minute with the carriage, then we'll take her home. I'll send him right back for you and the others."

"I'm coming with you," Harriet said, stoutly, scrambling unsteadily to her feet. "'Tis my fault this happened. If I hadn't thought up this skating party, China would be warm and cozy right now."

"'Tis not at all your fault," Jake countered. "If there's someone to blame, 'tis I for teasing her into leaving the main group. You needn't desert your other guests. I can take care of her. Here, Harriet, you're floundering like a demasted sloop. Fasten on to my waistcoat and I'll give you a tow to shore."

They made their ponderous way to the bank just as Obed brought the carriage to meet them. For one so slow and deliberate, he reacted quickly and calmly in a crisis. As Jake handed China up to him, Harriet said, again, "I want to come with you."

"Nay, Harriet," Jake said, firmly, vaulting in beside China. He lifted her onto his lap and nodded at Obed. He didn't want anyone's help; he wanted to be alone with her, to caress her, to cajole her back to life. He couldn't bear to share this precious moment with someone else, not even with Harriet. He looked down to where she stood, red-nosed and forlorn. A slight smile softened the grimness of his expression.

"Don't fret," he said, gently. "I'll take care of her. I promise I will." Even as he uttered the words, Jake realized they were an echo of what he had told Zacch. A wave of guilt swept over him. He hadn't done so well with that promise, so far, but he'd make up for it now, he thought fiercely. He held China tighter and turned her face toward his chest, placing a warm kiss on her forehead. "Hoist all sails, Obed," he said.

Halfway to town, China came around. As consciousness slowly reasserted itself, she was aware of feeling terribly, numbingly cold. It took her a minute to remember all that had happened: the pique that had led her onto thin ice, its earsplitting crack and her terrifying plunge into the frigid pond. More hazily she remembered Jake's voice softly prodding her to keep afloat and to stay awake. Slowly she opened her eyes and saw thick, blue wool. She turned her nose to it. It smelled like the sea. "Jake?" she said.

A grip she hadn't even noticed until now loosened, and her head lolled back. Jake's face came into view. China watched as relief replaced the tension in his blue eyes and on his handsome face. "Aye, China," he said tenderly.

"I'm cold," she said, as shivers overtook her.

"I know you are," Jake said, hugging her close to him again. "We're almost home."

Obed pulled up in front of China's house and jumped down. He held open the gate as Jake carried China through, then sprang forward to do the same for the front door. "I doubt you need me now," he said, bluntly. "And the horses oughtn't to stand around, all lathered like they are. So I'll be off."

Jake nodded his thanks and maneuvered his blanketed, dripping bundle through the narrow doorway. He set her down on the rug in front of the parlor hearth, then poked the banked fire to a blaze and threw some more logs on the grate. China leaned forward instinctively, but the heat only made her shiver harder. Her teeth started to chatter.

"Hang tight," Jake said, setting the poker back on its hook. He reached over and wiped a wet strand of hair away from her mouth, since her hands were still trapped under wraps. He rose to his feet. "I'll be right back."

China blinked her acknowledgment as she sat, miserable and dazed, in a puddle. She heard Jake's footsteps taking the steep steps two at a time, heard the bedroom doors open and shut, heard his footsteps on the stairs again, and then he was back with a heap of towels and quilts in his arms. He dumped them on the floor and knelt down next to her, a grin just beginning to pry at the corners of his mouth.

"It seems to me," he said, starting to unwind the horse blankets and overcoat around her, "that we've been in this situation before. Only the last time it was in June and caused considerably less alarm. I hope you don't mean to make a habit of falling into Nantucket ponds." He tossed the outer wraps into a soggy pile across the room, then started on the buttons at the back of her dress.

"Nay, don't," China protested, between clattering teeth. She tried to shrug his hands away, but was too stiff to coordinate her movements.

Jake easily overcame her struggles, his grin broadening. "Not this time, *ma pauvre petite*," he said. He finished unbuttoning the wet gown and pulled it over her head. He started working on the laces of her petticoats, pushing away her groping hands when she tried to stop him. "This time I'm not turning my back, nor am I making any chivalrous promises." His tone grew more serious as he added, "'Tis not the moment for modesty. We need to get you warm right away." The flannel petticoat followed the dress over her head, and he tackled the buttons on her boots.

China knew he was right. She had to get warm. The roaring fire was making no dent in her shivering, her fingers were too numb to have undone her clothes by herself. She was suddenly very glad Jake was here.

"Hmmm, blue silk stockings," Jake commented, rolling one down her leg. "I'm glad you haven't spent all your money on practical matters." He popped it off her slender foot and tossed it, with aplomb, on the growing pile. He reached for the other ankle. "'Tis also reassuring to know there's something sinful going on beneath your Quaker feathers, *corbeau*. There, that's off."

There was just her chemise and pantaloons, now. China shut her eyes while Jake carefully untied the white satin ribbons and peeled the thin cotton undergarments off her skin. She kept her eyes closed while he took a towel and rubbed her whole body, gently, at first, to blot up the wetness, then more briskly, to chafe away the chill. He rubbed her arms and legs, her back and her stomach. He ran the towel along the curve of her neck, down the slope of her shoulder, across the swell of her breasts. He toweled until a faint pink flush chased the deadly blue tint from her splendid skin, and until she tingled with reawakening warmth.

He wrapped a dry quilt around her and China opened her eyes. She found herself looking directly at him. His blue eyes, like the harbor in March, were deep and unreadable. His face, strong planes burnished by wind and weather, was still. China swallowed. "Now what?" she whispered. She was very aware of her skin against the quilt.

Slowly, Jake reached up and took two fistfuls of quilt, pulling until her face met his. Her eyes closed, again. He covered her cold lips with his own, hot and hard. Another shiver ran through China, but it wasn't from the cold this time. Jake eased her away and her eyes opened, again.

"Now we give you a hot bath," he said, hoarsely. But he didn't move for a minute, still holding on to the quilt. Finally, he sighed, arched his eyebrows in inner consent, gave her a quick kiss and released the quilt. China swallowed, again.

Jake went through to the kitchen, scooping up the sodden pile of wool and flannel as he went. China could hear him stoking up the stove and pumping kettles of water. She crouched closer to the fire. She was still not warm, though she had ceased shaking. When she heard Jake go into her father's room, her forehead wrinkled in puzzlement. A minute later, he came through the door with a grin and a glass of rum.

"I knew I could depend on Zaccheus," he said. "'Twas fine rum when he bought it six years ago, and since then it's only improved. I'll hot some up with butter, but down this for a starter. It will get your blood going."

"Thee knew right where to look?" China asked, astonished. Though she'd never done an intense cleaning in her father's room, she'd often been in there to lightly dust and sweep, without ever coming across any spirits.

"Of course I knew," Jake answered, chuckling. "We had to have some place to hide from Aunt Judith. Come now, take this while I go get the tub."

A short while later, China was up to her neck in warm water, a cup of hot, buttered rum in her hand. Jake slouched behind her on the sofa, reading aloud interesting tidbits from the *Inquirer*. Suddenly she giggled from the relaxing effects of the rum and the very thought of the ludicrous picture she must make. She felt very much warmer. In fact, she felt quite wonderful. She let her head lean all the way back on the edge of the tin tub, her neck making a lovely arch.

Jake noted her giggle with another quirk of his eyebrows, but he went on reading. He got up once to add more water to the tub and more hot rum to her cup. Evening was closing in now, and the only light in the room came from the fire, a warm, orangey glow. It lit China's skin, making it seem like polished bronze. Jake remembered the time they had lain in the light of the early autumn sunset, and she had looked like an Egyptian statue. They had spoken of their love that evening, of their deep, eternal love.

He set the paper aside. "Are you cooked, yet?" he asked, lightly. "Or should I get some more hot water?"

"Nay, I think I'm done to a turn," China responded, with another giggle. "In fact, I'm almost overdone. But I can't seem to hoist myself out of the pot." She flung her arm expansively, holding her empty cup. "I think I drank too much rum," she confessed, confidentially. She leaned her head back again and looked wide-eyed, and upside down, at Jake.

Jake was enchanted. Her magnificent eyes, with their charcoal accents, never seemed so seductive. Her long, slender body spilled gracefully, indolently, from the small tub. "Perhaps I'd better give you some help, then," he murmured, rising. "It would be unmannerly of me to ignore a maiden in distress."

China giggled again and let him lift her from the tub. She raised her arms languorously, unembarrassed as he toweled her dry, once more. This time, though, he didn't rub briskly, invigoratingly. He let the cloth slide slowly, sensuously over her body, drifting up her thighs, smoothing over her belly, grazing the tender tips of her breasts.

China cocked her head to one shoulder, her arms still extended. "Well?" she asked, softly.

"Well, well, well," Jake replied, dropping the towel and circling her waist with his hands. As he pulled her close to him, her arms swung forward and wrapped around his neck. She pressed against him eagerly, met his mouth hungrily. The feel of his lips and his tongue thrilled her, the touch of his sure, strong hands, following the curves of her flesh, sent shocks of pleasure shooting through her. She pushed even closer, wanting more, wanting to feel his hard, muscled chest crushed against her aching breasts, his thick curls twined between her fingers, his sea-scented skin fused with hers.

She alternately kneaded his steely shoulders and tugged at the clothes impeding her contact with his bare body. Her desire was pure and uninhibited. Between the hot buttered rum and the intoxicating aftermath of finding herself warm and alive, China gave in, utterly, to the passion coursing through her body. The inebriation broke the barrier of her resistance, it blurred old battle lines, but her love did the rest. It wasn't any man she wanted so ardently, it was Jake.

Jake responded with equal desire. This was the woman he always knew was underneath those dreary dresses and behind those somber avowals. This was the woman whose creamy skin felt like silk beneath his tongue, whose shiny, black hair smelled like a spring day on the moors. This was China, the woman he loved. He ripped off his own clothes and sank with her, naked, to the soft quilts strewn in front of the fire.

A long while later, their appetites temporarily slaked, Jake cradled China in his arms. With fingers, now gentle, he traced the patterns of the flames reflected on her skin. "You can't deny it, China," he said. "Nothing has changed. Time doesn't separate us, it doesn't pull us apart. Our lives will always be joined. We're destined for each other."

"Mmmm," China replied. She languidly turned her head and placed a kiss on his chest, then snuggled more comfortably in the crook of his arm. The light tickle of his fingertips was soothing, almost mesmerizing. She couldn't deny it, he was part of her. Only when she surrendered to her powerful love for him was she complete, alive and satisfied. Everything else was just marking time. She let her eyes close against his shoulder, blissful.

Jake rolled her on her back and shook her until her eyes popped open wide. "Say it," he demanded, leaning over her, propped on his elbows. "Say 'tis true. Say that you love me and that nothing can keep us apart."

China lifted her arms and circled them lightly around his neck. "I love thee," she said. "I love thee with all my heart." She pulled his head down and left a lingering kiss on his lips. "'Tis true that nothing can ever separate us." She tightened her arms around his neck as another thought struck her. "Nothing that is," she added, sadly, "except thy long voyages at sea."

Jake heard the despair in her voice, the unutterable wretchedness. Wincing as if physically slapped, he didn't answer her. There was nothing to say. It was an old argument, the major obstacle to their happiness. And it seemed unresolvable. He laid his cheek against the tender white skin on China's breast, luxuriating in its softness, listening to her heart beat. It wasn't as if he enjoyed those nights all alone on the *China Maid* or sharing his days with the likes of Samuel Easton. It wasn't as if . . .

"Nay, wait!" he cried, rising up so suddenly China was startled. "How stupid I've been!" He smacked his forehead with the palm of his hand, while China stared, astounded. "Oh, China, China, my love," he said, happily, scooping her into his arms and rolling on his back. He crushed her with hugs, covered her with glad kisses.

"Has thee gone mad?" China finally blurted out, fending him off by pushing her hands against his chest.

"Nay, my beautiful China doll, I have not gone mad," Jake said, pulling her down for another kiss. "I have just come to my senses." As she leaned, puzzled, on his chest, he cupped her face in his hands. "Marry me," he said, simply. "Marry me and come live with me on the *China Maid*. We won't ever have to be apart again."

China's mouth fell open in astonishment. There it was, the answer to all her years of anger and anguish, to her years of yearning to be restored to her childhood home, to her years of pretending she didn't long for Jake. Jake grinned at her visible amazement.

"There it's been, dead ahead of us, and we've sailed upwind and downwind of it all this time," he said. "What's your answer, now, China? Will you marry me? Will you share my life?"

China collapsed against him, her heart almost bursting with happiness. "Thee already knows the answer, Jake," she whispered into his ear. She ran her finger over the little gold hoop. "Of course I will." His arms drew tightly across her bare back, holding her next to him.

IT WAS CONSIDERABLY COOLER in the parlor when China woke late the next morning. She was still swathed in quilts, but she was by herself and the fire was just coals. Shivering, she reached one arm out and tossed a log on the grate, then quickly retreated inside her cotton cocoon, waiting for the fire to blaze up and beat back the chill. While she waited, she thought over yesterday's events, marveling again at the solution to their long-standing quarrel. It was so simple. So satisfying.

Rising cautiously and finding, to her delight, a pile of fresh clothes Jake had laid out before leaving, China thought of her promise to Shubael. As she grabbed for her chemise, she shook her head. No matter what, it would be impossible to marry him now. She wouldn't be tranquil and content; she would be miserable, and so would Shubael.

She felt a twinge of guilt, but it was overwhelmed by a feeling of relief. Relief at being released from a passionless, predictable future. And sheer excitement at the prospect of the love and adventure she would have, instead. More lighthearted than she had been in years, China finished dressing and set off for the shipyard to see Jake.

JAKE, TOO, was in the height of good humor. He couldn't imagine why he hadn't thought of bringing China with him a long time ago. Who knows how many arguments it would have saved, how much anxiety. But that was all in the past, now. As were those endless, restless nights in the doldrums, yearning to have her long, cool body next to his, and the fascination of ports of call that somehow weren't so interesting without her enthusiasm.

"'Tis a glorious day," he exclaimed, slapping the back of the man standing next to him.

Bobby Cronin jerked forward under the force of Jake's exuberance, nearly slicing his thumb on the wicked-looking chisel he was sharpening. He was a sturdy man with a gray speckled beard and faded blue eyes that managed to look ingenuous and alert at the same time. He was not a Nantucketer, but had come from Ireland to carve ships' figureheads and quarter boards by day and fanciful statues born in his fertile imagination by night.

Bobby's eyes darted from Jake to the dull, gray sky overhead. "Gawd in heaven," he exclaimed. "'Tis a glorious day only if you're fond of damp breezes and snowflakes. 'Tis enough of both you'll be having today to keep you smiling for a fortnight." He tucked his chisel and rasp under his arm and blew on his fingers.

Jake laughed, acknowledging his oblivion to the weather. "I'm feeling particularly fine, today," he admitted. He looked around for an obvious explanation for his good humor. "The work on the *Maid* is going well," he said. "She should be ready to launch on schedule. Have you started my figurehead, yet?"

Bobby nodded and pointed toward a log six feet long and two feet in diameter. "Right there," he said, walking across the yard to inspect his work. While Jake tried to make some sense of the rough hacks and slashes, Bobby scratched the back of his head and studied the piece. "You sure you want her shoeless?" he asked, at last. "'Tis easy enough now to button on some boots, but if you change your mind later, I'll have to chop off her toes."

"Barefoot," Jake said, firmly.

The sound of an approaching carriage cut off any further discussion. Jake looked up eagerly, hoping to see China. To his astonishment, however, the passengers were Sarah and Liddy Coffin, and a bulky, surly-looking boy of about sixteen. Jake had called once at their house on India Street, when he had first returned, to deliver Zacch's message to Sarah. It had been a superfluous visit, as he soon learned. Sarah hadn't waited to hear Zacch's dying words, but had gone ahead and married Barzillai Cartwright two winters ago. Despite Liddy's flirtations, Jake had cut short the call and left, disturbed by Sarah's fickleness.

Now he walked across the yard to meet them, more curious than condemning. He was in too marvelous a mood to bear any rancor.

"Hello, Jake," Liddy said, holding her hand out, delicately, for him to help her down. "You have been a man of mystery. We haven't seen you once since your visit two months ago." She pouted prettily. "If I didn't know you were so very *busy* with your ship, I might think you were avoiding us."

"Hello, Liddy, Sarah," Jake said, noncommittally. He helped the two sisters descend and nodded an obligatory greeting at the lumpish boy swinging clumsily to the ground.

"Jake, this is our cousin, Seth Mayhew, Mother's nephew," Liddy said, touching the youth lightly on the shoulder. "Seth, this is Captain Swan."

Seth just stared at Jake, his muddy brown eyes vaguely hostile in a pasty, moonlike face. Jake nodded again, then looked back to Liddy, annoyed by the boy's expression. "'Tis an unseemly day for you ladies to be driving about," he commented. "The wind is raw and 'tis set to snow."

Liddy gave a little shiver of her fur-clad shoulders. "You're right, of course, 'tis a wretched day, but we've been wanting for the *longest* time to come and see your ship.

373

Haven't we, Sarah?'' Sarah blinked once in bewilderment, but eventually agreed. Jake folded his arms across his chest and settled back to enjoy this performance, a sardonic light making his blue eyes bright.

"'Tis such a handsome vessel,'' Liddy continued, gazing rapturously at the *Josephine*. Jake suppressed a chuckle. "The pride of the fleet. Why, every day I hear someone speak of it in admiration. They praise the grace of its lines and its steadiness at sea. And they always say it never fails to come home from the Grounds gunnel deep. Of course, I am then forced to reply that 'tis not merely the ship to be credited, but also the skill of its splendid captain.'' She pursed her pink lips in righteous indignation.

"I am honored by your generous championship,'' Jake murmured, with mock modesty.

Liddy waved one hand, gloved in fine French kid, deprecatingly. The other hand she slipped under his elbow and artfully turned him around. "You must show us your ship,'' she said, steering toward the *Josephine*. "I'm so *eager* to hear all about it. Seth,'' she called over her shoulder, "why don't you go watch that man who is chopping up the log?'' Seth clumped glumly across the yard to stare at Bobby Cronin, but Sarah tagged uncertainly after Liddy and Jake.

Liddy drew to a halt by the corner post of the clipper's scaffolding. She glanced momentarily upward, with a look of practiced reverence, then immediately lost interest. "I must confess, Jake,'' she said, inching closer to him and speaking in a soft, confidential tone, so he was forced to bend his head toward her to hear. "We have a favor to ask of you. We were quite desperate and distraught, not knowing who to turn to, then I thought of you and knew you were the ideal person. The perfect man.'' She bit her bottom lip and puckered her brows, a lovely picture of helplessness.

Jake was amused. ''I think I better know the nature of this favor before my head is so swollen by your flattery, I agree to sell my soul for a two hundredth lay,'' he said dryly.

''I would *never* ask that,'' Liddy said, squeezing his arm in horror. '''Tis really much simpler. 'Tis about Seth.'' She cast her eyes quickly in the direction of her cousin, then returned them to fasten earnestly on Jake's face.

''You see, he came along rather late in Aunt Mary's life; she's older than Mother by nearly ten years. And he's been, well, to be quite blunt, he's been a bit of a *problem*. He's a tiny bit slow,'' she admitted, reluctantly, but hastened to add, ''though he's generally good-natured and very obedient. What he really needs is *guidance*. Poor Uncle Enoch is too old and bedridden to be a good example, so we thought, Sarah and I,'' she inclined her head toward Sarah, who was standing with her hands tucked neatly in her ermine muff, ''we thought that a voyage at sea, under a captain as strong and brave as you, would make a man of him.

''So there it is, Jake. Do you think you could *possibly* find a berth for him on your ship?'' She looked at him beseechingly. ''Aunt Mary's mind would be put at ease, I know. And we would all be so very *grateful*.''

Jake had been entertained by Liddy's tale until he understood exactly what she wanted, and then she had ceased, quite abruptly, to charm him. He glanced across the yard to where Seth was woodenly planted in front of the Irish carver. He wanted no part in the probably futile task of turning this dull-witted boy into an acceptable man. Nor did he want such a clumsy person in his crew. On board ship, agility could be the difference between living and dying.

He was about to firmly refuse when Sarah smiled at him. It was a sweet smile that brought dimples to her cheeks and a certain radiance to her peaches-and-cream complexion. He didn't think, then, of Seth, or even of Barzillai Cartwright. An image flashed through his mind of Zacch, with Sarah in his arms, on the beach at Coatue, her innocent blue eyes gazing at him in adoration. Zacch had gazed back, proud of her love, enchanted by her pink and gold beauty.

The thought of Zacch made him soften. "Let me think on it," he capitulated. "I've not had anyone sign articles yet. 'Tis too early still. I'll let you know." He regretted his words almost as soon as he uttered them, even more so when Liddy gave a cry of delight and threw her arms around his neck.

"Oh, *thank* you, Jake," she whispered in his ear. "I knew I could depend on you to help me."

As Liddy swayed against his thigh, her attar of roses fragrance filling his nose, he was vaguely aware of the sound of feet running across the frozen earth behind him. By the time he had untangled himself from Liddy's grasp, however, the runner was out of sight. And by the time he handed Liddy and Sarah back into their carriage and returned to work, he had forgotten all about it. Nothing, not even Seth Mayhew, could disturb him for long today.

China's high spirits, on the other hand, were crashing down around her. The running feet had been hers. Today, she had forgone a carriage, needing to stretch her long legs in exuberance, and arrived at the shipyard just in time to see Liddy slip her hand around Jake's arm and lead him, seemingly willingly, to a spot by her ship. As she had stood deathly still, staring, Jake had bent closer to the beautiful brunette.

China felt so betrayed, she could scarcely breathe. Her stomach was icy. How could he? How could he make love to her one day, swearing his eternal devotion, even asking her to marry him, then lock arms with Liddy Coffin the next, in an intimate tête-à-tête. China was nothing more than another woman in another port of call. When she thought of herself pressing naked against him, she felt nauseous with humiliation. No wonder he wanted to bring her along on his next voyage. What could be more convenient?

Since his back was to her, China could not see Jake's expression, but she could see him look down and nod to Liddy. And she could see Liddy respond with a suggestive embrace. She could take no more. She turned and fled, tears of rage and heartbreak blinding her.

BY THE TIME JAKE SHOWED UP at her cottage that evening, lustily singing, China's eyes were clear, cold and dry. She stood in the center of the kitchen, waiting for him to enter. When he opened the door, stamping snow off his boots, a smile of pure joy splitting his rugged face and softening his sea-blue eyes, she almost yielded. Almost.

"Thee needn't bother to take thy coat off," she said, her voice trembling slightly.

"Why not?" Jake answered, genially, crossing the room to kiss her. "Are we going somewhere? To Harriet's?" When China flinched away from his touch, he looked at her in surprise. Suddenly he noticed how rigidly she held herself and the grim set of her jaw. Her eyes, her incredible, seductive eyes, no longer shone with love and desire; they were as ominously gray as the sky before a thunderstorm. Dread trickled through him, tightening the muscles in his broad shoulders.

"Why not?" he repeated, more harshly this time. He reached for her arm, digging his fingers into her flesh.

China pushed him away and took several steps back, putting a kitchen chair between them. "I have rethought thy offer to marry thee and come live aboard the *Maid*," she said, her voice gathering strength as she spoke. "And I must reject it. I was intoxicated last night. I had too much rum and too close a call. It made me say things I didn't mean."

For a moment, Jake was speechless with disbelief. Then he exploded. "Nay!" he shouted, moving menacingly close to her. "Nay! 'Tis not what you said last night that was false, but what you are saying now. What kind of nonsense is this, China? What have you been drinking today to make you spout such bilge?"

"'Tis not nonsense," China said, gaining momentum, as always, from his anger. "I have made my decision and it does not include thee. I have my own ship to build and my own course to sail. There is no room on the charts for thee." Her heart was beating very fast, but she stood her ground.

Jake towered over her, glaring, hands on his hips. "Fine!" he finally spat out, his fury fueled by the intensity of his disappointment. "'Tis just as well to settle this now, because I cannot keep up with your damned hot and cold moods anymore. 'Tis difficult enough to deal with your madness on shore, where I can walk away. In the confines of a ship, I'd probably throttle you, then be swung from the yardarm for a murderer. I might be willing to die for your love, China Joy, but I am not willing to die for your indifference!"

He stalked to the door and threw it open, letting in a few flakes of snow that were flurrying. He turned to shake his finger at her stricken face. "As soon as the *Maid* is ready to sail, I'll be gone," he fiercely promised. "This time I won't be back."

18

ANTARCTICA
January 1846

SHUBAEL STOOD ON THE DECK of the *Justice*, muffled up to his eyes, but still feeling chilled. He watched the activity on board the *Eleanor*, anchored a few hundred yards away. The crew was moving quickly, scouring try pots, clearing the deck, lashing boats securely to the bulwark. Their hold was full of oil and pelts, and tomorrow they would thread their way through the ice floes and make for home. With all his heart, Shubael wished he were on that other schooner.

Sealing was even worse than whaling. It was a bloody, brutal business based more on land, and ice, than at sea. There wasn't even the deep sense of satisfaction he felt from steering his ship over vast stretches of ocean; the visual pleasure of seeing the blue sky meeting an empty horizon. With sealing they did not sail endlessly, infinitely, in search of their prey; they lay at anchor in an icy harbor in this barren outpost of the world and went about their work in whaleboats and on foot.

And the weather. Shubael shivered involuntarily. The weather was bitter beyond belief. There was never a moment when they could relax their guard against the weather, when they could forget to protect themselves from it. To do so could mean death. It was cold, mercilessly cold. Shubael could scarcely remember what it was like to feel warm.

"Shall we lower, sir?" Ephraim Myrick asked. His words were muted by the scarf wound around his face.

Reluctantly, Shubael tore his envious eyes away from the *Eleanor* and fastened them on his first mate. "Aye, Mr. Myrick," he said, in his usual disciplined voice. "Lower all boats. We'll spread out and follow the same course as yesterday."

An hour later Shubael guided his whaleboat into a small cove and quietly ordered the man in the bow to set an anchor in the ice. A large group of seals lounged not far off, their contented snorts and snuffles interrupted by the approach of the hunters. As Shubael and his crew stepped ashore, armed with lances, harpoons and heavy clubs, the seals rose gracelessly, and suspiciously, from their slouched positions.

At a signal from Shubael, the men fanned out, cutting off the animals' escape route to the sea. Barking in alarm, the cumbersome beasts wriggled away, moving with surprising speed on flippers and tails designed more for propelling them through water than over solid land. The men scattered in chase.

Shubael lost sight of the rest of the crew as he, and a single other bulky sailor, pursued a panic-stricken mother and her pup. They stumbled and slid along the edge of the cove, successfully thwarting the seals in their attempts to dive to freedom, and finally cornered the pair on a jagged little peninsula. While the sailor slipped around behind the mother, to prevent her from changing direction, Shubael raised his club and waited for the pup to come within range. For a split second, something inside him rebelled, but then it was time for action and his well-drilled reflexes took over. He slammed the club down on the head of the pup.

The mother's hoarse call of despair changed to a stran-gled moan of agony as the sailor's lance found its mark. In a moment she lay still. Except for the ever-present creak-ings of the ice, there was silence. Shubael stared in disbe-lief at the sight before him, at the bright red blood on the clean white snow. The mother's keening cry echoed inside his head, wrenching at his heart.

Suddenly he could bear no more. Emotions tore loose inside of Shubael, emotions he had been damming up for years. His soul seemed to scream in protest. Unaware of his actions, powered only by his frenzied feelings, he raised his club and brought it down on the dead body of the seal pup again and again. Tears streamed out of his eyes and froze on his cheeks, but he continued his crazed pounding. He sought relief, release. He wanted to smash the source of his suffering as he was smashing the body of the seal.

Only the wicked sound of cracking ice halted him, club in midair. Not quite comprehending, he looked up through tear-blurred eyes. For a fraction of an instant, he saw the face of the burly sailor, slack with fright. Then Shubael was thrown on his stomach as the ice split apart exactly where the sailor stood. The man's arms flew wide, a shriek of ter-ror filled his throat, then his body slid into the inky water. By the time he buoyed to the surface, a minute later, he had frozen, dead.

Still flat on his stomach, Shubael observed the scene al-most with detachment. It didn't seem real. Nothing did. His mind was drained by his violent outburst, robbed of its ability to react. It was as if he had emptied himself out and was only slowly refilling. By the time he realized that the little ice peninsula was now an island, it was ten feet from shore and traveling swiftly, with the current, out to sea. There was no way he could jump to safety.

The cold wind tugging his hair made him aware that his head was bare. Instinctively he raised his hand, feeling for his fur hat. At the same moment he saw it lying on the opposite side of the ever-widening gulf, where it had landed when he had been hurtled from his feet. Somehow, through the dullness fogging his mind, he remembered that he always carried an extra hat in his pocket, in case one got lost or wet. It was essential to keep his head covered in this frigid wasteland, essential to survival.

He rolled awkwardly on his side and fumbled in the pocket of his heavy fur coat for the thick cap China had knit. With clumsy, mittened fingers, he pulled it over his ears, then laboriously tightened the muffler wrapped around his neck and face.

When he rolled back on his stomach, the pulpy body of the baby seal lay inches from his eyes. A cry of horror choked in his throat. He flung the torn carcass off the edge of the ice with a back sweep of his arm. With frantic swipes, he shoved the bloody crust of snow after it until the frozen surface was clean. Gulping back his revulsion, Shubael lowered his head to his folded arms and waited.

The ice floe, barely bigger than his long, lean body, ran rapidly out the mouth of the cove and headed for open ocean. For some reason, Shubael didn't feel afraid; he felt patient. He had exorcised his demon and was too exhausted to think about what came next. It might be rescue, it would probably be death. He didn't care. He had lost control over his life when his club had struck the seal pup, and without control, he had nothing left. It didn't matter where the bobbing block of ice took him.

The day moved into night with no lessening of light. It was summertime at the bottom of the world. The constant wind and the chill of the ice worked their way through the layers of clothing encasing Shubael. At first it felt bitingly

painful to him, almost searing him with its sharpness.
Gradually, though, he ceased to shiver as numbness set in.
He couldn't feel his arms or legs, could barely lift his head
when an age-old instinct forced him to try. He let it drop
again. There was nothing to see but black, gelid water and
more bobbing floes of ice.

Then drowsiness overtook him, an indolent sensation
that brought with it warmth. It felt lovely, reminding him
of the languid heat of the Seychelles, hot, lazy days when
he had lain naked in the sand next to Amedee, letting bathtub-warm, blue water wash over him. He smiled at the
thought, smiled at the image of Amedee splashing in the
turquoise lagoon at Anse Banane, laughter crinkling the
corners of her almond-shaped eyes, tropical sun gleaming
on her silky, café-au-lait skin. He was just remembering
what it was like to slide his lips over those three delicious
dots on her smooth, round cheek, when darkness consumed him.

"HAVE THE HELMSMAN hold true to this course, Mr.
Whitbread. We needn't change until we arrive at the South
Orkneys. We've good luck with this weather. We should
make fine time."

"Yes, sir. And shall I take the midday sighting, as well?
Or will you be on deck to read the sextant?"

"Oh, no. Your young eyes are sharper than mine, Mr.
Whitbread. Carry on."

"Yes, sir."

The conversation floated under the blanket covering
Shubael's mind, prying, pushing, insisting that he become aware. He struggled to concentrate on what the
speakers were saying, to comprehend what was happening. The voices were unfamiliar and the accents were
clipped and British. He opened his eyes cautiously, almost

reluctant to leave the comfort and security of the darkness that had enveloped him. He saw, straight above him, a hefty wooden beam from which was suspended a brass lantern, swaying rhythmically. With an effort, he realized he was lying flat on his back in the cabin of some strange ship.

"Well, hello. Decided to join us then, have you?"

Shubael slowly rolled his head in the direction of the raspy voice. He saw a genial-looking man with thinning gray hair and sparse-looking muttonchop whiskers. His red veined cheeks and nose indicated a fondness for gin, but his eyes were clear and his manner was kind. Shubael didn't know who he was. He didn't respond.

"No doubt you are wondering who I am and where you are," the man guessed, seating himself by Shubael's feet. Shubael's eyes followed him, seeing, now, that he was lying on a sofa. "I'm Captain Dawson, and this is my ship, the trader *Charlotte*."

At that information, Shubael's eyes traveled slowly around the cabin. In one corner stood a handsome mahogany and brass chart rack. In another was a desk, upon which lay a leather-bound log. The center of the room was dominated by a large chart table and by an open chest containing dozens of glass-stoppered bottles of medicinal potents and powders. Shubael recognized the atmosphere. He was in Captain Dawson's dayroom.

"We found you four days ago, quite unconscious," Captain Dawson continued. "You were floating on an ice floe no bigger than a tea saucer. It's a damned miracle that you are still alive. By all rights you shouldn't be. When we found you, the sea was lapping over the edge of the ice. If you had gotten doused, I shouldn't think you'd be here now. This damned cold is a killer."

Settling himself more comfortably, he said, "You have a bit of frostbite. Mostly the toes. It's a queer thing how frostbite always goes for the feet first. But I shouldn't think you'll lose them. More of your good luck. Though I imagine they'll give you the devil of a time in cold weather for the rest of your life. My grandfather froze his toes as a lad. Soaked his shoes and socks out sledding and wouldn't go home to change. He was miserable every winter until he died at eighty-six. I remember him hobbling around with a great damned stick, swinging it at any poor sod who got in his way. He was in a foul humor from November 'til May.

"I say, though," Captain Dawson went on, bringing the subject back to Shubael. "You must have a damned strong will to live. That and the constitution of an ox. It's an unusual man who survives any mishap in this damned region."

He cast a look of distaste out the iced-up porthole, then turned back to Shubael.

"Every trip I make out here, I get news of some dreadful accident," he said. "The other day, in fact shortly before we found you, we bespoke a Nantucket ship. We came alongside to see if they had any pelts to sell, but they were just out from America and were in a damned tizzy to boot. They had lost two men to this wretched place. One was the captain. All they ever found of him was his hat. He must have been trapped beneath the ice, poor chap. The other fellow was wedged between some chunks of drift ice, frozen as solid as you please." Captain Dawson gave a shudder and looked longingly toward the mahogany cabinet, where a decanter of gin was locked.

"You are lucky to be alive," he repeated. "This is a nasty territory. Good for trade, though," he added with a resigned arch of his scraggly eyebrows. "Prime fur here. And now that we've settled that little fracas with the Chinese, we're back in business. That's where we are heading. Canton.

"I say, though. I'll wager you are off a sealer. Must be three dozen of them, hereabouts. You've the cut of a Yankee about you. Am I right? What's your name?"

Shubael still didn't answer. He just stared. First he stared at Captain Dawson, shocked to hear the report of his own death. Then he stared at the swaying brass lantern, wondering why he was alive. His crew assumed he was dead, gone forever underneath the glacier. Frozen, like the hapless sailor with him whose identity he didn't even know, his face hidden behind a scarf. The only clue they'd found was his fur hat, lying, he remembered, next to the body of the mother seal. No wonder Captain Dawson hadn't made any connection. The man he rescued was wearing a thick wool cap.

But he had survived. He hadn't perished beneath the ice, the body heat sucked out of him before he could even drown. Captain Dawson had said that he must have a strong will to live. But he didn't. Shubael shut his eyes. He would be better off dead.

He was tired. He was tired of turning his back on tropical sunsets and clean horizons to butcher whales and other beasts, of spending years in the lonely austerity of his ship at sea and of returning home to an even lonelier and more austere existence. He was tired to death of fighting the battle between his soul and his sense of duty, tired of accepting responsibility, only to have it unappreciated or unneeded, tired of striving, endlessly, for that elusive quality called success. There was no reason for him to live.

"Tut, tut," Captain Dawson said, sympathetically. He leaned forward and patted Shubael's shoulder. Shubael opened his eyes. "I've heard of this sort of thing happening before. Amnesia. A man's memory can be wiped as clean as a child's school slate when he's had a severe accident. I say, perhaps this will help you remember. At one point you called out 'Amedee,' over and over again. Could that be your wife? Does the name strike a familiar chord?''

''Amedee,'' Shubael whispered. In his mind he finished the image that had been with him when he lost consciousness. He felt the silky skin beneath his lips, skin scented of cinnamon and tasting like salt, skin warmed by hot sunshine and brushed by balmy breezes. His eyes shut again, blocking out the beams and the lantern and ship, seeing, instead, Amedee. She was his reason to live. She always had been.

When he was with her, he had felt alive, in the real sense. He had been filled with laughter and happiness. He had felt replete. He had burst loose from the constraints of his upbringing, from the colorless, humorless doctrine that gnawed away at him. He had basked in love.

In that instant he made his decision, completely and irrevocably. He would not return to Nantucket or to the *Justice* or to the slow death of an existence tightly bound by obligations and unreasonable morals. He would return to Amedee; he would live. He would fulfill the only duty that mattered, the only promise worth keeping: to love Amedee, always and forever.

With that resolution came tremendous relief, the release he had so violently and blindly sought by battering the carcass of the baby seal. He was freed, freed by his tie to Amedee. And with the freedom came a sudden understanding. He realized, now, why his father had been a failure. It wasn't because he had invested unwisely, or because he had mismanaged his affairs; it had been because he married a woman he didn't love. Another burden lifted from Shubael as the haunting refrain of his youth vanished.

What had Benjamin Swain said? ''You can't spend the rest of your life paying for your father's mistakes.'' Shubael finally relinquished his debt. The only person he now owed anything to was Amedee. He owed her his love. And that was a payment he would gladly make.

He felt guiltless, and oddly unsurprised, at the thought of succumbing to the fate he had been avoiding all these years, of following his father's footsteps and of disappearing. For a moment he considered telling Captain Dawson the truth, of saying that he was Shubael Brown, and he wasn't dead, but that he was permanently retiring to a little island in the Indian Ocean called La Digue. After a quick inventory of those he was leaving behind, however, he changed his mind.

Benjamin Swain might miss the rich cargoes he brought back to port, but there were always other, eager and able, young men who could take his place. His mother might miss the money he regularly and dutifully presented to her, but she was too consumed by the waste of her own life to grieve long for his. Besides, his younger brothers were fully grown up, now, and capable of contributing to her support. In the end, it would probably hurt the whole family less if they thought he was dead, rather than that he was abandoning them.

Then there was China. Of them all, she alone would probably feel genuine sorrow, but it was better this way. It was better that she mourn him only once, and only for a little while, than to spend the rest of her life mourning a loveless marriage. He couldn't bear to think of her as an embittered old woman like his mother, her magnificent spirit turned sour. In time, her memory of him would fade and then she would feel free to indulge in her love for Jake, just as he was now indulging in his love for Amedee. Really, it was better this way.

Shubael opened his eyes and looked at Captain Dawson. "My name is Jones," he said easily, enjoying the irony of happily imitating his father after all these years. "Alfred

Jones. I was the third mate on the *Eleanor* out of New Bedford. We were making for home when I fell overboard and landed on the ice. I must have been knocked out for a few minutes because when I came around, the *Eleanor* was long out of hailing range. I just stayed on the ice floe and waited.''

Captain Dawson nodded. ''You're a lucky man,'' he said, again, almost awed by the magical powers protecting Shubael. ''Damned lucky.''

''I am,'' Shubael said, agreeing this time. He felt very lucky. And elated.

''Well then,'' Captain Dawson said, slapping both hands on his thighs in conclusion. He rose. ''As I've said before, we're bound for Canton, so I can't go chasing the *Eleanor* to hand you back. I'll let you down in Payta or Valparaiso, though. Shouldn't have to wait too long to find passage back to your New Bedford.''

Shubael hesitated a minute, visualizing charts and trade routes in his head. ''If 'tis all the same to thee,'' he said, ''I'd as soon stay on to Canton. I've nothing or no one waiting in New Bedford. I'd only turn around and come back here.''

Captain Dawson shrugged. Now that his curiosity had been satisfied, he was more interested in his noontime nip than in Shubael's itinerary. ''Fine, fine,'' he said, heading for the mahogany cabinet.

IN CANTON, Shubael sold his heavy sealskin coat and bought passage on a British merchant vessel bound for Madras, India. In Madras, he made a deal with an Arab dhow bound for Mombasa, but the Arab stole his money and threw him off the boat in Ceylon. He waited for a month on the beach in Ceylon before finding a berth on a Dutch East Indian tea ship stopping in Mauritius. Once in Mauritius, he wangled his way on board a government courier, which brought him to Mahé.

After five days in Mahé, he found a schooner going to Grand' Anse in Praslin. From Grand' Anse, he walked over the island to Baie Ste. Anne. Squatting on his heels in the shade of a palm tree, he chatted with a lean, leathery fisherman who finally agreed to take him the rest of the way. Shubael took a deep breath and rose slowly to his feet. He stared over the purple water to the green island across the way. Only five more miles.

Seven months after waking up on the *Charlotte*, fingers and toes tingling with frostbite, Shubael set his bare feet on the hot white sand of La Digue. All he owned were the clothes on his back, now tattered and stained. As he walked along the beach toward Napoleon's house, he was suddenly seized by apprehension. In all these months, he had never doubted that Amedee would be waiting for him, keeping the promise that had haunted him halfway round the world. He had been so wound up in his eagerness to reach her, so immersed in his visions and expectations, he had never considered she might not be here for him at the end of the voyage.

His feet moved more slowly along the sand. He was reminded of the last time he arrived in La Digue. He was then the prosperous, and proper, master of a ship, but he had been plagued by similar feelings. What if Amedee had forgotten him? What if she had married someone else? What if she rejected him now that he was ragged and penniless? This time it wasn't a year that he had been gone, but three, almost four. What if that idyllic week at Anse Banane and her whispered pleas for him to return were just a dim memory, a part of her past?

Almost opposite Napoleon's comfortable home, he stopped, gathering courage to continue. A small boy was crouched naked by the edge of the water. The sun glistened on his light brown limbs, still round with baby fat, and shone on his silky, straight hair. He was trying, desperately, to keep his coconut-husk sailboat from capsizing. His frustration was obvious from the hunch of his tiny shoulders and the determined downward turn of his face. A smile tugged at Shubael's mouth.

"Shall I show you how to set the sail?" he asked, glad for the distraction.

Eyes still intent on the boat, the little boy nodded. Shubael knelt down beside him and pulled the craft ashore. "The mast must be sturdy and straight, to start with," he said, snapping the bent end off the palm frond mast. "Then the sail must be placed to catch the wind." He adjusted the takamaka leaf accordingly. "Now she is ready for launching." He gently pushed the boat back in the warm water, where it bobbed easily in the breeze.

The little boy squealed in delight. "My boat, my boat!" he cried, looking up at the tall stranger who had helped him. His face broke apart in a fearless grin, making deep dimples in his round cheeks and crinkles of his huge, almond-shaped brown eyes.

Shubael caught his breath. The little face was so familiar, it was imprinted in his heart. "What's your name?" he asked, touching a finger to the smooth, brown skin. "What do they call you?" He had to know.

But the boy was too enchanted by his boat to answer. He shrugged away Shubael's touch, eyes on the toy once more. He rose on his sturdy legs and ran two steps along the water's edge, following the progress of the coconut-husk hull. Shubael rose, too, and took two steps after him, capturing him by both arms. The boy's flesh was soft and warm beneath his fingers.

"What's your name?" he asked, again, more urgently this time. He squatted once more in the sand, but didn't release the child. He searched the boy's upturned face, waiting for an answer.

The boy returned Shubael's gaze, trying to decide if he was afraid or not. Finally he glanced at his boat and saw it sailing away. He struggled to free himself so he could chase after it. "Ti-Shoobell," he said, in the interest of ending the conversation.

Shubael let his hands fall abruptly, and the boy scampered down the beach. Ti-Shoobell. Petit Shubael. This was his son. He hardly had time to comprehend that fact, to absorb the rush of joy swelling inside him, when he heard the name again.

"Shoobell," called the husky voice. "Shoobell. You've come home."

Shubael's head snapped up and he saw Amedee running toward him, one hand clutching her kazak above the scudding waves, the other hand pressed against her heart. He was on his feet in an instant, his long legs closing the gap between them, his arms reaching out in desperate yearning. Amedee flew into them, crushing against his body, clasping him around his neck. Shubael held her fast, covering her with kisses, filling his senses with the scent of cinnamon clinging to her café-au-lait skin, with the feel of her lush body beneath the thin cotton of her dress, with the sweet taste of her lips, the satiny softness of her cheeks, with the innocence and ardor in her lovely almond eyes. He wrapped his arms more tightly around her and filled himself with her uninhibited love.

"Yes, Amedee," he whispered, his lips against her ear, "I've come home. Forever."

19

NANTUCKET
April 1846

THE *CHINA MAID* gave a hesitant lurch, then slid gracefully over the greased skids and plunged into the harbor. She followed docilely as two whaleboats towed her to deeper water and set her anchor. Back on the beach, Jake whooped with glee and pounded John James Henry on the back. "She looks good, doesn't she?" he asked, proudly.

John James Henry folded his arms in front of him and nodded placidly. "Very pretty, Ja-Jake," he answered. "Good as new. Even better than before. I like the picture on the bow."

He was referring to the figurehead, a life-size statue of China, precise in detail from her shiny bangs to her bare feet. Bobby Cronin had even managed to capture the spirit of her expression and the seductive quality of her gray eyes. She looked completely comfortable, entirely at home, on her perch above the sea.

John James Henry's mention of the figurehead dampened Jake's exuberance. After that brief, but bitter, battle with China, he had almost had Bobby Cronin stop working on the statue. Every time he had gone over that kitchen scene in his mind, every time he had heard China coldly asserting, "There is no room on the charts for thee," his fury had been renewed, and he had almost canceled the commission. But then he would remember her rising from the tub, rosy skinned and giggling, radiating love. His fury would ebb and he would say nothing.

While Jake wavered, enraged one moment, enchanted the next, Bobby worked steadily on, unaware of any problems. He applied the last touches of paint while Jake was off island in New York, then went ahead and had it fastened in place. When Jake returned, irritated by the ledgers and statements he'd had to review, China had greeted him from the bow of his ship. He had sworn and stormed, but by then it had been too late. He could no more remove her from the *Maid* than he could from his heart. As he himself had said, no matter what, they were meant for each other. And now he had her always, a paint and wood reminder of his love.

Jake cursed softly and turned away from the water's edge. For the hundredth time, he savagely wondered why she was acting the way she was. What peculiar thoughts were drifting through her beautiful head? What unfathomable emotion was making her deny her feelings, feelings Jake knew were as deep and strong as his own?

"Looks like she still floats."

The voice interrupted Jake's brooding. He halted his aimless retreat next to Bobby Cronin. The Irish carver stood with his hands in his pockets, his pale blue eyes scanning the harbor.

"They say that witches always float," Jake muttered, responding more to his irritation and frustration than to Cronin's comment.

"Witches?" Bobby sounded suddenly worried. His eyes flicked more rapidly between Jake and the *China Maid*. "Is it a witch, then, that she reminds you of? Did my carving go amiss? Every time you look her way you fall into a fit of fearful grumbling. 'Tis displeased you are."

"Nay, Bobby, 'tis not your work that causes me to scowl," Jake hastily reassured him. "'Tis my own thoughts. You've done a masterful job and I apologize for not saying so sooner."

Bobby scratched the back of his head in contemplation. "Are you sure then?" he asked. "I had to carve her mostly from memory. For a while the lady was coming here every day to see her pretty ship, and then, just when I needed to study her most, she disappeared. 'Twas a bit of by guess and by garry to finish her likeness. But hers is not an easy face to forget. Especially those eyes. They do stay with a man."

"They do, indeed," Jake said, grimly. He would have moved on then, involved in his own memories of those extraordinary gray eyes, but Bobby was in a mood to chat. While Jake shifted impatiently from foot to foot, Bobby pulled his hands out of his pockets and crossed them comfortably on his chest, ready to continue the conversation.

"They're like the windows to her soul, they are," he said. "Lovely glimpses of her thoughts and feelings." He rubbed his salt-and-pepper beard meditatively. "I remember one morning, aye, 'twas the last time I saw her, her eyes were almost the same cast as the sky. Stormy they were. But with that white skin and her black lashes, they stood out like beacons. Gawd in Heaven, what a sight."

When Jake made a noncommittal grunt in reply, Bobby kicked at a scallop shell and watched it skitter toward the water. "Aye, 'twas the last time I saw her," he repeated, nodding his head, as if confirming the fact. "You remember the day, don't you?" he asked, glancing slyly at Jake. "'Twas the day those Coffin sisters were here with their lummoxy cousin. And him standing and staring at me like I was a two-headed cow, while you gave the ladies a tour of the *Josephine*."

"Ummm," Jake said, again, preferring not to be reminded of that day that ended so disastrously. He was aware of Bobby watching him closely and was puzzled, until Bobby's words sank in. "Wait," he exclaimed. "She was here that morning?" he asked, incredulously. "China was here?" Even as he asked the question, he vaguely recalled the sound of running feet as Liddy had pulled him into a grateful embrace.

"Eh?" Bobby asked, innocently, seemingly intent now on a sea gull bobbing on a wave in the harbor. His faded blue eyes flitted toward Jake's anxious face. "Aye, she was here. 'Twas the last time I saw her."

For an instant, Jake stood stock-still, staring at Bobby Cronin, though he hardly saw the wood carver. China had been there that day. She had seen Liddy whispering in his ear and clutching him around the neck. She was jealous. Relief poured through Jake with the realization. She had misinterpreted what she had seen, and that was easy to remedy. He broke into a broad grin and clapped Bobby on the shoulders. Bobby grimaced, then grinned back.

Twenty minutes later, Jake was pounding on China's door, shouting, "China! Open up, *corbeau*. I've something to tell you." When only the imperturbable donging of the grandfather clock striking noon drifted through the closed door, he rattled the latch. It was locked. He went around to the kitchen door, which was always open, and let himself in. Again he shouted for China, and again the silence of the empty house greeted him.

Swearing softly, he stoked up the fire in the cookstove and set the kettle on for tea. She'd probably just gone to do an errand in town, he thought, to buy a piece of fish for supper or a brick of butter for the freshly baked bread cooling on the oak table. While he waited for the water to boil, he spooned tea into the pot and rummaged in the cupboard for a jar of beach plum jam and a bread knife. He moved easily in the comfortable kitchen, at home.

Jake poured the boiling water and cut several thick slices of bread. When the tea was brewed, China still had not returned, so Jake sat down by himself and ate. Three cups of tea and half a loaf of bread later, he started to feel frustrated. Where was she? While he washed up his cup and his plate, he wondered if she were with Zenas Swain, sipping sherry from a delicate crystal glass in his Persian-carpeted office. He felt his own jealousy creeping across his heart.

The longer he waited, alternately pacing the parlor and staring blackly out the kitchen window at the view of the moors that always fascinated China, the more irritated he became. His imagination waxed in the quiet house, torturing him with thoughts of China and Zenas. He couldn't believe that Zenas satisfied her in any way. He was no match for her, he could never keep pace with her. If Zenas couldn't see that, China surely should. What was she doing all this time anyhow?

By the time he finally heard the gate open and click closed, the ebullient humor he had arrived in was long gone. Although he had come with the benign intention of clearing the air between them of jealousy, he was now consumed by it himself. In the back of his mind he knew that his unreasonable temper would do nothing to ease the tension between them, but he seemed incapable of controlling it.

When China came in, a minute later, she was startled to see Jake filling the doorway to the parlor, long legs apart, arms across his chest, and a fierce look on his rugged face. "I've been waiting here for almost three hours," he growled. "Where have you been?"

Although China couldn't immediately assimilate all the feelings that raced through her at the sight of him, she could instinctively respond to his tone. She tossed her new, navy-blue pelisse over a chair and set her hands on her hips. "I beg thy pardon?" she said, indignantly.

"I asked you where you've been all this time," Jake said, taking a menacing step toward her.

China didn't retreat. "I've been to Harriet's house," she replied hotly, "though I can't see that 'tis any of thy concern. Nor do I know why thee has been in my house for three hours...." Her voice trailed off at the dramatic change in Jake's expression. The glower vanished, chased away by his familiar, and heart-melting grin. The grin crinkled the corners of his sea-blue eyes, momentarily disarming China.

In that moment, he closed the gap between them with two long strides, and grabbed her gleefully into his arms. He covered the astonished O of her mouth with a hard, hungry kiss and pressed her slim body close to his with the powerful span of his hands. A hot glow surged through China and she ached to respond, but her anger overcame her passion. She twisted herself away, wiping the back of her hand across her lips. Her cheeks were very red and her eyes were smoking.

"How dare thee?" she seethed. "I thought I had made it quite clear that I wished to sail separate courses. Does thee take me for a cheap tavern girl? Or one of thy wenches? Does thee think thee can parade in here whenever thee has the urge, spouting insincere phrases meant to turn my head? Thee might have fooled me once, but not forever. Thee can save thy pretty words for thy other women, Jake Swan."

Jake seized her hand, following along when she backed away, but refusing to relinquish it. "There are no other women, China," he said, earnestly. "There never have been. Not from the first day I saw you running down Straight Wharf almost seven years ago, with your bonnet falling halfway down your back. My love for you has only grown stronger and surer since that day.

"Nay, hush, let me finish," he said, laying a finger on her lips, silencing the scornful retort he could see rising in her eyes. "I know what you saw that morning at the shipyard. I just discovered, today, that you were there. I know you saw me talking to Liddy Coffin and I know you saw her embrace me. But it was not by my invitation, nor did I respond.

"She and Sarah came on the pretext of asking for a berth on the *Maid* for their cousin, who is a slow, slothful boy, and obviously a trial for his parents. I should have said nay on the spot, for I have no intention of taking that clod to sea, but when I looked at Sarah, I was reminded of Zacch, and something in me softened. I told them I'd think on it, and that was when Liddy took the opportunity to leap all over me.

"She was a silly flirt as a girl and she's even more of a vixen now that she's a full-grown woman. I don't deny that she has a pretty face and an appealing body, but there is absolutely no way I'd risk capsizing your love for even a minute with her. Besides," he went on in a huskier voice, "I much prefer your beautiful face and your lovely body and everything else that goes with you." He slowly pulled her toward him by the hand he was still holding, his blue eyes, darkening with desire, locked on hers.

China moved forward as if mesmerized. She wanted desperately to believe what he was saying. In the weeks since she had cast him out of her life, she had been wretched. His parting threat had gone round and round in her head, devastating her with its finality. The thought of never seeing him again, of never being able to hope for the sight of him striding down the dock, his strong shoulders cutting confidently through a crowd, his dark curls tossed by the wind, his rich voice booming out orders and greetings and laughter, that thought had almost made her forget her pride. Wasn't it better to have him at least sometimes than never see him again?

But she had resisted that impulse then and she was trying to resist it now. She was trying to decide if he were telling the truth, trying to unclutter the confusion suddenly filling her mind, when he drew her so close to him her breasts brushed against his chest when she exhaled. He let go her hand and brought his up to her cheek, carefully pushing aside a hank of shiny black hair. His face lowered over hers, his lips barely touched hers. His other hand came around the back of her head, softly twining her hair while he breathed kisses over her closed eyelids, across her flushed cheeks and down her slender, white throat.

As his mouth and hands pressed gradually harder, kneading her, melding her to him, China succumbed. She gave in to his scent of the sea, to his enveloping strength, to his sensuous caresses. She gave in to the thrills coursing through her, to the yearnings in her heart; she gave in to her love. Eagerly, she returned his kisses, straining closer, free of restraints, wanting to feel his flesh next to hers.

"China," a muffled voice called out, accompanied by a rapping at the door.

"Damn," Jake whispered, while China's eyes snapped open, startled. Her breath came in great gasps. "Don't answer," he begged, clutching her to his shoulder for one more moment. "Pretend you're not here. Whoever it is will go away." He let his lips trail around her ear and down her neck.

China shuddered in pleasure, but pulled away. "Nay, I must answer," she said, reluctantly. "'Tis Zenas. He'll persist till he finds me."

"Damn," Jake said again, more savagely this time. He held on to her hands as she tried to move away.

"Please, Jake, I must open the door," China protested weakly.

He dragged her back to him and circled his arms around her slim back, laying his lips roughly, urgently over hers. She felt his tongue filling her mouth, felt his thighs crushing her. She pushed closer, rubbing against his hard body, tangling her fingers in his hair.

"China," came Zenas's voice again, louder, more insistent. He followed it with another knock on the locked door.

With a sharp intake of breath, China spun abruptly away from Jake and started through the parlor. "I'm coming," she called, rearranging her crumpled fichu as she went. Her heart was thumping very fast and she was gulping for breath. Her hands were trembling as she turned the key. For one second, before she lifted the latch, she let her eyes close, trying to gain control over the delicious sensations sensitizing her skin.

"There you are, China," Zenas said, when she opened her eyes and the door simultaneously. "I thought you might not be home. I've been quite anxious to find you." He started in through the door that China wordlessly held ajar, but stopped just inside the parlor when he saw Jake lounging, arms folded across his chest, against the hearth. China shut the door, then squeezed around Zenas's still form to stand somewhere between the two men.

"I was at Harriet's most of the day," she said, a little nervously. Zenas was looking at her in a peculiar way. She was suddenly very aware of her heated cheeks and her bruised lips. She was sure her hair was in disarray. "I've only just come home," she finished, lamely.

"And I've interrupted a visit," Zenas stated, coldly. It was not too difficult to interpret the bright light in Jake's blue eyes, or the soft, seductive look in China's gray ones. His disappointment and disapproval hardened his tone.

"Hello, Zenas," Jake said, levelly, not moving from where he stood.

"Jake," Zenas replied, nodding imperceptibly in his direction.

"Please sit down, Zenas," China said, hoping he wouldn't. "Would thee like some tea?" It was an awkward situation, not made any easier by the difficulty China was having collecting her wits. She felt distracted, scattered, caught between disrupted desire and emotional confusion. She wanted a few peaceful minutes to sort out her thoughts; instead, she was faced with this almost tangible strain.

"Thank you, no," Zenas said, turning back to China. "*Mine* is not a social call." He spoke more brusquely, much more brusquely, than he had intended.

"I have just received a letter from the *Justice*, delivered by the *Eleanor* out of New Bedford. The letter was written on the twenty-ninth of January by Ephraim Myrick. He tells of a tragic accident in which an ice floe shattered. A sailor has been found frozen to death and Shubael has disappeared. They found only his hat. It is presumed that he was trapped beneath the ice."

When Zenas's crisp words penetrated the muddle in China's mind, her hands flew to her mouth, as if to suppress the wave of horror and nausea welling up inside her. She felt the heated flush drain from her face, felt her body sway weakly. She stumbled two steps to the sofa and collapsed on it in shock. All she could think of was her own fall through the ice, of the terror she had felt when the frigid water had closed over her head. She remembered the excruciating pain, then the paralysis, the numbing, utter exhaustion.

"Oh dear God," she moaned, wrapping her arms around herself and rocking back and forth. Poor Shubael. Poor kindhearted, gentle Shubael. At least she had had Jake to clamp a strong hand around her wrist and to pull her to safety, to wrap her in blankets and to rub her to life. She had had Jake to rescue her from the freezing pond and to warm her with his love. Shubael had had no one. He had died all alone, trapped in the icy sea, all alone with his pain and his fear and his melancholy secrets.

"Nay, nay," she sobbed, still rocking in involuntary chill.

Both Zenas and Jake moved forward when China sank to the sofa, and both stopped, eyeing the other up. In the end, it was Zenas, mostly because of his proximity to her, who reached China's side first. He was instantly repentant of the unflattering thoughts he had had when he arrived, and upset with himself for the careless way in which he had broken the news to China. He was reminded, to his intense mortification, of the scene on Straight Wharf, only four months ago, when he had castigated Jake for being similarly insensitive.

"I'm so sorry, China," he murmured, kneeling in front of her. "I wish there were something I could do to ease your grief." He reached for her arm, wanting to arrest her rocking, wanting to give comfort with his touch, but China flinched away. She seemed self-contained in her mournful motion.

Zenas felt useless and ineffectual, especially with Jake towering above. He tried to ignore Jake's glare as he leaned toward China, again. "Is there any way, at all, I can help you?" He placed his hand, sympathetically, on her knee. Again China twisted away, still rocking, rejecting his solace. Zenas felt increasingly uncomfortable, even superfluous. He was dimly aware that the tables were turned, now, but he stubbornly refused to yield to Jake.

"Shall I fetch Harriet?" he asked, desperate to find a way he could aid her, but China didn't seem to hear him.

"I'll take care of her," Jake said, quietly, but with such assurance Zenas was forced to concede.

"Very well," he said, stiffly, rising. "I'll come by tomorrow to see if I may be of service." When Jake shrugged doubtfully in reply, he pursed his lips and left.

As soon as the front door closed, Jake sat down on the sofa by China. More assertive than Zenas, he succeeded in halting her pitiful seesawing simply by putting his iron-hard arms around her and holding her tightly to his chest. "'Tis a sorry thing," he murmured, kissing the top of her head, tenderly. "'Tis a sad, tragic affair."

His direct words and actions seemed to pierce the fog of China's sorrow more than Zenas's conventional condolences had. She raised her head to look at him, and Jake was stunned by the anguish darkening her eyes. Despite himself, he again felt a stab of jealousy that another man could command so much emotion from her. He held her face in the palm of one hand, softly stroking her pale cheek with his thumb.

"He must have been a fine man," he said, trying to control his feelings. "Anyone who can bring such a heartbroken look to your face must have been a worthwhile person. I know he helped you when you were all alone. I know he was generous with his time and his money, but you're not all alone now and you won't ever be again."

He lifted her face up to his and lightly kissed her. "This changes nothing," he said, keeping her close. "'Tis a terrible end for a man who deserved much better, but it changes nothing. You still have me to turn to, to help you, to love you. We still have our whole lives to be together, just as destiny decided it long ago. And as brutal as this may sound, perhaps it is that much easier now for you to marry me and to sail with me on the *Maid*.''

China lay back in Jake's arms and stared at him for a long time, her dazed and distraught emotions finally coming into focus. Then she placed her palm flat against his chest and pushed herself away. ''Aye,'' she said, slowly, nodding her head. ''It does sound brutal. In truth, it sounds indecent.''

She set her head wearily against the hard, horsehair back of the sofa, her hand fell limply to the seat. She felt overwhelmed with guilt and shame. While she had lain naked in Jake's arms, blissfully betraying her promise to Shubael, he had died an agonizing death, alone. '''Tis disgraceful and indecent,'' she repeated, as much to herself as to Jake.

Another flash of jealousy jolted Jake as she retreated from him in disgust. ''Decency is a social luxury,'' he replied, exasperated. He grabbed up one of her hands and pumped it as if to make her understand. '''Tis for those with plenty of time to spend. I can't afford such luxury. The *Maid* is to sail three weeks from tomorrow. 'Tis trite but true, 'Time and tide wait for no man.'''

China pulled her hand from his grip. ''Go then,'' she said, wearily. ''Go with the tide. Take thy ship and be gone from here. Leave those of us who are left on land to satisfy our feelings of decency and sorrow in peace.'' She stood up and walked to the window, searching for an outlet for her overwrought emotions.

Jake rose, too, and shortened the distance between them. He quelled the resentment in him as he gruffly said, ''I apologize for my poor timing and for my lack of pretty manners. I've told you before, though, that they are not my strong suit. Too much time is wasted in bows and curtseys;

too many of life's vital juices are bled dry by polite phrases and proper form. We're beyond that, China. Our love is greater than some stilted code of behavior, some dreary sense of decorum.

"You know that. You feel it as much as I do. You've a wild spirit, a *joie de vivre*, the same as I. That's why we belong together, why we need each other. We're two of a kind." He reached his hand out, inviting her to take it, to accept what he was saying.

"Don't let this change things," he said, softly. "Don't let this interfere with our love. Come with me. Marry me and come with me on the *Maid*."

Although Jake's words sounded chords in China's heart, although she knew he was right about their souls being matched, in her head she had had enough. She was saturated with tragedy. She brushed his hand aside. "I, too, have told thee something before," she said. "I've told thee that I will never marry a man who goes whaling. I was a fool to go back on my word, to let slip my convictions. But never again."

She crossed her arms on her stomach and turned to stare out the window again. "'Tis a miserable business," she said, bitterly. "It has taken from me everyone I've ever loved. First it killed Maman, then Papa, then Zacch. And now Shubael. I can bear no more losses; I want nothing more to do with whaling or those who embrace it."

Inflamed as much by her slap on his hand as by the inference of her argument, Jake grabbed China by the shoulder and spun her around to face him. "You never loved Shubael," he shouted. "You are confusing gratitude and companionship with love. 'Tis me you love and you haven't lost me. I'm still here and wanting you. Whaling has not taken me away from you, it's brought me to you."

"Nay, thee is wrong," China stormed back, pushing his hand from her shoulder but looking him squarely in the eye. "I lost thee to whaling long ago. 'Tis useless for me to compete. Whaling claimed thee for her own: she has bound thee, shackled thee, beguiled thee with her magic. All else is second to thee, Jake Swan, and I will not be second to any mistress of thine."

Jake seized her arm, shaking it in fury. "You are exaggerating," he roared. "You are being melodramatic. 'Tis a job, is all, a job I do well, one that lets me be on the sea instead of on land. What would you have me do instead? Be a preacher? A farmer? Or would you have me be a businessman like Zenas?

"Would that suit you better?" he demanded, flinging her arm away in outrage. "Would you prefer me to be a prissy landlubber? A pale-faced man who hides safely at home, who never takes risks and, thus, never makes gains? An unimaginative man who limits his life to a schedule? Breakfast at seven, work eight till six, sherry at six-thirty, in bed at eleven. Roast beef on Wednesday night, cribbage on Friday night, a tumble with the wife on Saturday. Is that more appealing?"

"Infinitely." China spat the word out icily. Her anger had concentrated to a cold glow; her gray eyes were gleaming dangerously. "I would always prefer a man like Zenas to one who is oafish and vulgar. Zenas is a gentleman, something with which thee has very little acquaintance. He is kind and considerate, interested in my opinions, not full of bullheaded notions and schoolboy bravado. He *respects* me. And that is more important than any quicksilver pleasure."

"'Tis more than quicksilver pleasure between us, China," Jake retorted, hurt and incensed. "'Tis a lifetime of love, of sharing, of being happy and satisfied. Will you pass that by? Will you sail out of deep, free water, to go aground in a shallow, safe cove?''

China studied him a moment, considering. "Does thee intend to continue whaling?'' she asked pointedly.

For a moment there was a chance, a moment when he almost melted her resistance with the intensity of his love, if only he seized that moment. But he didn't. Instead, angry and defensive, he shouted, "I do indeed.''

Something inside China collapsed. This was her final loss. Whaling had won its ultimate victory. She had no one left. No one but herself. She pointed to the door, her eyes on his, defiant, but calm. "Go then,'' China said, quietly. "Go and forget thee ever knew the path back.''

Jake's eyes narrowed in wrath, but he didn't know how to reply. If only she would yell or rant, he would know how to handle her; he could easily match her. But this deadly composure unnerved him. For the first time, he felt a trace of fear, fear that he might truly have lost her. Still, his pride and his pique prevented him from yielding. Instead, he gave a mocking salute and followed her pointing finger out the door.

THREE WEEKS LATER, Jake stood at the rail of the *China Maid*, watching Nantucket fade from sight. He hadn't exchanged so much as a word or a glance with China since their fight. He felt miserable, almost giving orders to come about and return to port. In the end, though, his stubborn streak prevailed. He kept on course, his natural confidence finally restoring his faith.

He was sure they were meant for each other, sure she would eventually realize it. Clutching to that thought, Jake resolved to keep reminding her of their love. He would send her another shawl from Valparaiso, some beads from the Sandwich Islands. On every homeward-bound ship he saw, he would send her letters, teasing, bantering letters that would make her rise to the bait. She couldn't resist. He would bombard her with messages, with recollections, with tokens of his affection. He would badger her into confronting her feelings. She would relent.

From her hidden spot above Capaum Pond, China watched the *Maid* sail away, her wooden likeness bobbing joyously toward the sea. She gripped her shawl more tightly around her, to ward off the chilly April air and the icy feeling of loneliness and loss numbing her heart. It was finally over.

As a tear started to form in her magnificent gray eyes, China shook her head stubbornly. No more of that, she vowed. No more sentiment and self-pity. She had plenty to satisfy her. She had her ship, her ambitions, her career as a merchant. No longer would she be enticed by one night of bliss or a few stirring promises. It wasn't enough. She would not relent.

20

NANTUCKET
July 13, 1846

IT WAS A WARM, MUGGY EVENING and China's clothes clung damply to her skin. Although she had been thrilled with the pale pink gown of fine Swiss muslin when she had bought it two months ago, its long, lace-trimmed sleeves, tight-fitting bodice and volumes of skirt now seemed no more luxurious than the drab Quaker dresses hanging in her closet. In this weather, all clothes were unbearable. She thought longingly of that afternoon on Coatue so many years ago, when she had slid, half clad, into the clean, refreshing sea and swum exultantly toward Jake.

"'Tis so hot," she said, quickly, to distract herself from such memories. As she walked, she fanned herself vigorously with the paper program for the melodrama they had just seen at the Atheneum. "If only it would rain and clear the air."

Beside her, escorting her home, Zenas nodded. "It has been an unusually dry summer, despite the heavy air. It always seems on the verge of rain, but it never comes to anything."

Now it was China's turn to nod, but she made no further comment. It took too much energy to talk, especially on such a futile topic. She would rather think about the *Josephine*, three weeks off the ways and ready to make her maiden voyage to England. She was sitting right now, snug, at Straight Wharf, partially loaded with casks of oil, waiting to be towed out beyond the Bar, to receive the rest of her cargo. She looked trim and saucy and very fast.

Between building the clipper and purchasing her cargo, China had invested almost all her money, but she expected to see handsome dividends. She felt confident about the business decisions she had made, based partly on her own instincts and experience, and partly on advice generously offered by the Swains. She had worked hard, compiling ship lists, writing dozens of letters overseas, studying the market, carefully laying her plans. In time, she should have a very solid foothold in shipping. It made her proud.

The only flaw in the realization of her ambition, the only vague disappointment, was the fact that she wouldn't be accompanying the *Josephine* to England. She had reached that conclusion somewhat reluctantly; being back at sea had always been an essential part of the dream. It wasn't wholly feasible, however, from a financial point of view. There was just enough money in the bank for her to sit tight and wait for the expected returns, but not enough for her to spend time in London. China shrugged. There would be other trips.

Besides, Harriet's baby was due next month and she shouldn't be away for that. Harriet would need some help after the baby was born and China wanted to be on hand to volunteer. Clarissa Swain, Harriet's mother, was a well-intentioned and kindhearted woman, but completely ineffectual when it came to domestic duties. China often wondered what she would have done had she married a man less well-to-do than Benjamin. She seemed incapable of running a household without several servants to aid her. China knew Harriet would want someone efficient, but familiar, in the house.

"Perhaps we could take a drive tomorrow afternoon," Zenas said, interrupting her musings. "It might be cooler out of town. We could just go out to Dionis and be back in time for your birthday dinner at Harriet's."

"That would be pleasant, Zenas," China said, slowly, as she refocused her thoughts. "I had almost forgotten it was my birthday. My mind has been occupied with the *Josephine*."

"You are like a fretful mother," Zenas said, teasingly. "You worry about that ship day and night. In fact, you've become almost as single-minded as Papa on the subject of ships. I never thought I'd tire of the discussion, but I shall be quite relieved when she sails and there are no more details for you to fuss with. Perhaps then, I can bring your attention back to more entertaining subjects."

Although he spoke lightly and smiled benignly, there was a serious undertone to his words. The subject he most wanted to broach, when China was less engrossed in her ship, was marriage. It had been on his mind for months, ever since he had received news of Shubael's death. He'd felt obliged to observe a decent mourning period, though after her initial shock and horror, China hadn't appeared too distraught. Really, it seemed the biggest obstacle to having her consider his proposal was her obsession with the *Josephine*, especially now that that lout, Jake Swan, had sailed over the horizon. He had only to be patient a little while longer.

"Just think," China said, pensively, "I shall be twenty-five tomorrow. 'Tis a quarter of a century."

"Practically ancient," Zenas said, in mock dismay. He took the opportunity to ruffle his fingers through her silky, black hair. "Hmm," he said, "no sign of white hairs, yet. Although perhaps you rub stove black into your hair every morning to fool the public into thinking you are still young."

"Nay, be serious," China protested, suddenly quite caught up in the idea. "'Tis not so much a question of young or old, but of all that has happened to me in that quarter-century span." She stopped where she stood, in the bulky, night shadow of a clapboard-fronted mansion.

Zenas stopped, too, surprised that she was so intense. "It has been a full life," he agreed, easily.

"More than full," China corrected, straining through the darkness to make him understand. "It has been up and down like a child's teeter toy. Or like a tropical storm, with fierce winds and high seas one minute, and sunshine and rainbows the next. I've come from a miserable stone cottage in France to a whaling ship around the world to a snug home in Nantucket. I've been so poor I couldn't buy a loaf of bread and so wealthy I could buy a beautiful ship."

She started walking again, at a slow, reflective pace. Zenas followed. "For the first four years of my life, I didn't know I had a father, and then I didn't have a mother. And now I have no family at all. I was a twin, and now I'm sailing solo; I was to be wed, and now I'm more or less widowed. I was a lowly shop clerk, and now I'm a shipowner. Nay, Zenas, thee must admit, it has been a remarkable quarter century. I feel there ought to be a milestone set somewhere."

"A remarkable quarter century for a remarkable lady," Zenas replied, sincerely, squeezing her arm in the dark.

China sighed, but said no more. Zenas was sweet, but he simply didn't understand her. Not the way Jake did. Jake would have recognized the momentousness of this occasion. He might even have gone out and carved the granite marker she envisioned, like the milestone by the Pacific Bank. He would have set it firmly in her garden, officially

declaring one era over and another begun. He would have
rocked back on his heels, his arms wound around her waist,
carefully examining her face for signs of the passing years,
his blue eyes deep, searching.

She hurriedly switched her thoughts. She might have
added more events to her quarter-century chronology, she
decided. She might have added two narrow escapes from
death, one unjust assault on her honesty and three proposals of marriage. If Obed's years of stuttering devotion could
be considered a proposal.

China glanced at the slim, young gentleman by her side.
She sighed again. Unless she missed her guess, there was a
fourth proposal in the making, too. There was no mistak-
ing Zenas's intentions. The interest he had taken in helping her with the *Josephine* went beyond even Benjamin's
kindness and concern. China knew he wasn't doing it as a
favor to Harriet, or even because of an obligation to Shubael. And it certainly wasn't out of charity for a possible
competitor. The plain truth was Zenas was falling in love
with her.

China snuck another glance at him. His neat blond hair
shone around the edges of his summer hat, even in the
murky starlight. His dim profile was elegant. She turned
her gaze back to the street in front of her. As she studied
the dark lumps of cobblestones, twisting at her feet, she
tried to tell herself that her difficulty in visualizing such a
union was only due to her absorption with the *Josephine*.
All her energies were wrapped up in her ambition, in her
desire to prove herself a success. For the moment that was
the most important thing in her life.

Perhaps when her ship came in, laden with profitable
merchandise, a credit to her business acumen, perhaps then
she would consider the proposal that Zenas was probably
going to make. Walking along in the dark, she nodded

briskly, trying to convince herself. Of course she would. It was only her preoccupation that caused her to hesitate, she told herself, stoutly, only her immersion in shipping affairs. Jake's unflattering description of Zenas had nothing to do with it.

A giggle started up in her throat as she remembered the daily routine Jake had contemptuously recited. Just in time, she turned it into a cough, eliciting no more than a mildly curious glance from Zenas. Poor Zenas, she thought, with a flash of mischief. He would die of embarrassment if he knew what Jake had said about him. Jake had painted such an unappealing portrait.

As quickly as she had quelched her giggle, China repressed her sympathetic thoughts of Jake. However accurately or inaccurately he had assessed Zenas's character was beside the point. His opinion no longer mattered. He had sailed away and she would never see him again. Which was the way she wanted it, she thought, vigorously nodding her head to underscore her sentiment. She tried to ignore the involuntary ache that accompanied the idea. Less vigorously, more forlornly, she thought she ought to marry Zenas just to prove Jake no longer had any impact on her life.

"I think the heat has gotten to you," Zenas said, teasing again. "You are practically scurrying down the street, your head bobbing like a cork in the waves, and here you've almost missed the turn to your lane. I should have thought you'd know the way blindfolded."

"Oh," China said, halting abruptly. She looked back two paces to where Zenas stood at the head of the lane. A blush flooded her cheeks, fortunately hidden by the night. "Indeed I have," she murmured, retracing her steps.

Perhaps to salve her guilty conscience, or to keep further unwelcome memories at bay, when they arrived a minute later at her gate China invited Zenas in for a cup of tea. "I know it sounds absurd,'' she said, ''but Aunt Judith always claimed the most refreshing beverage in the heat was hot tea. She said it equalized the temperature inside and out. There's a clump of mint by the clothes pole that we can pick as we go in. And I believe I have a lemon in the cupboard. Would a cup of lemon-mint tea suit thee?''

Zenas unlatched the gate and held it open for China, then followed her in. ''With all respects to Aunt Judith,'' he said, ''I think I will decline the tea. I've no doubt that it is most salubrious, but the thought of lighting a fire to boil the kettle is very disheartening. I'd be delighted to stop for a brief visit, and, perhaps, a glass of lemonade, but please don't start a fire.''

''Of course,'' China said, relieved at his answer. She unlocked the front door and let them in. ''Thee is being most sensible. I've often meant to buy a small, ship's stove for summer cooking, but something else always comes up.'' She tossed her program, her reticule and the new straw bonnet she had held by its pink ribbons onto the pine table. She gestured toward the sofa as she walked past it to the kitchen. ''Come sit down while I squeeze the lemon into a pitcher. Does thee like thine sweet?''

''Moderately so,'' Zenas replied, settling comfortably on the sofa.

China returned a few minutes later with the two glasses of lemonade and a plate of cinnamon shortbread made slightly soggy by the humidity. They were passing a pleasant while, sipping their sugary tart drinks and amiably discussing *The Drunkard, or the Fallen Saved*, the play they had seen, when the frantic clanging of the Lisbon bell came quite clearly through the open windows. China moved to the edge of her chair, instantly taut with apprehension.

''At this hour it can only mean a fire,'' she said. She glanced at the grandfather clock. It was just past eleven.

"Does thee suppose it could be on Straight Wharf?" She didn't care if Zenas teased her and called her a mother hen, worry was starting to work on her nerves. The *Josephine* lay bound to the pilings along the wharf, a highly flammable cargo stowed beneath her decks, and on the wooden walk beside her.

But Zenas didn't laugh. He rose immediately, his own concern mirroring hers. Although he had no ships at the dock, he did have valuable oil sitting in warehouses, as well as his offices, to consider. Neither made mention of it, but both were remembering the terrible conflagration in 1838, which started in Joseph James's ropewalk, and destroyed almost thirty buildings before it was brought under control by blowing up neighboring houses with gunpowder.

"I'll go find out," he said. "It's probably only a haystack catching a chimney spark, or a lamp knocked over in a tavern brawl," he added, attempting to reassure her. "But I shall go investigate and come back with a full report."

"Thank thee, Zenas," China said. She rose, too. "Thee is always so considerate. Thee indulges my whims almost too much." She gave him a grateful smile that belied her occasional annoyance with his eagerness to please. In this instance, she was glad to accept his chivalry.

Zenas hesitated a minute before leaving, his mind suddenly diverted from the emergency. "I can never indulge you too much, China," he said softly. "It gives me great pleasure to take care of your needs."

He stood with his hat in his hand, regarding her intently. China felt her cheeks turn red, as her gratitude changed to uneasiness. She didn't know how to respond to Zenas's obvious overture, and, more importantly, she didn't want to think about it right now. Fortunately, the urgent pealing brought Zenas's mind back to the problem at hand. He lightly touched China's shoulder, promised to return immediately with news and left.

With the house empty and nothing to do but wait, China started uncertainly in one direction and then in another. The insistent clanging of the Lisbon bell, no matter how muted by distance, made it difficult to ignore the situation or to ease her mind. She finally forced herself down in Zaccheus's rocker and took up a piece of mending. Between the dim light of the oil lamp and the anxiety absorbing her concentration, the torn chemise didn't fare so well. After pricking her finger a third time, China tossed the garment back in the basket and got to her feet.

Still aimless, she wandered from one window to the next, leaning for a time, looking out, then abruptly moving away. She kept telling herself she was being irrational, that she was allowing her imagination to get the better of her, but the gnawing apprehension persisted. The solemn donging of the grandfather clock cut through her thoughts and made her jump. She looked at the time. Midnight. Zenas had been gone almost an hour.

China started for the door, then, at the last minute, let her hand fall indecisively from the latch. An hour really wasn't so very much time, after all. By the time Zenas walked into town, found the source of the problem, had gone to assess it himself, and possibly even lent a hand or offered advice, an hour could have easily passed. And then he still had to walk back. Grudgingly, China returned to the rocker, though she left the mending untouched. She sat perfectly still, gripping the arms of the chair, waiting for word.

When another half an hour had gone by, she could take the tension no more. Like a watch spring released from its case, China sprang out of the chair and raced for the door. Almost as soon as she opened it, she knew something was wrong. It was not a minor accident that was keeping Zenas from returning, but something of frightening dimensions. Over the tops of the trees, in the direction of town, the sky was orangey bright and billowing with black clouds, like the sunset at the end of a storm. There was no longer any question of waiting. Barely bothering to close the door behind her, she started off for town.

Her stomach twisted in cold fear as China quickened her pace. By the time she reached the end of her lane and turned into Main Street, the unnatural glow had become more vivid and the smell of smoke was heavy in the damp air. She broke into a run.

The closer she came, the more her heart pounded. Fire was no longer an abstract possibility, it was real. She could hear it now, the roaring and the snarling of flames devouring wood, the bangs and blasts of buildings exploding from the heat, the shattering of glass, the crash of collapsing roofs. She could hear the screams of frightened horses and the shouts of frantic men.

And when she came around the curve by Trader's Lane, she could see it. Great, tall shafts of fire licking through shingles and clapboard, out of windows and doors. Smoke and soot spewed forth in greasy black geysers, staining the brilliantly lit sky and searing China's lungs as she gulped hoarsely for breath. Still she kept running, stumbling over her feet, sides aching for air, propelled by the horror of the spectacle before her.

A crowd of people by the bank finally brought her to a gasping halt. She looked down the street, down the two square blocks that were the commercial heart of Nantucket, at the banks, at the grocers, at the milliners, at the butchers, at the dry goods, at the dress shops. She stared, stunned. They were all aflame. All of Nantucket was on fire.

"China! You shouldn't be here! Go home!" came a shout in her ear. She turned toward the voice, only barely heard above the tremendous din. It was Zenas, and he was tugging on her arm, trying to pull her back from the fire. Still in shock, China allowed herself to be led away a few steps, away from the overwhelming heat and the fierce draughts of furnacelike air, but then she got hold of herself. She shook off Zenas's grip and turned back toward the fire.

"You can't go down there, China!" Zenas shouted, seizing her with both hands this time. "It's dangerous! Go home! The fire could swing in this direction any moment!"

China cast a wild look in the direction of the wharves, impossible to see through the flames and soot and mobs of people. She looked back to Zenas, desperate. "What of the waterfront?" she asked, her voice almost lost in the noise. "Has the fire reached the waterfront?"

Zenas shook his head, not because the wharves were untouched, but because he couldn't answer the question. "Go home," he repeated. "Go home and keep safe. I'll come tell you as soon as I know something, China. Don't worry."

"Don't worry?" China screamed, pulling free from Zenas. In the back of her mind it vaguely registered that Zenas's tie was still smartly knotted in place and that his linen jacket was still stretched smoothly across his slender shoulders. "Don't worry?" she screamed, again, too frightened to remember her manners. "How can I not worry when the *Josephine* is in danger? I've invested all my money in that ship. All my money and all my hopes. I must know if she is safe!"

"Please, China," Zenas said, trying to reach for her again, trying to steer her back to safety. "There is no way I can get through to the *Josephine* just now. Please go home and wait for me to come. Don't worry about the money. I'll take care of you when this is all over.''

That was not the reply that China wanted to hear. She shoved Zenas's hands away in exasperation and darted around him to run up Fair Street. Clutching her skirt well above her speeding feet with both white-knuckled fists, she cut through alleys and yards, leaped over rows of flowers, paralleling Main Street beyond the fire line. She half slid, half tumbled, down the bluff on Orange Street, to land on Union Street, one block from the wharves.

Even at this distance from the fire, the air was hot and thick with soot, barely breathable. Cinders fell on China's face and hands and burned holes in her pretty pink gown. Still, she paused only long enough to draw in great gulps of scorched air before continuing on, staggering slightly, to Straight Wharf.

Through the night lit by a burning town, through dense clouds of smoke and ash, China could see the tall masts of the *Josephine* standing proud and whole. "Thank God!" she cried, in deep relief, and started toward her ship. An instant later she was lying flat on her face on the rough planks along the edge of the dock, her head reverberating with the boom of a warehouse that had exploded beyond her and knocked her down.

She crawled to her knees, oblivious to the splinters stabbing her palms and stuck in her face. As she watched, terrified, hunched on all fours, oil poured out of the ruined building like a river, a bright flame racing along the top of it, spilling into the sea, and setting even the saltwater on fire. The flames moved across the harbor with the current and the tide, snapping at anything in their path, cutboats, lighters, whaleboats, dories.

Panic forced China to her feet. It took only a moment to reach the *Josephine*, to see her ship in the eerie light. She could see the fresh paint still gleaming on the rail, see the new brass shining on the wheel. Sobbing with fear and futility, China struggled to release the heavy dock lines holding the clipper ship securely to the wharf. She threw the wrist-thick hawsers off the pilings, but the *Josephine* remained serenely where she was.

"Nay," China cried. "Don't stay! Float away!"

She gave a mighty shove on the *Josephine*'s bow, with every bit of strength she could command. The clipper's nose bobbed slightly and inched around. China turned to move farther down the dock, to try pushing amidship. She had taken one weeping, choking step, when a rough arm circled her waist and yanked her back.

China shrieked in fresh fear and beat at the iron arm holding her. Her fist fell limply, though, when a flaming cask of oil rolled down the dock and settled only a foot from where she had stood. The burly sailor, clutching her to his sweaty side, had just saved her life. Before she had time to mumble her gratitude or to elicit his help in saving the *Josephine*, she found herself swept unceremoniously into his arms and carried at a trot around streams of fire to a safer spot.

He set her down with a thump and she staggered a moment before regaining her balance—a moment in which she saw flames chewing along the neatly furled new sails of the *Josephine*, then climbing up the rigging and masts, making a bright outline in the night. It was a sight repeated all down the dock as whalers and schooners and vessels of every description caught fire.

Another explosion slammed against the air, causing fierce, hot gusts to rock both China and the sailor backward. For another fraction of a second, China watched, almost beyond horror, as the *Josephine* burst apart, her valuable cargo an inferno, her beautiful woodwork an eruption of flaming planks. Then she found her face buried against the sailor's sooty, soaked jersey, as he shielded her from the shower of cinders raining down around them. When China looked up again, coughing and gasping, the *Josephine* was a blazing ship, sinking in a blazing sea.

Before the magnitude of the sight could penetrate China's numb mind, before she could fully grasp the scope of the destruction she was witnessing, she felt herself being led away. The stocky sailor clamped his calloused hand around her upper arm and steered her briskly past the burning buildings and scattered debris. Everything was in flames, everything was shattering, smashing, snapping, collapsing. Only a small, perilous path existed on what had once been an open street, paved with shells and bordered by wooden walkways.

"Ye'll be awright, here," the sailor shouted in her ear. "Just stay along the sand." He pointed a soot-blackened finger in the direction of the narrow harbor beach along Washington Street, looking cool, white and calm in the hideous light of the fire.

"Thank thee," China mumbled. She looked up at the sailor. His face, too, was pitch-black with oily ash. Dazedly, China assumed hers was as well. "Thank thee," she mumbled again. The sailor nodded and wound his way back into the hellish spectacle to be what help he could elsewhere.

China stumbled through the spiky dune grass to the strip of beach below. She sank down on an overturned dory and stared, mesmerized, at the fire. A slight breeze, innocent of the searing winds within the town, drifted off the sea and brushed her cheek. It soothed the skin, which, she was suddenly and painfully aware, was burned, blistered and scraped.

"Happy birthday," she said, softly, though the words sounded loud. She realized, then, that she could hear the steady ripple of the water lapping on the shore. On this little spit of beach, the fire seemed remote and distant. China lay back on the dory and studied the sky overhead. It was cast in an orangey glow. She threw her forearm across her eyes, blocking out the terrible night. "Happy birthday," she murmured again.

She thought bitterly of the quarter-century milestone she had been envisioning only hours before. Her catalog of events hadn't been complete then, but it was now. She had the one element necessary to turn her, full cycle, back to the time of her birth: financial disaster.

She was impoverished, now. She was as poor as a washerwoman in France, twenty-five years ago. She had her cottage, her gray clothing and nothing else. There were no overdue ships she could hope for, no absent brother, or father, or husband, to wait for. Nothing. In a quarter of a century, she had sailed around the world and found a fortune, to arrive, now, with less, far less, than she had had when she had started.

China sighed, a deep, defeated sigh. The *Josephine* was gone. It meant more than just poverty; it meant much greater failure, too. It meant an end to her illusions. She had thought she was capable of running a business, of making her way in the world on her own. She thought that she could prove to herself, and, she reluctantly admitted, to Jake, that she could combine her love for the sea and for ships with a career that wasn't whaling. But she couldn't. She had failed.

DAWN BROKE UNNOTICED in a town already as bright as day. Nine hours after it started, in the rear of William Geary's hat shop, the fire was contained. It had collected its price. Fully one third of the town was nothing but ashes. Almost four hundred buildings had burnt. Seven oil factories, three banks, the County offices, two newspaper offices, a dozen warehouses, practically every store, shop or commercial enterprise, even the Atheneum, where they had watched that forgettable little melodrama. All gone.

Slowly, China made her way up the still-hot cobbles of Main Street. She thought she had finally realized the fearful extent of the fire, but she was stunned by the devastation around her. All the way over to Jared Coffin's big brick house, two blocks away, all she could see were smoldering timbers and free-standing chimneys. The smell of smoke and oil and gunpowder lay heavily in the air. People moved about in shock.

"China! Thank God you're alive!" Zenas cried, hurrying from the charred pile of rubble that had been his elegant offices. "But look at you! What happened? My God, are you all right? Where have you been?"

While Zenas babbled, his frantic tone indicating the level of his worry, China calmly peered around at herself to see what was causing the expression of horror on his pale face. Her hands were filthy black and full of festering splinters. Her dress was an indistinguishable color, ripped, scorched and ragged. Though she couldn't see her face, she could feel the burns and cuts. What she couldn't guess, however, was how frightening she appeared, just two huge, gray eyes staring from a grimy, battered mask.

"My ship has burned, Zenas," she said. "The *Josephine* has burned." Then she turned and started toward home. She wasn't interested in Zenas's hovering, in his solicitousness. He was still wearing his finely tailored jacket, though it was smudged and creased.

She waved him away in disgust. He was weak. Weak and prissy. Unconsciously, China used Jake's own description of him. Prissy. She knew for sure, fortune or no fortune, there was little chance she would ever consider his proposal. She was more apt to marry the burly sailor from the dock than to marry Zenas.

"Happy birthday," she said, again.

21

INDIAN OCEAN
OFF MADAGASCAR
December 1846

"BLOOOWS! THERE SHE BLOOOWS!" As the words rang out, Jake stuck the needle into the shirt he was mending and let it drop from his hands. He waited a moment before rising wearily and trudging topside. He was exhausted.

Although he had left Nantucket with the intention of cruising in the South Pacific, halfway to the Azores he had suddenly changed his mind. Whether it was restlessness or rebellion, or just a whaler's instinct, Jake had decided to head south around the Cape of Good Hope instead and to cruise the Indian Ocean. It was proving to be an extremely sound decision. Their luck had been uncommonly greasy, so far. Almost overwhelmingly so.

No sooner did they stow the oil from one hunt, when more spouts were sighted on the horizon. For months, their lives had been a continual round of giving chase, killing, cutting in and trying out. Jake hardly remembered what clean clothes felt like, or what it meant to have a moment's leisure. His mind was drugged with fatigue, and he knew the men were in no better shape than he. Only the thought of their rapidly mounting lays kept them from mutinying. Even so, there were defiant mutterings and frequent fights in the fo'c'sle.

When Jake emerged on deck and saw the gaunt, slack faces of the crew, he was almost at the point of admitting China was right about whaling. At the moment, there seemed little that was ennobling about it. It was simply a dirty, brutal grind that devoured a man's youth and vitality. There had to be a better way to make a living.

Jake rubbed at the stiffness in his back while automatically scanning the horizon. This was the last time he would buy a whaling ship just to prove a point of pride, he thought ruefully. But out loud, he demanded, "Whereaway? Sing out, man!"

"Blows! And again! Dead abeam to the larboard!" came the answering cry from the crow's nest.

Jake located the spouts easily and focused Zaccheus's old glass in that direction. It was only a small school, today, just four spouts, but he decided to lower all boats anyway. Right now they were glutted, seemingly overloaded, with opportunities. Every seaman knew, however, that their luck could change tomorrow, and they would curse themselves for allowing even one whale to swim off unchallenged.

Minutes later, they were all in boats, pulling tiredly toward the whales. As they approached the unsuspecting school, Jake saw that it was a single family. A bull, a dam and twin calves. He felt sick. It seemed like a macabre joke. At this moment, when China's objections to whaling were so much in his mind, it was somehow significant that he should come across such a group of whales. It was witnessing the slaughter of a similar school that had first set China against whaling twenty years ago.

The men stroked steadily nearer, but Jake remained motionless, transfixed. His limbs were heavy, his thoughts were leaden and dull. He suddenly wanted very much to be in Nantucket, holding China, soft and sweet smelling, in his arms, forgetting the dirty, lonely life at sea.

"Ja-Jake?" John James Henry asked, quietly, from the bow of the boat. "Ja-Jake, is it time? I'm ready when you say so."

Jake stirred. He forced himself back to the present. This was no time to daydream and to wish for what wasn't. As China had said, he'd charted his course, and now he must sail it. His business was whaling and it was time for business. Four men were waiting for his orders; John James Henry's hand was hovering near his harpoon. They were closest to a fat calf. He had to kill it.

"Ship oars," he murmured, so as not to alarm the whale. The oars came silently aboard. "Ready when you are, John James Henry."

The big man nodded and rose. He turned deftly, his iron in his giant fist. He wedged his knee firmly against the clumsy cleat for balance, took careful aim, then sent the harpoon, straight and true, deep into the hide of the whale. He instantly snatched up a second iron and it, unerringly, followed the first.

"Stern all!" Jake shouted, his blood racing with reflex excitement. Oars dipped swiftly into the sea, again, and propelled them away from the mortally wounded whale. Jake skillfully steered them out of reach of its thrashing flukes, then yelled, "Up oars!" as the enormous beast sounded. Line whirled from the tubs in which it was coiled. It hardly took Jake's command for the men to bail buckets of water over the sizzling loggerhead. Jake and John James Henry scrambled to change places so Jake would be in position to deliver the death blow.

It was all routine, all perfectly normal. Jake had gone through the same motions a hundred times. Adrenaline and experience carried him along. Time rushed by as their boat bounced in roiled seas. Concentration was intense. And then it broke.

Out of the corner of his eye, almost with another sense, Jake saw the starboard bow boat get an iron in the mother whale, swimming anxiously near her harpooned baby. Before he had time to absorb that information, to separate it from the situation demanding his attention, he saw the whale's massive flukes beat the ocean in rage. Almost at the same time he felt the sturdy whaleboat he was in flipped from the water as if it were dandelion fluff, spun over and smashed into the waves.

Jake's arms flailed wide, trying to right himself, to regain control of his catapulting body. He collided with the water at the same instant as a sixteen-foot oak oar. It caught him across the chest and across one arm, driving the breath out of him and sending sharp pain shooting through him.

Off balance and in agony, Jake felt himself sinking deep into the ocean. His left arm was useless. His lungs screamed for air that wasn't there. In vain, he fought for the surface. Through the shock, through the excruciating searing, through the franticness and futility, one thought registered clearly. He was going to die.

Images flashed through his mind, images of his life and the people in it. He saw his grandfather downing a tot of rum, his father hunched over his desk, Zaccheus peering amiably across a chess board, Zacch, bare chested and brown, laughing down the length of the deck. And then he saw China.

He saw her splashing helplessly in Miacomet Pond, her lips blue from the cold, and sprawled sleeping against a log, her lips blue, now, from eating berries. He saw her swimming exultantly toward him in the summer sun off Coatue, and standing naked and rosy in the firelight of her parlor hearth. He saw her clear lovely face and her great, seductive, gray eyes. He saw them lit with laughter as she sat next to him on the buckboard, luminous with desire as she stood

431

beneath a tree, the rain beating against her porcelain skin, and brimming in grief as she quietly told him she lost him to the sea long ago. Then he saw nothing.

22

NANTUCKET
Christmas Day 1846

WITH SLOW, carefully tempered motions, China knotted a clean fichu around her neck, smoothed her skirt and brushed her silky, black hair. In the months since the Great Fire, she had learned to stretch out the simplest tasks so as to fill the long, empty hours of each day. She had given up searching for a job some time ago; there were none to be had. The whole commercial section of town was only partially rebuilt. There were hardly any shops, let alone positions for shop clerks. China had more idle time than she knew what to do with.

Today, at least, she could look forward to Christmas dinner at the Swains'. Although Aunt Judith had never acknowledged that this day was special, Harriet's family had always celebrated Christmas with a huge roast goose and a pile of presents. Since Aunt Judith's death, China had joined them. As she shrugged into her cloak, she grimly reflected that this year the festivity would be considerably subdued.

There wasn't a person in Nantucket who hadn't suffered from the fire. Even the Swains, with their seemingly endless resources, were less comfortable than usual. Although all their ships had been at sea, and thus had escaped damage, they had lost their offices and their warehouse, and the oil stored in it. It would take them some time to recover, but at least it seemed likely that they would. Obed's father, for example, had nothing to show for what had once been a profitable sail loft but ashes and a minuscule insurance settlement. Obed had been cod fishing in a dory, off 'Sconset, to support his young wife and his son, Edward, born three weeks after the disaster.

China conscientiously banked the stove before going out. Fuel cost money and she had to conserve every penny she could. She had very little left in reserve. What hadn't burned up with the *Josephine* in July had gone for her living expenses ever since. She had made sure to set aside enough for taxes. She couldn't bear the thought of confronting Mr. Hawkins again, though this year many property owners would have trouble paying their tax bills.

China closed the kitchen door behind her and started along the scallop-shell path to the gate. She shivered a little and wrapped her cloak more tightly around her. It was a raw, bleak day, not unlike her future, she thought ironically. She unlatched the gate, let herself through and latched it shut again. Walking as slowly as she could in the chill wind, she made her way to Gardner Street.

As she plodded, she reviewed, for the hundredth time, the meager options available to her. Both Harriet and her father had invited her to come live in their homes, but she was unable to accept either offer. Partly it was pride that prevented her, but there were other reasons, too.

Knowing how straitened Harriet and Obed's circumstances had become, China felt awkward about adding to their burden. And anyway, she had relinquished Obed's support when she had rejected his advances; it didn't seem fair to change courses now. She still spent a good part of every day helping Harriet with Edward, and she allowed

Obed to keep her supplied with fish fillets in return, but she wouldn't let it go any further than that.

Her reason for refusing Benjamin's generous offer was much more direct: Zenas. He had asked her to marry him twice since the fire, once immediately afterward and once only a few weeks ago. Both times she had said no. She couldn't think of him as anything but weak. His elegance, his fine manners, his solicitous demeanor no longer appealed to her. They were overwhelmed by her perception of him as impotent. In fact, without the *Josephine*, and shipping in general, to lay a common ground, China found she had nothing to talk about with Zenas. There was no way she could live under the same roof as he.

China lingered on the corner of Gardner and Main Street, waiting for the noontime bells to ring. She shifted from one cold foot to the other, not wanting to arrive too early. Those were some fine choices, she thought bitterly, as she clapped her hands together to keep warm. She could marry a man she didn't respect, impose on friends who couldn't afford it or face destitution alone.

And truthfully, she admitted, grudgingly, she had no one to blame but herself. If she hadn't been so determined to invest all her money in the *Josephine*, she would not be in such trouble now. Zenas had warned her, but she had wanted to show that she could run a business that didn't depend on whaling; she had wanted to show that she could be independent and successful. She kicked at a clump of cold mud. This was the last time she would buy a ship just to prove a point of pride, she decided.

When she finally entered the Swains' big parlor, she found the mood there not much gayer. Except for Edward, who wanted only to eat, sleep and, occasionally, coo, the topic on everyone's mind was still the fire and its long-term effects. China sighed as she let Zenas lift the cloak from her shoulders. She was heartily sick of the subject and was hoping that she could forget about it for at least a few hours.

"May I get you a glass of sherry?" Zenas asked, while Benjamin filled the background with a monologue on fire insurance and the reliability of the companies that handled it.

"Thank thee, Zenas," China replied, settling onto a striped silk settee. "'Tis just the thing I need at the moment."

"Nay, Zenas," Benjamin said, interrupting himself. "Belay the sherry and fetch China a cup of eggnog. And don't be stingy with the rum. She's looking a bit light in the water. We need to give her some ballast."

Zenas cocked a questioning eyebrow at China, wishing neither to disobey his father nor to offend China's sensibilities. But China grinned for the first time in months. "Aye, Zenas," she said, "don't be stingy with the rum." Benjamin grinned back. Zenas shrugged.

"Now, let's see, what was I saying?" Benjamin asked the room at large. He glanced from Harriet, absently rocking Edward's cradle with her foot, to Clarissa, obliviously crocheting a cap for her grandson, to Obed, sitting with his arms crossed sturdily on his chest, a look of extreme patience on his face.

"Thee was talking about fire insurance," China offered, sipping the cup of eggnog Zenas handed her. The rich, rum-laced drink warmed her stomach and lifted her spirits.

"Aye, fire insurance," Benjamin said, pulling at his chin. "I swear, 'tis all underwritten by the devil. They're all a proper lot of pirates."

"Benjamin," Clarissa murmured, chiding. "Not on Christmas Day."

"On any day, Clarissa," Benjamin countered, his blunt face turning red with rum and indignation. "They're quick enough to collect their premiums. Usurious rates they are too. But come time to pay out and where are they?

"Did you hear about poor Isiah Starbuck?" Without waiting for the vague head shakes from his audience, he continued. "His was one of the houses they had to blow up with gunpowder trying to contain the fire. 'Twas right in the path of that inferno, and there's not a bit of doubt it would have gone up in flames if it hadn't been blown up first. Kezia had just time to grab the baby and her mother's candlesticks before they ran out the door. They lost everything else. And what did the insurance company say?"

Again he barely gave anyone else time to make a reply before he answered the question himself, practically shouting, "They said, 'Sorry Mr. Starbuck, but we can't pay you a penny. We have you covered for loss due to *fire*, not due to *explosion*.' Now, what do you think of that?"

"You're waking Edward, Papa," Harriet said, gently. Even she had reached a saturation point with hearing hard-luck stories. There were so many.

"Is there any more eggnog?" China asked, holding out her empty cup. She felt very relaxed and comfortable.

"Fetch her some more eggnog, Zenas," Benjamin said, in a more moderate tone. "'Tis doing her a world of good. 'Tis putting the wind back in her sails."

Zenas looked disapproving, but did as he was bid. No matter how indelicate it might be for a lady to swill rum, he couldn't deny that it made China more captivating than ever. Her gray eyes were dreamy; a lovely pink flush warmed her white cheeks.

"He's gone," Obed said, cryptically, from his chair.

"Who is, dear?" Harriet asked, while everyone else looked puzzled.

"Isiah Starbuck. He's gone," Obed repeated, still stuck on the subject the others had already forgotten. "Left last week with Kezia and the baby. I saw him go on the New Bedford packet. Just two bundles of clothes that came out of the barrels from the mainland churches. Kezia's got a cousin in Ohio who sent them money for the trip. I presume it likely they'll make a new start there."

Silence greeted Obed's addendum to the Starbucks' story. It was one thing to overlook the myriad injustices and hardships wrought by the fire, it was more difficult to hear of Nantucketers accepting defeat. Hundreds of island families were leaving, heading for such landlocked places as Ohio or Missouri and upper New York State.

There were no jobs on Nantucket and few prospects for the future. Even the mighty whaling industry, pioneered by Nantucket ships and Nantucket men, seemed vulnerable. It had been declining imperceptibly on the island for the past three years, hindered by the damned Bar blocking the harbor. This disaster would only accelerate its downfall.

"'Tis a pity," China said, feeling less easy and more frustrated. Even if she had the money to relocate elsewhere, she couldn't imagine leaving Nantucket for good. As often as she dreamed of sailing to interesting ports around the world, she never meant to abandon her home in Nantucket. She would always return here. This was where she lived. For better or for worse, her life was tied to this sandy, little island.

"Aye, 'tis," Benjamin muttered, for once at a loss for further words. He pulled his chin fiercely.

"Every day there's a new story," Clarissa said, shaking her head, sadly. "This island is emptying like a barrel with a hole in the bottom. Just Tuesday, Betsy Coffin, my laundry lady, told me she's leaving right after the New Year. Her husband worked in the candle factory and now can't find a job. They're going over to Edgartown to try their luck there. Betsy's been with me for eleven years, too.''

While Harriet tsked in sympathy and Benjamin looked grim, China felt her pulse quicken, her instincts for survival coming to the fore. ''Will thee hire someone else to do thy wash?'' she asked, cautiously.

''Of course,'' Clarissa answered, momentarily setting down her crocheting, surprised that there could be any doubt.

China took a deep breath to steady her suddenly twisted nerves. ''I should like to apply for the position,'' she said, softly.

For an instant, there was silence again in the room. Then everyone began speaking at once.

''Nay, China, you don't mean it,'' Harriet cried, leaving the cradle to come sit by her friend and seize her by the hand.

''China, please,'' Zenas said, almost simultaneously. ''That's not necessary. I can take care of you, if only you'll let me.''

''Bilge!'' Benjamin roared, oblivious of baby Edward. ''You're like my own daughter. I can't let you wash clothes for a living. You weren't born to be a laundress.''

''On the contrary,'' China said, strangely calmed by all the objections. ''I was indeed born to be a laundress. I can remember carrying buckets of water with Zacch, from the well to my mother's big washtub, when we were only three or four. Maman did laundry to make ends meet while we waited for Papa to come back. In fact, she did wash before she ever met Papa on the beach. So thee can see, I'm really quite qualified.''

439

"I can't let you do our wash," Benjamin insisted, again. "I'll gladly give you the money, you know that, but I can't let you take in laundry. 'Tis one thing to work in a shop selling ribbons and mustard seed; 'tis another to turn your pretty hands red and raw scrubbing clothes. Tell me how much money you need."

"And thee knows I can't take thy money," China responded. "Though I appreciate thy kindness with all my heart. I'll earn my own way, however, whether 'tis by washing thy clothes or someone else's." She patted Harriet's hand, still holding on to her own.

The Swains looked doubtful, but Obed nodded in approval. He had always been doggedly realistic; the fire had wiped away the last of his illusions. "She'll do a good job," he said.

"Of course I shall," China agreed, looking gratefully his way. She glanced around at the other faces, still showing shock and dismay. "Don't fret," she said, in an attempt to leaven the mood. "I won't put starch in thy underdrawers." No one laughed.

WALKING HOME AFTER DINNER, the mellowing effects of the eggnog long faded, China let her facade of cheerfulness and determination fall. It took too much effort to maintain. In its place came something quite close to despair. It seemed fate hadn't finished with her yet. It had not finished mocking her.

"Oh, Jake," she murmured into the foggy dusk, as she had once before, years ago. "Where is thee now? I need thee."

As soon as she uttered the words, she chastised herself for softening her attitude. She had sent him away for good reason, she reminded herself. She had ordered him out of her life.

He didn't have to obey, though, she thought forlornly, in instant response. It wasn't like him to meekly submit. Today she was too downhearted to stand on principle. She longed for him to suddenly appear, a mischievous grin on his handsome face, a gleam of delight in his deep blue eyes. She longed for him to pull her possessively into his arms, to tenderly stroke her hair, and to hold her tight until the devastating hopelessness disappeared.

As was the case the last time she wished it, though, no tall, rakish figure materialized from the fog. Tears trailed down China's cheeks. It wasn't a very merry Christmas, and the New Year, all alone, didn't promise to be very happy either. She wiped at her wet eyes with the back of her hand. She felt miserable.

23

INDIAN OCEAN
OFF MADAGASCAR
Christmas Day 1846

JOHN JAMES HENRY's broad, grinning face came hazily into view as Jake lifted heavy eyelids. For a few seconds he just stared dully, without thought or sensation.

"Merry Christmas, Ja-Jake," John James Henry said. "Welcome home, too. You scare me good and plenty, falling so far into the sea, but now you've come back."

As John James Henry's words penetrated, memory poked at Jake's mind. Almost instinctively he struggled, remembering sinking deep toward the ocean floor, knowing he was going to die. He was rewarded for his unconscious efforts by pain burning through his chest and clawing at his left arm. With it came the clear-headed realization that he couldn't possibly be dead, because this certainly wasn't heaven.

"Nay, nay, Ja-Jake," John James Henry clucked, his grin giving way to a worried frown. His huge hands moved fussily around the pillow under Jake's head. "Don't go flip-flop, flip-flop, like a fish in a pail. Stay still. I'll help you."

"What happened?" Jake asked, through gritted teeth. As the first flash of pain slowly subsided to a gnawing throb, he became increasingly aware. He was lying on his bunk aboard the *China Maid*, and, except for a corset of bandages around his chest and some splints strapped to his arm, he was naked. And hot. "What happened?" he asked again. He had more specific questions, but they took too much breath to ask.

"Hush, hush, I'll tell you everything," John James Henry said, guessing at his curiosity. "'Tis like this: Mother whale got very angry when we fasten on her baby. Even angrier when Sam-Samuel fasten on *her*. She gives swish with her flukes and throws our boat into the air. Like a pancake in a pan. Very bad." He smoothed the sheet beneath Jake as he talked.

"I fell into the sea feet down, easy, but I saw you fall on your belly. Saw oar go bang bang and hurt you bad. Saw you sink deep. Like lead line measuring fathoms. Quick, quick, I swam over and dive after you. Like diving for conch on reef in Rarua. I went down, down chasing you. Finally catch you and haul you back up. You didn't look so good, Ja-Jake." He shook his head grimly.

"You weren't breathing too much and your face look very pale. Like poor Za-Zacch when cask smack him. But we hoisted you on board and I fix you up. You got two broken ribs and one broken arm. I put on bandages and splints and then make medicine tea and talk to the spirits. I told them they got to let you live. I guess they listened." His big, brown features broke into a tender, crooked smile.

Despite the pain pressing down on him, biting with every breath, Jake felt a rush of warmth. He was overwhelmed with gratitude. He remembered the hollow horror of knowing he was going to die, the utter helplessness and dread. No matter how much it hurt at the moment, he was very glad to find himself alive, and he was extremely touched by John James Henry's solicitude.

"Thank you," he murmured. "I'm—"

"Hush, hush," John James Henry said, again, interrupting. "Hurts too much to talk." He gently patted Jake's shoulder. "No need to make such talk anyway. 'Tis why I'm here. The spirits gave me dream in Rarua and send me along so I can catch you when you fall into the sea. The spirits chart the course."

"Perhaps," Jake acknowledged, with a wince, "but I'm still quite pleased that they put you at the helm."

"Stop, stop!" John James Henry said, raising his hands in alarm. "No more talk. No more thank you, thank you. I know you're happy I save your life. But I'm happy, too. First thing, I pay my debt with Za-Zaccheus. Second thing," he said, his grin coming back, "I keep Sam-Samuel from being captain. He's too crabby. Never laugh." He patted Jake's shoulder again and rose, his head scraping against the ceiling. "'Tis enough gam, gam. Now you must sleep."

He started to leave, but Jake weakly called him back. "Wait," he said. "What of the boat and the other men?"

"Boat stove in," John James Henry said, shrugging his massive shoulders. "Looks like inside of Aunt Judith's kindling box. Everyone else fine, fine. Made eighty-three barrels of oil, too. Now go to sleep."

He left the cabin, closing the door quietly behind, but Jake didn't fall asleep again. His mind was too occupied with what had happened. He remembered, very clearly, the images that had flown past him as he had sunk toward death. Most especially he remembered seeing China, remembered the grief and the certainty on her beautiful face as she had banished him forever.

"Oh Jesus," he whispered as a fresh pain struck him. This one was not caused by his battered ribs or by his broken arm, but by the sudden realization that China had been absolutely serious. She had told him to leave, she had eliminated him from her life, not in a passing fit of pique, but because she had had a surfeit of sorrow. She had lost her whole family to the whims of whaling and she could bear no more. She was simply barricading herself against further heartbreak.

And instead of understanding her, instead of sympathizing with her, he had only underlined the tragedy by walking out on her. He had somehow imagined himself to be immortal; he had scoffed at her fears that he would never return. Now he knew better. The only reason he was alive right now was because of a dream John James Henry's spirits had sent him. It was a pretty thin margin on which to base such arrogant avowals that he would come back to her.

A deep sense of shame filled Jake. How shallow of him to think that he could cajole her with cheap beads and a flamboyant shawl, that he could tease and taunt her into changing her mind. What blinding conceit and overbearing pride had made him believe she would relent and have him back?

He had thought it enough that they loved each other, that the strength of their love would overcome all obstacles and objections, but he realized now that he had been wrong. Love would be little comfort to China if he were dead, flung deep into the sea by an enraged whale. He had misused their love; she had wanted him and needed him and he had let her down.

"Oh Jesus," he muttered, again, as the pain searing through his chest reached his heart. He felt miserable.

24

SEYCHELLES
April 1847

JAKE WATCHED IN FASCINATION as the *China Maid* glided past the lush, little islands guarding the entrance to Mahé harbor. There was something different about this tropical port. Partly it was the verdant mountain in the middle of Mahé, so unlike all the flat coralline islands they'd come across so far. Partly, too, it was the interesting array of vessels at anchor or tied along the stone quay. There was a British ship, a Chinese junk, an Arabian dhow and a French frigate. There were island schooners and pirogues and double-ended fishing skiffs. A lazy-paced, but international, air hung over this Indian Ocean island.

They had been following the whales north from Madagascar for the past four months, their greasy luck unbroken. The hold was almost full, two years' fishing completed in less than one. A tremendous storm, accompanying the change in monsoons, had blown them off course, away from the grounds. It had done little to damage the *Maid*, but the men were more irritable and exhausted than ever. Jake had decided that some fresh provisions and a spree ashore were in order. He'd set the helm for the Seychelles.

As much as any member of the crew, Jake was looking forward to getting smashingly drunk and to finding a willing and winsome woman who could help him forget the mess he'd made of his life. By now he was thoroughly healed. At least his bones had all knit nicely. His soul still felt bruised and sore. He had no idea what distractions there were ashore, but he was anxious to find out.

The words of the British customs official, who rowed through the heat of midday to meet them, put a damper on his anticipation, however. "This is a civilized port," the man said, his boiled-red face getting brighter with bureaucratic righteousness. "This is not some heathen island where one may disport oneself in an immoral and raucous manner. Any violations of our laws will be punishable with fines and incarceration. We will not tolerate drunken destruction. Have I made myself understood?"

"Aye, perfectly," Jake growled, sympathizing with the inspector's position, but disliking the man's attitude. He turned to the assembled sailors, who were listening dubiously to the pompous speech. "Any violations of local laws will be further answerable to me personally," he said. "Now is *that* understood?" He fixed an icy blue glare on the men until they nodded their heads sullenly and shifted their feet. Jake nodded, too, corroborating their agreement. Then he swung toward the first mate.

"Your watch, and Henry's, will stay on board, Samuel," he said. "Everyone else is free to go ashore. I want every man jack on board by ten o'clock, though, or there'll be hell to pay." While the lucky half of the crew raced for the fo'c'sle to find shirts and shoes, the shipkeeping half muttered and glowered.

"Belay that talk," Jake ordered. "Your turn will come tomorrow. In the meantime, I'll see that you get fresh food for supper." The men looked somewhat appeased and Jake headed for his cabin to dig out his going-ashore clothes.

As his boat approached the long, stone quay, Jake was torn between his desire to search out a cool, cozy tavern and his duty to reprovision the ship. When they tied alongside and he stepped ashore, however, he was greeted by a new diversion. The activity on the quay told as interesting a story as the ships in the harbor.

Sacks of cinnamon bark, coffee beans and copra were stacked in front of thatch-roofed warehouses. Shirtless men, with brown, black and beige skins moved indolently between ox carts laden with vanilla. Small schooners lay next to the pier, off-loading or receiving cargo, or just idling under the hot sun and the cobalt blue sky. The air was full of wonderful smells, all mingling agreeably with the scent of the sea.

Suddenly untroubled, Jake watched his men take off for the low, scattered buildings of town, down at the end of a long, dusty road. He chose to wander around the wharf, inhaling the aromas and inspecting the island vessels. He stood for a while, watching burlap bags of copra being hoisted off the deck of a thirty-foot schooner and being flung onto the back of an open-sided wagon. While the hundred-pound sacks thudded onto the cart, the patient ox yoked to the traces alternately licked at the brass ring in his nose and flicked his tail at the flies on his flanks.

After emptying the schooner, most of the longshoremen went to stretch out, laughing and gossiping, in the shade of a pandana palm. A lone twelve-year-old boy with coal-black skin, whom the others called Bien Noir, was left to crack a whip and shout authoritatively at the ox. Despite the boy's urging, the ox moved with slow, indifferent steps down the quay to a warehouse. When the warehouse was full, the copra would be loaded onto ships bound for Africa and India, where the sun-dried coconut meat would be pressed and processed into oils, soaps and medicines.

Jake followed the copra as long as he could, until Bien Noir left the big ox to flick flies and lick his nose while he went to have his dinner. Wholly absorbed in the atmosphere, Jake moved on down the quay to where a fifty-foot schooner was being loaded with sacks of rice, some cast-iron cooking kettles and several bolts of cloth. It was like watching international trade in miniature. Instead of trading barrels of refined oil and boxes of spermaceti candles for porcelains and silks and fine wines, piles of coconuts were being exchanged for pieces of calico. With a pang, he realized that this was what China had in mind for merchant shipping.

She wasn't thinking of the boring facts and figures of his father's business, the endless ledger columns waiting to be totaled, the pages of inventory lists waiting to be filed. She was thinking of ports such as this one, where profits and pleasure overlapped.

Once again, Jake felt a stab of guilt and misery. He cursed himself for not listening to China more carefully, for stupidly ignoring her arguments. It wouldn't be half bad to put into lovely islands such as these, fill up the hold with vanilla and coffee and sail off to London or Le Havre. The ship would certainly smell sweeter, too.

"Damn," Jake muttered. He'd given up the woman he loved and an enjoyable life, for the rigors and the stink of whaling. And for the privilege of claiming he was right. He glanced out across the placid purple harbor to where his ship lay at anchor, the wooden statue of China poised above the water. What a fool he was.

Thoughts turned inward, Jake barely saw the scene before him. He leaned against a piling, thumbs hooked casually into the wide belt around his trousers, vaguely watching as a chain of men passed the cumbersome sacks of rice from one to the other, until they were lowered into the hold. A white man, whose skin was tanned the color of polished mahogany, crouched by the hatch, his back to the dock, directing the operation in the singsong Seychellois patois called Creole.

A boxlike cabin was stuck on the deck, just aft of the jury-rigged fireplace, where several succulent-smelling kettles of curry steamed. From the cabin came the sound of a woman humming happily. In its doorway a small boy, with dark, silky hair and huge brown eyes, was laboriously constructing a boat from coconut husks and takamaka leaves.

The longboat bearing the boiled-red customs officer came past, four black men rowing, and the British bureaucrat looking wilted in his heavy uniform. At the sight of the schooner captain, he raised his hand in a semisalute and called, "Good afternoon, Captain Brown. It's a hot one, eh?"

Captain Brown looked up from the hold and rose. He was tall and lean, taut as a whip. His back was still to Jake, but Jake could hear him reply, "Good afternoon, Mr. Bodge. Aye, 'tis a hot day, indeed."

Immersed as he was in his own reflections, it hardly registered with Jake that this Creole captain had a decidedly Anglo name and an American accent. Just then, the humming woman stepped from the cabin and Jake's attention was further distracted. She was lovely. Shiny black curls escaped from a pink ribbon, spilled over her shoulders and framed her round face. As she smiled at the captain, her almond-shaped eyes slanted away. Three tiny dots enticingly decorated her creamy, cocoa-colored cheek.

Jake stared in admiration, but the woman was unaware of him. She only looked at the captain. "Shoobell," she said, in a husky voice. *"Ou faim?"*

The captain turned to smile affectionately at the woman, and Jake went rigid with shock. All the details slid into place, the name, the accent, the angular profile. Shubael Brown. He was seeing a ghost.

Perhaps it was the intensity of Jake's stare, or perhaps it was his stiff stance. Whatever the cause, just as Shubael was about to tell Amedee, yes, he was hungry, out of the corner of his eye he caught sight of Jake. He turned to stare back at this imposing stranger, puzzled by the man's expression.

As Shubael studied the vivid blue eyes fixed on his own, searching for some clue to his unusual behavior, the man's head turned slightly and the bright noon sun glinted off the gold hoop in his ear. Unbidden, bits of information and images came together in Shubael's mind. He linked the news of an American whaler in the harbor with the memory of a jaunty figure, morning light gleaming off an earring, guiding the *China Maid* the last few miles to home. A heaviness filled him, a sense of melancholy he had not felt since the ice floe in the Antarctic. This was Jake Swan.

For a few moments the two men simply looked at each other, while Amedee watched apprehensively from the stern of the schooner. She didn't know who this handsome stranger was, but she was suddenly afraid. She used to see the same look of bleakness drawing Shubael's face and saddening his eyes when he told her he had to leave her, when he said he didn't know when he'd return. She clutched Ti-Shubael's shoulder, waiting.

It was Shubael who shook himself free of his trance, first. With a few agile strides, he was over the bulwark and standing on the quay beside Jake, two tall, powerful men. He held out his hand. "'Tis unnecessary, I think, to introduce myself, but I am Shubael Brown," he said, evenly.

Numbly, Jake shook the proffered hand. "Jake Swan," he said, totally confused. Quite obviously this was the man he thought he was, but Shubael Brown was supposed to be dead, frozen to death in the inky sea at the bottom of the world, not stowing rice on a rough-cut island schooner under the hot, equatorial sun. Moreover, Shubael Brown was a correct Quaker captain, a disciplined, duty-bound Nantucketer, not this sun-burnished man clad in white duck trousers and nothing else, not this contented man speaking mellifluously in Creole and casting looks of adoration at a Seychelloise beauty.

Shubael saw Jake's bewilderment and relaxed. Jake wasn't here to condemn or accuse him; he was just curious. Shubael gestured toward his schooner. "Come aboard?" he invited.

Still speechless, Jake nodded his head and stepped aboard. He looked the length and breadth of the schooner, as if somewhere he could see an answer.

"I was just about to eat. Will thee join me?" Shubael asked.

Jake swung his gaze back to Shubael and finally found his voice. "Thee?" he questioned, incredulous. The plain speech seemed completely out of place.

Shubael shrugged his shoulders. "Old habits die hard," he said. Then he grinned, his dimples magically chasing away any residual gloom.

The grin disarmed Jake, too, setting him at ease. "'Tis not the only thing that seems to die hard," he commented dryly. "You appear fairly sound for a corpse."

Shubael grinned again, more sheepishly this time. "I suppose I must tell thee all about it," he said. "Shall we eat first? We caught a tuna coming across from La Digue yesterday and have a great pot of tuna curry, now. 'Tis quite tasty, though it might be too highly spiced for thy palate."

"Not at all," Jake responded. "After lobscouse and whale steaks, anything else is like manna from heaven."

A shadow flickered briefly across Shubael's face. "Aye, I remember," he said, soberly. Then he shrugged again and the unpleasant memory vanished. He turned to Amedee and spoke quickly in Creole.

Jake watched while she nodded, a look of relief flooding her lovely face. She stepped momentarily into the cabin and reemerged with a pair of coconut-shell bowls, which she took to the fire and heaped with snowy, white rice and rich, aromatic curry. Shubael took them from her, his smile of thanks reflected deep in his eyes.

"This is Amedee," he said to Jake. His tone was a trifle wary, ready to spring to the defense, but Jake made no comment. He merely accepted a bowl of curry and gravely bowed in greeting. Amedee dipped her head shyly and fled back to the cabin.

Shubael led the way forward, to sit cross-legged in the welcome shade of a carelessly furled sail. He made no further attempt at conversation while he attacked the huge helping of curry. A bit more cautiously, Jake followed suit. Despite his brave declaration, the pungent spice was a jolt to his tongue. It didn't take long, however, for him to overcome the fieriness and to relish the wonderful flavor. The two men ate their meal in silence.

When his bowl was empty, Shubael set it on the deck, wiped his fingers down the side of his pants and settled back against the mast. "Has thee ever been sealing?" he asked, quietly, easing into his explanation.

His mouth still full of rice and curry, Jake just shook his head.

The shadow slipped across Shubael's face, again, as he said, "'Tis a wretched occupation in a godforsaken corner of the world." He stared at his hands, lost in remembering. "A vicious occupation," he murmured.

Jake swallowed the last chunk of tuna and leaned back against the bulwark. Shubael didn't seem inclined to say any more, so Jake prompted him. "They wrote that you were dead," he said. "They wrote that the ice had broken and you had fallen through. You were trapped underneath it, drowned. Frozen. You and another sailor."

Shubael roused himself. "Aye," he said, slowly. "The ice broke. It broke right where he was standing." He paused, and it seemed that he had retreated into his memory, again, but after a moment he lifted his gaze.

"I was standing at the end of a tiny peninsula," he said, looking at Jake. "When the ice broke, I was on an island, a floe, carried with the tide and the current out to sea. I don't know how long I was stranded on that chunk of ice. I lost consciousness." He flicked his hand in the air, as if tossing away that unknown time.

"But they found your hat. They found it on the ice next to the body of the sailor," Jake said, trying to sort out the story. He felt his bafflement building again.

"'Twas my fur hat they found," Shubael explained. "When the ice cracked, I was thrown on my face and my hat fell off. As I floated away, I could see it on the far shore. But I always kept an extra in my pocket, a good, thick wool one. In that region, a bare head is an invitation to death. It saved my life." He paused again, and once more regarded his hands. "China knit it for me," he said, looking back up.

It was the first mention made of China. Jake felt his stomach twist into knots. This was the man who was meant to marry China. And he was alive.

"That was a year and a half ago," he said, tersely. "And ten thousand miles away." He asked no questions, but his query was implicit. What happened in between?

"When I came to, I was on board a British trader," Shubael answered. "I was bound for Canton with a bad case of frostbite. From Canton I went to Madras, from Madras to Ceylon, from Ceylon to Mauritius, and from Mauritius to Mahé. It took seven months."

"Why that route?" Jake persisted. "'Tis the long way home."

"I wasn't trying to go home," Shubael replied, softly. "I was trying to come here."

Now Jake was really stunned. "Here?" he asked.

"Here," Shubael answered, firmly.

Jake was so torn between relief and disbelief, between astonishment and bewilderment, he didn't know what to say next. The whole tale was becoming more bizarre by the moment.

Shubael read the confusion in Jake's face and tried to think of a way to explain. He heard the edge come into Jake's voice when China's name was mentioned, and he knew he had to tread carefully. In the end, he simply called to the little boy sailing his finished ship over a pretend sea. "Ti-Shoo," he said, *"Venir ici."*

Ti-Shoo trotted eagerly down the deck and plopped into Shubael's lap. Shubael wrapped an arm around the brown little boy's belly and pressed a kiss into the silky dark hair. He smiled fondly at Ti-Shoo and Ti-Shoo grinned back. "This is my son," Shubael said to Jake. "He'll be four years old in September."

Jake started to nod automatically, still trying to untangle what was going on, when realization struck. He looked quickly from Ti-Shoo to Shubael and down the length of the schooner to Amedee. Then he looked back to Shubael. It was Shubael's turn to nod.

"Amedee is his mother," he said. "And now my wife."

Jake should have been satisfied. Shubael's answer should have set his mind at ease. But it only raised more questions. Shubael had been to the Seychelles before he'd ever met China. He'd known Amedee and sired a child. Why had he left? And then why had he come back? Why had he asked China to marry him? And why had he married Ame-

455

dee instead? He looked at Shubael, unsure of how to phrase these questions. "'Tis complicated," he said, hoping for further enlightenment.

"Aye, 'tis complicated," Shubael agreed, offering none.

Both men sat silently for a few minutes, brooding about fate, then Shubael shifted his son from his lap and got up. "I must take advantage of the tide," he said, almost apologetically. "We're sailing soon for La Digue." As Jake rose, too, he added, somewhat hesitantly, "Would thee care to spend a few days there as my guest?"

There was nothing hesitant about Jake's reply. "I would," he answered, instantly. He wasn't sure why Shubael had extended the invitation, but he accepted it gladly. Gone were all thoughts of getting drunk and finding a girl. He was more intent on unraveling the mystery of Shubael's motives. It went beyond common curiosity; he suddenly felt there was something very important about understanding the situation.

By the time Jake rowed out to the *Maid*, told Samuel Easton to carry on with the provisioning while he was away for a few days and rowed back to shore, Shubael had the mainsail up on his schooner, and stood ready to cast off the lines. The breeze was light, but it was constant, and they made steady progress toward La Digue. If Jake expected any revelations on the overnight trip about Shubael's actions, he was disappointed. Except what he could interpret from the atmosphere on board, Jake learned very little.

Although he couldn't really be called rude, Shubael made almost no attempt at conversation. Mostly, he seemed utterly content to stand at the helm, or to sit on the boom crutch and steer the schooner with his bare feet, watching the blue Indian Ocean beyond him. Once or twice Ti-Shoo wandered aft to help his papa, and Shubael let him grab hold of the wheel while he kept his long, strong hands gently on top of the smaller ones of his son.

When the sun set, in a dramatic display of bright rose and flame red above a dark purple sea, Amedee filled the coconut-shell bowls, again, with rice and rich curry, and they ate. After supper, Jake offered to take a turn at the wheel, but Shubael smilingly declined. Instead, Jake lay on his back on the flat roof of the cabin, his stomach warm and full, studying the high, wide, night sky, velvet black and full of stars. He thought of China and felt very alone.

In the morning, Amedee made a rice gruel with tiny hot peppers, which Jake found to be a startling breakfast, but, on the whole, a satisfying one. By the time lunch came, he was not only lulled by the creak of the sails, the giggles of Ti-Shoo and the humming of Amedee, he was also ready for his coconut-shell bowl, loaded this time with rice and fried fish, caught that morning with a line held over the side. During the long, drowsy afternoon, he napped and taught Ti-Shoo how to make a cat's cradle with old twine.

The sun was setting again, splashing the sky with brilliant orange and streaks of green, when they dropped anchor outside the reef at La Digue. A lone pirogue poled out to meet them, though a laughing, shouting crowd was gathered to greet them on the white, sandy shore. When the single oarsman, a serene-looking man of middle years, climbed aboard, beaming and embracing Amedee, Shubael introduced him to Jake.

"This is Napoleon Mussard," he said. "He is my father-in-law and my partner. He built the schooner and I run it."

Napoleon was also Shubael's nearest neighbor, Jake discovered, when they reached land. Their houses stood next to each other, across the road from the beach. They even shared a stone kitchen. It was Amedee's mother, Mathilde, who prepared the meal that evening, a simple supper before they went to bed.

"Tomorrow evening they will make a feast," Shubael promised. "Tonight 'tis just enough food to keep from having bad dreams."

Jake nodded complacently. Though still mystified by Shubael's behavior, it no longer seemed so urgent to unravel it. He was caught in the slow island pace, calm and unhurried. He was at least beginning to understand what attracted Shubael to the Seychelles, even if he didn't know quite how China fit in. Time would tell.

They spent the next day unloading the schooner. Shubael protested that Jake needn't help, that he should wander around the island and find a deserted lagoon for a swim, but Jake insisted on pitching in. Relaxed though he might be, he didn't want to get too far from Shubael. He couldn't escape the instinctive feeling that there was something important to be learned. He heaved sacks of rice out of the hold and handed them into pirogues, marveling again at what a different approach to trading this was from his father's.

Just as Shubael predicted, Amedee and her mother prepared a sumptuous meal that evening. Jake ate with relish, tears streaming down his face from the diabolical little "pimonte," hot peppers, that the Seychellois favored. There was grilled fish, its slitted sides stuffed with ginger and garlic, barbecued sea turtle steaks, an oniony salad of hommard, or lobster, fresh chutneys with pineapple and green oranges, baked breadfruit and plenty of rice. Jake sat back, sated.

"And now an island specialty," Shubael announced.

"Nay," Jake groaned. "I cannot eat any more."

"Thee needn't eat this one," Shubael said, his charming dimples disguising the devilish light in his eyes. "'Tis bacca and 'tis for drinking.'' He poured a syrupy, amber liquid into three mismatched cups and handed one to Napoleon and one to Jake. Amedee and Mathilde rose to leave, clucking their age-old disapproval of this masculine sport, though Amedee snuck a sip from Shubael's cup before she followed her mother, giggling, through the door.

"Salute," Shubael said, raising his cup.

"Salute," Napoleon echoed.

"Good health," Jake said, then took a swallow. The sweet sugar cane liquor slid easily down his throat and spread through his body. Delighted, he took another taste. A wonderful, warm sensation traveled all the way to his toes, pinning them in place. Jake slouched in his chair.

He let the cool evening breezes from the sea blow against his skin as the musical Creole conversation of Shubael and Napoleon rolled around in his head. He downed some more bacca and closed his eyes while another wave of paralyzing warmth swept through him. It was an idyllic life, Jake thought. No wonder Shubael had stopped in La Digue.

He seemed perfectly at home here. He blended into the atmosphere. When he walked along the dusty, red road, people called to him and smiled. He had the expressions, the gestures, the temper of the islands. He had a beautiful Seychellois wife, a lovely family. He had found a way to give up whaling without giving up the sea. He had everything.

Across Jake's heavy limbs, across his awed mind, crept a tiny shred of envy. It somehow didn't seem fair that Shubael should be sitting here, talking happily to his father-in-law, his friend, satisfied, contented, sure that he loved and was loved, while Jake was so desolate.

"*Bon nuit, Jacques,*" Napoleon said, interrupting the resentment rising in Jake. Jake opened his eyes and saw Napoleon standing before him, his hand lifted in farewell.

"He's off to bed," Shubael said, lazily, from his chair. His long legs were stretched out in front of him, his elbow leaned on the rosewood table.

"Good night, then," Jake said, struggling to his feet.

Napoleon laughed and waved him back into the seat. Jake collapsed. He took another gulp of bacca while Napoleon said some final words to Shubael and wandered out of the room. With the fresh rush of liquor came renewed annoyance, turning his jumbled emotions into self-righteous indignation. Emboldened by the bacca, he let his thoughts slide along his tongue.

"'Tis a shipshape setup you have here," he said, rancorously. Shubael cocked an eyebrow in surprise. "You've settled nicely into a cozy berth, without so much as a glance in your wake. Doesn't any of your Quaker conscience remain with your plain speech? Do you ever think what effect your actions have had on those you've left behind?"

He swallowed his last drop of bacca, then reached across the table to refill the cup. Another sip and he finally said the name most on his mind. "What of China?" he asked, in an injured tone. "You made plans, promises. She was counting on you. Then you turn up dead." He wagged an accusing finger at Shubael, who was examining the bottom of his cup. "She is a fine woman. A clean-sailing and honest woman. She deserves better than to be deserted without a second thought."

"Aye, she is a fine woman," Shubael agreed. For a moment his eyes took on a distant look as he remembered the past. He sipped, meditatively, from the chipped cup he was studying. "I'm sorry. I only meant to help her. I never wanted to cause her any distress."

"Ha," Jake snorted, washing the single syllable down with a slug of bacca. "'Tis a novel way of helping, leaving her all alone and in mourning. Couldn't you at least have

written to her? Couldn't you at least have let her know you
are alive? Can't you imagine what she was going through
with her whole family gone?''

Shubael looked up at Jake. "But I didn't think I was
leaving her alone," he said, evenly. "I thought thee was
there. The moment I saw the *China Maid* making for port,
I just assumed thee would see to her worries whether I was
absent at sea or living in Nantucket. When I saw thee on
the deck that morning, I knew I was of no further use to her.
In truth, I was one sail too many. 'Tis thee she needs and
wants, not me."

It was obvious that Shubael felt neither remorse nor regret. His clear, direct tone somehow embarrassed Jake, and
it stirred, deep under his protective ire, the hint of suspicion that he was really foisting his own failure onto Shubael, that it was himself that he was admonishing for
abandoning China. He had gone too far, however, to back
away now.

"And quite clearly 'tis Amedee that *you* need and want,"
he said gruffly, covering his chagrin with further attack.
"And just as clearly, those needs and wants are well satisfied. I've never seen a man more content, more pleased with
his lot in life. If you knew all this was waiting for you, what
were you doing in Nantucket? Why did you propose to
China? 'Twas most generous of you to pay her taxes, and I
know she is indebted to you for nursing her when she was
ill, but why marriage? How could you have one woman in
the Indian Ocean, a woman who plainly adores you, but
want to marry another woman in the Atlantic Ocean? You
hardly seemed the sort to practice bigamy."

Shubael gave a rueful semismile at that remark. "Nay,"
he admitted, "I'm not a bigamist. I simply made a mistake." He was silent for a moment as he tried to compose
an answer to the rest of Jake's questions. He thought som-

berly of his mother's insistent harping, of his father's haunting lack of success and of his own rigid adherence to a sense of duty invented by others. One glance at Jake, though, and he knew he couldn't explain those things to him. He might have been able to tell them to China, now, but not to Jake.

Shrugging fatalistically, he said, "Aye, that's it. I made a mistake. I had my life rigged out for the wrong weather. I set too many sails for heavy weather and not enough for cruising."

Through the blur of bacca, Shubael's words again pricked at Jake's conscience. He sensed that he, too, had set the wrong sails, that he had misplaced the importance of things, but, as before, he turned his frustration and self-reproach back on Shubael before he could think it through.

"A mistake, is it? A mistake?" he bellowed, picking up the word and using it like a refrain. "How can you make false promises to a woman as wonderful as China and then slough it off as a mistake? You came within hours of marrying her. But for an icy step on Josiah Folger's back porch, she'd be your wife now. And then what would you say?"

His own heart leaped in horror at the thought, and he almost wondered why he was condemning Shubael for leaving China when he was just as glad he'd done it. The idea never properly penetrated the haze hovering over his mind, however, and he only asked again, hoarsely, "What would be your excuse then? Another mistake?"

Though he was not unaffected by the bacca, either, Shubael shrewdly guessed that he wasn't the only one who had made a mistake where China was concerned. A trifle irked by Jake's belligerence, he replied, "'Tis useless to debate what would have happened if she were my wife. She is not." He paused to let his silence emphasize that fact.

"But at least I was able to help her when she needed me," he continued. "I was there to give her comfort and security when her tide was at an ebb." He drained his cup, set it carefully on the table and squinted across the room at Jake. "And then I left her in thy care. If 'tis China's happiness thee frets over, then 'tis not my presence in the Seychelles that thee should question, but thine."

For a moment, the rebuke brought Jake up short, articulating the thoughts he hadn't been able to admit. His anger changed to surliness. He was obliged to concede that Shubael was right. He rubbed his eyes with weary fingers. If anyone was guilty of abandoning China, making false promises to her, it was he. No amount of bacca could disguise the truth or shift the blame to Shubael.

He had promised her love, total, complete, eternal love, and he hadn't delivered on his promise. He had been too occupied with his own satisfaction and convenience to ever truly, and lovingly, consider hers. Shame filled him as he suddenly remembered the vow he had made to Zacch, as his friend lay dying. He had sworn he would always take care of China. But he hadn't and he wasn't. Another promise broken.

It wasn't enough to overpower her with kisses and to keep her coffers full. Loving her, caring for her, meant more. It meant joining themselves, each giving to the other, uniting, blending, contrasting, compromising and ultimately setting sail on a course together. Love was not just an emotion, a passion, an urge; it was a way of life. He'd said as much himself, not even realizing the depth of his words. He'd told China that there was precious little else in the world worth more than love.

Jake let his hands fall from his face, and he looked across the table at Shubael. Shubael had done it. He'd given up success and respectability, his home in Nantucket, for the sake of Amedee. In return, he'd gained the same serenity he'd seen in Napoleon's smile, the same slow, mellow pace in the air in the Seychelles. He'd gained a comfortable, gratifying life; he'd gained love.

"Well, what am I supposed to tell her now?" he finally growled.

Shubael studied him intently for a moment, sensing the change in his attitude. Then he shrugged again and heaved himself to his feet. "That is between thee and she," he said, quietly.

"Nay," Jake protested. "I meant, what am I supposed to tell her about your death, about why you disappeared?"

"Oh that," Shubael said. A grin spread across his lean face, chasing away all shadows of the past. "Tell her that the yards are squared. The cap she knit me saved my life; our accounts are even." He picked up his coconut-oil lamp and started weaving for the door. Halfway there, he turned and looked again at Jake. "And tell her that thee loves her," he advised. Then he headed for his bed and the waiting embrace of Amedee.

After Shubael left, Jake sat alone in the room lit only by the moon. He slumped against the table, utterly down-hearted. He still hadn't learned very much about Shubael, but that no longer seemed to matter. Instead, he'd learned about himself. He'd learned that he was a fool, a stubborn, blind fool, who'd wasted his one chance for happiness. He should take a few lessons from Shubael about putting his priorities in order, and rigging his ship for smooth sailing.

Jake absently ran a finger around the edge of his empty cup, then, suddenly, sat bolt upright. That was exactly what he'd do. He'd put his priorities in order. He would go back to Nantucket and tell China what was most impor-tant to him. He'd load up the hold with sweet-smelling cinnamon and vanilla and tell her it was his token of a new

career. He'd tell her it was a tribute to her. He'd tell her....
Jake grinned into the tropical evening, then shrugged just
as Shubael had, taking his advice. He'd tell her that he
loved her.

25

NANTUCKET
August 1847

"DAMN! 'TIS HOT," China muttered to herself. She brushed her damp bangs off her forehead with the back of her hand, then dispiritedly laid another shirt on the oak kitchen table for ironing. She paused a minute to rub her aching back. She was too tall to be bent over the table for so long. There was still an enormous pile of clothes to be done, however, and it was already late.

She vaguely wondered what the hour was. She'd had to sell the grandfather clock last winter to pay for firewood, and now she knew the time only when the wind blew the chimes of the Lisbon bell her way. It didn't really matter, she supposed. One day or one hour was depressingly like the next. If she wasn't scrubbing someone else's clothes, she was draping them on the line to dry, or spreading them out for pressing.

If only it were not so hot, she thought, she might not mind it so much. She was dressed in just her chemise and petticoat, all alone in her cottage, late at night. Still, she had to keep the stove going so her irons would be warm. The heat was intense. Even the thin batiste of her undergarments clung uncomfortably to her skin. The kitchen door stood open to let in any cool air she could catch.

As if on the lookout for a chance breeze, China glanced briefly up. And then again, her gray eyes flying wide open, her breath coming in a gasp. Jake was lounging casually against the door frame.

"I see you still talk like a sailor," he said, his familiar rich voice sending a sudden flock of goose bumps over China's flesh. As his arresting blue eyes swept the length of her barely clad body, he added, "And dress like a mermaid."

China's heart was banging as she tried to think of what to say. After that lone vulnerable moment last Christmas, she had shut him from her again, determined to forget him and his magical pull on her emotions. One look at him, however, at his handsome face with its tropical tan, and his dark, unruly hair curling carelessly around the gold hoop in his ear, at his strong arms, shirt sleeves rolled high, crossed against his hard, flat chest, one look and she knew she had not been successful. It was all she could do to keep from rounding the table and running into his embrace, from letting his strength and his desire envelop her.

"Hello, Jake," she finally said, holding on to the edge of the table as if to hold herself in place. She hoped her voice didn't sound as quavery as it felt. She had banished him before with good reason. She had refused to battle with whaling for his time and attention, had refused to take second place to an occupation that had only brought her devastating grief. To capitulate now would destroy her self-respect, and without that, she literally had nothing.

Besides, she told herself, he'd been gone a year and a half. It was wholly possible that he'd found a less insistent woman than she, one who would unquestioningly accept the risky life he led, the life filled with long, fretful absences and brief respites ashore. China swallowed. Her throat felt dry. Though she told herself to behave sensibly, the thought of Jake with another woman in his arms was appalling.

"Hello, *corbeau*," Jake replied, sauntering forward, a grin, outrageous and roguish, breaking across his rugged face. China's legs felt rubbery and she gripped the table harder. Jake came to a stop on the other side. Just three feet of oak planks separated them. She could smell the salty scent of southern seas clinging to his skin, and she was suddenly aware of how very little she wore. Her body was aching beneath the sheer cotton, tingling against the lace of her chemise.

"I've brought you something," Jake said, reaching into his pocket and extracting a small cloth sack tied with twine. He set it on the table between them.

"What is it?" China asked, eyeing the sack suspiciously. She was afraid to reach for it, afraid to stretch her hand toward Jake.

"'Tis a gift," Jake answered. "A tribute. Open it." He nudged it closer to her, then let his hand retreat. In the dim glow of the single sooty lamp, she looked radiant. The skin on her bare shoulders and arms was cool and silky, though her cheeks were flushed with the heat. Her thick dark lashes feathered down against her face as she studied the sack. "Open it," Jake urged, again.

China reached a tentative hand across the table and took the bag. With fingers that did not quite respond to her command, she undid the string. A delicious aroma wafted out of the open sack. When she peered inside, she saw chunks of cinnamon bark and long, dried pods of vanilla. Her apprehension temporarily turned to puzzlement. It was a nice present, a useful one, but very unlike Jake. She knew he didn't imagine her in the kitchen, always baking.

"Thank thee," she said, politely. "'Tis a lovely gift." She was determined not to encourage him in any way, either by questions or by comments or by reverting to their old, easy bantering. She set the sack and the string on the corner of the table and turned her attention back to the shirt in front of her. At least her eyes were on the wrinkled cloth; her concentration was three feet away.

Her stomach was fluttering as she nervously adjusted the sleeves and fussed unnecessarily with the collar. It suddenly felt unbearably hot; the flush on her face seemed to spread all over her. The air was terribly close. It was as if Jake's body, standing before her, was blocking the breeze from the door. Why was he doing this to her? She had willed herself to forget about him. Why couldn't she?

Hand trembling, China reached for the iron. Unable to focus, her fingers slipped against the scorching surface. "Owww!" she cried, yanking her hand back. It was only a slight burn, but tears came to her eyes, less in reaction to the minor pain than to the frustrated emotions pounding within her.

In an instant, before she could wave him away, or withdraw from his reach, Jake was around her side of the table and scooping her into his arms. For a moment, the familiar excitement of his flesh next to hers overwhelmed her, and she couldn't resist. In that moment, Jake carried her into the parlor and settled onto the sofa, with her in his lap. He found her injured hand, clenched in the folds of her petticoat, and pried open the fist. Then he placed a soft kiss on each singed finger.

The touch of his lips, his sure grip on her wrist, the strength and intimacy of his arm circling her shoulders, sent thrills through China. She had to shut her eyes, to cut off his powerful presence, and regain control. "Put me down, Jake," she finally protested, struggling weakly. "Let me go."

But Jake held her fast. "Nay, China," he said. "I'll not let you go until you hear me out, so the sooner you stop thrashing like a gallied whale, the sooner you'll be able to make your escape." He paused, his blue eyes deep and demanding, intent on hers. "If that is what you wish," he added, soberly.

By now, China had gotten hold of herself and had turned her pent-up passion into self-righteous indignation. "Aye," she said, twisting against him. "'Tis what I wish. I have ironing left to do and no time to waste with thy childish pranks."

"Ah, your pious pose," Jake said, giving her a little shake in exasperation, but not releasing her. "You know it does not become you. And you also know it doesn't fool me. So stop being silly and forget about the ironing. It can keep for another day."

As always, China responded readily to the provocation in his tone. She ceased fighting and sat as still and primly as her scanty dress and trapped position would allow. "It will *not* keep for another day," she said, stiffly. "I promised Mrs. Barnard I would finish her laundry by tomorrow and I must keep my promise or risk losing her business. I can't afford to offend my customers."

"What?" Jake exclaimed, incredulous. Shock filled his face. "What the hell are you talking about? Since when do you do laundry for a business?" he demanded. Then he looked quickly around the room, as if its emptiness were only now registering. "Wait," he said. "Where is the clock? And the chess table?" His tone grew more accusing and he looked back to her, shaking her again, in genuine anger this time. "And where is Zaccheus's rocker?"

China set her face stubbornly, refusing to be bullied. She was no more happy than he with the loss of her family's furniture. "Sold," she said, shortly. "Sold to pay debts."

Jake's anger subsided as rapidly as it had risen. "Tell me what happened, China," he said, quietly. "When I left port sixteen months ago you were a rich woman. Why are you now washing other people's clothes?" When she didn't reply, when she only fixed her great, gray eyes obstinately beyond him, he took her chin in his hand and guided her gaze back to him. "Eh, China?" he prodded. "What happened?"

She looked at him, steadily, a moment, then wrenched her face free and stared at her knees. No matter how much she had rationalized, it still hurt to think of her failure. "Perhaps thee is not aware of the Great Fire," she said grudgingly. "It was a year ago in July. It destroyed two thirds of the town."

"Aye, they told me about it on the lighter," Jake said, prompting her to say more. "And I saw the new buildings on Main Street as I walked here. But how did that affect you? You had a ship at sea."

China let her head drop until it almost touched her chest. "'Twas not at sea," she mumbled. "'Twas tied to Straight Wharf...." Then she gave a gasp and covered her face with her hands. "She burned to the waterline, and sank. What cargo was not on board was on the dock beside her," she said, her voice barely audible in her misery.

"Oh China," Jake said, softly, "I am sorry. I am truly sorry." He pressed his face against the top of her head, laying a kiss of sympathy in her silky hair. She didn't have to give him any more details; he could guess the rest. She had gone from wealthy woman to washerwoman, all alone.

That stirred a question in his mind, a question that had been gnawing at him, plaguing him, for the past four months. "What of Zenas Swain?" he asked, tersely. "Why didn't you marry him? They couldn't have been completely wiped out by the fire. He could have taken care of you well.''

When Jake had first crushed close to her, China had almost welcomed his embrace, finding comfort in his compassion, release. But his new questions brought her tensely upright again, her lips tightly compressed in reply.

Jake chuckled, relief flooding through him. He had his answer. There was no danger of losing China to that deskbound dandy. He covered her pursed lips with a kiss, quickly, before she could protest. ''Good,'' he said, his blue eyes taking on their teasing light. ''Then as soon as you finish Mrs. Barnard's wash, I assume you'll be free to come cruising with me.''

''What bilge is thee spouting now?'' China asked, angrily, wiping her lips with the palm of her hand, trying to remove the feel of his lips on hers, trying to calm the frantic beating of her heart. She struggled again to free herself, banging her bare feet futilely through the air. ''Set me down,'' she ordered.

Jake ignored her command and held her tighter. He darted close and set another kiss on her satiny skin. '''Tis not bilge,'' he said, his impossible grin making her blood race. '''Tis an invitation to come cruising with me on the *China Maid*. Shall I have it scribed on parchment and hand delivered to you?''

''Thee may have it carved in marble, for all it matters to me,'' China retorted, truly angry, now. She tried to push him away, all too aware how undignified she appeared, perched on his lap in her underclothes. ''Thee has momentous gall inviting me to cruise on thy wretched whaler. Thee knows what I feel about it. Does thee think I talk only to hear myself speak? Has thee no respect, at all, for me?''

''On the contrary,'' Jake replied. ''I have tremendous respect for you.'' His expression was serious now, his goading grin gone. "And I think you talk so *I* can hear you speak. At least, I hope so. And I want to listen. That is why I'm inviting you to come cruising with me, so I can listen to all the things you have to say." He smiled again, and rubbed his chin on her shoulder. "Well?" he asked, a hint of his former mischief returning. "When will you be ready to sail?"

China ceased her squirming and looked at him sternly. "What does it take to make thee comprehend that I will not play thy games anymore?" she asked. "I will not let thee cajole me with thy empty flattery. Nor will I allow thee to draw me into argument. The first exercise is an insult, the second a waste of air. It will only lead to loud noise and long-buried rancor. I have no wish to battle with thee."

Jake completely abandoned his teasing tone. "I have no wish for battle, either," he said. "In truth, the only argument I will ever give you again is if you refuse to marry me.

"Hush," he ordered, placing his hand over China's mouth as she opened it to lash out angrily. "Hear me out. I stopped whaling four months ago. On your recommendation, I've turned to trading. You were right, 'tis more enjoyable. At the moment, I'm hauling coffee and spices from the Seychelles. But if you prefer, or you think it more profitable, we can carry wine from the Azores, or rum from the Caribbean, or furs from Alaska. Or all of them in turn."

He dropped his hand from her face and smiled gently at her. She was staring at him openmouthed, her gray eyes wide in wonderment. He put his finger under her chin and tenderly pushed closed her mouth. She gulped and blinked.

"Or none of them," he said. "More than anything else, I want you for my wife, China Joy, for my partner in life. I'll sail around in a bathtub, if you'll sail with me." He paused a minute, as another thought struck him, frowned a bit, then shrugged. "If you don't like the sea, we can live on land. We can have a farm, if that's what you like. We can raise pigs and chickens and sheep.''

"I don't want to raise pigs," China said, dazed, disbelieving what she was hearing.

"Then we won't," Jake said, relieved. "We'll only do what pleases us. If we want to sit out a trip in Nantucket, that's what we'll do. We can spend our summers visiting Harriet and our winters calling on John James Henry. He's gone home to Rarua. He decided we can take care of ourselves.

"We can go to California. Or to France. Or to Mexico. Or Japan." He no longer needed to restrain her, to forcefully hold her in his lap. With both hands, he brushed her shiny black hair away from her cheeks, then framed her face with his fingers.

"We'll make good partners," he told her, touching his lips to the tip of her nose. "We'll make shrewd investments. And a happy family. And lots of love." He bent his head over China's, kissing her, his lips warm and insistent.

"Now what do you say?" he asked, sliding his cheek down her smooth white neck and tracing his tongue along her bare shoulder.

"Aye," China whispered, pressing herself toward the source of her pleasure. Her heart was swelling inside her, spilling over with joy. She felt all her experiences, her emotions, melting together. She felt the exultation of swimming toward Jake in the ocean off Coatue, the ecstasy of lying naked next to him in the pine grove above Capaum Pond, the excitement of sharing secrets with him on the beach at Miacomet, the euphoria of emerging, warm and alive, from a hot tub into his waiting arms. She felt the elation, the exhilaration, the unhindered happiness of love.

Jake turned his head and placed a kiss on her throat. "To which part are you agreeing?" he asked, his voice deep and husky.

"To all of it," China answered, without a moment's hesitation. She wrapped her arms around his neck, and ran her fingers through his curls. "There is no need to argue," she murmured, brushing her lips across his brow. "I agree to all of it."

Without another word, Jake gathered her into his arms and stood up. He blew out the single, sooty lamp, leaving only the moon and the stars to light the parlor. Then he carried China up the steep steps toward her soft, feather bed.

Sarah

MAURA SEGER

Sarah wanted desperately to escape the clutches of her cruel father.
Philip needed a mother for his son, a mistress for his plantation.
It was a marriage of convenience.
Then it happened. The love they had tried to deny suddenly became a
blissful reality... only to be challenged by life's hardships and brutal
misfortunes.

All men wanted her,
but only one man would have her.

Her cruel father had intended
Angie to marry a sinister cattle baron twice her age.
No one expected that she would fall in love with his
handsome, pleasure-loving cowboy son.

Theirs was a love no desert storm would quench.

JULIE ELLIS

author of the bestselling
Rich Is Best **rivals the likes of**
Judith Krantz and Belva Plain with

It sweeps through the glamorous cities of Paris, London, New York and Hollywood. It captures life at the turn of the century and moves to the present day. *The Only Sin* is the triumphant story of Lilli Landau's rise to power, wealth and international fame in the sensational fast-paced world of cosmetics.